Praise

"Sophie's Run goes far beyond any expectations I had set. I did ...vant this story to end! Once again, the story was ...ıal, full of bits and pieces that add depth to an already ...tful, hard-to-put-down story. I just plain LOVE it all!"
~Nova Reylin

...e's Run is a rollercoaster of emotions that draws you in ...ves you hanging for the 3rd book! If I could, I would go ...r than 5 baskets! Seriously! I enjoyed *Sophie's Turn* but *Sophie's Run* has surpassed it in my eyes!"
~Tobi Helton

...s always interesting when a sequel is launched following a ...rill...nt debut. Did it live up to the first? OMG—it **so** did! I got so lo... in this delightful, delicious story, that I had to keep telling ...self that I wasn't Sophie! I love Nicky's writing style, so na...ral, and so funny as well as warm, romantic and adorable ...you are kept guessing till the end. If the third one in the ...es was ready, I would have picked it up right away and de...d that one too! What will I do when this series finishes? I have no idea!"
~Kim Nash

...I...as thoroughly drawn in to the continuing escapades of S...p...ie Penhalligan. Will the alluring rock star win her back, or ...id s...e just meet the true love of her life? I was almost as eager as Sophie to find out! Endearing, warm, and funny, *Sophie's Run* is an utter delight!"
~Bonnie Tra...... ...tically Yours

Nicky Wells

Sophie's Run

Part 2 in the Rock Star Romance Trilogy

Sapphire Star Publishing
www.sapphirestarpublishing.com
First Sapphire Star Publishing trade paperback edition, February 2013

The characters and events in this book are fictitious. Names, characters, places, and
plots are a product of the author's imagination. Any similarity to real persons, living
or dead, is coincidental and not intended by the author.

ISBN-13: 978-1-938404-49-8

Cover design: Chad Lichtenhan

Cover image: Holbox

Author photograph by Deborah Smith

www.sapphirestarpublishing.com/nickywells

Dedication

For my Mum.
Because you never, ever once doubted that I would write all my books, one day.

PART ONE:
UP IN THE AIR

Prologue

The ferry bumped gently against the pier, and I took a deep breath to steady my jangling nerves. I was here.

I arrived on this tiny, car-free island in the remote German North Sea, and I was all alone. It was strangely thrilling to think that no one knew where I was. No one was expecting me. I had made no arrangements for my stay. In fact, I didn't even know where I would sleep, but that was fine. It suited my mood. I wanted a clean break, a fresh start. No links to the past, no connections to the mess that I left behind.

Just briefly, I wondered whether Steve would notice that I was gone. Steve, who I had thought was definitely *the one*. Would he even care, after everything that had happened? And what about my best-friend-in-the-whole-world, Rachel? Or Dan, for that matter, my other best friend, singer and rock star extraordinaire, who also doubled as my ex-fiancé — well, one of my ex-fiancés, actually. Would he notice I had run away?

While I waited for the ferry to finish docking, I drank in every detail of my chosen exile. The calm sea with little white-

1

crested waves lapping gently against the quay. The green and white of the sandy dunes standing stark and fresh against the wide-open, deep-blue sky. The tiny harbor with only a handful of buildings and a few fishing boats bobbing on the incoming tide. Seagulls wheeling overhead, their mournful cries carrying on the gentle breeze, augmenting my sense of emptiness, newness. Fresh, clean, salty air. I took another deep breath, feeling calmer already.

Yes, I had done the right thing. I had come to the right place. Here, I would find the space and the peace to think things through. I would figure it all out, everything that had happened, and a few things that hadn't. And I would put my life back together.

Chapter One

"*Sanctus, sanctus dominus...*" I hummed under my breath as I walked up to the church from South Kensington Tube Station. "*Pleni sunt coeli...*"

I was lost in the music and my heart soared. The thought of taking part in tonight's impending choir concert—my second—was intoxicating and terrifying at the same time. Normally a rock-chick at heart, I had found a second musical home in the small choral group that I had joined on an impulse a few months ago.

I hurried my step, knowing that the orchestral rehearsal was due to begin and berating myself for being late. Why was I always late? I couldn't even blame the Tube on this occasion. Although I *could* blame Dan Hunter, lead singer of legendary rock band Tuscq and, owing to a complicated set of circumstances, one of my closest friends. He had called me at *Read London*, the newspaper where I worked as a deputy-editor, just seconds before I was due to leave.

"Sophie," he had drawled down the line as he always did. "Is it still okay if the band and I come to see your show tonight?"

I had giggled. He might be a rock god, but he didn't quite 'get' the classical scene. "I would love it if you came to the concert tonight," I had responded, swallowing butterflies of excitement. Singing was one thing; knowing you had a friend in the audience was another.

"Great. Looking forward to it. It'll totally rock, I'm sure." His enthusiasm was overwhelming. I sincerely hoped he had checked out Fauré's *Requiem* beforehand so that he knew what was coming.

"It will," I had concurred weakly. "In a manner of speaking."

"See you after the show?" Dan was keen to verify this point.

"That would be lovely." I nodded my head even though he couldn't see me. "Oh and —" I shouted before he could hang up.

"Yes?"

"Don't forget Rachel and Jordan are meeting us there, too."

"Excellent." Dan sounded genuinely delighted; he had always liked my spiky, sparky, colorful best friend and partner-in-writing at *Read London*. He wasn't quite so keen on her boyfriend, soon-to-be-husband, although he couldn't explain why.

Hence, by the time I left the office, I was running late. I would have to hurry to get to the church where we would perform and…

"Oomph!"

I tripped over a paving stone and launched myself missile-style at a passing couple. The man caught me by the arm, but I still dropped my handbag and music. I bent down to retrieve my scattered belongings, muttering apologies all the while. "So sorry," I panted. "All my fault, I was totally lost in thought and…"

The words died on my lips as I straightened up and faced my rescuer.

Tim. With Dina.

Dina beamed at me delightedly. "Sophie! So good to see you. How've you been? And are you all right?" She took my arm gently and inspected me for any damage. Tim said nothing, but his face had turned into an icy mask.

"Dina, hi!" I returned her greeting uncertainly. "And Tim!" I addressed my ex-fiancé. Squirming with discomfort, I didn't quite know where to look. I forced myself to meet his eyes, which flashed with contempt.

"How *are* you?" My determinedly cheerful question didn't yield a response. Dina stepped in quickly.

"We're fine," she buzzed. "We're engaged and…" She waggled her ring finger bearing an enormous engagement ring in my face. It was certainly bigger and flashier than the one Tim had given me, and I gasped in awe.

"That's so beautiful," I exclaimed before I could help myself. "Congratulations! When's the big day?"

Dina opened her mouth to speak, but Tim finally woke from his trance and took his fiancée roughly by the arm. "Nice seeing you but we must be off," he barked, and pulled Dina onwards.

"Ouch," I muttered to myself, temporarily rooted to the spot. Tim was clearly still bearing a grudge but I couldn't blame him, really. I had ended our relationship in unusual circumstances, having returned from a three-week tour of Europe with Tuscq and having fielded and declined a proposal of marriage from Dan Hunter himself. I had tried to explain to Tim that I was leaving him because we weren't making each other happy, but he had focused entirely, and quite mistakenly, on the Dan angle. *Nonetheless, it didn't take you long to get it back together with Dina,* I mentally told him off. *You started dating her mere weeks after we broke up. So you couldn't have been* that *heartbroken.*

Shaking myself out of my stupor, I glanced at my watch and broke into a run. Now I really was late!

The orchestra had finished tuning and the dress rehearsal was in full swing by the time I finally crashed through the church doors. I slowed my step and prayed that my heart rate would slow down, too, while I carefully tiptoed down the aisle to find my place in the choir stalls. Mouthing an apology at the choir director, I tried to make myself invisible as I crept past her and squeezed myself into the end of a pew. I opened my folder of sheet music and told myself to focus. Yet I appeared to be in the grip of a delayed stress reaction; I started to shake so badly that the music slipped right out of my grip and fluttered prettily to the floor. When did I become so clumsy?

"Don't be nervous," my pew neighbor whispered to me. "You'll be fine."

I smiled wanly at her and bent down to retrieve the sheets of paper, bumping my head against the pew and momentarily seeing stars. *Great.* At this rate, I wouldn't make it through the concert.

Breathe, Sophie, breathe.

Rehearsal finished with me barely noticing it had taken place. It was only a short twenty-minute break before the actual concert would begin. Most of the singers disappeared from the choir stalls, grabbing a drink or catching up with friends as the audience began to arrive. I simply remained in my seat, staring vacantly into space. My heart was still beating fast, and I had a strange sensation of heightened awareness. Every noise, every sound was amplified tenfold, and everything I saw appeared to be overly sharp, overly bright, extremely clear. I wondered if that was how Dan felt before he went on stage.

All too quickly, the orchestra musicians returned to their places and re-tuned their instruments. The high-pitched whining of violin strings being adjusted hung in the air and tugged at my nerves. I looked away from the audience and instead examined the intricate carvings in the woodwork of the choir stalls facing me, currently filling with basses.

I watched with wry detachment as they all sat down and took their music, readying themselves for the beginning of the concert. Yet abruptly, one man got back to his feet again, squeezing past knees and unsettling everyone in an effort to reach the end of the pew.

"What *is* he doing?"

"Who?" my pew neighbor chimed in curiously. She followed my gaze and sighed. "Isn't he gorgeous? That's Steve. He's reading the dedication tonight."

Something weird was happening to me. I had a strange tingling sensation, a kind of jubilant foreboding in my tummy that I had never experienced before. I heard myself speak without knowing what I would say.

"Has he always been in the choir? I've never seen him before."

"He comes and goes. He's not here very often. I think it's a work thing..." My neighbor's voice seemed to come from a long way away. My eyes were trained on Steve as if my life depended on him.

Suddenly, he looked up. His gaze met mine and our eyes locked. Time stood still.

Those eyes. Round and sparkly, they were like pools of melted chocolate sprinkled with stardust, mysterious and warm and oozing tenderness. A prickle ran down my spine, and the hairs at the nape of my neck rose in anticipation.

I knew without the slightest shadow of a doubt that this was the man I would marry. And I also knew that this recognition was mutual. Steve stood stock-still and I could practically see the electricity arc between us.

The moment passed; it had seemed like minutes but had probably been mere seconds. I rose to the surface as though I had been in a trance. *Entranced.*

"Are you all right?" my neighbor whispered.

"Fine," I whispered back. "Absolutely fine."

Chapter Two

The concert went well until somebody arrived with the proverbial bang right in the quietest moment of the piece. The slamming of the church door made everybody jump, and the ensuing shuffling of feet and muttered excuses distracted most of us. I could see our conductor frowning, but she continued without missing a beat.

Everybody surreptitiously craned their necks to see who might be causing this disturbance. Everybody but me. I would have recognized that voice anywhere, at any volume, however muted or whispered it was. Plus I had been waiting for this moment, knowing that Dan would make an entrance of some description when he and the band arrived. Yet I blushed deeply, feeling responsible for bringing this rock-god, classic-klutz into the church.

I fiddled with my necklace. *The* necklace. The half-engagement-ring pendant with the beautiful sapphire that Dan had had made for me after I turned down his proposal on the plane back from Paris. He usually wore the other half—a kind of symbolic "we're not really together, but we'll always be together" gesture that summed up our friendship perfectly. To me, the pendant had become a good luck charm, and it reassured me now. It wouldn't matter whether Dan liked the music or rated our performance; he had made the effort. And yet… part of me wondered whether this was actually a good thing. Had I made a mistake by inviting Dan into this part of my life that I had so carefully carved out for myself as a new beginning?

Distraction, double distraction, and now triple distraction. First Tim, then Steve, now Dan. And *now* I had lost my place. My pew neighbor actually clamped a hand over my mouth to stop me from having an unintentional solo moment, and I snapped to with a jolt.

Calm down, Sophie, I told myself. *No harm done. Nobody will have noticed.* Nobody except for… I could see Steve winking at me. I blushed some more, suppressing a wild giggle. *No more!* I admonished myself, turning my attention fully to the music. I resolved to meet Steve after the concert and, after that, tell Dan off for making such an entrance.

Best laid plans! The concert ended and before I could grab my chance, Steve loped off to the front to speak to the conductor and a group of people I didn't know. I remained in my seat and speared Steve with looks while the other altos filed out one by one. *Come on, come on, come on,* I urged him under my breath, knowing I was running out of time, knowing that any minute I would be claimed.

Too late. While I was still trying to generate some sort of invisible tether between myself and Steve, Dan had found me, dragging Rachel, Jordan and the rest of the band along with him as I had known he would. They swooped down on me full of kind words and congratulations, eager to let me know how much they had enjoyed themselves. General mayhem ensued as six people crowded into my pew, but Dan somehow managed to sit himself down next to me. He gave me a boisterous hug that nearly toppled me over. I was sure his voice could be heard all over the church as he half-roared, half-sang, "Sophie, that was beautiful. I am *so* impressed." He regarded me critically and gently touched a finger to the bruise on my forehead.

"Who have you been upsetting tonight?" he joked, yet the gesture was undeniably tender. Out of the corner of my eye, I noticed that Steve was watching us closely, and I squirmed uncomfortably. *This wasn't meant to happen.*

"No one," I said, rather more abruptly than I had intended. "It's nothing."

I didn't know where to look, but Dan was full of beans and didn't even notice my agitation.

"Come on," he said, pulling me out of my seat and onto my feet. "Come on," he repeated for everybody's benefit, motioning for the band and Rachel and Jordan to get up and get moving. "Let's go have some dinner."

And when I remained rooted to the spot, trying to make some kind of visual farewell connection with Steve, Dan took a formal bow, doffed an imaginary cap and boomed, "Milady, your carriage awaits." I giggled despite myself.

If I was reluctant to leave, Dan utterly failed to notice. I was swept along in his slipstream, and a little part of me was excited that Dan had come to collect me. It felt quite nice to be made a fuss of. But the bigger part of me shrank and shivered in dismay as I finally caught one last look at Steve, watching Dan's exuberant Sophie-extraction-performance and looking— disappointed? Sad? Amused? Impossible to tell. *Still,* I reasoned as I was being dragged out of the church, *he was a member of the choir even if his attendance was patchy; there would be more rehearsals and more concerts after the summer break,* I would *find this man.*

Chapter Three

It turned out that Dan hadn't been joking about the carriage. That man certainly was full of surprises. I was half-expecting the customary stretch limo, but certainly not a horse and cart. Dan exploded with laughter.

"I told you your carriage was awaiting!" he exclaimed gleefully.

"Well, I know," I muttered back. "I didn't think you meant an actual... What *is* this?"

"This," Dan announced, gingerly patting the horse's head, "is our transport for right now. You know...rock gig, big limo. Classic gig, classic transport. Fits the occasion, don't you think?"

I observed the horse cautiously, not sure what to make of this equine encounter. "Where on *earth* did you find a horse and cart in Central London?" I persisted.

"Oh, you know, there are hire companies about," Dan responded airily. "And anyway, this isn't a cart, this is a proper carriage. Won't you go and check it out?"

Before I could say anything else, Rachel opened the carriage door with a great squeal of excitement and climbed in. "What are you waiting for?" she shouted back at me. "Come on in."

"You've got to be joking, right?" I challenged. "This... this is too over the top. I mean, who *does* this kind of stuff?"

"*I* do," Dan responded, looking slightly crestfallen. "I thought it would be a laugh."

Seeing the sadness in his face, I finally caved. Anyway, I was only protesting for form's sake, lest *Candid Camera* or something should pop up any minute.

The inside of the carriage was simply sumptuous. It was done out in red velvet upholstery with two sets of seats facing each other. Small imitation candles in all four corners cast a soft, but barely sufficient, glow. Rachel and Jordan sat on one side with Joe (Tuscq's drummer) and I sat on Dan's lap on the other side, squeezing in beside Mick (the bassist) and Darren (lead guitar). There was the teensiest fridge stuck under one of the benches, and Joe swiftly produced a couple of mini bottles of champagne.

"It's like way back when on that coach..." he commented, giving me a wink as he popped the first cork. "Let's try not to spill it all this time."

I grinned back. I had always liked Joe and he had a knack of defusing situations with his easy-going, happy demeanor. We all clinked glasses, holding on for dear life as the carriage rocked and wobbled through the London streets. I let my misgivings and confusion drain away and allowed myself to relax.

Dan had reserved a table for us at *Zeus!*, the flagship restaurant of one very flamboyant and multi-Michelin-starred TV celebrity chef. If the maître d' was astonished by our mode of transport, he didn't bat an eyelid. Instead, he greeted us like royalty and showed us swiftly to a secluded table. A couple of years ago, occasions like this one had featured quite heavily in my life, and I recalled the initial heady excitement and disbelief at my good fortune in having linked up with my favorite band, and taking part in their lifestyle. I smiled to myself, feeling a little nostalgic for the innocence and naivety of those early dates. Now, of course, I was much more sophisticated and worldly-wise. Well, possibly, a little bit. I could be serene, and poised, and elegantly glamorous with the best of them, I applauded myself inwardly, skillfully shooting an olive across the restaurant while trying to spear it with a toothpick.

Rachel gave me a strange look. "Are you all right?" she mouthed into my ear.

"What?" I whispered back. "Why wouldn't I be?"

Rachel shook her head. "You're being weird."

Weird? Who, me?

Trust Rachel to read me like a book.

"I'm not being weird," I hissed. "I've got something to —" The "tell you" stuck in my throat as I knocked over my glass of wine in the effort of communicating with my friend without being heard by the others. Rachel jumped up and flapped about with a napkin, wiping at her trousers and shooting me murderous looks.

"Sorry, sorry, sorry," I gabbled, joining my own napkin to her dabbing efforts, and seizing the opportunity to whisk her off to the ladies' room. Five pairs of male eyes regarded us with amusement as we ambled off, holding a napkin over the incriminating wet patch.

The doors had barely shut behind us when Rachel turned on me.

"Right," she announced. "There'd better be a jolly good reason why you just spilled an expensive glass of wine over my favorite designers, so I'm listening."

I looked at her, trying to gather my thoughts, trying to work out how to communicate the enormity of the situation.

"Rach…" I started, then caught sight of her wet patch and erupted in involuntary giggles. "Let's tidy you up first." I grabbed a few luxury paper towels from the dispenser, but Rachel wasn't having any of it. "That'll dry. It's only white wine. Go on."

I gulped. *Okay. If I must.*

"Rach, I saw him. My thunderbolt-and-lightning. My man."

She looked at me uncomprehendingly, so I elaborated. "The one I'm going to marry."

Chapter Four

"You *what?* Where? When? *Who?*"

Rachel's eyes lit up with a sense of intrigue. "You dark horse! When did all of this happen?"

"Keep your voice down," I hissed back, "I don't need the whole world to know just yet. I haven't even really met him yet. I just know—"

"You just *know?*" she repeated, somewhat incredulous.

"Yeah, I just know. *You* told me all about thunderbolt-and-lightning. You said, one day I would just know. Well, I didn't believe you, but you were right, and now I know."

"I said that?" Rachel wondered out loud. "When?"

I gave a big sigh. "Don't you remember? When I called you from Paris all that time ago, and I didn't know what to do? *You* said that obviously Dan *and* Tim weren't right for me, and that I'd know when I met the right man."

"Oh." There was a small silence. "Yes, I did say that." Rachel acknowledged.

"Well, don't tell me you didn't mean it?"

"Of course I meant it. I just thought you'd forgotten. You never mentioned it again until just now."

"How could I forget something momentous like that?" I asked back. "I've been thinking about it for almost two years, doubting that you were right. But tonight—" I paused.

"Tonight...what?" Rachel breathed. "What happened? What did Dan say to you?"

"No," I wailed, "this is nothing to do with Dan. Dan is all over, it's all history. This is..." I paused again, visualizing the chocolate eyes, recalling that moment.

"This is—what?" Rachel prompted once more.

"This is... *real*. This is really it."

"Yeah?" And, when I still said nothing, "Go on, don't make this like pulling teeth." She adopted a Sheriff-of-Nottingham voice. "I will extract the truth from you even if I have to dig out your heart with a teaspoon."

I laughed. "I think you've got your films mixed up. Okay, okay...right, so at choir tonight... Oh Rachel, it was unbelievable. I locked eyes with this man. I think his name is Steve, and we looked at each other, and I just know I'm going to marry him."

Rachel looked at me expectantly.

"That's it?" she eventually queried, when nothing more was forthcoming from me.

"Yes," I said, "that's it."

"You looked at a man."

"No, I *locked eyes* with a man," I corrected, lest she should get this vital detail wrong.

"You *locked eyes* with a man," Rachel repeated, making speech marks in the air with her fingers, "and you know you're going to marry him."

"Well, yes. But it was more than that," I tried to explain.

"Oh good," Rachel interjected, "I'm glad there was something more, let's hear it."

"Well, it wasn't *more* more," I started again. "Rach, it was like you said. Thunderbolt-and-lighting. I felt like I'd been electrified. I could practically *see* the sparks fly between him and me. It was real. It was incredible. He felt it, too. He looked at me the whole time and we couldn't move."

Rachel regarded me gravely. Her eyes seemed to penetrate right to the back of my head. Suddenly she started whooping with joy, jumping up and down, pumping my hands and twirling me round and round.

"Oh my God," she finally uttered. "It's happened, it's really happened!"

"It's happened?" I echoed.

"It's happened," she confirmed gleefully. "You've had your real, bona fide thunderbolt-and-lightning moment."

"So you believe me?" I needed to hear it again.

"Totally. You lucky cow." And she punched me playfully on the shoulder. We stood in silence, regarding each other's reflections in the softly lit mirrors. Idly, I picked up a bottle of exclusive, expensive hand lotion and squirted some on my hands. Rachel was overcome by another wave of hilarity.

"It's brilliant, it's brilliant, it's absolutely bloody brilliant," she sang, dancing around me again. She spoke in her best newsreader voice. "Sophie Penhalligan today clapped eyes on the man of her life. She hasn't met him yet but intends to fix that situation as soon as humanly possible. Sophie" — she pushed a soap dispenser in my face as a pseudo microphone — "how does it feel to have your own personal thunderbolt-and-lightning after all this time?"

"Err…electrifying," I offered, and we collapsed in giggles again.

Still laughing, we returned to the table, and I put in my best effort at being charming and funny. I caught Dan looking at me quizzically a few times. Like Rachel, he was very much tuned into my emotions and he probably sensed something was up. I wasn't ready to 'fess up, so I simply flashed him my biggest smile and raised my glass in a silent toast. He gave me his devastating rock-star smile and shrugged, toasting me back.

Chapter Five

A few days later, it was my birthday. I hit the big 3-0.

In the grand scheme of things, that wasn't really *that* momentous. Statistically speaking, I wasn't even a half-lifer yet. But still — I was thirty.

Dan, being ever magnanimous, offered to host a big birthday bash for me in a club or a hotel. He painted a wonderful picture of Tuscq playing, lots of champagne, canapés, the lot. "Anything you want," he tempted me. And tempted I was.

But I thought better of it. Yeah, it would have been great to have a big bash, but it wouldn't have been *my* bash. It wouldn't have been me.

After much consideration, I decided that I wanted to welcome my thirties by celebrating Sophie-style, in my flat, with my friends, with random bottles of wine brought by my friends, with my badly cooked food, my ancient stereo, my music. It would be crowded and noisy, and the neighbors would complain, and wine would be spilt and I would regret it all the next morning when I had to tidy up on my own. But it would be *my* party.

And so there I was, on the evening of my thirtieth birthday, rolling up rugs, moving the sofa beneath the window, tidying away any breakables, and drinking cava along the way. I was having a great time already.

Suddenly, I collapsed in a heap of giggles as I realized that something dreadful had happened to me. I *had* grown up after all. Only a few short years ago, it would never have occurred to me to clear the decks and protect my belongings. And yet here I was, in best ex-fiancé Tim-mode, party-proofing the flat. I raised a glass to Tim, wherever he was. "Here's to learning from the best."

"Learning what from the best?" asked Rachel. She had let herself in and was carrying a big bag of groceries.

"Party-proofing," I giggled. "Don't I remind you of someone?" I adopted my most serious expression and commanded myself in a stern voice, "Don't forget that vase, now, Sophie. It's a priceless heirloom."

"Oh... Yes, I get it," Rachel wheezed, then looked thoughtful for a second. "I suppose it happens to the best of us, imitating our exes. *Only* kidding!" She thumped me lightly on the shoulder. "Anyway, better get on with this lot, the food won't cook itself."

For the next hour, we took a rather nostalgic trip down memory lane, back to our student days, when, like today, we had also prepared toasted pitas and hummus and taramasalata, sausages and pizza.

And when we were done with memory lane, I turned the conversation to Rachel's Big Wedding to Jordan. How could I not? I was going to be chief bridesmaid, after all, and it was my duty to ensure that the bride-to-be remained happy, relaxed and organized. Especially organized.

In fact, the wedding had been meant to happen in the spring. Not so. The happy couple had been so delirious with excitement over their long-overdue engagement that they had not managed to get their wedding off the ground. I had warned and ranted and raved and admonished...and in the end, I concluded that it really didn't matter. If they weren't ready for a spring date, it would have to be an autumn wedding. Or a winter one.

Obviously, as March had turned into April and there was no actual date set, no plans made, Rachel had become a little agitated that plans weren't progressing. *Then* I had sprung into action, and together, Rachel and Jordan and I had finally selected the August bank holiday weekend for the big day. Gradually, I had assumed a role of wedding coach. I had done the research and presented options, gently and subtly coaxing them in the right direction. And after they had finally settled on a venue and a caterer, I gracefully backed out to let them work out the details for themselves.

Every now and then, I surreptitiously checked in to make sure they were still making progress. Like now.

"How's that dress coming along?" I asked while arranging a pile of napkins on the kitchen counter.

"What dress?" Rachel shot back, unaware of my change of subject.

"Your wedding dress," I clarified.

"Oh...that..." Rachel blushed. I put the napkins down.

"What did you do?" I demanded.

"Err...well...nothing, really. I just..."

She fidgeted with the hem of her cocktail dress. "Um, well, I changed my mind."

"You what?" I screeched, incredulous. It had taken *weeks* of trawling through all the wedding boutiques of Greater London to find The Dress for Rachel, and another couple of weeks to convince her to buy it. It was a sleek, elegant sheath dress in creamy satin. Rachel looked like a princess, especially after the dressmaker suggested embroidering the bodice with tiny little pearls and glittery fake diamonds. I had never seen a prettier dress.

I leaned against the wall. "What have you done?" I whispered. "Please don't tell me you canceled the dress."

Rachel looked sheepish. "I didn't think it was really me," she responded softly. "Sorry."

I gulped. Of course, her dress was her choice, but her taste had proved somewhat dubious.

"Have you got a picture of the new dress?" I demanded weakly, prepared for the worst. Rachel's eyes sparkled.

"Have I got a picture of the new dress?" she mimicked, teasingly. "You bet I do. You *know* I do. Here." She searched in her handbag for something, finally retrieving her phone. "Let me show you."

She scrolled through the menu, clicking her tongue impatiently while trying to locate the right file. Eventually, she found it and handed me the phone triumphantly.

"*Oh. My. God.*" I squealed delightedly. "Oh my God, Rachel, you tease, why did you give me such a fright? I thought you'd changed it all."

Rachel grinned wickedly. "Do you like what we've done?"

"It's beautiful." She had only gone and made the perfect dress divine. "How did this come about?"

Rachel blushed. "The dressmaker suggested it, knowing how much I wanted a meringue. She said it would be stunning, and that she'd always wanted to do this for someone. So we're all happy."

I regarded the photo again, feeling my face split into a broad grin.

Rachel had kept the sleek sheath dress, and the dressmaker had embroidered the bodice. But she had also added a single layer of the most beautifully delicate organza to the sheath. It was absolutely magical.

"This is the most incredible dress ever," I breathed, choked with emotion.

"Isn't it fantastic?" Rachel agreed happily, taking her phone from me and regarding herself critically. "I do love that organza layer. It makes the whole thing so…floaty."

"It's adorable," I agreed, feeling hugely relieved. At least the major pieces of her wedding were now successfully in place. It wouldn't matter whether Jordan wore a morning suit or an ordinary suit, or whether there was a grand color scheme in operation or not. They had a beautiful venue, a delightful caterer and a magical bride. It would be perfect.

"Now for you," Rachel cut into my thoughts. "We need to find you a dress, and soon."

I gulped. The bridesmaid's dress was the one aspect of the wedding that I had cheerfully neglected. I was fairly certain that Rachel wouldn't inflict undue pain on me, but when she had pulled hideous wedding dress after hideous wedding dress off the racks, I had begun to panic slightly.

"I've got more photos," Rachel announced gleefully, scrolling through the files again. "Look at these!" She proffered the phone once more. I regarded a selection of bridesmaid's dresses in pinks and lilacs, and I had to concede, the lilac one didn't look too bad. I was about to make a comment when the kitchen timer pinged.

"Time for the garlic breads to go in," Rachel diagnosed and got busy once more. She started to peel the garlic breads out of their packaging, but interrupted herself to give me a big hug. "I'm so glad you're my best friend, and my bridesmaid," she told me. "What would I do without you?"

I didn't know what to say, so instead I hugged her back extra hard, feeling all emotional and gooey.

Chapter Six

By nine o'clock, my little flat was heaving. Dan had arrived, bringing the rest of the band with him. Some old school friends had come, some of them making a rather long trip from Newquay. My work friends were there, and my choir friends as well as the downstairs neighbors, whom I had invited on the premise that they couldn't complain about the noise if they helped make it. It wasn't a massive party by Dan's standards, but with thirty-odd people crowding into the lounge and spilling over onto the landing and right into the kitchen, it certainly felt as packed as a nightclub.

The music was pumping and people were dancing. The kitchen was a riot of random bottles of wine and spirits, food was going in and out of the oven, and Dan had donned an apron and was taking great delight in playing butler. At ten o'clock, the doorbell rang and two men wearing chef's hats and white tunics struggled up my stairs with an enormous pink cardboard box. Dan intercepted them before I could take a look-see and steered them toward the lounge.

As the delivery chefs left, the music stopped and the lounge lights went out. Excited whispering and muffled voices emanating from the lounge suggested that something was afoot. Suddenly, Rachel pressed a glass of champagne in my hand and propelled me toward my dark sitting room.

"Happy birthday to you... Happy birthday to you... Happy birthday, lovely Sophie... Happy birthday to you!"

Everyone had crammed in the lounge to sing my birthday song, and while my eyes were struggling to take it all in, the cake exploded on the table. Dozens and dozens of sparklers ignited, and an indoor Catherine wheel fizzed away colorfully.

And the cake. *Wow.*

It was a three-tier pink and silver affair with sugary stars and pearls distributed artfully but liberally over each tier. The base was decorated with dozens of tiny little pictures of me, from birth to thirty. I was speechless.

"Sophie," Dan piped up, clearing his throat somewhat nervously. "I know you didn't want a big posh bash in a fancy place, and that's all fine. We're all having a terrific time. But..." he looked a bit sheepish. "Well, I know you, and I know you wouldn't have bothered with a birthday cake for yourself."

I had bothered, actually, on this occasion, but the outcome was nothing compared to this amazing creation. I decided to keep quiet on the matter of the mess that was my own brown squidgy chocolate cake, I could always have it for breakfast.

"Anyway," Dan continued, "I thought it would be okay if we treated you to the best birthday cake ever...so here it is. Happy birthday, Sophie!" he shouted once more.

I felt oddly moved, but before I could get tearful, a chant erupted all around me.

"Cut! Cut! Cut! Cut-cut-cut-cut-cut!"

I turned to get a knife from the kitchen, but Joe had thought ahead and stood behind me, wielding my best bread knife and nearly stabbing me in the chest.

"Sorry," he muttered. "I can't seem to find a cake knife."

"You can't find a cake knife," I giggled, "because I don't have one. But this'll do." I turned to attack the cake.

"*Hold it,*" came a shout from the depths of the lounge. Rachel emerged, brandishing a camera. "Photo opportunity! This moment ought to be preserved for eternity."

"Okay," I grumbled. I hated having my photo taken, especially doing something where I would show off how clumsy I was by, for instance, toppling the cake over while cutting into it. But Dan had read my mind.

"Don't worry," he whispered, "I'll hold the cake while you cut."

Bless him. So I cut, and with Dan standing behind me holding the cake stand with both hands reaching around me either side, the resulting photo looked strangely like the "happy couple" shot at a wedding. Strangely, that is. Not necessarily attractively.

The party carried on with people dancing, disco lights in the lounge, and lots of laughter and raucous singing. I was feeling mellow and happy and a little drunk, flitting back and forth with more food and drink for my guests.

Unexpectedly, I heard shouts of, "Ooh, a smoke machine, how cool!" from the lounge. This was slightly odd because I didn't have a smoke machine, hadn't hired one, and also couldn't remember anyone bringing one.

Before I could investigate, I heard mutterings of, "Eugh, but the stink."

Abruptly, the music stopped and the lights went off again. This time, the lights went off everywhere in the flat.

People had opened the windows in the lounge to let out excess smoke, and as I stood pondering, a large whitish flame emanated from one of the sockets by the fireplace. Everyone stood and stared, transfixed in the twilight created by the orange glow of the outside lamp post. A thin black line appeared above the skirting board, spreading rapidly along the room accompanied by a horrendous stink and an ominous sizzling sound.

What appeared like minutes could only have been seconds, before Mick shouted at the top of his voice, "Everybody out, *now*! Fire!" He was at the back of the room, and he was the first to comprehend the situation.

"Sophie, dial 999" he commanded, and I duly sprinted to the telephone. "Dan, go and open the front door. Everybody move, move, move!" Mick shouted, now with a tinge of panic in his voice as people weren't leaving fast enough.

And that did it.

Within two minutes, we were all outside, listening to the sirens of fire engines neeh-nahing their way to my flat, and contemplating our lucky escape. By now, flames were evident through the still wide-open windows, and my flat was lit up from within with a flickering orange glow like a Halloween pumpkin.

My flat. My lovely flat. All my lovely things.

I started back to the front door. I had to get my much-loved teddy, and my insurance papers, and books and CDs, and photos, and degree certificates, and my passport.

"Oh no, you don't!" Mick and Dan caught me before I could go back in. Dan shook me roughly. "What the hell do you think you're doing?" he demanded.

"I need to get my stuff," I gabbled. "It's all going up in flames. My stuff. My life." I let out a long wail and tried for the front door again.

Dan slapped my face. "Listen to me," he screamed, trying to make eye contact while I was frantically twisting my head to look past him toward my burning flat.

"Listen to me," he screamed again and turned me bodily around so I was no longer facing the house.

"You've got your life."

When I still didn't seem to get it, he repeated, louder still, "You've got your *life*. Nothing else matters. You are alive, and so is everybody else. Nobody is hurt. We were very lucky. You may not have any of your stuff tomorrow, but you've got your life."

"Sophie?" Rachel cut in gently from behind me. "Look!"

She proffered something. I was so startled, I couldn't see properly at first.

"Oh, Rach!"

Rachel had rescued my childhood teddy. She had also grabbed my handbag containing credit cards and mobile phone from the hook by the door, and my cherished photo cube from my bedroom.

"How…? Why…? I thought…?" I couldn't quite get my sentence out.

"It was easy," Rachel explained. "I was right by your bedroom when Mick started shouting. I knew this was going to be bad" — I winced — "so I grabbed the first things I could reach without really stopping."

She pressed Teddy in my arms and hung the purse round my neck. "At least that should cover the basics…you know, money, and that stuff," she added gruffly. I hugged her tightly. Dan shook his head. "That was very risky, Rachel," he admonished. "Thoughtful, but risky."

"I know," Rachel said. She gave a watery smile.

Meanwhile, the fire brigade had arrived. Two engines parked up, and there were at least ten fire fighters busily rolling out hoses. One of them was talking earnestly to Mick, but I could only hear snippets of conversation. He seemed to be trying to find out whether anybody was still inside. "No," Mick said confidently, "I was the last one out. I was furthest back and there was nobody left when I got out."

The water started shooting out of the hoses through the windows and right into my flat. The flames had consumed the curtains and the first floor was properly ablaze, like something you saw on the news. Two of the fire fighters were pointing their hoses high, so that the water shot up in the air and arched over the roof. Two others were dousing the neighboring roofs and houses with water. What a mess.

Thirty bedraggled partygoers looked on silently as the fire fighters put out the blaze that ended my birthday party in a flash. When the fire was under control, gradually, one by one, people left with offers of help and asylum.

Soon, it was only Rachel, Dan and the band, and me left outside the ruins of my flat. And the downstairs neighbors, of course, who looked utterly shell-shocked. I didn't blame them. In fact, I was surprised that they weren't ranting and raving at me for setting our house on fire. Then again, I hadn't actually done anything. I had no clue what had happened.

Right at that moment, the chief fire officer came to talk to me.

"I gather you own the flat?" he started without much of an introduction. I guessed this wasn't the time for social niceties.

"I do, yes. I was having a birthday party."

"Any idea what happened?" he wanted to know.

I gulped. Dan spoke on my behalf.

He explained about the flash and the smoke. "We couldn't see any evidence of fire to start with." The fire officer wrote something on a pad.

"How long before there were actual flames?" he inquired.

I spoke up now. "A few minutes...maybe five? We were all out here by then."

He nodded again. He was very calm, but I couldn't make out whether he was judging us.

"Why are you nodding?" I challenged him. I couldn't help myself, I was all muddled up and I wanted someone to say that this wasn't my fault.

He ignored me, and asked another question instead. "Anybody smoke anything at your party?"

"No," I declared firmly. "I'm a strictly no-smoking girl."

"Good. How many appliances were you running at the time?"

Appliances? What, like a washing machine? Or a kettle?

"Um, I don't know. The lights were on..." I tried to reconstruct what had been happening when it all went wrong. "The stereo was on and a couple of lamps, probably... The oven was on in the kitchen, and maybe somebody boiled a kettle. I can't think of anything else. Can you?" I sent Dan and the others an imploring look. Lots of shaking of heads.

"I can't think of anything out of the ordinary," one of my neighbors piped up. I could have kissed her.

"Hm..." mused the fireman, scratching his chin. "Sounds like a cable fire to me. Maybe there was a short somewhere. We'll have to investigate." He turned to go. The group of us remained standing on the same spot, feeling bereft.

Eventually, Dan pulled himself together. "Wow, what a night," he pondered. "Not quite what we had in mind, perhaps, but certainly unforgettable."

That comment broke the ice, and I giggled. I chortled. Then I burst into hysterical laughter.

Pretty soon, Rachel was in hysterics as well, and we were clinging on to each other for dear life.

"I'm going to wee my pants," Rachel snorted, doubling over with laughter. I noticed the firemen shooting us sympathetic looks. "Shock," one appeared to be mouthing to the other but they left us to it.

The four band members regarded us hysterical girls with bemusement, unable to comprehend our sudden mirth.

Eventually I calmed down again.

"Where am I going to stay?" I wondered out loud.

"You can stay with me," Rachel declared eagerly.

"You could stay with me," Dan offered simultaneously.

I looked from one to the other.

So did Mick, Darren and Joe.

Everybody looked at me.

"I..." I started, not knowing what to say. "I don't know what to say."

Chapter Seven

That night, I moved in with Dan. On a strictly temporary basis, of course.

Rachel backed down gracefully once she was certain that Dan's offer was both genuine and innocent. Her flat, while lovely, would have felt very crowded, and there was the gorgeous Jordan to consider.

Incidentally, it occurred to me, where had Jordan been? The two of them, Rachel-and-Jordan, were practically inseparable these days. I felt a pang of guilt at not having noticed his absence or asked Rachel about it.

Anyway, Dan packed me and my meager rescued belongings into a taxi as soon as the fire brigade had given us the all clear to go. I was to come back the following morning to hear the verdict on the state of disrepair of my flat.

It was almost four a.m. by the time we arrived at Dan's house, damp, overtired and reeking of smoke. Dan installed me in one of his guest rooms and ordered me to have a shower. He grabbed all my discarded clothes and stuck them straight in the washer. And no, I had no idea that he even knew how to work a washing machine. I kind of imagined that a housekeeper would take care of all of that.

"Humble beginnings," he grinned when I teased him about it. "Some things you never forget. I can work a dishwasher, too. *And* I can cook." He threw me a probing look, brow furrowed, before he added, "There are quite a lot of little things you don't know about me yet, my sweet. You know the big stuff, but you never had a chance to find out the everyday matters."

He said it lightly but I took his point. However, I simply smiled sweetly and let it pass. This wasn't the time or the place.

By the time I emerged from the bathroom, clean and slightly pink, Dan had deposited a pair of his pajamas on my bed for me. Much too big, of course, but there was something extremely comforting about snuggling into a pair of laundered, oversized men's pajamas. Even if they were slightly unexpected. In days gone by, Dan had worn silky designers or even slept completely without. This pair was weird. They were thick cotton pajamas in a red-and-green tartan pattern. Quite unlike Dan, in fact. Still, they were soft and smelled fresh, and I was very, very tired. I crawled under the duvet and was asleep before I could put the lights out or reflect further on Dan's pajama aberration.

Barely six hours later, there we were again outside my flat in Tooting, bleary-eyed and quite unable to take in the scale of devastation.

"Structurally unsound" and "uninhabitable" were the two words that lodged in my brain out of Fire Officer Thomson's assessment. He and his crew had investigated the flat closely earlier that morning and concluded that a faulty connection in one of the sockets had short-circuited, creating that massive flash flame that we had seen and igniting the cables under the plaster, eventually causing carpets and curtains to catch fire, and so on.

I was still taking all of that in when another fireman handed me a rather large, very soggy bag.

"What's this?" I wondered out loud.

"These are the clothes and a few other things that we salvaged from your bedroom this morning," he explained. "I'm afraid everything else has been destroyed either by fire or water. Oh, and most of the kitchen is still intact," he added cheerfully, "but I figured you'd probably not be wanting your crockery just yet."

"Err, no," I concurred weakly, regarding the bag in my hand. So that was it. That was all that was left of my stuff. I swallowed hard.

"Chin up," advised the fireman. "No one got hurt, and everything else is replaceable."

"Um, yes," I mumbled uncertainly. "I suppose it is."

So we returned to Dan's house, where I set about instructing my insurance to send somebody out to complete a claims assessment, where I rang Mum and Dad to let them know what had happened, and where I sent out a text to all my friends to make sure they were all okay. Afterwards, Dan helped me hammer out a rudimentary strategy for hiring builders to fix the flat, and then he took me for a walk in the park.

We didn't talk much because there wasn't much to say. I hadn't fully comprehended what had happened to my life yet. I *knew*, but I couldn't seem to understand.

Dan was brilliant. Bearing in mind our history, he was careful not to create any ambiguous moments. There was no innuendo, just all-out, full-on friendship. He invited Rachel and Jordan over that evening for dinner; this time Jordan turned up, but I didn't get a chance to find out why he hadn't made it the previous night.

And suddenly, Sunday was over, somehow, and on Monday morning I had to go to work. Taking a different route to a different Tube station, walking past different coffee shops and different newspaper vendors. How very odd and unexpected life could be.

Chapter Eight

It turned out to be slightly surreal, sharing a house with a rock star. Our lives seemed to move on different planes, and in more ways than one. When we were alone together, we made a careful point of being just friends. Meanwhile, every morning at six thirty, I would trundle down to the kitchen to find the remains of Dan's entertaining from the previous night cluttering up the kitchen surfaces. Mostly there would be glasses and bottles, frequently accompanied by takeaway cartons and used plates. Very occasionally, there was evidence of rudimentary cooking using a disproportionate amount of pots and accessories which would also languish in the sink.

Dan would be fast asleep, blissfully unaware of my early morning work-drone existence and leaving the tidying up to Jenny, the housekeeper, who would arrive at about nine o'clock. Incidentally, I fell into the habit of adding my breakfast dishes to the general debris, thus granting myself an extra ten minutes to lounge around watching breakfast television before heading out

to work at seven thirty. Sharing a house with Dan certa:
some perks.

Jenny also took over my laundry and my ironing
asking and without comment. I didn't have to lift a finger
of cleaning or hoovering, and so I led a very relaxed existe
a few weeks. Apart, of course, from all the stress of tryin;
the insurance to settle my claim, which had risen to q
astronomical sum. Also, keeping on top of the builders re
my flat proved quite a challenge, until Dan suggested app
a project manager and adding the cost to the insurance
The latest estimate was that it would be three to four
before I could move back in.

So in the interim I stayed at Dan's, and I was g
dangerously used to my cushy lifestyle there. The only fly
ointment was that, after the first few days, I barely saw
gathered Tuscq was working on a new album, but sometim
was clearly just "out." I made a point of not asking whe
went or what he did on those occasions, and he made a po
not telling.

When he *wasn't* out, he would often bring home a rar
woman. His conquests were all attractive models with pe
figures, generous endowments in the chest region, and
identical faces done up with artful makeup. Somehow, tho
they never seemed to make Dan happy. *That* bothered
intensely.

Without meaning to, I started mildly discomfiting D.
lady-friends at every opportunity. Once I posed as Dan's lc
suffering wife, and one time, when Rachel stayed over,
pretended that we were all part of one happy love-in. And s
went on until…until George changed everything.

George had had the privilege of staying for three nights
a row. Having emptied the fridge of any vegetable matter

reens and oranges, having consumed all of my bread even though she was on a strict no-carbs diet, and also having liberally made use of my Orient shower cream without asking, George tried to make friends. Presumably, she figured that buttering up the incumbent resident would improve her chances of hanging on. Anyway, she couldn't have got off to a worse start when she called me—

"Sadie!"

Of course I didn't react.

"Yoo—hoo, Sadie, *hello!*" she warbled, sounding vaguely like a songbird in distress.

I looked up from my book.

"Are you talking to me?" I inquired.

"Sure am," she issued with a total lack of concern. "You must be the lovely Sadie. Dan's told me all about you."

I heaved a sigh. "Has he, now?"

"Yeah, like how you're just staying for a while and how you're definitely moving out and how you're totally like not into him and how—"

I had to stop her in mid flow.

"Yup, that would be me. Except my name's not Sadie."

"Not Sadie?" she echoed.

"No. Definitely not."

"Are you sure?"

I snorted into my tea cup. "Quite sure, darling. And you must be..." Now it was my turn. She opened her mouth to answer, but I got in there first. Not in her mouth, of course. I spoke first, was what I meant.

"No, let me guess. You must be..." I regarded her critically as if to get a clue from her appearance.

"Candy," I offered.

She shook her head, looking offended. I ploughed on.

"Crystal." Another shake of head.

"Teela...? LaLa...?" More shakes of head, with mouth opening and closing, ready to speak. I was faster.

"Barbie? Nala? Babsie? Shelley? Brie? Davinia?" I was on a real roll here, with no idea where all these names were coming from.

"Arabella-Georgiana," she interrupted me suddenly at top volume. "My name is Arabella-Georgiana."

I stared, wide-eyed. The words left my mouth before I could stop them. "Do people really call you that?"

To my great surprise, she burst into tears and sat down heavily at the kitchen table. I felt bad. After all, it wasn't her fault that her parents had saddled her with an impossible combination of names. I sat down next to her. What to do? I couldn't really hug her, I didn't even know her.

"I'm sorry," I offered eventually, when she had calmed down enough to be able to hear me. "That was really rude. I'm sorry, really."

When I didn't get a reaction, I decided to dig my hole deeper. "It's a pretty name, really..." I continued. "It's just...well, a little unexpected."

She snorted and signaled for me to pass her a tissue to blow her nose. *Harrumph!* My goodness, that girl could blow. I blushed at the inadvertent innuendo as my mind imagined her... No, no, no, I didn't want to go there. Arabella-Georgiana wiped at her eyes, smearing mascara all over her face and suddenly looking really vulnerable.

"My friends call me George," she hiccupped eventually. "Anyway, it's not you teasing me about my name that's upset me." She paused. "Has...has Dan really had all those women...?" she asked, then hastily turned down the tone of her question. "I mean, not *had* had…well, obviously that, too…but, what I meant is, is he really bringing back so many others?"

I flinched at "others." Not a good sign.

I heaved another big sigh, but spoke much more gently.

"I made all those names up, George, because I don't really meet Dan's conquests most of the time. But…" I stopped to see how she was taking this in so far. "Yes, he does bring home quite a lot of different ladies…"

She looked crestfallen. I took pity on her. "Look, it's just how he is. He can't help himself. I think he's looking for something but he doesn't even know what it is."

She hiccupped again, looking waif-like and forlorn.

"I'm fairly sure that he hasn't made you any promises of any kind…has he?" I suddenly had this awful thought he might have forgotten himself. When *I* first met him, he had been absolutely, brutally honest with me. *I'm bad news,* he had said. *I love to have sex, but I'm not in love with you.* That was his default mode when he took someone to bed. Or at least, it used to be. Obviously, there was always the possibility that he might develop feelings for someone; he was only a man, after all. He had nearly believed that he loved me, back then. *Nearly.*

"No," George acknowledged, abruptly cutting into my ruminations, "no, he hasn't. He told me he was bad news…but I thought…" She petered out.

Bless her.

Suddenly, she fixed me with a surprisingly inquisitive stare with those red-rimmed, black-ringed eyes of hers. "How do you cope with it all?"

I gave a start. "What, who—me?"

"Yes, you. I mean, after all, you live here. You must be…pretty serious about him?"

I burst out laughing. "Oh my gosh, no. I was, at one time. A long time ago. But I knew that he would always seek out other women, and so I broke it off. We've stayed friends though, as cheesy as that sounds. I'm only staying here while my flat is being redecorated."

She looked a question mark at me.

"It burned down. On my birthday. While I was having a party."

"*No*," George breathed, "really? How awful for you." She was momentarily distracted from her own misery. Abruptly, something clicked, and she looked at me with recognition.

"I knew I almost had it right. It's not Sadie, it's *Sophie*, right?" I nodded my head, astounded at the sudden insight.

"I knew I'd seen your picture before. You were engaged to Dan a couple of years back, right? And you dumped him?" I cringed at the stark summation of events, but yes, I acknowledged, that was me.

"Wow." George was awestruck. "Wow," she repeated. "I don't know if I could have let him go."

Oh dear. She was *still* stuck on him. I sidestepped her comment by focusing on her own predicament.

"Honey," I said as gently as I could. "You should let him go. *Now*. He's not yours, not anyone's. You'll get hurt. He might ring you tomorrow, you might go out again, you might even come back here another night. But...the day after, it'll be somebody new. Trust me."

So, I had turned from model-baiting to model-counseling. Perhaps I wasn't such a mean person after all. George sat at the kitchen table like in a dream, and Dan—as always deploying impeccable timing—chose that precise moment to walk in.

"Hello, my two favorite ladies in the whole wide world," he joked, not even remotely perturbed by George's destroyed appearance. "Lovely to see you having a cozy chat."

George looked at him with confusion.

"Is it true you don't love me?" she asked abruptly, in a voice that was only ever so slightly wobbly. Dan shot me a look. I shook my head.

"No, George," he said, as gently as he could. "I'm sorry, sweetheart. I don't love you. I never told you I did, or would. I did say I was bad news." He, too, sat down at the kitchen table. We made quite a tableau, the three of us.

George suddenly got up and left the table. Five minutes later, she was back, dressed in demure jeans and sweatshirt, face clean of makeup, hair in a ponytail. She looked much younger now, eighteen or twenty at the most. Like a lost fresher. Dan and I both realized at the same instant that that was exactly what she was.

"I'll be going now," she said in a small voice. "Thanks for…um, everything." And before Dan could say anything, she turned and left.

Chapter Nine

"Oh my God, Dan" I admonished. "Have you *any* idea what you're doing? Poor old George here...she was practically a babe-in-arms. She was only putting on an act to get to you. Don't you ever *see* those things?"

I was surprisingly angry. Dan looked sheepish.

"She said she was twenty-five. I believed her. What should I do, ask for ID?"

"Well, maybe you should!" I shot back. "One day, you might not be so lucky. Dan, for God's sake, what's the matter with you?"

"I don't know," he said, then muttered something about midlife crisis.

"Oh, come off it," I advised. "You've got almost everything you want. We've talked about this whole relationship thing, remember? I really don't care who you shag, but make sure you don't pick someone who'll get really hurt. Poor old George..." I petered out.

To be fair, Dan looked shocked to the core. He retreated to his studio and I didn't see him for the best part of a week. He barely left the house, and he didn't invite anyone back. Perhaps George had done him a favor and taught him a lesson.

One Friday afternoon, when I finished work early and had nothing to do, what with Rachel and Jordan busy planning their wedding… Well, I got home to Dan's house and he was there, and he was out of his studio. In fact, he was in the lounge reading a book, a rare pastime for this here rock star of mine, and he was also humming a tune. I had been hearing snippets of this tune on and off all week on the few occasions when I had seen Dan, and it was very catchy. I had found myself humming bits of it at work today.

Anyway, there he was, not busy, not sulking, but just there. When I walked in, he jumped off the sofa and greeted me like a long-lost friend, big hugs and all. He pressed a gin and tonic into my hand and dragged me into the kitchen.

"I told you I could cook," he announced, and opened the oven door with a flourish. I could just make out a dish filled to the brim with what looked like hot cheesy sauce. It smelled delicious. I took a closer peek but he shooed me away, telling me to sit down at the table, which he had already laid for two.

"What is this?" I managed, totally taken aback.

"Just a little treat," Dan announced cheerfully, pulling the rack out of the oven and revealing a perfectly cooked, mouth-watering lasagna. "To apologize for my very bad behavior and my long sulk." He set the steaming dish on the table, narrowly avoiding knocking over an open bottle of red wine.

"I got garlic bread, too…" he continued, deftly retrieving it from the oven. "Oh, and salad." He scurried to the fridge.

I sat in awe. "This is fantastic," I managed eventually. I was eyeing up the garlic bread which looked homemade. "Did you make this?"

"Of course," Dan assured me. "I did tell you I could cook. I just need time, and inspiration." He spread a napkin on my lap like an expert waiter and sat down to join me.

"Wine, madam?" he asked in a serious sommelier voice, bottle already poised and pouring.

"Oh yes, please," I breathed, somewhat overcome. Then I spied a fancy-looking envelope lying on the kitchen counter. Ever curious, I got up to retrieve it. It was addressed to me.

"Hold on..." I muttered, "what have we here?"

Dan was looking a bit nervous. "Erm," he started, and cleared his throat. "Uh, I have a pretty good idea what that is. I was going to feed you first though... You know...soften the blow a bit."

Blow? What blow? What *was* he talking about? This wasn't a dreaded brown envelope, nor a bill. The envelope was thick lilac paper with little printed daisies scattered prettily in an arch along the left hand side. In fact, it looked like a wedding invitation. I smiled. Who did I know who was getting married? Oh, what fun.

I turned the envelope over in my hands, ready to open it, when I caught sight of the sender.

Dan caught me looking and got up quickly. He took my hand, the one with the envelope, and looked me in the eyes.

"You don't have to open this now," he said gently. "Have some dinner first. Here, finish your drink at least..."

He knew. He was such a kind man, trying to distract me from this disaster in the making, but I had to open it. I had to read it.

I slid my index finger through the top of the envelope before he could stop me. Out fell several bits of paper, but I caught the lilac card in my hands.

Ms. Dina Erin Belling
and
Mr. Timothy Renfrew
request the pleasure of your company
at their marriage
at Portreath Castle, nr Plymouth
on Saturday, 14 July,
at 2p.m.

I turned the card over and over in my hand, but there was nothing else. No name, no personal address or note of any kind. I felt like somebody had kicked me in the stomach.

Dan had been reading over my shoulder. "Oh dear," he announced, somewhat too cheerfully for my liking. "They might at least have put your name on it."

Well, yes. That, and a few other things, I thought. And what was the point of this? Overcome with strange emotion, I felt jittery and I had to sit down. Tears were pricking the back of my eyes, and I had to sniff to keep them at bay. Dan was making a good job of trying to ignore my discomfort.

"Cheeky buggers," he announced to no one in particular. "Leaving the invite so late."

I ignored him and picked up the envelope again. The handwriting was definitely Tim's, and I shivered in dismay. "I'm not going," I declared.

Dan laughed at me.

"Don't laugh. It's not funny." I sulked, but he laughed harder still.

"I'm not going, and you can't make me," I declared once more.

Dan sat me down at the table again and spooned out some lasagna for me.

"Here," he pronounced. "Eat. It'll make you feel better. And drink, too," he added as an afterthought.

I dutifully took a large gulp of wine.

"Steady on, now," Dan warned. "I didn't mean, get plastered out of your mind. Here, eat something." He picked up the spoon for me, making as though to feed me like one would a child. I glared at him.

"Just why exactly are you so upset?" Dan probed gently.

I duly considered the question. Why *was* I so upset? I supposed the answer was that Tim and I hadn't exactly split up on amicable terms. I couldn't possibly show my face at his wedding.

"I. Am. Not. Going."

Dan gave a theatrical sigh but took the bull by the horns.

"Of course you're going," he told me in his most insouciant voice. "In fact, we're both going." And, seeing my shock and horror, he added, "It'd be rude not to, after they sent *such* a kind invite. Come on…" he coaxed. "It'll be a laugh."

"But…" I stuttered, feeling flustered at the turn of events. "But," I continued, "you're not invited."

"How do you know?" Dan was being obtuse. "It doesn't say anything on the card."

"Well, exactly. That would be how I know."

"Rubbish," Dan stated. "Who goes to a wedding on their own? Who?" He looked a challenge at me. I refused the bait.

"Not many people," I started cautiously, but was mercilessly interrupted.

"Bollocks. Nobody, that's who. And you're not nobody. So, we're going, both of us." He rubbed his hands with glee.

I tucked into my lasagna while I mulled this over. Actually, the food was rather fantastic, and as it warmed my insides, I warmed to the idea of going to this wedding with Dan. I gave an involuntary smile.

Dan had been watching me closely and saw the weather change on my face. "There now," he grinned back, "that's my girl. We'll have a great time. We'll be the evil guests... We..." he paused for thought. "I know! We'll get blindingly drunk and disgrace ourselves by singing loudly. We'll be the worst guests ever. We'll..."

"Hold your horses," I interrupted. "I think utmost grace and poise would be much better weapons here."

"Hm," Dan concurred doubtfully. "But not much fun. However, if it's grace and poise you're after, let's send an acceptance card, right now. Make it official, before you change your mind."

And so we sat down companionably on the sofa, laptop between us, another bottle of wine on the go, while designing our very own acceptance card.

"Tim might not like this," I surmised, examining the end result a little dubiously.

"Tim can go to hell!" Dan declared, but quieted down quickly when he saw the thunderous look on my face.

"Grace and poise," I reminded him.

Dan raised his eyebrows. "Okay... He might be a tad surprised, that's all," he backtracked obligingly. "Now...for expedient delivery..." He scrolled through the contact list on his smartphone. "There."

He dialed a number and spoke briefly. Within twenty minutes, a bicycle courier had turned up and collected our masterpiece.

"Mission accomplished," Dan announced happily. "Ah, it'll be great. I love a good wedding."

Meanwhile, I was having second thoughts. About going, and about our hasty means of accepting the invite.

"Now don't you go looking glum," Dan warned me. "I need your help with something." And, when I didn't react, he persisted. "Right now, if you please?"

"Okay," I shrugged. "What is it?"

Dan jumped up with extraordinary alacrity. "Come on," he urged, "I want to show you my studio."

"Studio?" I echoed. "I thought you needed my help with something?"

"I do, you'll see. Come on, this way."

Chapter Ten

Down the stairs and into the basement he took me. I had never been down here before, hadn't needed to visit his sanctum. We reached a sturdy door that led into a smallish, wood-paneled room. Three empty music stands graced the center of the room, and at the back nestled a drum kit, several six strings and two bass guitars. By the opposite wall, an impressive-looking keyboard sat on its stand. Immediately to the left there was a thick glass door, leading up a few steps into the mixing room.

"Go on up, have a look," Dan encouraged with a proud smile. I dutifully heaved open the heavy door, climbed the steps and sat down in one of the leather-padded executive swivel chairs.

"Wow," I said, commenting on the comfort of the chair and the fact that it rocked slightly as well as swiveled. Oblivious to my meaning, Dan glowed with pride.

"It's great, isn't it?" he beamed. He made a sweeping hand gesture, taking in the mixing area with all its little buttons.

"This is" — Dan broke into a voice-drumroll — "a 24-track recorder with switchable balanced or AES/EBU digital inputs, balanced analog insert points, metering and controls on the front panel, and it is also compatible with a USB 2.0 drive."

He looked at me expectantly, but I had absolutely no idea what he had said.

Indulgently, he offered, by way of clarification, "The 24 tracks make it really easy to get amazing live and rehearsal recordings, and it sets up very quickly. This little baby can deal with analog inputs, records to a quality broadcasting format and also lets me plug in a standard USB 2.0 drive so I can transfer it all to my workstation."

All right, I had understood bits of that. I could compute "live and rehearsal recordings," I understood "sets up quickly" and I had in fact heard of a "USB drive," although the meaning of the numbers escaped me.

"Wow," I breathed, deeply impressed if still confused. "Amazing."

Dan burst out laughing. "You haven't got a clue what any of that means," he guffawed. "And why would you?"

"No, indeed," I concurred. "But it sounds impressive... even if it doesn't look like much."

Dan chuckled. "Technology has come such a long way. You were expecting a huge mixing desk with hundreds of buttons and dials, right?"

I nodded.

"Well, this little thing here does all of what the old desk would have done, plus a lot more. It's simply amazing. It's powerful enough to lay down tracks with the band that could be put straight on an album... I only got it a few months back. Anyway, this is where I need your help."

Before I could ask anything, he had lightly tapped a button and the song that he had been working on filled the room.

A beautiful, mournful electric guitar opened the song, with an acoustic guitar mimicking the theme and setting the rhythm. Very gently, the drums took over and a bass tap-tapped along. The sound gave me goosebumps.

Dan's beautiful, throaty, powerful voice came in on a sad and soulful lyric.

> *You and me…*
> *We were meant to be…*
> *Now it's history…*
> *Why can't you see…?*

There was a rather lengthy gap while the instruments continued their work, and then his voice was back, this time in what was obviously going to be the chorus. Another verse, another gap, another chorus.

Dan let the music fade out before he spoke. "What do you think?"

"It's beautiful," I offered truthfully. "But—I don't know, it feels a bit unfinished."

"Unfinished?" he probed.

"Well, there seems to be something missing. What's with the long silences?"

"Ah," Dan said jubilantly, "I was hoping you'd pick that up. See, this is meant to be a duet, man and woman singing to each other. I wanted to try something new. Obviously, I'd like to sing the male part but I don't know who's going to take the female part yet." He paused.

I was still rubbing emotional goosebumps out from my arms.

"And?" I prompted, when he didn't continue.

"It's kind of getting difficult to finish the song without a female voice. I *think* it'll work but I can't tell for certain. Would you help me?"

"Sure. But what could I possibly do?"

Dan regarded me levelly. "I want you to sing."

I nearly fell off my chair. "What, me? You are kidding."

Dan shook his head. "I kid you not."

"But Dan! I can't sing. I'm the world's worst singer. I can't even hold a tune alone in the bath."

"Yet you sing in the choir," Dan offered calmly. He had clearly given this some thought.

"Well, yes…but that's different," I tried to explain. "There are lots of us and I've got sheet music—"

"Aha," Dan pounced with a flourish. "If it's sheet music the lady be needing, I can help you." He rifled around in a big pile of paper and extracted a handwritten score.

"There you are. That's your…that's the female part. Please?" He gave me his best little-boy-lost look. "Just try? I want to hear what it sounds like with the two voices together. Please?"

One gin and tonic and the best part of a bottle of wine spoke before I could think.

"Okay," I heard myself agree. "But you better coach me. And if it's terrible, you've got to wipe it all out."

"Deal," Dan said, and we formally shook hands. Thus we set to work. First of all, he taught me my lines. Having a score actually made things a lot easier. As long as I started off on the right note, I could do it. I was jolly impressed with myself.

After twenty minutes, Dan declared me ready for a trial. He installed me in the recording room with a microphone and a music stand, put headphones on my ears so I could hear the backing track, and off we went.

I had never, ever had so much fun before. It was intoxicating, heady, mind-blowing.

Dan had me sing the female part in a number of different ways before deciding on one he wanted to keep. He played it back to me a few times and recorded me all over again. I nearly melted when he gave me a big beaming thumbs-up from the mixing room.

Next thing I knew, he was warbling on about two-part harmonies, and we were in the recording room together, singing *together*, laying down the chorus.

"Shouldn't we do that individually?" I asked when we took a little break. "Wouldn't that be much…cleaner? Safer?"

"Well, yes," he agreed. "It would. And we will go back and record it individually as well. But doing it together gives it a lovely live feel, a real feel. I'll play around with it all for a while and see what's best." He looked at me briefly, then added as an afterthought, "Best for when, you know, I do the actual recording, with whichever singer is in on the project."

In all the excitement, I had forgotten that we were only doing a demo. I felt the teensiest stab of disappointment, but stamped on it quick and hard.

"Unless…" Dan continued softly. "Unless you've changed your mind? What do you think about it being you?" Seeing my confused expression, he thumped me lightly on the shoulder and gave me a hug. "Nah, only teasing. Let's finish this up and see what we think about it by the light of day, shall we?"

And that was exactly what we did.

When I finally fell into bed, exuberant and overexcited, at three a.m., I was convinced I wasn't going to be able to sleep with the fizz and enjoyment of it all. Not so! I dropped off quickly and had a long and dreamless sleep.

Chapter Eleven

When I woke up to sunshine streaming into my room, the whole recording interlude seemed totally unreal. *Had we really done that?* I wondered, as I lay in bed, idly watching sun-beamy patterns on the ceiling. This was almost as surreal as having a one-night stand. Not that I had much experience in that department, but it seemed like a good analogy.

I flexed my toes under the duvet, luxuriating in my lazy lie-in. But suddenly, I remembered the invite to the dreaded wedding. My heart thudded in my chest. Had we really sent an acceptance card? A homemade one? By courier? Worse still, had I somehow committed to actually going?

Oh. My. God.

What a totally awful thing to do, all of it. How did I get into these messy situations when Dan was around?

Oh yes, and Dan. *What had he been playing at?* I ruminated, pulling my knees up to my chest. *Had his grand dinner been merely a ploy to get me to agree to this stupid wedding plan?*

And while I was thinking about ploys, had dinner been merely a prelude to the vocal seduction? Had *that* been his grand plan?

I nibbled my thumb. That was much more likely. He'd clearly had this whole thing mapped out before I got home. I turned and stared out of the window, where I could make out wispy shreds of cloud scudding by on an incredibly blue London sky.

Yes, he had probably planned a dinner to make me more receptive. I giggled. I would never have put my voice on some sort of 24-track extra blah-di-blah device without a full tummy and a bit of Dutch courage. I thought about this some more. Should I feel outraged, or something? I wasn't really sure. I felt like I had been manipulated, but in a good way.

Contrary to all my protestations of the previous night, I actually found the prospect quite exciting, in a purely hypothetical kind of way, of course. After all, we had shaken hands on the recording being only a demo. But I did quite fancy hearing it again, maybe one more time. Just for me.

So I went to look for Dan, but no Dan could be found. I padded all over the house, right down to the studio—but it was empty and deserted. I consulted a clock; it was only midday. Dan never left the house before midday, he didn't even *get up* before midday. Where the heck was he?

I tried calling his mobile, but I heard it ringing upstairs somewhere, so he had not taken it to wherever he had gone. Bummer! I paced around the kitchen, agitatedly nibbling my index finger. What was he up to?

First things first, I needed some breakfast. I chumped on my toast with a vengeance, and I drank several gallons of coffee. Gradually, I forced myself to slow down. There was no way of tracking Dan down while he didn't carry his mobile. And in actual fact, there was no great urgency, either. I would probably see him later tonight, or some time tomorrow, and he could play the demo to me then. Who knew, if he had enough time, perhaps he might be convinced to play around with it a bit more. Meanwhile, I had a Saturday to get on with.

I picked up the phone again to ring Rachel, but only got her answerphone, and her mobile went straight to voicemail as well. Where was everybody today? Grudgingly, I left a message, suggesting afternoon coffee on the King's Road somewhere, and got dressed and left the house for a spot of shopping.

Several shopping bags later, I finally sat down in a little coffee shop at the Sloane Square end of the King's Road and ordered a mocha. I sat by the window, looking out at the busy comings and goings, and felt quite calm and content. Sometimes, you had to stop and say, "Life's good." This was one of those moments.

I surveyed my shopping exploits. I had bought several throws and cushions for my soon-to-be-refurbished lounge. I had found some fabulous crystal candlesticks. Admittedly, I didn't know if they were real crystal, but they looked very boho and chic.

I had also been very naughty and ordered new sofas. After all, the insurance would pay for it all, and there was quite a long delay before the shop would deliver, so why not get organized? I had spent a good hour trawling around a specialist little sofa shop that would make my sofa to spec. I had trial-sat on dozens of sofas, looked at yards and yards of fabric, and finally made my choice. Soon I would have an L-shaped five-seater sofa with lovely fat cushions in a dusky off-pink. It would look stunning on my new cream carpets with the throws and cushions I bought.

The only thing missing was my best friend to share in my triumph. I had rung several more times and left another voicemail, but Rachel was AWOL.

I chewed on my lower lip. There was something going on for her today. I knew there was, I simply couldn't quite remember *what* it was. Something to do with Jordan; some kind of party.

I shrugged, resigned to the fact that she was busy. I could have rung someone else but I didn't really feel like it. And anyway, Rachel would ring me back eventually.

Chapter Twelve

The call came at ten to ten that night.

I was in the middle of a DVD and halfway through a bottle of wine when my mobile chirruped into life. I was still alone in the house, having seen neither hide nor hair of Dan all day. So after a yummy takeaway from the local pizza place, I had decided to relax, all by myself, with a glass of wine or three, a huge bag of chili flavor crisps, and Jason Bourne.

Given the late hour and my slobbed-out state, it took me a few seconds to locate my phone. "Don't ring off, don't ring off," I muttered under my breath while I paused the DVD and brushed crisp crumbs onto the floor. Quickly, my search led me into the kitchen and to my handbag, which I had left sitting on the counter. Naturally, the phone stopped ringing just as I finally found it and the display went blank. I stared at it, annoyed.

"I jolly well hope you'll ring back, whoever you are," I announced to thin air, and sure enough, the phone rang again. I nearly jumped out of my skin.

"Rachel?" I answered, having clocked from the display that it was her. A torrent of sobbing unleashed through the earpiece. I had never heard anything like it.

"*Rachel?*" I asked again, trying to make myself heard over the crying. "Is that you?"

More sobbing.

"What happened? Rach?" An ice-cold finger of dread tingled its way down my spine and a terrible sense of foreboding lodged in my tummy. "Rach? Are you okay?"

"Sophie." Rachel's voice eventually emerged from among all that sobbing, although I had to strain to hear it.

"Sophie, please come quick. Please. Come now. Please!"

Goosebumps spread all over my arms, and the kitchen tilted slightly with transferred panic. I tried to stay calm, and to instill calm.

"Of course I'll come," I said loudly and clearly. In fact, I was already slipping on my shoes and grabbing my keys.

"Where shall I come to?" I asked. "Where are you?"

"Please, please, hurry," Rachel sobbed into her phone. "You've got to come. Please!"

She was hysterical; she was completely beside herself. Had she been with me, I might have slapped her to shock her out of it. As slapping wasn't an option, I opted for shouting instead. "I'M ON MY WAY," I yelled. "WHERE ARE YOU?"

I left Dan's house, slamming the door shut without locking or alarming it—sorry, Dan!—and frantically tried to locate a taxi.

"WHERE ARE YOU?" I shouted again.

My mobile crackled and hissed. It sounded like Rachel was calling from Outer Mongolia.

"...party..." I eventually made out. Progress.

"WHOSE PARTY?" I inquired. "WHERE?"

I saw a yellow light working its way down the road. "TAXI" I shouted even louder, and practically jumped in front of it to stop it. I wrenched open the back door and fell inside.

"Steady on, love," the cabbie advised me. "Where's the emergency?"

"I don't know yet," I replied hurriedly, returning my attention to the mobile phone.

"Rachel," I pronounced as clearly as I could. "Rachel, focus. Where are you? Where do I need to come?"

More sobbing and hysterics. I was about to blow a fuse, when some words came forth.

"Party boat." Sobbing and sniffing. "Putney."

Right, I could do something with that. Not very much, but at least I could get the cab moving.

"I'm in a cab," I told Rachel, putting on my most reasonable and reassuring voice. "We're on our way to Putney. Where in Putney should I come?"

"Party boat," was all Rachel would say. And then, chillingly. "I can't do this anymore."

The line went dead.

I swallowed hard, trying to contain my rising panic.

"I need to find somebody on a party boat in Putney," I said to the cab driver. "Where should I go?"

"Moored or sailing?" was his laconic response.

Moored or sailing—how should I know?

"I don't know," I admitted. The cabbie gave a resigned sigh.

"All right, love, I'll take you to Putney pier, shall I? We can take it from there."

"Okay," I agreed. "But please hurry. It's—"

"—an emergency," the cabbie cut in. "Yes, I got that impression." And, under his breath, "It's *always* an emergency in this business."

The journey seemed to take forever but could only have lasted about fifteen minutes. Soon the river came into view and I started looking out for a party boat.

The cabbie was doing the same, because he suddenly offered, "Look out there to your right... That's the boat you're looking for."

I followed his gaze and sure enough, there was a pleasure cruiser blazing with fairy lights right in the middle of the Thames.

"Looks like it might be heading for the pier," the driver suggested. "Probably best if I just take you there and we can see."

Another couple of red traffic lights later and we veered off sharply to the left just before Putney Bridge. The cabbie pulled up by the pier, and I fumbled in my purse for the fare. Then I fell out of the cab as ungracefully as I had fallen in, straightening up swiftly and scanning the river for the approaching party boat.

Alas, it didn't seem intent on mooring after all. I could hear snippets of music and gales of laughter. And—

My heart stopped.

Well, okay, it didn't, but it felt like it.

I had found Rachel. She was hanging by her very fingertips off the front railings of the boat. I could see her distinctive ponytail and her very favorite party frock.

What on earth was going on?

"She's gonna let go, you know," somebody spoke to me. I nearly passed out with shock. It was my friendly cab driver, having got out for a look-see.

"Never," I assured him with as much authority as I could muster. "That's my best friend out there. She's not going to let go. That must be some kind of stunt."

The cab driver watched thoughtfully.

"Uh-uh," he ventured. "Not a stunt. That looks pretty desperate to me. We should call an ambulance."

I opened my mouth to protest again, but Rachel let go. Things seemed to be happening in slow motion. Her fall took forever. Her body turned in the air and she hit the water slightly lengthwise. A little splash showed where she had hit the water, then nothing. Nothing at all.

Someone was screaming. "*Rachel! No!*"

It took a couple of seconds for me to work out that it was me. Subsequently, I vaguely heard someone else and turned to see who it was. The cab driver was speaking urgently on his mobile phone, but I couldn't understand what he was saying. I felt like I was under water myself, sinking, drowning, unable to hear or make myself heard.

Quite suddenly, the sensation cleared. It was like I had unmuted the television and could follow the action again.

"...off the boat, yes, by Putney pier... No, I'm a cab driver... Her friend took me here... No, the people on the boat don't seem to have noticed... Yes, the boat is still moving... No, she's not come up again yet..."

Chapter Thirteen

My mind was racing.

What had happened to my cheerful, happy-go-lucky friend to make her jump off a boat? Why wasn't she coming up? Was she still alive? Should I jump in? Why wasn't anybody helping her? Where was the ambulance?

Where was bloody Jordan? *Where?*

What would an ambulance do, anyway?

And always, always, that central question—why had she let go?

Suddenly, the party boat was lit up from above as a helicopter hovered and switched on its search lights. At the same time, a rescue boat came zooming up the Thames. I breathed a sigh of relief. Somebody had alerted the coastguards. With a boat and a helicopter, Rachel would stand a chance. If only she would come up.

The rescue boat homed in on one area and I saw her. In the glare of the search light, I could just see a head bobbing above the water.

There were tears running down my cheeks as I whispered, "Swim, Rachel, swim like you've never swam before. Swim!"

I had grabbed the cab driver's hand in my emotional turmoil, and it was only when he gently pried my fingers off one by one that I realized I had been squeezing rather hard. He flexed his fingers gingerly. "Steady on, love," he advised. "Breaking my hand won't save your friend there. But look!"

He pointed out toward the boat, and I focused once more on the unfolding drama. Rachel was rather halfhearted about swimming. She would do a few strokes and then let herself float, sinking back into the water until her head was nearly under. At that point, she would do a few more strokes before letting herself go under again. It didn't look as though she wanted to be saved at all.

The coastguard rescue boat had assumed a position in the current below Rachel. It wouldn't have taken much for her to reach the boat, yet she appeared to be turning away from her rescuers.

I was dizzy with frustration and inability to help. It was through a thick haze of emotion that I noticed an ambulance rolling up the pier, deftly reversing so that the doors faced toward the river. Two paramedics got out, opened the back and disappeared inside. Within seconds, they reappeared with a stretcher and a green emergency case. They strode purposefully up onto the pier and waited for things to come.

Meanwhile, the coastguard rescuers had decided that Rachel wasn't going to join them willingly. They had lowered a dinghy into the water, and when it drew level with Rach, one of the coastguards threw her a life ring but she pushed it away and went under instead.

"She's not wanting to get out of that water, is she now?" the cab driver observed dryly. "It's not often you see a death wish written over somebody quite so clearly."

I was stunned.

How dare he? How *dare* he?

What was he even still doing here? He had no place commenting on my best friend like that. I turned to shout at him, to let out all my frustration and anger, but I caught myself in time.

He was right. He might have been extremely callous about it, but he was right. Rachel did seem to have a death wish. Or rather, she didn't seem to have a desire to live. What was it she had said on the phone? *I can't do this anymore...*

Down in the water, it was becoming more and more obvious that she couldn't do any more swimming. Her movements had slowed right down and the flailing had stopped. She looked like a broken ragdoll, jetsam on the tide.

The party boat had come to a stop a few meters up river. All the party guests were now standing by the railing, watching Rachel's plight. I hoped to God that Jordan wasn't among them—if I found out he had been there and watched Rachel drowning herself, I wouldn't be responsible for my actions.

Now there were two people in the water. There was Rachel, only barely afloat, and another swimmer, a strong, purposeful swimmer, making his way toward her. He had to be a lifeguard, and he swiftly reached Rachel. I breathed a sigh of relief; she was safe.

Not!

The appearance of her rescuer had inflamed in Rachel one last effort to resist, and once more she was thrashing wildly. However, the lifeguard was having none of it. He took Rachel in the classic arm-lock while he was side-stroking toward the dinghy. Within a minute, he had reached the dinghy, dragging a lolling Rachel with him. She looked more like a broken ragdoll than ever.

Suddenly, things were moving really fast. I had started running toward the pier, and by the time I reached it, the coastguard had already handed Rachel over to the paramedics. They placed her on the stretcher and were fitting her with an oxygen mask.

I knelt down beside her, trying not to get in the way of the paramedics. One of them looked at me, taking in my tear-stained face and shaky appearance.

"Do you know her?" he probed. "Is she your sister? Your friend?" His voice was deep and calm.

"She's my best friend," I offered, resisting the urge to stroke her pale face. The other paramedic had brought blankets to wrap her up and was now inserting a cannula in her right hand.

"Do you know what happened to her?" the first paramedic asked. I shook my head.

"I have no idea," I tried to explain.

"Was it you who called 999?" the other paramedic cut in.

"The cab driver...the cab driver who took me here, he called." I looked over to the car park. "He's still there, look."

But before anyone could look anywhere, Rachel gave a moan and a splutter. She started coughing up water, and the paramedic deftly pulled her oxygen mask off so she wouldn't choke. "It's okay," he soothed, crouching down low to look at her face. "You've been in the river, and we've got you out. You're safe now. Do you remember your name?"

Rachel started shivering all over and mumbled incoherently. I made eye contact with the other paramedic — should I talk to her? He nodded, *yes*.

"Rach?" I started, also crouching down low. "Rach? Can you hear me?" My voice wobbled a little, and I tried really hard to keep my fear from showing.

Rachel turned her face toward me.

"Sophie," she said after what seemed an eternity, and the paramedic and I let out a joint sigh of relief.

"Rach," I said again, taking her un-cannula'd hand this time. "What happened?"

"What happened?" she repeated. "What happened?"

The paramedic next to me rose to his feet, pulling me up with him.

"We'd better get her to the hospital quickly now," he explained. "She's conscious, breathing, and appears to remember you. But we've got to have her examined and make sure she doesn't secondary drown on us later."

Secondary drown?

I was confused. I had assumed that they would let her perk up and let me take her home. I longed to ask questions but this wasn't the time. The paramedics loaded Rachel into the ambulance. When they started closing the doors, I turned to go, unsure of what else to do.

"Hey…are you coming?" one of the paramedics shouted after me. I turned back.

"Am I allowed?"

"Of course. A familiar face will really help," he assured me.

So I climbed into the back of the ambulance and sat on a pop-down chair next to Rachel. The driver got in the front and the ambulance moved off. No sirens, no blue lights—Rach wasn't in mortal danger. Still, being in back with her and the paramedic, seeing her bundled under all the blankets, with that oxygen mask back over her mouth, the enormity of what had happened finally hit home. I felt shaky all over and ever so slightly woozy. I reached out a hand to steady myself against the ambulance wall. The paramedic, still fussing over Rachel, glanced up briefly.

"You okay?" he inquired. "You've gone quite pale. Take a few deep breaths," he suggested calmly.

"I'm fine," I replied, taking deep breaths as instructed. "Just a bit...you know." I didn't want to say it in front of Rachel, didn't know how much she would hear or take in.

"I know," he said. "You should get a drink of something when we get to the hospital."

"Where are we going?" I wanted to know.

"St George's," he said. "In Tooting."

"That's good," I responded. "That's where we both live."

Chapter Fourteen

Within minutes, we arrived at the hospital. The paramedics took Rachel right through and I trailed after. A brusque nurse took me aside to expedite Rachel's admission. While I wasn't exactly next of kin, having arrived with the patient apparently gave me authority to supply important information such as name, date of birth, and place of residence. Meanwhile, Rachel was taken into an examination room.

I was allowed to wait in the relatives' area and sat down wearily. The paramedics came by, obviously on their way out, but stopped to talk to me.

"You still look very pale. Have you had that drink yet?" the one who had looked after Rachel in the ambulance asked. I shook my head.

"Let me sort that out for you," he offered. "We wouldn't want you to keel over now." He disappeared and quickly came back with a steaming mug of milky tea.

"I put three sugars in for you," he said, pressing the mug into my hand. "Drink it slowly, and good luck." And before I could say anything else, they loped off.

Time passed in a blur as I observed the comings and goings. Various doctors went into Rachel's room and came out again, and I was getting anxious all over again. Finally, one of them sat down next to me.

"I'm Dr. McKendra," she introduced herself. "Your friend is okay now. She's warm, and coherent, and quite comfortable. We've given her a sedative and will keep her in overnight, just in case..."

She petered out.

"I know," I volunteered. "The paramedics said something about secondary drowning."

"Yes, that is a risk," Dr. McKendra conceded, "but—"

"What *is* secondary drowning?" I cut in.

The doctor paused for a second. "If your friend has inhaled any water, even a very small amount, that could impair her breathing process later, even in a few hours."

I struggled to take that in, but Dr. McKendra continued speaking.

"That isn't what we're most worried about," she announced. "Were you aware of your friend being depressed at all?"

"Depressed? Rachel? No!" I exclaimed. "She's been happily planning her wedding and all that..."

Dr. McKendra sighed. "Well, it appears that she did jump into the river, rather than fall or be pushed."

"How do you know that?" I asked defensively, even though I clearly remembered watching Rachel let go.

"The police have been talking to the guests on the pleasure cruiser, and there was no incident as such. Nobody even remembers her disappearing."

The good doctor might as well have stabbed me through the heart with a shard of ice. The police had been on the boat? Investigating? And where the hell had Jordan been through all of this? How did nobody notice her disappearing? Would she have to speak to the police, too? Was she, like, in actual trouble for jumping off a boat?

"Well, that doesn't mean anything," I objected, pushing my concerns aside and focusing on the matter at hand. "There could have been an accident or somebody could have pushed her over, secretly, without anyone else seeing…"

I stopped, aware that I was sounding like an extra from a CSI show.

"Rachel told us that she jumped," the doctor informed me carefully. "She just won't tell us why. And that's why we can't let her go tonight."

I nodded slowly, reluctantly. That did make sense, especially given the frantic phone call I received and everything I observed. I simply didn't feel like sharing that with the doctor, however kind she seemed. I was wary of digging an even deeper hole for my friend, and I was convinced that there had to be a perfectly good, one-off, catastrophic reason for her action. Rachel wasn't a suicide candidate, even if she had been put on suicide watch.

"Will she have to speak to the police?"

"Probably not, for now. I've told them what she's told us and advised them against questioning her. So…" The doctor trailed off.

"Can I stay with her?" I needed to know.

"Sure," Dr. McKendra agreed. "We need to finish some checks before you can go in. She'll probably go to sleep quite quickly though. It would be good if you could come back early tomorrow."

"Of course," I immediately agreed. "I can stay the night if that would help...?"

The doctor smiled. "I don't think that will be necessary. You look like you could do with some rest, too. Is there somebody who could pick you up later?"

"Err, yes, I guess so, but—"

"Good, that's settled. You can go in when the nurse tells you. Thank you for all your help. You probably saved your friend's life."

And with that, she got up and left.

I sat in a daze for a few moments, then reluctantly got out my mobile to text Dan, blithely ignoring the "no mobile phone" signs plastered all over the place. Mission accomplished, I sat back and waited.

And right there, in this most unlikely of places, after this most horrendous of events, in the most awful of circumstances, I saw him again.

Steve.

I nearly didn't recognize him in scrubs, but our eyes met once again, and it was definitely him. He was walking alongside a trolley carrying a badly injured man. He was busily monitoring the patient's vital signs, and yet he caught my eye.

For one second, his step faltered as he saw me, but he got swept along by the movement of the trolley, disappeared through some automatic double-doors. And the moment was over.

My heart leapt in my chest and all my senses were jubilant. There was definitely something there. He had seen me.

He had nearly stopped. I hadn't imagined it, I knew I hadn't. I very nearly did a little jig. Just wait until I could tell Rachel about this and —

I crash-landed back in reality after my short but intense flight of fancy. I almost felt guilty at the joy and exhilaration I had so briefly experienced.

A nurse stood in front of me. "You can go in now," she repeated, a tad impatient.

"Oh, oh, right, thanks. Sorry," I gabbled, gathering up my things and entering Rachel's room.

"Only a few minutes, mind. We'll be moving her to the ward shortly," the nurse shouted after me.

Rachel looked small and frail, but she had some color back in her face.

"Sophie," she croaked. "You came."

"Of course I came, silly," I chided, trying not to burst into tears.

"Can I have a hug?" Rachel pleaded.

"'Course you can." I bent down to give her an awkward little hug.

"Sit," she invited me, softly patting her bed. So I sat, and held her hand.

A fat tear escaped from Rachel's right eye and slowly trickled down her cheek. She didn't even bother wiping it away, so I did it for her. That brought on more tears, but she didn't seem to have the energy for a full-on sobbing fit like she had had on the phone.

"I'm sorry," she whispered. "I'm so, so sorry. I know they all think I'm going to do myself in, but I'm not. I lost it. I'm sorry."

I hesitated. Was this the right time to talk?

"Do you want to tell me what happened?" I asked, as gently as I could. "You don't have to if you don't want to, I don't want to be nosey or anything… Just if you want to…"

"He dumped me," Rachel cut into my clumsy ramblings.

I stared, uncomprehending.

"He dumped you?" I repeated before I could think better of it. It was too big a fact to take in.

"He did," Rachel confirmed. "He didn't even warn me. He simply turned up with somebody else. The bastard. The evil…."

"Hold it, hold it, backtrack a little for me here," I pleaded. "What was this thing on the boat anyway?"

"I don't really know, some posh function. A launch party, I think. Well, it had a launch all right," she suddenly snorted. "Just not the kind they'd expected."

Humor. That was a good sign, surely?

"Right, so you turned up at this party on your own?" I verified.

Rachel nodded. "I didn't really want to go, it's not my scene. I didn't know anybody there. We've had some friction over that lately. Anyway…" she trailed off.

"You went, and he met you there?" I offered.

"I went, and he didn't meet me there. He brought somebody else. He didn't even acknowledge me."

I must have looked like a question mark, because she reiterated. "He pretended he didn't know me. He blanked me. I tried to talk to him but he had security take me away."

I gave a sharp intake of breath. *Oh my God.*

I was going to find him. And when I had found him, I was going to kill him. No, better still, I was going to tear him apart alive, bit by bit.

But Rachel was still talking.

"So I flipped. I went to the railing and took my ring off and threw that over the side. I thought I'd feel better, but I didn't. And then it seemed like a really good idea to go after it. I mean, what's the point of it all?" She shrugged her shoulders. "I hadn't even drunk anything. I threw my glass of champagne at him before they dragged me away. What a waste, huh?" She gave a hysterical giggle. "Anyway. What a stupid thing to do. I felt I couldn't go on. But you can always go on. Of course you can. Remember Gloria Gaynor, right?" And unbelievably, she burst into song. Very softly. "I've got all my life to live, I've got all my love to give, I will survive… I will sur*vive*…"

Her eyes glazed over and she bore a crazed expression. A rash of goosebumps spread from my arms to the nape of my neck. I hated seeing my friend like this, veering between her calm, rational self and hysterical, defiant self-pity. Yet before I could say anything to comfort her, she passed out. A nurse—a different one from before—gave a little cough. She seemed to have been in the room for a while.

"Sorry," she said. "I had to be here. I didn't mean to listen. Anyway, looks like she's asleep now. That'll be the sedative kicking in."

I nodded. "Was this…was this really her talking, or was that the sedative, too?"

The nurse smiled. "A bit of both. What a shock, though. You can kind of understand her reaction, can't you?" She busied herself straightening Rachel's blankets.

"You'd better go and get some rest," she suggested. "Come back in the morning. She'll have a jolly good sleep. Everything will be better in the morning."

Chapter Fifteen

When I emerged from the hospital, more shaken than I had realized, I found Dan waiting outside the lobby. He looked slightly disheveled and very pale.

"What on earth happened?" he greeted me. "Is Rachel all right?"

I started talking, but he interrupted me immediately. "You look done in, let's get you home. You can tell me on the way." He took my arm and led me toward the car park. I filled him in on the evening's events on the drive home, and his face assumed a grim, and a grimmer still expression.

"Low," he mumbled under his breath. "That's really low." He drove on in silence, but at the next red traffic light he suddenly erupted. "Bastard," he announced forcefully and smacked the steering wheel as hard as he could.

"I know," I concurred. "Bastard. Scum. Evil son of a bitch. I've gone through the whole catalogue but nothing's quite strong enough."

Another silence ensued as we neared Dan's house. Soon, we were sitting in Dan's kitchen, me with a gin and tonic — for medicinal reasons — and Dan with a whisky on the rocks.

"You don't think..." Dan pondered, sounding hesitant to express his thoughts. "Well, is it possible that Jordan might have tried to break up with her for a while and she didn't get it?" he finally ventured.

I spluttered into my drink.

"*No!*" I issued with considerable emphasis. "How can you even think that? They were *engaged*." I took a deep breath to steady my voice. "Rachel picks up on these things, she would have known something was wrong. No," I reiterated, "this was a complete surprise to her."

"I guess you're right." Dan was crestfallen. "I never really liked the guy that much but I find it hard to believe that he could be so cruel."

"*I* liked him," I confessed. "They seemed so good together. But this...well, this is something else."

"Oughtn't we to find out why?" Dan ventured once more.

"No. Absolutely not. I don't care about his side of the story." I banged my glass on the table for emphasis this time, noting absentmindedly that it appeared to be empty. "What he did was inexcusable. Unforgivable. No matter *what* the reason, you don't do that to a person." And, as a classic non-sequitur, "Can I have another, please?" I waved my glass in the air.

"Sure," Dan jumped up and busied himself with the ice cube maker.

"I guess you're right," he said again as he sat down once more. "I just don't know what else to say."

"There's nothing *to* say," I pondered. "He dumped her, and she threw herself off a boat. Now she's in the hospital, and they think she's at risk of inflicting more harm on herself. That'll look *really* good on her health records. That'll stay with her all her life."

"Okay, okay," Dan soothed as I was getting myself worked up again. "Calm down. It's done now. And she didn't have to jump, nobody made her."

I snorted again. "Only a man could say that. Of course she didn't have to bloody jump. Of course nobody made her. That's exactly the point. She flipped. She lost it. Temporary outage, if you will. She will regret this bitterly in the morning. She'll feel really stupid. But she felt she had no way out. Have you never felt that way, ever?" I challenged him.

Dan considered this. "Nah, not really. But!" Something occurred to him. "When Irene left me…"

He paused while I waited with bated breath for what he would say next. Even though that was way before my time, I knew he had been heartbroken after the divorce.

Smiling ruefully, he continued, "When she'd gone, after I'd been all patient and calm… Well, when I was on my own, I guess I lost it a bit." He stopped and turned red.

"What did you do?" I pounced, intrigued.

"I…" he faltered.

"Go on, you've got to tell me now."

"I smashed up my Les Paul."

I sucked in my breath. "Your Les Paul? Your *Black Beauty*? Your beloved electric guitar?" I confirmed, incredulous. "The really, really expensive one?"

"Yup, my baby. I smashed it against the wall. I don't know what came over me." He looked sheepish all over again.

"See," I pounced. "You *do* get it. You destroyed something really precious to you. That's not a million miles away from throwing yourself into the river on an impulse. It's certainly the same range of emotion."

"Okay, all right, I get it," Dan conceded, not quite convinced. "Anyway," he drew circles on the table top in the condensation puddles that had run off our glasses. "What now? Where does Rachel go from here?"

"I don't know," I sighed. "First of all, we've got to get her out of hospital as soon as possible."

Dan walked in through his front door carrying a hold-all when I stumbled bleary-eyed down the stairs the next morning.

"Morning," he greeted me cheerfully, looking gleeful and excited.

"Morning," I greeted him back. "Where have you been?"

"I," Dan announced, clearly bursting to share his story, "tracked down the elusive Jordan *and* I collected all of Rachel's things from his flat."

"You *what?*" It was too much to take in so early, and I allowed myself to sit down on the bottom step while I digested the information.

It turned out that after I had gone to bed, Dan had driven round to Jordan's flat and waited. Waited, until a very drunk Jordan finally rolled in in the wee small hours of the morning in the company of the very same long-legged blonde bimbo whose appearance had driven Rachel to her desperate deed.

"I can tell you," he said, joining me on the bottom step, "I nearly lost the plot. I was so bloody angry when the two of them rolled up together, totally unaware of the misery they had caused." His brow creased with cross lines as he recalled his emotions.

I had never seen him seriously angry, but I could imagine that that would be a frightful sight.

"But then I remembered that that's not my style, really," he carried on, "so I came up with something else instead. I sent the blonde bimbo packing and told her to have herself checked over at her local STD clinic, just in case she'd picked up something nasty."

"You didn't," I breathed. "That's slander."

"I sure did, and I don't care if it's slander," he retorted cheerfully.

Having dispatched the offending female, he made Jordan admit him to his flat and confronted him.

"What the fuck are you playing at," he had yelled. "You were planning a wedding with Rachel and you dump her for a slut?"

Jordan, or so Dan said, had been quite taken aback by this turn of events. "I... I..." he had started, unable to string together a sentence.

"Too dumb, or too drunk," I snorted, feeling vicious.

"Precisely," Dan concurred. "Anyway, I pressed him and I pressed him and do you know what he said?"

I shook my head, uncertain whether I wanted to hear. Dan didn't give me a choice. He was on a roll.

"He said," he hollered, swept away by remembered anger, "he said he was *bored*. He said Rachel was *suffocating* him with all that *wedding* stuff and he just wanted to have some fun. Some *fun*!" Dan was furious even as he retold the conversation.

"I've done some pretty stupid stuff in my time, you know I'm not a saint," he reflected on his own misdemeanors. "But what Jordan did on that boat, the way he treated Rachel so callously, so very carelessly, that was in a league of its own. That was contemptible." He thumped the stairs with his fist to vent his feelings.

"Anyway, without another word, I collected every last little scrap of Rachel's belongings that I could find, plus the keys to her flat. Jordan collapsed on the sofa in a blubbering heap while I put her stuff into my bag."

He lifted the hold-all for emphasis. "He was crying like a baby, and it made me even more cross. I said to him, 'Save the drama, mate, you're too late, what you did was inexcusable.' And then I just left him there."

Dan, the avenging angel. I felt a warm glow of hero worship and affection, and if I hadn't been quite so determinedly over this guy, I might have fallen in love all over again. I gave him a big hug, just for good measure.

After a quick breakfast, Dan drove me to Rachel's flat so I could get some of her clothes and toiletries before visiting her back in the hospital.

When I got to the ward, Rachel was finishing her breakfast. She still looked very pale, but her eyes were alive and her demeanor was animated. The cannula had gone and there was little evidence of medical attention still being given. I pulled the curtain round her bed to give us some privacy from the other five ward-mates and we got talking. Rachel launched straight in.

"I'm so sorry to have given you such a fright," she said, grabbing my hand and making me sit with her on the bed. "I don't know what came over me." She shrugged. "Well, I do actually, but it all seems so silly now."

I nodded, not knowing what to say.

"It's just...I was so *hurt*. Can you understand that?" She looked at me with pleading eyes. I nodded again.

"And I'd thrown the ring overboard, which you have to admit is *quite* a reasonable response, and it looked so pretty as it glittered and fell...and it was gone, and I thought, wow, I bet it's nice and peaceful down there...and suddenly, I don't know. The water looked so...inviting."

I inclined my head to indicate that I had listened and motioned for her to go on.

"And then I was in it. In the river. It was cold. And quiet. I couldn't hear any noise from the boat anymore, only the water whooshing past and my breathing in my ears. And I was so tired." She trailed off and shrugged. "It all seemed so easy. Just to let go. No more worries. Just…flowing."

"Is that why you turned away from the lifeboat?" I had to know. Of all the events I had witnessed, that was probably what had disturbed me most.

"I didn't know it was a lifeboat. I couldn't see properly. I thought it was Jordan coming to taunt me," she explained.

I digested this. Okay, I could accept that. It sounded within the realm of the plausible.

"But didn't they call to you?"

"They might have done, but it is really hard to hear in the water. And the engines were making a lot of noise. And frankly, I didn't care. I just wanted to get away."

That sentence hung between us for a while.

"But why?" I eventually persisted, holding up a hand to stave off a quick response. "I know what Jordan did, and it's truly despicable." I took her hands and made her look at me. "But Rach, you've got so much going for you. Your friends, me, your job, your lovely flat… You can't have wanted to throw all that away just because Jordan did something truly evil?"

She looked at me levelly.

"I simply couldn't face picking up the pieces of my life all over again," she finally offered. "I'd done it once before, and it took me years to put the light back into my life, and I didn't think I had the energy to do it again."

This was news to me. "What are you talking about?" I asked, gingerly.

Rachel sniffed. "My own thunderbolt-and-lightning man, and what happened with him," she elaborated. "I never told you this before because it was too painful...but... Well, maybe it's time I did."

"Okay," I coaxed, "go on."

"What, here? *Now?*"

"No time like the present. Go on, out with it," I ordered.

"Okay. I guess you're right," she said, but a nurse interrupted us, using that awful over-cheerful voice that set my teeth on edge every time.

"Good morning, Rachel," she trilled, "and how are we feeling this morning?"

Rachel rolled her eyes at me.

"*I* am feeling much better," she retorted.

"Jolly good," the nurse continued, unperturbed. "I can see that we're feeling better. We must have a little chat with another nurse before we can go home later today, and our mum and dad will be picking us up, I think. So"—she whisked Rachel's covers off briskly—"we might need to go for a shower to make ourselves a bit more presentable."

Rachel snorted but obediently sat up. I proffered the bag of toiletries.

"Here, knock yourself out," I suggested and gave a big start as the nurse snatched the bag right out of my hand.

"What's in there?" she demanded, sounding terribly officious and rummaging through the bag. "These are only soaps and creams."

"Yes," I explained sweetly, "they're her favorites, that's why I brought them. I meant 'knock yourself out' in the sense of 'make yourself happy,' you see?"

The nurse handed the bag to Rachel and glared at me. Then she harrumphed her way down the ward. Rachel rolled her eyes at me in a sympathetic manner.

"You've been told," she snorted. "Naughty girl. Right, I'll be off to make myself look human. Don't go anywhere." With that, she swung her legs off the bed and trotted off to explore the hospital showers.

Chapter Sixteen

When Rachel got out of the shower, she made the bed, rolling pillows and covers together to make a sofa-like shape, and we settled down for a chat.

"His name was Alex," Rachel launched in abruptly.

Just as abruptly, the curtain was opened and a short, rosy-looking nurse popped her head through the gap. "Rachel?" she asked.

Rachel raised her hand like a child in school. "That would be me."

The nurse stepped into the curtained area. "I'm Rosie. I am the mental health nurse on duty. I'm hoping that you'll have a chat with me about what happened yesterday."

Rachel held the nurse's gaze and answered evenly. "Of course." The nurse cast a quick glance my way before continuing. "Based on our conversation, I will be able to assess whether we can discharge you today."

Rachel nodded. "Okay." Inwardly, I applauded loudly; she was doing so great being composed and reasonable.

The nurse stepped back and held the curtain open like a door. "Shall we go somewhere private?"

"Of course, yes, that would be good," Rachel acquiesced, swinging herself off the bed yet again. I watched her walk down the corridor with Rosie and prayed for the best.

Half an hour later, she returned, looking a little drained but calm.

"She'll ask the doctor to sign the discharge notice," Rachel explained. "I did good, apparently. She doesn't think I'm a danger to myself anymore." She smiled sadly. "What a mess. Anyway…"

Rachel sat cross-legged on her bed and patted her side. "Pull them curtains again and let's talk." I did as instructed while she launched into her story again.

"His name was Alex. I met him in the library at college. No, this was before our time in Cambridge," she clarified before I could query the statement. "Don't interrupt me now. Right, so I met him in the library. I saw him across an aisle and I dropped the pile of books I was carrying. You should have heard the noise. It was like a tsunami." She chuckled at the memory.

"Alex burst out laughing while the librarian was telling me off, and he came to help pick all those books up. We went for coffee, then dinner, skipping a few lectures… and that was that. We were an item. 'Alex'n'Rach. Rach'n'Alex.'"

She sighed wistfully. "He was *gorgeous*. Delicious. Edible. He had dark brown hair that kept flopping into his face. Not like a toff." She intercepted my look and punched me on the arm. "It was lovely. He had to keep pushing it back with his hand. And he had the most piercing blue eyes you've ever seen. They were like searchlights, and when he looked at you, it was like he could look straight into your soul. And when he was laughing, they seemed to be dancing. And when he was sad, they looked frozen and cold. I've never met anyone with eyes like that before or since."

She gulped.

"He was tall, taller than me. He had the most gorgeous behind and…"

"Enough," I laughed, "I get the picture. Spare me the graphic details."

"I wasn't going to give you the graphic details," Rachel sulked. "I was going to say that he could wear Levi's 501 as though he was born in them." She grinned, and continued.

"So, we had this whirlwind romance. It was unbelievable. Heady. Exciting. I was swept off my feet, and he was the same. He was one year older than me, so he was in the throes of his final year when we met. But that didn't bother him one bit, and we never thought beyond the end of the academic year."

Rachel gathered her thoughts.

"That was a bad mistake. It turned out that he'd signed up for Voluntary Service Overseas for after uni. He was going to some remote place in Africa to help build a settlement and a well. When I realized that he was serious about going, I got really upset and we had lots of rows. He kept saying, 'it's only a year.' And I kept saying, 'but something might happen to you and I might never see you again.' And so it went on for a few weeks."

She paused.

"…and?" I prompted eventually.

"And? The morning he had to go, we had another big argument. I started it, I was so upset about it all. I can see now that I was being stupid and selfish, but we were both still so young… Anyway, he got on that plane without speaking to me again. But he wrote to me. He wrote me on the plane and when he got there. He sent a letter every day, and photos. He was missing me, and he was sorry and apologetic."

"That's good, right?" I tried to feel my way into her emotions here.

"It would have been. Except..." she swallowed.

"Except what?"

No answer.

"Rachel, what did you do?" I sounded like a mother.

"Nothing," came the confession. "That's it. I did nothing. I never responded to his letters. Ever. I didn't send him a single one. I went back to uni for my final year, and I pretended he hadn't happened. His letters became more and more sad. He couldn't understand why I wasn't writing back. He tried to call me a couple of times. And then it all stopped, letters, calls, everything."

She halted. "I never saw him again."

At that, she bit back the tears.

"It's all right to cry," I offered.

"No, it's bloody not," she disagreed, wiping her nose on her sleeve. "They already think I'm a loony and seeing me in more floods of tears isn't going to improve matters now, is it?"

She had a point.

"Anyway," she continued softly. "That's when it hit me. What I'd done. That it was all over. *That's* when I went to pieces. In a big way. I nearly failed my finals. I thought my life was over."

More shoulder shrugging and biting back of tears. "It took me a long time to realize that he hadn't dumped me. That I had, in effect, dumped him." Rachel gave a start and looked at me with big eyes. "You don't think Jordan thinks I dumped him, right? That's not what happened, is it?"

I gave her a don't-be-silly-look. "Of course not. You mustn't ever think that." I stroked her arm for extra reassurance, and we held each other in a hug.

An hour later, she went home to Cardiff with her mum and dad, and I went back to Dan's.

What a roller coaster.

What an insane turn of events.

This wasn't what I had expected from the summer.

Suddenly, my best friend's wedding was off the cards, which was a terrible and inexplicable pity. As a direct result, my best friend had had a tragic episode and had gone off to recover miles away from London, leaving me desperately sad for her as well as feeling lonely and bereft myself. My birthday party had seen my flat going up in flames, and I ended up living with a man whom I once loved and was trying very hard not to get attracted to again. At the same time, I had had this amazing thunderbolt-and-lightning experience not once but twice, with the same mystery man, whom I just couldn't seem to be able to track down.

Where everything seemed to have been steady and ordered a few weeks back, now all the balls were up in the air, and I absolutely did not. have the slightest idea where they would land.

My life had been turned upside down and inside out. And I did not like it, not one little bit.

PART TWO:
TRUE LOVE

Chapter Seventeen

"Please will you come with me?" Dan wheedled. "Please? I don't want to go on my own."

He waved the air tickets under my nose. "Come on. It'll be fun! And innocent."

I took the tickets out of his hand and looked at them thoughtfully. Two seats, business class, to Berlin. Leaving tomorrow.

Oh gosh. Why was everything so complicated at the moment?

It was just over two weeks since Rachel's little swim in the Thames. She was still at her mum and dad's, but I had spoken to her every day. Her parents had swiftly, efficiently and very discreetly canceled the wedding. She was reading lots and went for a swim every morning, partly to exorcise the ghosts and partly to get some proper exercise. She sounded a little better all the time.

My flat was nearly ready to move in. The builders needed only a few more days for painting and laying new carpets. And in all this time of staying at Dan's, I had womanfully restrained myself from falling for my rock star all over again. I had worked hard at keeping things simple and innocent. Plus, of course, I couldn't get the lovely Steve out of my head. If only choir rehearsals would resume sooner.

In the meantime, this. An invitation by the dangerous Dan to have a little mini-break to Berlin with him to celebrate his fortieth birthday. Business class travel, five-star hotel, the works. Everything that turned my head first time round, all over again.

Dan was still looking at me expectantly.

"Explain to me one more time why you can't have a big party like you normally have? Are you running away from your own birthday?"

Dan sighed. "Look, I'll be forty in two days. That's a fairly big deal to the press. I *am* a bit of a celebrity, after all." He gave a boyish grin belying his imminent descent into old age.

"Since when have you been adverse to a bit of media circus?" I gently teased him.

"I..." he shrugged helplessly. "On this occasion, I'd just rather avoid being plastered all over the papers with my age written in big fat letters. Who likes being called a sad old rocker?"

I giggled. "You know full well that you're neither sad, nor old. I didn't realize you had a complex about your age!"

"I haven't!" There was a vehement edge to his voice. "But you know what reporters are like."

I winced. I knew *exactly* what reporters were like, for obvious reasons. "That's an occupational hazard for me, and an unfair generalization. *I'm* not like that. Hey!" I had an idea. "*I* could write a piece about your birthday!"

Dan smiled and shook his head. "No coverage on my birthday, thank you, not even from you, sweet angel. I'll just celebrate it in private, please. Although I'd like to do it with you."

I disregarded the ambiguity in his last utterance and turned my mind to more practical matters concerning evading an ever-curious press.

"Surely they know already that you have a big round birthday coming up, they must be all over it by now?"

By way of response, he hit the play button on his answerphone. Message after message rolled by saying things like, *Dan, hey, old boy! Tom-Peter-Mick-Chuck here from RockMag-RockRadio-RadioRocks-HardRockTimes... I gather it's your birthday soon. Care to send us an invite/do an exclusive/come for interview? Speak soon.*

The messages came to an end and I sat in contemplative silence while Dan ran a hand self-consciously through his hair. "See?"

"Wow," I said at last. "That's quite something. What are you going to do with all of these? Isn't it bad publicity to ignore all these folks?"

Dan shrugged. "The label is dealing with them. So...in fact, I *must* disappear. I'm sure the paparazzi will be camping outside the day after tomorrow."

"So I'd be doing you a favor?" I suggested. Dan nodded.

"You'd rather go with me than the rest of the band?" I asked.

"Yup," came the dry reply. "I wouldn't want to do this trip with anyone else but you."

Gulp. Why?

"And you'd like to pay for everything?" I double-checked. Dan nodded again.

"Because you'd like to. As a treat for your birthday." I deadpanned. Dan nodded patiently once more.

"And there'd be absolutely no strings attached whatsoever?" There, I had delivered the killer blow. Dan took it in his stride, nodded yet again.

Not good enough.

"There's to be no expectation of funny business, rumpy pumpy, hanky panky or any of that. None at all?"

Now I had rattled his cage. "No," he finally spoke. "None at all. But what do you need by way of assurance? Should I wear a chastity belt?"

I giggled. "Of course not. Although that *would* be quite a picture…"

"Then why are you doing this?" he asked.

"Doing what?"

"Making it all so excruciatingly plain? Harping on about how we definitely can't have sex?"

Aha, methinks he might have had an agenda after all.

"Because…because it was hard to let you go last time. And because I'm not going there again. And because this *could* be really awkward without ground rules. And last but not least" — I took a deep breath — "because I don't want you messing up my mental health again."

Dan flinched.

"Was it really that bad last time?"

"Yes. *No!*" I didn't know how to explain. "You know I loved it all, loved you. But we put all that behind us and… Well, I don't want it all getting messy."

He digested this for a moment.

"Okay," he held up his hands in defeat. "I admit…I thought…perhaps…maybe…just once…"

I knew it.

Dan looked at me gravely. "Don't give me that *I knew it* look," he demanded. "I'm not that obvious. But will you please come?"

Those puppy dog eyes again.

"Yes, I will," I finally agreed.

"Great!" Dan enthused. "Here, let me show you where we're staying." He spread out a glossy brochure over the table. *Humboldt Hotel*, I read. *Five Stars. Close to the Ku'damm.* I gazed at sumptuous suites, exquisite dining rooms, a spa, a swimming pool, a fireplace lounge...

"This is yours," Dan pointed at one of the photos. "And I'm staying here." He pointed at another. Two rooms.

"I'm stunned," I confessed. "When did you organize all this? And why Berlin, of all places?"

He grinned. "Oh, a few days ago," he said airily. "I knew I wanted to go away but I couldn't work out where, so I closed my eyes, opened an atlas at random and stuck a finger on the page."

"And you hit Berlin," I breathed. "Incredible. How very fortunate." I wasn't quite buying this.

"I didn't, actually," Dan admitted. "I hit a place just to the north of Berlin, but it didn't look like there was much there, so I figured I was meant to go to Berlin instead."

"And so we're off tomorrow?"

"We're off tomorrow," he confirmed once more.

Well, what else could I say?

"Yippee!" I burst out. "This is so exciting."

Obviously, being an office slave rather than a loaded celebrity, I had a few things to take care of before we could leave. Like convincing my boss, Rick, that I had to have a few days off. Yes, to accompany rock star extraordinaire Dan Hunter on another trip. No, not to write a feature about, this time. Just for fun. No, not for *that* kind of fun. Rick relented, as I knew he would. He had raked in millions from my coverage of Tuscq's revival tour, he could hardly refuse a favor for his old friend, Dan Hunter.

Next, I boxed up my various belongings that had made their way to Dan's house and arranged for them to be couriered to my flat while I was in Berlin; I would move straight back in upon my return. Dan's housekeeper very kindly agreed to be at the flat to take delivery of my sofas and other new furniture in my absence.

Last but not least, I called Rachel to fill her in on all these developments. Refreshingly, when she heard my news, she turned into the old, perceptive, challenging Rachel instantly.

"What do you mean, you're off to Berlin with Dan?" she bellowed. "Are you insane?"

While I should have felt ever so slightly insulted, it was lovely to hear my friend on top form again.

"'Course I'm not insane," I protested. "It's just an innocent trip."

"Dan doesn't do innocent, and you know that full well," Rachel admonished. "I'm astounded that you two have cohabited for so long without crumbling. Or..." she paused. "Am I too late?"

"No, you're not too late, and no, we haven't crumbled. This is all totally platonic."

All I got was a snort.

"You know I'm a bit of a slapper, and I've always advised you to go for it," Rachel said earnestly. "But do you really think this is a good idea? And what about the lovely Steve?"

"What about him?" I said defensively. "I haven't even met him yet. I can hardly betray him, can I?"

"No," Rachel conceded. "You can't betray him. But you can betray your idea of true love, and your conviction, and your thunderbolt-and-lightning."

I sighed. "It really isn't going to be like that, I promise. We even have different suites."

"Correct me if I'm wrong, but you *always* had separate suites," Rachel reminded me. "Only you never used them."

One-nil for Rachel. Oh God, she was right. I faltered, but only for one second.

"Dan gave me his word. Of honor. There will be no funny business."

"You believe him?" she challenged.

"I do. And I trust him. Implicitly. He's never, ever given me cause to doubt him, or done anything that he hadn't warned me about."

"Also true," Rachel conceded and let me off the hook. I came off the phone jubilant. This verbal grilling was a great sign; I was almost one hundred percent certain that I had my best friend back. Things were looking up.

Chapter Eighteen

There was a light drizzle when the taxi deposited us at the Humboldt Hotel the next day. Dan had been true to his word. While we both had beautiful and extravagant suites, they were nowhere near each other. Mine was on the sixth floor, and his was on the eighth. There would be no clandestine midnight openings of magically unlocked interconnecting doors.

I eyed the four solid walls of my suite with mixed feelings. Obviously, I didn't want temptation, obviously I was totally, totally over Dan, and obviously I was still holding on to my Steve-moments, but this brought back so many memories that I couldn't help but feel overwhelmed at the similarities and dismayed at the differences.

Depositing my pink carry-on suitcase in the wardrobe, I took a quick tour of the suite. A bedroom, a small sitting room, a sumptuous bathroom with a spa bath and surround shower. As always, Dan wasn't stinting, bless him.

I was eyeing myself up critically in the mirror when there was a knock on the door followed by Dan's impatient voice, "Hurry up, woman, we've got a city to explore."

I snapped to and we were off.

Dan's excitement was contagious. We fair skipped out of the hotel together and walked up the *Ku'damm*, taking in the traffic driving on the right side of the road, the big plane trees lining this major boulevard, and all the fancy shops. I was worried that Dan would drown me in extravagant gestures, but all we did was window shop and look at the sights. We stopped at a bakery-cum-coffee-shop where Dan ordered two coffees and two *Pfannkuchen*, which I assumed would be pancakes but turned out to be doughnuts. They were still warm and freshly rolled in sugar and absolutely to die for.

"My clever book," Dan announced, unexpectedly brandishing a guide to Berlin, "tells me that these little delights are known as 'Berliners,' which translates into 'doughnuts,' all over Germany. Except in Berlin, these darlings are actually called Pfannkuchen, which the rest of the world would translate as pancake."

My mouth must have been hanging open in shock because Dan nudged me playfully and said, teasingly, "Do close your mouth, darling, we are in polite company."

I did as instructed. Then I snatched Dan's book out of his hands. "What *is* this?"

"A guide to Berlin," he replied deadpan. "I thought it might come in handy."

Berlin for Kids, it read. "This is a children's guidebook," I stated, stupefied.

"Why, of course," Dan acknowledged cheerfully. "It's so much more interesting that way. Look, it's got treasure hunts and puzzles and picture clues, and there are little tips about where to eat…"

I must have looked utterly confused. I hadn't known Dan was into kiddie-style sightseeing, or any kind of sightseeing. When I had accompanied Tuscq on tour, there had been next to no free time for doing touristy things, and nobody had brought any guidebooks.

"I find city guides for adults boring," Dan explained. "There's always so much information in there, and it's all educational. And okay, it's really interesting but there's always so much of it. So I prefer children's guidebooks." He winked and tugged at my elbow in a *c'mon* kind of way.

"I think it's—" I never got round to saying what I thought it was as a flash light went off. Dan gave a soft little curse.

"So much for not being recognized round here," he muttered. "Come on, let's go!" He pulled me to my feet, past the counters and behind the tills, and we boldly left the bakery through the kitchen. "Years of practice," he whispered to me as we muttered excuses to the kitchen staff.

We emerged in a little alley and randomly turned right, and right again. Mercifully, we ended up on the *Ku'damm* once more and were just able to see a little conflagration of photographers outside the bakery.

"Damn," Dan muttered. "And off we go."

He turned around and we walked briskly the other way, then stepped swiftly onto some escalators descending to a *U-Bahn* station.

"Where to now?" I questioned him when we were traveling safely—and at least temporarily incognito—on one of the cute little underground trains.

Dan flicked through his book. "We should really take in the Wall and the *Reichstag*…" he offered, but added reluctantly, "but I don't fancy that today. How's about..." He held up his children's guide book at a page saying, *Alexanderplatz and TV Tower*.

I nodded agreeably. It was his trip after all, and this looked quite exciting.

Once at *Alexanderplatz*, we discovered that we had about an hour's wait ahead before we could go on the forty-nine second elevator ride up the TV Tower. So we took a stroll, admiring the glorious old station building that was *Bahnhof Alexanderplatz*, trying to work out how the amazing world time clock functioned, and finally buying a helping of sausage and chips from one of the nearby stalls.

We sat down on a bench on the north side of *Alexanderplatz* to eat our *Currywurst mit Pommes*.

"This is great," Dan said once more with a huge grin.

Afterwards, we went up the TV tower, and once there, Dan got it into his head that he wanted to sit in the revolving restaurant. Somehow, he secured a table, and we installed ourselves in the bar for pre-dinner cocktails. The drinks were fizzy and deadly sweet, and mine went straight to my head. Dan was unperturbed, his eyes fixed on the vista of Berlin stretching below us and all around.

"Isn't this amazing?" he kept enthusing.

We lingered in the bar for a couple of hours, enjoying each other's company and ordering drinks and snacks as the mood took us. When we were well and truly stuffed, Dan suggested taking a tram ride round the former Eastern sector, just for the heck of it, and I happily obliged.

At ten p.m., I begged to go back to the hotel. My eyes felt gritty and my feet were hot and heavy, a sure sign that they had done too much traveling. They wanted a rest. *I* wanted a rest. And a bed. And preferably a bath before that.

Dan didn't seem to mind. He told me that he was thinking of checking out the hotel bar, or of grabbing an early night, too. *Yeah, right.* I left him to it.

Safely ensconced in my suite, I drew a lovely hot bath and submerged myself in fragrant luxury bubbles.

Lovely.

My poor mistreated feet tingled in the warm water, their muscles finally relaxing. I nearly fell asleep, feeling content as the cat with her cream, and I let my mind wander at random. Images of the past weeks flashed before my inner eye like constellations in a kaleidoscope but suddenly, a picture stuck. The moment of locking eyes with Steve.

I analyzed every second and wallowed in the memory. "Steve..." I whispered through a handful of bubbles. "I hope you're out there waiting for me." I blew hard and the bubbles dispersed, describing pretty arches in the air before settling on the walls and water like freshly fallen snow.

Thinking of snow... "I hope I don't have to wait until the Christmas concert to see you again." The thought filled me with panic, and I squashed it hard. It wouldn't be that long, surely.

But how and when *would* we next meet?

Probably at a choir rehearsal after the summer break. That would mean waiting another ten weeks. I would be there really early. I would probably wear...what would I wear? I didn't want to be too obvious but I wanted to look great.

Maybe I would wear — oh, idea! I would wear my snuggy favorite jeans with some sort of funky top, depending on the weather.

He would wear... I didn't really care what he would wear. He would look good in a potato sack as long as he kept that hair and those eyes. Those lovely, lovely eyes.

I paused for a minute, mentally zooming in on those eyes again.

Hm-mm. Hm.

We would probably not get to speak until after rehearsal, but then he would come over to me and say something like, *here's looking at you, kid.* Oh, a movie quote! I shivered with excitement and glee. How subtle. I hoped he had the speaking voice to match.

And he would take my hand and without awaiting my consent—in fact, knowing that I would agree to pretty much anything—he would whisk me away for dinner somewhere.

Uh.

"Somewhere" wasn't good enough. It needed to be somewhere special, yet close. Or perhaps not close, maybe that didn't matter. But it definitely couldn't be anywhere where I had been with Dan. Or with Tim.

Well, that would rule out most London restaurants, wouldn't it.

Hm.

He couldn't very well take me home, that would be too forward. Too fast.

I sighed. Darn it, he would just have to know a charming little restaurant that was virgin territory as far as I was concerned. He would come up with something. I was sure of it.

So, we would go for dinner and —

What, then, Sophie?

I let some more hot water into the bath, but then decided that I would rather get out. My fingers and toes had turned all pruney. Grabbing the fluffy white towel from the heated rack, I wrapped myself up tight and lay on the bed.

Staring at the ceiling, I realized I couldn't take this any further. For one, I really couldn't imagine what Steve's body might look like. And for another, I was starting to feel all...lonely. And needy. And uncomfortable in my skin. I had daydreamed myself into a hot spot.

Chapter Nineteen

"And this is Sophie, my awful ex. Bitch!" Tim took a sip of his drink and adjusted his buttonhole ever such a tiny amount. Then he continued. "She dumped me for a rock star. The stupid cow! Yes, take a good look, that's what an adulterous bitch looks like. I've invited her so that I could say it to her face, after all this time."

Tim went on and on, and I stood there with my face burning. I couldn't move a muscle, couldn't speak out to defend myself. *For starters*, I wanted to shout, *I didn't dump you for him! I dumped him before I ended it with you. Because we weren't right for each other.*

But I couldn't get the words out. I was clutching my glass of champagne so hard that I was in danger of snapping the stem.

Now it was Dina's turn to speak. Bizarrely, she had acquired an awful, squeaky voice that made my skin crawl like somebody scratching fingernails on chalkboard. "Lies, lies, lies, that's what Sophie told my poor, lovely Tim. It took him months to get over her cruelty and mistreatment."

Gathering up her absurdly long train in one hand and still holding a glass in the other, she left the dais and walked up to me in tiny, hoppy steps. She looked like a mouse in heels.

"I spit at you," she declared, and followed through right away.

Her glob of spit was well aimed and hit me on the forehead. I could hear the other wedding guests gasp in horror but still I couldn't move. Her spit, viscous as nasal snot, slowly ran down my forehead, down my nose and eventually dripped, ever so slowly, into my drink.

I wanted to die.

I—

Somebody was at the door, and I woke up with a start, heart racing, forehead wet with sweat. I rushed a hand up to my face—was it sweat? Or was it spit?

Sweat. Had to be. I was soaking all over. And I had no idea where I was.

Somebody was still knocking at my door and calling my name. Shakily, I got up from the unfamiliar bed and discovered to my great surprise that I was wearing nothing but a rumpled bath towel. Then I remembered—Berlin, Dan, the hotel.

Phew. I sat down heavily on the bed again, weak with relief.

A bad dream. Nothing but a dream. But one that could easily turn into a nightmare. The dreaded wedding was only a few days away.

The knocking and name calling got increasingly frantic and it occurred to me that perhaps I ought to let Dan in. I padded to the door, wrapping the towel back round me, and opened it.

Dan caught sight of the towel first and my bare legs next.

"Well, hello!" he enthused with a cat-whistle as he walked in. "Are we up for something after all…?"

The question died on his lips as he took in the rest of my appearance. I didn't blame him, having caught a look at myself in the mirror. My hair was standing on end in big, straggly strands. My face was blotchy from the crying I had done in my sleep, and my eyes were red-rimmed and bloodshot from ditto.

"What on earth happened to you?" Dan inquired softly. He retrieved a bathrobe from the closet and wrapped me in it, then sat down on the sofa and pulled me on his lap.

"What's going on?" he prompted once more.

By way of response, I burst into tears.

He knew me better than to ask any questions. Instead, he stroked my hair and made gentle soothing noises. Eventually, when I calmed down enough to speak without hiccupping, I related the whole nightmare.

"It was so real," I concluded, still shaking. "Like I was really there..."

"Now, now," Dan encouraged. "It won't be that bad."

"It will," I burst out furiously, and petulantly. "And I don't want to go. It'll be awful."

Dan continued to be unyielding. He eyed me up carefully.

"No matter what you dreamt, little one, we *are* going," he warned me. "Otherwise, this will haunt you forever. Trust me."

"It'll be awful," I reiterated.

"So what? It'd be great if it were awful. More laughs!" He had a merry twinkle of anticipation in his eyes.

How could anyone be so self-assured?

"Anyway," he continued, "as it is somebody's birthday, I suggest you get into the shower and make yourself presentable. We have things to do!"

"Oh God, I'm so sorry," I burst out, blushing deeply with embarrassment. "Happy Birthday, Dan!" I gave him a big kiss on the cheek and a big, strong hug. "Happy, happy birthday," I gabbled again. "Sorry I forgot, it was this stupid dream…"

Dan grinned benevolently. "Never mind, get yourself ready. I'll order breakfast."

"But-but-but," I stammered with confusion. Breakfast? Room service? This was more like the Dan that I knew of old, but I wasn't entirely sure whether I should tolerate him. "I got your present here… Let me get it." I made for my suitcase, but Dan propelled me toward the bathroom, laughing.

"I can wait. I know what you're like, get yourself sorted and you'll feel much better." He shut the bathroom door behind me, nearly forgetting to switch the light on for me.

"Thanks," I yelled, reluctantly yielding to the wisdom of his suggestion.

"Welcome," he yelled back.

Half an hour later, freshly showered and blow-dried and made-up, I felt more like a human being again. I had told myself sternly to chin up for Dan's big day—I wanted to make it fantastic, and I had a very special present indeed to give to him. Finding a good present for Dan was almost impossible as he owned nigh on everything he had ever wanted. Yet a birthday required a present, however small, and a round birthday *definitely* merited a gift.

He was a sensitive chap and he loved words. He always wrote his own lyrics, and I knew he appreciated a nicely turned phrase. So I had decided it had to be a book. He did own books. Quite a few, actually. A lot of them were technical ones relating to music and composition, and he had a few biographies of famous musicians and fellow rockers. He even owned a few novels, including at least one Booker Prize winner.

But this one was different. This one was *mine*.

Well, technically, it was ours.

It was a very personal present, but I thought he would appreciate that most.

I had written it over a couple of years, in little bits here and there, and even done a bit of editing on it. Nobody else had seen it, and I didn't think anyone else would ever see it. But for Dan, today, it was perfect.

It was the story of us, our story, or our not-story, as it were. It was a funny, and honest, and occasionally a little bit sad rendering of our romance two years previously. I had printed it out, at great pains, on paperback-size paper, double-sided and formatted like a book. I had added a dedication to him, and just for him. I had designed a cover. Finally, I had used all my contacts at work to persuade a printer I knew to run off a one-time-only copy of the cover, and bind it all together like a proper paperback with the pages that I had already printed. It looked and felt absolutely real.

There was an awful lot of me in that present, and I had my heart in my mouth when I retrieved it from my bag.

"Oh, a present!" Dan was wide-eyed with surprise. "How lovely. Sophie, you shouldn't have." He looked at me with big, excited eyes.

"Now, now," I warned awkwardly, "Don't get too excited. It's only a little something."

Dan shook his head in a "yadda yadda yadda" kind of gesture and picked at the wrapping paper. "May I?"

"Of course," I said, "just don't... Well, don't expect too much. It's—"

But Dan had already opened it. "It's a book," he exclaimed, sounding quite delighted. Then he did a double take on the title and the author.

Sophie's Turn.

"It's your book," he squealed, sounding almost girlish. "Oh my God, oh my God, why didn't you tell me?" He flipped through the pages eagerly.

"There's nothing to tell," I qualified. "It's not like I signed a mega publishing deal. This is a one-off copy, for you."

Dan paused in his perusing. "A one-off? For me?" he repeated, then clicked. "You *made* this? For me?"

I nodded, having temporarily lost the power of speech in the effort not to cry. I was feeling unaccountably emotional.

"I wrote it, too," I added, somewhat superfluously.

Now Dan was speechless. Instead of a response, he sat down and had a proper read of the first few pages.

"This is about us," he stated.

I waggled my head noncommittally, trying to gauge his reaction.

"Is it a diary?" he pondered out loud.

I latched onto the idea gratefully.

"It is, and it isn't. What we had was so beautiful, and so unique... Well, I didn't want to ever lose it. I didn't want to ever forget those days. Not one tiny little bit of it. How I felt. What we did. What *you* did."

He flinched.

"No, no, I mean the wonderful things you did," I amended hastily. "It's all in there. It's a happy story. And really, it ends happily for both of us, you'll see. If you don't like it—"

"I do. I *do*," he said emphatically. "I'm just surprised. And touched. Nobody has ever given me something quite so special before. This is unbelievable. All that work, and that effort..."

He petered out and turned the book over in his hands. "It looks so real, like it's been properly published. I can't believe you went to all this trouble for one copy, for me."

I could have sworn he was moved.

No, looking at him reverently turning the book over in his hands, I *knew* he was moved. And that, in turn, moved me.

Goodness, I was going to cry again. I couldn't cry *twice* on his birthday.

Thankfully, our breakfast arrived and we were both distracted from our musings. Saved by the bacon! We both tucked in hungrily.

Chapter Twenty

Dan wouldn't tell me his plans for the day. "You'll simply have to play along," he kept reiterating as he dragged me out of the hotel and onto the *Ku'damm*.

It was midmorning on a sunny Tuesday in July. The amazing boulevard was busy with tourists and office workers, but the atmosphere was relaxed. There was a definite hint of holiday in the air.

Dan walked me down the *Ku'damm*, past the *Gedächtnis-kirche* and right down another unpronounceable road, always consulting his children's guidebook.

"Where *are* we going?" I asked again, but I only got a suppressed murmur of "nearly there, nearly there" by way of response.

Suddenly, I realized that we were approaching the famous *KaDeWe* department store. How exciting. Would Dan want to go for an explore, or would that be too boring for a man?

But yes, we stopped outside and Dan looked at me expectantly.

"We're here," he announced with a flourish of his hand. "Kah-Dey-Wey. Or" — he looked in his guide again — "*Kaufhaus des Westens*. Department Store of the West."

I nodded eagerly, keen to get in.

"Hold it, hold it," Dan urged me, grabbing my hand. "You have *got* to appreciate this before you go in. This" — he waved at the department store — "isn't just a department store. This is Europe's *biggest* department store. Welcome to" — he took another quick look at the guidebook to be sure of his facts — "welcome to over sixty thousand square meters of shopping. I'm sure we'll find your dress in there."

I was rooted to the spot. Dress? What dress? What for?

Dan snorted with laughter. "The wedding? On Saturday? Let's get your amour."

The wedding, of course. I had never even considered what I would wear. I had assumed I was going to find something suitable in my wardrobe. In a flash I realized that wouldn't do. Dan was right. I needed something new.

Oh no, I bloody didn't. What I needed was not to go.

My emotions must have played on my face, because Dan held on more tightly to my hand and cajoled me along. "Come on now, it'll be fun."

I muttered a murderous comment under my breath and dug my heels in. We must have looked like an exasperated father with a truculent five-year-old, Dan pulling and me dragging my feet. But Dan was stronger, and he was determined. Suddenly, we were at the information desk on the ground floor, and Dan negotiated with a customer service lady. He was talking about an appointment with a personal shopper.

Ha. Fat chance, you probably needed to arrange a date three weeks, nay, three months in advance.

But — what?

The lady picked up her phone and spoke rapidly in German. In all that foreignness, I latched on to the few words that I could understand. Two of them were extremely familiar, involving as they did, "Dan" and "Hunter." The third one appeared to be *"Freundin"* — girlfriend?

Dan held a finger to his mouth, indicating I should hold my silence. The lady put the phone down and offered Dan her most dazzling smile.

"Mr. Hunter," she began in excellent English. "A personal shopper is expecting you. She will be delighted to assist you and your friend. If you'd make your way to the ladies' department on the second floor, please, she is waiting for you there."

And then—I swear she was blushing, and I could tell what was coming—yes, she summoned up the courage. She proffered a piece of paper and a pen. "Would you mind... I'd love your autograph." She blushed more deeply still. "I'm a huge fan."

"Of course," Dan agreed graciously and swiftly wrote out his name for her. "There you go." He handed her back her piece of paper and their hands brushed against each other. I had to suck in my cheeks to stop myself from laughing out loud. Not at her, per se, but because it was all so cute. And obvious. And because I had been there, myself. Dan intercepted my look and nudged me in the side.

"Stop smirking," he admonished in a barely audible voice. I obediently rearranged my face into a less irksome expression and even managed to give the lady a big smile myself. She was so excited, she barely noticed me anyway. She was already busy showing off her trophy to her colleague.

"I'm surprised," I ventured. "I thought you wanted to remain unrecognized."

"Well..." Dan sounded evasive. "This wasn't really anything much to do with me. You'll see."

I was intrigued, but he didn't give me an opportunity to ask more questions. We went up on the escalators in the central light well, and I had to admit, this truly was a spectacular place. Everything was bright, airy, and very elegant. Every floor boasted high ceilings, and there was plenty of space between the extravagant displays. The escalators rose toward a glass roof that looked to be spanning the width of the top floor, and I longed to go all the way up.

"Later," Dan whispered, his eyes having followed my gaze. "The top floor is all food, we'll have lunch there." He took my hand and pulled me off the moving staircase on the second floor.

Soon we were ensconced in a private dressing room with a cup of coffee each and a big prospectus of ladies' fashion, while the personal shopper was off collecting a selection of dresses for me based on rather cryptic instruction from Dan. "Get the lot," he instructed her.

The lot?

And there, she was back with a rail full of amazing looking dresses. Dan sprang to attention and flicked through the dresses one by one, muttering under his breath, "Too long — too green — too flouncy..."

He caught me looking. "What?" he laughed at my surprised expression.

"I didn't know you were a regular Gok Wan."

"I'm not," Dan chortled modestly. "But I know you. Remember that black Donna Karan number I got you once?" I nodded dumbly. The man had the memory of an elephant. And anyway, how could I have forgotten that memorable date, when he whisked me off in his stretch limo and handed me a bag with a suitable dress for the evening? I had slid it on, in the limo, completely dubious. And it had fit like a glove. In fact, that little black number still ranked among the best-fitting dresses I had ever owned. Dan had bought that dress completely blind, with no size guides or measurements or anything. Just his image of me in his head.

"…and anyway, I've done plenty of shopping with my sister," he continued merrily while I was reminiscing.

I latched onto this new piece of information.

"You have a sister?" I asked, utterly surprised.

Dan merely nodded, still sorting through dresses.

"How come I didn't know about her?" I demanded. Dan puffed out his cheeks and exhaled. "We don't see each other often. And she's just never come up in conversation before. You never asked whether I had siblings, so…"

I spluttered into my coffee. "Sorry," I retorted a tad archly. "It's not exactly the first thing that springs to mind when you date a rock star, is it?"

"No worries," Dan shot back. "I never did ask you whether you had any siblings, either."

I decided to ignore that barb and persisted. "So what's her name?"

"Jodie. She's my kid sister. I've kept her private but she's become famous in her own right, in her own way. She's always jetting off to places like LA and New York and Paris and Sydney."

"Why? What does she do?" I was intrigued now.

"She's in fashion," he mumbled vaguely.

In fashion. Jodie.

I nearly dropped my coffee cup.

"She's not Jodie Chase?" I burst out. "*The* Jodie Chase? The UK's hottest fashion designer, like, ever?"

In her corner, the personal shopper looked studiously disinterested.

"One and the same," Dan acknowledged. "She designed these garments. What do you think of this one?" He held up a dress for me to examine. It was a gorgeous creation, lovely and flowing sky-blue silk, gathered at one side and flaring out in an A-line. I longed to try it on, but Dan had already put it to one side.

"So!" I had a light bulb moment. "You came here because they stock your sister's clothes."

"Um... Yes."

Another light bulb moment—this one definitely a most ecologically-unfriendly, two hundred Watts, traditional bright glare, not your modern, dim, energy-efficient light bulb.

"That's what you were talking about at the information desk."

"Uh-huh." Dan responded matter-of-factly.

"So that's why you got to see a personal shopper. Nothing to do with being a rock star at all."

"Nope." Dan smiled mischievously. "I got you to see a personal shopper here today because I made an appointment in advance so that you could try on Jodie's dresses."

I was so wrapped up in my own thoughts that I didn't immediately react to this nugget of information. I needed to clarify something else first. "And she downstairs wanted your autograph because you're Jodie Chase's brother, yes?"

"Well..." Dan hesitated, refusing to relinquish his own claim to fame. "I'm sure she recognized me, too."

I giggled. "I'm sure she did. But hang on..." The penny finally dropped. "Did you just say you made an appointment in advance?"

Dan regarded me with somber eyes. "I did."

"Why? I mean, why here? Surely you can get her dresses in London, right?"

"The idea came to me on the plane. I texted Jodie to see if she supplied any stores in Berlin, and here we are."

Abruptly, he handed me four dresses. The magical blue one wasn't among them. "Try these on," he commanded. Fingering one of the dresses lightly, I sighed heavily. They looked divine. And expensive.

I stepped back, my arms folded across my chest. "I don't think I can afford these."

Dan rolled his eyes as though to say, "Not that old chestnut again." Grabbing a random dress off the rack, he disappeared in a cubicle and pulled the curtain shut behind him. This got the personal shopper's attention. She jumped up from her chair and walked over to me swiftly, eyes swiveling between me and the cubicle. She cleared her throat, uncertain how to handle this.

"Did he...did he go in there?" she confirmed unnecessarily.

"It looks that way," I offered, trying not to laugh at her disconcerted expression.

"He's not—is he trying the dress on?"

"Err, yes." I breathed. "Why, is that a problem?"

Meanwhile, Dan had run into trouble in the changing room.

"I need some shoes," he shouted woefully. "Could you get me some shoes to match? Size ten please, for me, and size six for the lady as well. Please?"

Confronted with a direct request, the personal shopper sprang into action. "*Schuhe...*" she murmured. "Size forty-four and size thirty-nine.... Hmm..." She bustled off.

Finally erupting into laughter, I bounced into Dan's cubicle. I was going to ask him what he was doing, but the words stuck in my mouth. There he was, in a bright orange, low-cut, floor-length dress with a big bow at the front. He had filled in the missing curves using his socks, and he hadn't managed to do up the zip. He looked disturbingly attractive in ladies' fashion.

"Will you do me up?" Dan turned his back to me and tugged experimentally at the fastening. I swatted his hands away and closed the zip to halfway up Dan's back.

"It won't go any further," I informed him dryly. "By the way, did you know your dress is called GaGa?" My eyes had caught on the flashy black-on-orange label sown inside the back.

"I didn't, but it makes sense. It's a wild dress." He gave a little twirl. "What do you think?"

"I think you're nuts," I snorted. "You be sure not to ruin this dress or else we'll have to buy it."

"Never fear," he grinned wickedly. "It would look much better on you, though."

I shook my head. "I don't do orange. Not if you paid me."

A discreet cough disturbed our whispered conversation.

"Excuse me, sir? Madam? I've got your shoes…"

"Great," Dan enthused and stepped out of the cabin. "Let's have them." He took a pair of orange flats out of the assistant's hands and regarded them critically.

"I was hoping for heels," he announced with a straight face, and I almost peed in my pants with laughter.

The assistant was now in professional mode. "I can't offer you heels in this style in your size," she announced, "but I do think we have some silver-colored shoes that would work with the dress. The heels are—" She looked attentively at Dan. "The heels are probably about six centimeter stilettos. Would you like to try them?"

"Why, yes!" Dan enthused. "I most certainly would."

The personal shopper went off to fetch the silver stilettos, and Dan grinned his wicked boy smile at me.

"Do you reckon she'll let us take a picture?" he wondered out loud.

"Hm…possibly, why?" I wondered back.

"It'd be cool to stick up on our website, don't you think?"

I regarded him critically. He was most probably joking, but with Dan you never did know.

"Yeah. But perhaps you ought to tuck those socks in more carefully," I suggested, tugging playfully at a black-and-pink striped heel that was protruding from his chest area. "It does rather kill the look."

He peered down his front appraisingly. "D'you reckon?" he asked. "I think it has something, this unexpected flash of black sock."

"Well, it does rather go with your hairy chest," I conceded. "If you're serious about the dress, you might consider shaving."

"I thought you liked my chest hair?" Dan mock sulked.

"Yes, but it doesn't work with a dress. It's just wrong."

"That's sexist," Dan declared, then changed the subject abruptly. "Here, try this." He handed me the divine-looking blue silk creation. "It's perfect for you."

I gave in.

The dress was so delicate, I barely dared breathe while I unzipped the back and gingerly stepped into it. It floated around me but clung in all the right places. It picked up the color of my eyes fantastically. It was perfect. It could have been made for me.

I looked at myself in awed silence for a few seconds. I had to have the dress. I twisted, trying to catch the label to figure out whether my bank balance would stretch to it. But of course, there was no label. It was probably very expensive.

I swallowed. Still, I had to have it.

"Are you okay in there?" Dan cut into my musings. "Don't tell me you don't like it..."

I pulled back the curtain and stepped out.

No, correct that—I *floated* out.

Dan and the personal shopper, who had returned from her shoe retrieval mission, gasped in unison. The personal shopper recovered more quickly, instantly homing in on my delight and offering gushing praise. Dan just stared, looking slightly incongruous in his orange dress clutching a pair of silver stilettos.

"Do you like it?"

Dan nodded. "She did a great job designing this dress."

I flounced around the room a bit more, tiptoeing all the way. The price question was still singeing holes into my financial consciousness, but that couldn't be helped. However, "I need some shoes," I announced to no one in particular.

"Of course," the assistant concurred. "These really won't do." She waved dismissively at the heels she had fetched before. "I have the perfect pair in mind, I won't be a moment."

And off she went again. I felt a little embarrassed, giving her the runaround like that.

"Don't worry," Dan said. "The commission on that dress will make her day."

I gulped. "Is it hideously expensive?" I asked, knowing the answer.

"No, not hideously," Dan replied. "Hideously *outrageously* expensive, if I know my little sister. But don't worry about it, I'll take care of it."

Moral dilemmas. This was a reprise of everything that had happened two years previously, and my, had I had some criticism from unexpected places. *Immoral, immature, indecisive* and *silly* were only some of the adjectives the women's journals had ascribed to me after the whole story had come out. That had hurt.

"I can't accept that," I said out loud, and Dan let out an exasperated sigh.

"Come on, now," he coaxed. "We've been through all of that."

"You can't go round buying me dresses like that." I protested. "I won't have it."

The personal shopper chose this precise moment to reappear, and she looked dejected.

"You won't have it?" she repeated. "But it is so very beautiful on you."

"She'll have the dress," Dan immediately reassured her.

"I'll have the dress," I confirmed at the same time. "I was merely telling Mr. Hunter here that I will pay for it myself."

"Oh no, there's no need for that," the assistant declared cheerfully. Dan and I looked at her, equally mystified.

"You see," the personal shopper continued eagerly, "this dress is part of Jodie Chase's Perfect Little Dress collection. It's called Sophie—"

I had to sit down. This was too much. I *knew* it. I knew it from the way the silk picked up the exact color of my eyes.

Jodie Chase was renowned for her daring couture, but the most famous collection of all was her Perfect Little Dress line. She dedicated dresses to women whom she admired or who inspired her, choosing a material and cut that she believed would most flatter. She *named* the dresses, but she never told her muses about it. She simply put the line with selected stockists all over the world.

Her first Perfect Little Dress had allegedly surfaced when she was still at fashion college. It was for Princess Diana, "because she always looked so sad." Word had got out and over time, Meryl, Kate, Pat, Bette and even Cheryl had been united with their very own Perfect Little Dresses. Rumor had it that Jodie gave the dress as a gift if and when it "met" its rightful owner. Which meant that this dress *could* be mine. But why on earth would she make one for me?

"Did you ever show Jodie a picture of me?" I asked Dan abruptly. Dan shook his head, but offered, "I didn't need to. We were in all the mags, once upon a time."

True.

"And...and when did she make this dress?"

"I don't know," Dan admitted. "As I said, I don't see her that often."

I fingered the material. "It's beautiful."

"Would you like to try on the shoes?" the personal shopper inquired discreetly.

"Oh, yes, of course." I stepped into the shoes as though in a dream. Needless to say, they fit, and needless to say, I took them.

And the dress. How could I not?

Dan had already disentangled himself from the GaGa dress and was ready to move on. I changed back into my ordinary clothes, reverently fingering the material of my dress and admiring the needlework. Surreptitiously, I was also looking for the tell-tale name and finally found it discretely stitched in the back, light blue on blue: *Sophie*. It really was mine. Smiling broadly, I handed the dress to the personal shopper and paid for the shoes. Dan asked for everything to be delivered to our hotel.

Then we had a lunchtime snack in the sixth-floor gourmet corner. Dan ordered champagne and caviar and smoked salmon on delicate little rolls. It was heavenly, but I found myself distracted of visions of myself in my perfect little dress. At least I didn't have to worry about wedding attire anymore.

Chapter Twenty-One

"So, what's next?" I questioned the birthday boy when we had sated our respective appetites for food and shopping.

"Surprise," he twinkled and hailed a taxi. We left the built-up area of Berlin and drove through increasingly leafy streets and suburbs. About half an hour later, the taxi pulled into a car park and I could vaguely make out a children's play area and some boats, with an expanse of water sparkling in the sunshine.

Right on cue, Dan offered an explanation of sorts. "Good day for a boat trip, don't you reckon?"

I nodded eagerly. Boat trips were *quite* my thing. We could sit on the top deck and quaff some wine or even champagne. I would buy, of course, it being Dan's birthday. It would be delightful.

"Is this the *Wannsee*?" I contemplated aloud.

"It certainly is," Dan confirmed happily, and ushered me out of the taxi. He had already paid the driver and dragged me toward the boats eagerly. He pulled me past all the lovely pleasure cruisers and walked on, and on. Suddenly, I saw a little boathouse tucked away at the far end of the quayside. Dan walked right up to it and whooped with joy.

"Awesome! Let's go rowing on the lake." He rocked backwards and forwards on the balls of his feet and pumped my hands excitedly. He was completely oblivious to the fact that I struggled to share his elation.

I had never rowed in my life.

Buck up, I told myself. *He's going to do the hard work and I'm going to sit there looking pretty. It could be worse.*

But Dan had other plans.

He hired two boats—one for him, and one for me. As the boat hire man effortlessly slid the two vessels into the water, Dan gave a theatrical bow. "Milady..."

My jaw dropped.

"You can't be serious," I uttered. "I'll fall in. I'll drown."

"No, you won't," Dan reassured me gaily. "It's easy. Come on, in you hop."

And he propelled me toward one of the boats. Before I knew it, I was sitting in it, an oar clutched in each hand, and the boat man gave me an almighty push into the wide expanse of lake *Wannsee.*

I pulled myself up by my bootstraps.

Oh, I didn't have bootstraps. Try again.

I pulled myself up by the straps of my strappy sling-backs.

There, that was more like it.

Regarding the oars critically, I experimentally dipped one in the water and lifted it out again. In, and out again. In, and out again. My rowing boat appeared to be moving.

Best try the other oar as well. *Hm.* I was turning on the spot. The left oar didn't seem to be working too well.

I turned to see what Dan was up to. *He* was still ashore, chatting with the boat man and laughing uproariously. *What is he laughing about?* I wondered, but was distracted by my right oar making a bid for freedom. I grabbed it hastily, leaning heavily to the right and the whole boat leaned with me.

Whoops!

Sitting up straight and keeping myself still, I waited for the little vessel to stop rocking and my heart rate to slow down.

Then I heard a *thud* on my other side and found that I had somehow rammed a wooden pole. Somewhat belatedly, I noticed that there was a whole row of wooden poles, some bearing signs instructing rowers to stay away.

Easier said than done. I was still drifting, and the current was pulling me right into the shallows.

Gradually, I became aware of some distant shouting. Turning again, I saw that Dan and the boat man were trying to attract my attention. They were both doing the Funky Chicken on the quayside.

No, hang on. Not the Funky Chicken.

They were trying to show me something. They were miming, arms going back and forth...

Oh. Of course. The oars. I was supposed to be use them both at the same time. I burst out laughing and tried again, but all I managed was a wild wobble.

I twisted round once more, casting desperate glances ashore. Behold, Dan was in a boat. He was coming after me.

"I'm stuck," I yelled, somewhat superfluously, and burst into more hysterical laughter. With fierce determination, I retrieved the left oar from an unscheduled diving mission in the water and grabbed both oars firmly, holding them level to the water. Ready, set, go!

In went the oars, ever so slightly, and I pulled them back with all my might, leaning, leaning; and yes, I was off! The muddy shore receded. Bump, there went another wooden pole, but never fear, I was on my way out now. Another dip-and-heave of the oars, and I was in open water.

"Easy now," a voice advised me, then issued an abrupt, "Watch out!"

A foreign oar appeared at the side of my boat, poking it aggressively. My boat obediently turned, and suddenly I was face-to-face with Dan.

"We nearly capsized each other, young lady," he informed me in a mock-serious voice. "Just what do you think you're doing?"

I shook my head, erupting into more peals of laughter, and I literally could not speak. Dan held the boats together as he waited for me to calm down.

"That looked adventurous," he finally commented in a voice quivering with laughter also.

"Hm-hm," I uttered noncommittally.

"Silly moo." Dan gave me an affectionate pat on the arm, moderated by a sweet smile. The boats rocked ominously, and he withdrew his hand quickly. "Right, let's turn you around properly and I'll give you a crash course in rowing," he offered. "We'll make a pro out of you yet."

Not likely, I thought, but I was glad of the instruction.

Lo and behold, once I had found my stride, it was actually quite easy. Emphasis on *quite*, mind.

Our hour was up much faster than I thought possible, and after I had somehow managed the nigh-impossible maneuver of getting myself back to the boathouse without ramming the pier or breaking the boat, Dan and I were on terra firma once more.

Dan gave me a big bear hug. "That was fantastic," he exclaimed. "Thanks so much. And now for the real boats."

So after all that, we did sit on the top deck of one of the pleasure boats, and while they didn't sell champagne, they had a very nice and immensely drinkable white wine.

All's well that ends well, I silently toasted myself. Aloud, I inquired of Dan what he intended to do with the rest of his day.

"We'll go back to the hotel, and tonight," my big birthday boy laughed, "tonight I want to go out dancing. To a club. Like I used to, with a lovely girl. Are we on?"

"Of course we're on," I agreed. That sounded more like a Dan-style birthday to me, and I was only too happy to oblige.

Chapter Twenty-Two

Oh, oh, but the hangover! As the plane took off, I was certain I would leave my head behind. Or at least my brain. The pain was excruciating, and I ached all over—head, back, tummy, and all. I put it down to too much booze. And too much laughter. And too much raucous shouting and heckling. How was I to have known that Dan was taking me to a club that did karaoke specials? That just proved that you could take the singer out of London, but not out of the man.

Anyway, I pondered, as I reclined limply in my business class seat, eyes firmly shut, hands clenching the arm rests. *What a night.*

I sat back up again and fumbled blindly in my handbag for some ibuprofen. I dry-swallowed two and lay back again, waiting for the drugs to do their magic.

After two days of living almost like a normal person, Dan had finally cracked the previous night. We had dinner in a Michelin-starred restaurant. Actually, we had pre-dinner cocktails in the hotel bar, after which, lightweight that I was turning out to be, things were a little bit hazy. So when Dan bundled me into another taxi, I didn't pay the slightest attention where we were going. I was concentrating on not creasing my perfect little dress that I had donned in honor of the occasion.

Dinner at the fancy two-Michelin starred restaurant was truly fantastic. We took our time over ordering and eating, and we even had a sedate little dance in a private corner. It was magical. And innocent, honestly. Just to keep myself rooted in reality, I made every effort to cast my mind back to my mystery man, Steve, and it worked. I even talked about him over dinner. Dan seemed…amused about that. He had never seemed amused while I had been with Tim. Then, he had always been very straightforward and adventurous. Now, he was being straightforward and decorous. Hands-off. Weird, actually. But nice.

After dinner, we had ourselves driven back to the hotel and changed into suitable dancing attire before going clubbing. How on earth Dan found this rock-club-cum-karaoke-place was beyond me; it was classy and glitzy, all mirrors and fairy lights and beautiful people. The rock music blasting from the speakers was a little incongruous with the décor, but it appealed to me. We secured a table, ordered drinks and relaxed.

Until. *Oh God.*

The sounds coming over the sound system were distinctly, almost intimately, familiar. His voice. *My* voice.

Love Me Better.

He—he had done it. He had released it.

Without consulting me. Without even *telling* me.

I felt hot and cold. My heart beat faster than the rhythm. I stared daggers at Dan, who held up his hands in an apologetic gesture.

"I was going to tell you; in fact, I was going to *ask* you but I was worried you'd chicken out and..." he launched into a somewhat feeble explanation.

"Too right I'd have chickened out. And what?" I prompted him to continue his thought.

"...and, well...it was just so great. I couldn't *not* use the vocals." Cue semi-apologetic, dead-devastating grin. The smile that no one could resist, not even me.

I whacked him with my handbag. I wasn't normally given to violence, but this was for form's sake, and I had to vent my feelings somehow. Only I hadn't quite worked out what feelings they were. Embarrassment, probably. Yes, definitely present. But also excitement? Pride? *Surely not.*

Meanwhile, our recorded voices reverberated around the club, loud and clear. It was surreal. Dan was watching me carefully. As he noticed me succumbing to the magic of our music, his face relaxed and he smiled again, lightly touching his nose to my nose, then nuzzling his face into my neck.

"I know you, Sophie Penhalligan," he whispered into my ear. "Secretly, you're thrilled. Come on, admit it."

"I am not thrilled," I objected, trying to sound dignified but failing miserably. "I am annoyed, actually. You promised me—"

"I promised you nothing, only that we would see how it went," Dan jumped in quickly.

Too quickly. I whacked him a second time, but only very gently. *Man, we sounded great.*

"You had this planned all along," I concluded. "You knew, even then."

"Of course," Dan admitted, unabashed. "You were bloody brilliant. This is the best song I've ever written. Of *course* I knew."

"So," I faltered. I couldn't help but listen to the music. Was that really *me*? Was it possible that I could sound so rock'n'roll? So cool? So authentic? Like I was, actually, a singer?

"It really is you," Dan confirmed, reading my mind as of old. "I told you, you were amazing."

"But how?"

"Easy. I had all the vocals I needed, and the guys and I did the rest. Well, not exactly; the engineers mixed it and produced it, but you and I, we laid down some pretty damn good groundwork, that night."

"And now—" I couldn't finish the sentence while trying to grapple with the implications of it all. Tuscq, a huge rock band. Me, providing the vocals for a single. What did that mean?

"And now we've released it as my fortieth birthday celebration single. Still rocking, but with a gentle edge."

"Still rocking, but with a gentle edge?" I echoed. "Did you come up with that?"

"Of course not. That was the PR guys." Dan laughed out loud. "I've always had a gentle edge, the world just doesn't know it."

"Shouldn't you be at some sort of launch party?" it occurred to me. "If this is your birthday single?"

"Ah no, I've explained that to you. Anyway, it's worked out quite nicely. I'm gone to no one knows where, and this single is out with a mystery voice that nobody knows whose it is. Perfect. It'll be number one by the end of the week, I guarantee it."

I nodded; yes, I could see that. But something disturbed me about this notion.

"What do you mean, a mystery voice...?" I suddenly pounced.

Dan looked a little bashful. "Um… Well…we didn't put your name on there for now. Obviously, we say thanks to the wonderful unnamed singer and all that, and there *is* a picture of the band and you, except you're blanked out. I didn't know how to ask you and I thought you'd say no, and if you're not on it and really don't like it, you can always deny, deny, deny… And if you do like it, we can have a relaunch in a few weeks' time and hit number one again. If you want."

I shook my head, trying to digest all this information. So I was going to be an incognito chart-topping singer with no name. Did I like that, or not?

"D'you reckon they'd play it again? I…I can't believe that's really me. Us. I want to hear it again."

"I'm sure they will," Dan agreed. "Shall I go and ask?"

"Would you?" I blushed. "Yes, please."

So Dan went off, like an ordinary Joe Bloggs, and requested his own single to be played once more. When he returned to our table, he informed me that the song was also available as a karaoke version, and how did I feel about that? I shook my head. I wasn't quite ready for that. So we simply sat back and enjoyed the music. Next thing I knew, Dan took off and requested all sorts of silly songs for karaoke, like the Funky Chicken, for crying out loud. He did some incredible things with his voice, weird high falsettos for a Pretenders number, and nobody realized who he was or what he was doing. I had rarely seen him so high on excitement and adrenaline. By the end, he went on merely for the thrill of not being recognized, and would he get away with it again. It was hilariously funny and, now that I thought it all over again, quite unbelievable.

I was reasonably certain that was what had happened the previous night, along with a few too many strawberry margaritas, of course.

What I wasn't certain about still was *The Song*.

I opened my eyes and stared out of the window. There was nothing to see except cloud cover, so I closed them again and imagined a wide-open sky with fluffy clouds above a calm ocean… What on earth would Mum and Dad think?

And Rachel?

And Steve? Would he realize? Would it give him the wrong idea about me?

The ibuprofen finally kicked in, and I fell asleep before I could finish the thought.

Chapter Twenty-Three

I went home straight from the airport. *Home* home, that was, to my very own flat. I was still feeling a little raw and hung-over, and now anxiety crept into the mix as the cab pulled up in front of my house. What would it be like?

The smell of fresh paint and new carpets greeted me as I unlocked the front door. *Oh, lovely.* It reeked of newness and a fresh start, and I knew that everything was all right.

Up the stairs I trudged, dragging my pink carry-on case, and stopped at the top of the landing to survey all that was mine.

Oh yes, I had come home.

You wouldn't have known all of this had been black with soot and damp with water just a few short weeks back. The cream carpets made the place look bright, and the walls were all pristine white.

Into the lounge, and yes! The sofas and the new bookshelves were there, the curtain poles were up and my lovely dusky-pink and cream patterned tab-top double-lined curtains were hanging neatly either side of the three sash windows.

The overall effect was overwhelming. I pushed all thoughts of lost belongings firmly out of my mind as I took in my restyled surroundings. The cushions I had picked on that fateful Saturday afternoon on the King's Road were doing a great job of making the place feel like home, and the ornaments and knick-knacks I had acquired were stacked tidily on the shelves, waiting to be liberated from their packaging. With only a few short hours of work, the place would be *mine* again. I let out a deep breath and sat down on the sofa.

Home.

While it had been undeniably lovely to live at Dan's house with all the perks that had brought, I hadn't realized how much I missed my own space. And even though there was the tiniest sense of feeling a little lonely in there, I knew I would soon fill the void with someone else's presence. I just knew. This absolute certainty came to me as I was sitting on my brand new sofa contemplating my future. I could almost see Steve sitting there with me, drinking a glass of wine or a cup of tea, idly flicking the remote.

The vision was so real, so vivid, I had to blink a few times to ensure that I was imagining it, that he wasn't actually there already.

It was like a strong premonition, but a good one.

I busied myself unpacking my suitcase and loading the washing machine before unwrapping new ornaments and furniture. I also, very carefully and quite reverently, hung my perfect little dress in the wardrobe, squashing my other dresses to the far side to give this one plenty of space.

At some point, I got hungry and did a mercy-dash to the supermarket by the Tube station, stocking up only on essentials for now. Milk, bread, butter, honey, chocolate, crisps, wine, a bottle of cava, pizzas, prawns, pasta…

At least I was ready. I picked up the phone to ring Rachel, still at her parents' house in Cardiff. It was a good call.

"*Sophie!*" she exclaimed with glee. "Were you good? Or were you…really good?"

I smiled. "We were both good. It was brilliant. But it was all innocent. I swear." I gave her a detailed rundown of events in Berlin. She grew very animated when I told her about *The Song*.

"I heard it a few times," she gushed. "I nearly called you because I was sure that was you, but I didn't know whether it was public knowledge."

It occurred to me that Rachel probably felt a little out of the loop on this matter.

"I'm really sorry I didn't tell you," I offered quickly. "This happened just before…" I faltered. "Um…well, it happened a few weeks ago," I continued evasively, not pinning down the dates. "We were alone in the house — *no*, not like you think, I can see you smirking right through the phone line."

"Sorry," Rachel admitted, not sounding contrite at all. "Go on."

I huffed. "Okay, right. Well, Dan had cooked me dinner and I got this invitation for Tim and Dina's wedding —"

Loud screeching interrupted my explanation. "What? You're invited to Tim and Dina's wedding?" Rachel sounded beside herself with shock. "When did this happen? Why haven't you told me? I can't believe this is the first I'm hearing of this."

"Err, I got it in the post, on a Friday. I tried to ring you but I couldn't get hold of you."

"Why not? Where was I?" Rachel demanded to know.

"I don't know," I tried to evade. "Anyway, I couldn't reach you and —"

"When was this?" Rachel asked impatiently, sounding cross, angry, and riled at being left out of a vital gossip loop.

"Um. About, well, about three or four weeks ago, I guess."

There was a pause while Rachel digested this information. "Was it more like…four weeks, or more like…three?" she eventually asked in a small voice.

I swallowed. Demons had to be braved.

"More like three," I replied gently. "This happened the night before Jordan hurt you so bad."

Another little pause.

"So I guess we never got a chance to talk about all that." Rachel finally reflected. "The wedding invite, and the song."

I shook my head, even though she couldn't see me.

"No, we never got a chance to talk about all that," I repeated her words. "It didn't seem important. To be honest, it didn't even occur to me."

"Okay, I can see that. Well, fill me in now," Rachel encouraged briskly.

Next it was her turn to catch me up on her life. As it turned out, she had mended quite quickly. Probably not completely — that would take a long, long time — but certainly superficially, she was functioning and projecting her old, buoyant, funny self with the trademark abrasive humor.

"I swim a lot, for obvious reasons… And I cook, for ditto, because I've got to learn *sometime*… Oh, and!" Her voice lifted with excitement. "Rick's asked me to write some features about life out Cardiff way for the *Read London* blog and I'm loving it."

She was positively brimming with enthusiasm about writing, but abruptly she returned to more urgent business.

"So, this wedding," she prompted in classic Rachel let's-resume-our-chat-from-ten-minutes-ago fashion. "When is it?"

"On Saturday," I whispered. She heard me anyway. "On *Saturday*? *This* Saturday?"

As she drove home to me how close the wedding really was, I experienced a sudden and quite unexpected pang of— what, exactly, I wasn't quite sure. Nostalgia? Dread? Disquiet?

But with Rachel prattling on, the moment passed before I could get a hold on the fleeting emotion.

"Please tell me you're wearing the perfect little dress?" she implored.

"Of course," I reassured her. "Dan wouldn't have it any other way."

"You go, girl!" Rachel approved.

"I'm still not so sure," I confessed. "I'm a little uneasy about going. I wouldn't want to spoil the day or be in the way..."

My heart sank to my feet in a sudden fit of panic. "What if all goes horribly wrong?"

Memories of my nightmare came flooding back.

"It'll be fine," Rachel soothed. "We're British, remember? We keep the party going against all odds. And anyway," she delivered her imperious parting shot. "I command you to go. To close that chapter of your life, and his. And to give me a detailed gossip afterwards. I want to know everything. *Everything*."

Chapter Twenty-Four

The Saturday morning of Dina and Tim's wedding dawned bright and clear. I had lain awake most of the night with a dull ache in my tummy that I put down to nerves. Heaving myself out of bed required a super-human effort.

I had some breakfast and threw on some jeans and an old T-shirt. Dan would be picking me up at ten a.m. to drive up to Portreath. We would stop somewhere nearer the place to change into our party gear—there was no point creasing our couture by sitting in a car for three hours. I placed my perfect little Sophie dress into a clear garment carrier and put all the other necessary accoutrements into a handbag.

Dan turned up right on time with the big limo and a driver. I was a bit embarrassed, but Dan insisted on traveling in style. Complete with food and bar and everything.

"Okay, okay," I surrendered to the inevitable, stroking the leather banquette fondly. "I might just grab some more sleep on the way."

Dan eyed me carefully. "Are you all right?" he inquired gently, dropping the jokes and the buck-up demeanor. "You look a bit pale."

"I didn't sleep too well," I explained. "Probably a bit worried."

"If it's that big a deal, let's not go. We can be the rude no-shows," Dan suddenly relented.

"No," I waved his suggestion away. "Let's not. We've got the car, and the dress, and the morning suit. Let's do this. I bet Rach is right. It's a good idea to close this chapter of my life properly, once and for all."

Dan grinned. "Atta girl."

I snuggled down on the seat and let myself look at the clouds through the big skylight. Soon, the gentle purring and rocking of the limo sent me fast asleep, and I woke up a couple of hours later feeling much refreshed.

"Hello, sleepyhead," Dan greeted me from across the limo. "You look better now. Had a nice rest?"

I nodded my assent, sat up and yawned.

"We're nearly there, it's time to get changed." Dan signaled to the driver and we pulled into a little service area for a pit-stop. It was twenty to one when we got back in the car, and we arrived at the wedding venue comfortably on time.

The castle was imposing. As we walked toward it on the gravelly pathway from the car park, the grounds opened up before us, offering a stunning view of the gardens, the headland, the beach far below, and, of course, the sea.

It was breathtaking. It was beautiful.

On the central lawn reaching up onto the headland, the happy couple had a big marquee. The tables were laid with pretty white and burgundy flowers with gypsophila tucked in between. Tall chandeliers with long white candles stood ready to provide illumination by night, and I suspected that they would later be backed up by scores of fairy lights that would be discreetly hidden for now.

It was amazing, and tasteful.

While I was busy admiring the setting, Dan had observed the comings and goings of the other wedding guests. "Come on, let's go in the Chapel," he encouraged, taking my arm and guiding me to join the stream of people entering the church.

Dignity and grace, I told myself, taking a deep, steadying breath. *You can do this.*

There he was, Tim. Waiting for his bride right by the altar while the guests filed in. My steps faltered, but only for a second. Dan guided me swiftly toward a pew at the back, and I sat down gratefully. For one moment, I was distracted from the glorious surroundings by a sharp, painful stabbing sensation low down in my abdomen. My head swam as nausea rose in the back of my throat. I swallowed hard, clutching Dan's hand hard for reassurance.

He mistook my iron grip for anxiousness and made soothing noises. "It'll be fine," he said for the hundredth time.

I didn't have time to explain the nature of my discomfort because the bride made her entrance and the music swelled, drowning the chatter of the wedding guests. We stood.

Dina looked resplendent in an elegant white gown made of satin and covered with delicate lace. Tim looked suitably relieved at the arrival of his bride, yet he seemed very nervous, and very keen. I had never seen him thus affected while we were together, and I was deeply moved by his apparent joy.

At last, the vicar geared up for the long-winded marriage wows, uttering the first line, "Do you, Timothy Renfrew, take this woman, Dina Erin Belling, to be your lawfully wedded wife?"

He paused to honor the measured rhythm of this ancient phrase, preparing to go on with the customary "to have and to hold," but—

"I do," Tim burst out.

Oops.

There was a moment of stunned silence as everybody held their breath. The vicar looked flustered, then gave a little smile.

"That's admirable, young man, but we're not quite ready for that yet," he announced in his most fatherly voice. The tension broken, a good-natured tinkle of laughter rippled through the church and Tim blushed deeply.

Dina reached out and briefly held his hand. The vicar calmed the couple down with much muted whispering, and the three of them tried again. This time, vows were said and exchanged without a hitch, and the deed was done. Everybody clapped wildly at the first kiss, and I found myself smiling like the Cheshire cat.

"Ah, weddings," Dan mumbled in my ear. "You can't beat them."

Unsure how to react to this unexpected confession, I merely smiled and squeezed his hand.

The service over, we stepped back out into the brilliant sunshine and I blinked.

"You okay?" Dan asked quietly.

"Of course I'm okay," I responded briskly.

People were spilling out of the church and milling about, and Dan took my arm yet again. "Let's perambulate and look busy," he suggested.

So we ambled about, reveling in the views and the summer sunshine. After the third circuit of the grounds, however, my feet were starting to ache and I needed a sit-down. And I really, really fancied a drink.

"Do you think the bar might be open?" I asked hopefully.

"Let's go take a look," Dan concurred eagerly.

We located the bar inside the castle itself, in one of the downstairs reception rooms. A long oak counter stretched the length of one wall, and the tables scattered across the room were equipped with candles and glasses. Dan swiftly installed himself behind the deserted counter and tried to work out how to get a drink without breaking anything.

"Get out from behind there," I hissed, feeling the giggles rise. "I'm not that desperate, and we'll get caught."

"The lady fancies a drink," Dan intoned solemnly, "and so a drink the lady shall have."

"Too bloody right," someone concurred forcefully behind me. Dan and I turned as one to see who had found us out. A little old lady in a pink tweedy dress with an impossible hat had banged her handbag on one of the tables and sat down heavily on a nearby chair.

"Ah, good. A server," she continued brusquely in a clipped, very posh accent. She had to be one of Tim's great-aunts. "Get on with it, young man. Don't stand there like a nincompoop. Open the bloody bar and come across with some fizz," she instructed regally, if somewhat rudely.

Dan sprang to with glee, never once batting an eyelid. He gave a mock salute and declared, a tad jokingly, "Yes, ma'am. Of course, ma'am."

"Champagne, if you please. And not the cheap stuff. I know what they have. I paid for it."

Definitely one of the great-aunts, then.

I scrabbled in my handbag for a tissue to stifle the laughter that was building in my chest. I barely concealed it as a cough before I got told off.

"You, young lady, stop that slouching. It does nothing for your posture, or your appearance. And whatever could be the matter with you? Take that hanky out of your face and let me see you properly. Do I know you?"

Mutely, I shook my head. I didn't trust myself to speak. Dan interrupted our little malentendu by waving a champagne bottle about. "Will this do, ma'am?"

Unidentified Great Aunt duly turned her attention away from me.

"Yes, that'll do. But for heaven's sake, stop waving it about. You'll spoil the bubbles."

"Certainly, ma'am."

Dan took a step back and grabbed a white napkin, which he wrapped carefully and expertly around the bottle. He turned the bottle with a flourish, turned, and turned it some more, and the cork came out with a satisfying *plop*. Nothing spilled, not a drop. I felt like applauding but caught myself in time.

For a second, Dan stood there, bottle in his right hand, cork in the left, surveying the situation. Then he set the cork down and took the bottle in the proper grip, four fingers cradling the base of the bottle and the thumb inserted in the little indent in the bottom.

It was a magnum bottle, and it was full, and no doubt it was insanely heavy.

It was also chilled, and now sweating with condensation. It was a recipe for disaster.

Dan threw me a look. "Ready?" he asked.

"Ready," I responded automatically.

"Okay…" Dan said, his tongue flicking over his top teeth in concentration. "Here goes…"

He stepped up to the counter and took position in front of a large triangular arrangement of champagne flutes which was at least ten rows deep. Dan stood by the base, and the very tip of the triangle was furthest away from him.

He lifted the bottle.

He leaned forward, holding his jacket tight to his body with his left hand so as not to disturb the glasses as he leaned.

He reached out his right hand, the one holding the bottle.

He reached out to pour into the top glass.

He reached—

And he leaned—

And—

CRASH!

The bottle slipped out of his hand, fell, and smashed at least two dozen champagne flutes in one go. The bottle itself smashed into several pieces. Champagne sprayed everywhere. Dan jumped back. Unidentified Great Aunt fell sideways off her chair with shock and surprise. Smithereens of glass shot across the room almost as far as the window.

And thus it was all over. The silence was deafening.

I was mortified. Dan seemed unperturbed. Unidentified Great Aunt recovered first.

"Now that wasn't terribly clever," she commented from her prone position on the floor. "I daresay that was several hundred pounds of damage you've just inflicted, young man. Perhaps you ought to consider a change of career."

She tried to get up, but couldn't manage to get her limbs in order. "Would you terribly mind giving me a hand up before you go about tidying up this disaster?" she asked pointedly.

Dan jumped out from behind the bar and helped her to her feet. He sat her back down at the table and asked, quite conversationally, "Would you like a drink while I tidy this fiasco?"

"Why, yes, certainly," she responded.

"Me too, please," I chimed in, inadvertently sitting myself down at the table with Great Aunt.

She gave me a hearty pat on the arm.

"That's been quite a shock, dear, hasn't it?" she said bracingly. "You might have been hit by shrapnel. Still, nothing that can't be mended. Except of the spilled champagne, of course. Terrible waste, that. Never mind."

I nodded dumbly, unable to figure her out. *Shrapnel?*

Dan appeared at our table with a fresh bottle, which he opened with as much aplomb as the previous one but poured in a more pedestrian manner, using both hands in fact so as not to lose control of the slippery surface again. He poured two glasses, one for Great Aunt and one for me, and, after a moment's thought, he poured himself one and sat down with us.

"Cheers," he offered with a sunny smile. Great Aunt was absolutely scandalized, but I clinked glasses happily.

"I don't know," Great Aunt muttered to herself. "The help sitting down with the guests, what are we coming to?"

Dan and I exchanged a look, and he decided to let himself off the hook. "I'm not the help, actually," he declared mildly. "I'm a guest. I couldn't find any help, so I thought I'd help myself, so to speak. Which is, of course, terribly rude and uncouth."

Somehow, he had struck the right tone of endearing contriteness. Great Aunt did a dramatic opinion U-turn.

"Not the help... I see, I see. Just taking the initiative. Right. Of course. Yah. I do apologize. You see, I thought..." She actually petered out, which was probably a first in her entire life.

"No need to apologize," Dan said. "And I will, of course, reimburse your family for this terrible mess."

"Oh, no, no, no, I won't hear of it. The caterers can claim it on their insurance. No, don't you worry yourself, young man, I will set it right." And, clutching her champagne glass in one hand and her handbag in the other, she tottered off.

Dan and I sat in silence for a minute, then burst out laughing.

"You didn't do that deliberately, did you?" I inquired of him between gasps.

"Of course not," Dan snorted. "I would never waste champagne like that."

"I could see it happening," I confessed. "I just couldn't stop you."

"Me, too," Dan admitted, wiping a tear from his eye. "Although I didn't anticipate it being quite so spectacular."

He took a big sip of his drink. "It is mighty nice stuff," he commented. "Probably quite expensive, I should think."

"Oh, at least a few hundred pounds worth of damage," I intoned solemnly.

"Yeah, yeah," Dan waved me off. "That includes the glasses, though."

We giggled again, and I defiantly ignored another attack of sharp, stabbing pain in my tummy. It was probably just a stitch.

"Come on, let's tidy up," Dan eventually rallied. "We can't leave this mess."

He located a dustpan and brush, bucket, broom and mop in a little cupboard just outside the bar.

"How did you know about this?" I stared in wonderment.

"It was a guess. As I told you before…humble beginnings. Once upon a time, I worked behind the bar as well as singing in front of it, as it were." He grinned and handed me the dustpan and brush.

"Be careful not to cut yourself while you swipe the debris off the counter. I'll take care of the rest."

We left the bar spick and span, with the pyramid of glasses restored and a note on the till with the telephone number of Dan's agent so the staff could contact him about payment for the damages. The wedding reception was just beginning to get under way and we went to investigate the table plans. Soon we discovered that we had been placed with some of Tim's relatives—and who should be presiding over our table, but Unidentified Great Aunt! When she saw us approaching, she rose from her seat and exclaimed joyfully, "Yoo-hoo, you two, over hee-aaar."

Dan gave me a conspiratorial smile. "This should be interesting," he whispered.

Ever the networker, he greeted Great Aunt warmly as though they had known each other forever. She gave him a quick kiss on the cheek and offered hers to be kissed in return. Then he introduced me formally as his companion, which elicited a round of excited whispering around the table. But he refused to be drawn, and, smiling gracefully, we sat down on our assigned chairs.

After the meal, of course, there came the speeches. I felt myself grow tense with apprehension.

"Relax," Dan breathed into my ear. "Soon we can dance."

I did as instructed, holding on to my champagne glass for moral support, breathing deeply and smiling widely. And happily, nothing bad happened. The speeches were short and sweet with lots of gracious things being said. We toasted the bridesmaids, the happy couple, and parents, family and friends, and that was it. My nightmare remained just that—a stupid, self-inflicted and completely unfounded worry. I mentally sent my most sincere apologies and deepest gratitude to Tim and Dina, glad now that I had come along to witness their union.

The newlyweds performed their first dance to much rousing applause, and all of a sudden the sit-down part of the evening was over.

"I want to dance," Dan reiterated.

"And so you shall!" I nudged him to look at the dance floor where a folk band was setting up on the stage. Right on cue, their caller announced that the ceilidh would commence in five minutes.

"A ceilidh!" My excitement levels rose to dramatic heights. I *loved* Scottish dancing.

"Excellent!" Dan rubbed his hands together energetically. "Let's get hot and sweaty."

I laughed. "I'm sure we shall. I might have to take these shoes off, though, they'll kill me. Or I might accidentally stab someone with the heels!"

The caller asked for the first set of people to join him on the dance floor.

"Come on, you good folks," he coaxed. "I need two sets of eight people here. We're doing the Cumberland Square Eight"

I slipped off my shoes and Dan pulled me to my feet. We were second on the dance floor after Tim and Dina, and we bowed to each other ceremoniously. Dina wore the brightest smile, and even Tim looked me squarely in the eye.

The caller put us through our paces, circling, stepping left, stepping right, toward the middle and back out again, doing baskets, round and round, and then dance it all again with the next partner down the line. I waved a temporary goodbye to Dan and surrendered to the motion of the dance.

Inevitably, before too long it was my turn to dance with Tim, and we smiled at each other uncertainly. The pace of the music was too fast for any hesitation, and within seconds we boogied, holding hands, swirling each other, clinging tight then letting go, as though it was the most natural thing in the world.

"Thank you," Tim said sincerely while we promenaded round the floor. "I'm enjoying myself. And thank you for coming."

"Thank you for inviting me." I injected more gratitude in my voice than I could express in words.

"It was good to see you," Tim elaborated carefully. "And Dan, too."

My cheeks tingled with a rising blush. "It's not...we're not...he's just a friend. We're not together," I felt obliged to explain.

"It doesn't matter either way," Tim absolved me graciously. "That's all history."

The jig ended and I pulled Tim aside for a moment to continue our conversation.

"Why...why were you so cross when I bumped into you a few weeks back?" I blurted out before I could stop myself. "You can't imagine how surprised I was when you sent me a wedding invitation shortly after that encounter."

It was Tim's turn to blush. "I don't know why I was so cross. I guess I was being stupid. Dina and I chatted about it later that night and I realized that I was hanging on to a grudge that I'd actually given up a long time ago. Dina suggested inviting you, and it seemed like a good idea. I'm glad you made it."

"So am I," I agreed. "I wasn't sure about coming, I was worried I...might somehow be in the way, but it was good and it was a great wedding. Congratulations to you both, I'm so happy for you," I added somewhat belatedly.

Tim inclined his head in silent acknowledgement of my good wishes.

I caught sight of Dan downing a drink back at our table, and I realized that I was desperately thirsty. And exhausted. "I think it's time for me to go," I said.

Unexpectedly, Tim folded me into a hug.

"Goodbye, Sophie," he spoke solemnly. "I'm glad we got to say our farewells properly at last."

"Goodbye, Tim," I returned his valediction, feeling unaccountably choked up. A great weight lifted off my shoulders. Maybe Rachel and Dan had been right. Maybe I had needed to close this chapter of my life. Tim and I let go of each other, and I walked away slowly. Next thing I knew, Tim had reclaimed his bride and they were dancing happily. And so it was that Tim and Dina's wedding ended on a high and happy note.

As I ambled toward Dan, fragments of emotion and memories skittered around my head like so many colored glass beads, forming pretty, ever-changing patterns, spinning round and round like the ceilidh dancers, and making me dizzy. That awkward stitch in my side was back, too. Breathing was painful and the shallow gasps I took only amplified my dizziness. Quite without warning, I was in the grip of overwhelming, crippling fatigue, so I begged Dan to call for his limo, and we took off twenty minutes later.

"Just take me home," I mumbled as I stretched out on the long seat, "just home."

Thus I passed out.

Chapter Twenty-Five

I woke up in the early hours of the morning, completely disorientated. I had been dreaming about the wedding, and the fire, and Dan's house, and the single, all rolled into a swirling nightmare of confusion and claustrophobia, and when I first woke up, I didn't quite know what was going on.

The clock on my bedside table said three a.m. I had been asleep for over two hours. And I felt awful. *Really* awful. I was dizzy and cold. My tummy hurt. *Really* hurt. I wanted to be sick.

I dragged myself to the bathroom and sat down next to the toilet, waiting for the inevitable. Yet after a few minutes of sitting shivering on the cold tiles without vomiting, I decided I was probably safe to go back to bed. I made a clumsy detour via the kitchen to make myself a hot water bottle, and I sank gratefully back into bed. I slept fitfully through the rest of the night, waking up every hour or so and repeating the bathroom expedition several times, without success.

At nine in the morning, I really wanted to see a doctor. Of course, it being a Sunday morning, I only got the answerphone for the out-of-hours surgery. Still, I left a message and went back to bed.

Two hours later, I left another message. I vaguely thought about ringing Rachel, but remembered she was still in Cardiff. I thought about ringing Dan, but felt silly. I could look after myself, dammit.

A nurse rang me back at noon. She listened to me carefully and asked me whether I could make it to my surgery for an emergency appointment. Easier said than done. My tummy was so tender, I could barely stand upright, and as for pulling up my trousers or, heaven forbid, doing the button up... No can-do, not today.

It wasn't far to the surgery, only a few streets away really, but it seemed to take an age. A nurse buzzed me in and bid me to take a seat in the waiting room. There were a few other people there, all in various stages of distress, and I chose a seat at the far end, for fear I might erupt and do some collateral damage.

The chair was uncomfortable, and I struggled to keep upright or balanced so I lay down on the floor instead. I curled up into a ball and concentrated on breathing. Unsurprisingly, things happened quite quickly after that. Within a few minutes, I was whisked off into a treatment room and a doctor tried to determine what ailed me. He asked me a lot of questions, and he took my temperature and my pulse. Then he handed me a small bottle and asked me whether I could possibly pee in it.

I regarded the tiny thing incredulously and tried to imagine hovering over the toilet, balancing awkwardly while...ugh.

"Do I have to?" I checked.

"Yes," he informed me. "I need to rule out a pregnancy."

Pregnancy? I gulped. Not likely. My addled brain couldn't work out what would be worse, admitting to not having had sex for at least six months, or trying to pee in the bottle. I opted for the bottle.

The doctor helpfully handed me a cardboard cup that looked like an oversized egg box with a spout and encouraged me to use it. Seeing by befuddled expression, he clarified. "You pee in it. When you're done, you tip it..." He gestured for emphasis.

Obviously, the result came back as expected. "Well, you're not pregnant," the doctor announced. He gently prodded my tummy here and there and disappeared, only to return with another doctor. Together, they prodded some more, mumbled something about how I was apparently "guarding" and rubbed their chins, then left me alone for a little while.

I nearly dozed off, feeling cold and clammy and sore. But a few minutes later, both doctors came back and informed me that I was to be taken to hospital. St George's was only round the corner, so one of the doctors loaded me in his car while the other phoned ahead.

"Thank you," I said, making a feeble attempt at polite conversation.

"No worries," came the dry response. "The sooner you get seen, the better. Look, we're here. An ambulance wouldn't have even got to the surgery by now." He parked his car in the ambulance bay and walked me straight through the emergency reception, handing me over to a nurse who was expecting me.

The nurse immediately took my temperature and pulse again, then handed me a bottle to pee into, together with another egg-box-spout contraption.

"I already did that at the surgery," I pointed out weakly, knowing at the same time that resistance was futile.

"I know," she told me apologetically. "But we have to make sure."

Bottle once more filled, I was given a trolley to lie on, a thick blanket, and two paracetamols. I must have slept, because the big clock on the wall suddenly showed two o'clock. I had been there an hour. I felt lonely and frightened. I wanted someone to hold my hand. With Rachel still away, it had to be Dan.

I fumbled to retrieve my mobile phone from my jeans pocket and, half-hiding it under the blanket, I tapped out a quick message to Dan.

Please be at home, I prayed. *Please come.*

Half an hour later, I was still lying on my trolley under my scratchy blanket, feeling cold and numb with discomfort. Suddenly, somebody said my name, and hurried footsteps came up the corridor, stopped by my trolley. Dan had come, oh thank goodness. He had also brought a nurse with him and immediately asked her a lot of questions, before he had even said hello to me. I felt giddy with relief. Somebody else to take charge.

The nurse scuttled off again, and Dan perched on the side of the bed. He took my hand in one of his and stroked my face with the other. "Now what have we here?" he asked gently.

I shook my head, unable to speak for a moment.

"It's all right," he soothed. "I'm sure they'll sort it out soon."

Whether his appearance had expedited matters or whether my turn had come, I couldn't know, but suddenly there was action. My trolley was wheeled into an examination room, a doctor appeared as well as a nurse, the GP's notes were being perused, the pee test discussed, my temperature taken again, my tummy prodded some more.

Finally, the doctor filled me in. "We think you have acute appendicitis," he declared. "We're not entirely sure because you're not quite presenting right, but the best candidate for your symptoms is an angry appendix." He paused while I took that in.

"We want to operate as soon as possible. We're waiting for a bed to become available on a ward, and we'll get going." He rubbed his hands together energetically, as though he couldn't wait to get stuck in.

"Meanwhile, we'll make you a little more comfortable." He addressed another person who had joined us and issued some incomprehensible instruction. "I'll be back as soon as we are ready," he informed me cheerily and left.

The other person introduced herself as a trainee doctor. She announced she would get me ready for the operation. The first thing she did was to close the door, for some privacy. Next, she switched the radio on. Ah, a woman after my own heart.

Dan sat on a stool by my bedside, observing critically and holding my hand.

"Let's get you hooked up with a line," the resident announced. "Are you afraid of needles?"

I shook my head. I didn't particularly like them, but I could deal with them. She tapped the veins in the crook of my elbow a couple of times, *um'd* to herself and tried the other arm. "Not great," she announced. "You're a little dehydrated. But let's have a go."

Dan looked on aghast as she tried to put a needle in with very little success. One stab, two stabs, three stabs; "Let's try the other arm, shall we?"

I obediently offered my other arm. While Dan was appalled, I was past caring.

The resident kept trying while the three of us kept a religious silence, and the only thing to be heard was the chatter of the radio.

There, finally! The resident sat back and breathed a sigh of relief. The needle was in. She started fixing it up with surgical tape. Meanwhile, the news had started on the radio and the newsreader was updating us on local events.

...and a man was arrested today following an armed hold-up at an off-license in North London. It was later revealed that his weapon of choice was a cucumber...

Given the palpable tension in the room, this was simply the funniest thing I had ever heard. All three of us erupted into laughter at the same time. Unfortunately, as I was shaking and the resident was jittering, the needle that she had so very carefully inserted popped right back out, leaving a big gash in the skin and a resident back to square one.

Suddenly somber again, she wiped her forehead and said, quite apologetically, "Look, this isn't working for me today. I'll get a nurse to put your line in, just hold on a second."

Within seconds, she was back with the promised nurse, who got the line sorted out with no fuss at all. Finally, they gave me some painkillers and started a saline drip. Just as I was starting to feel relaxed for the first time that day—whatever they had given me was powerful stuff, I felt like I was floating on a cloud—the first doctor returned, brandishing a small bottle and an egg-box-spouty thing.

Buoyed by the new absence of pain, I giggled. "Please don't make me do another one. I've already done two."

"I know," he acknowledged. "But if I am to cut you open in an hour, I want to be absolutely sure that I'm not going to stumble across an ectopic pregnancy."

"Okay," I sighed theatrically. I felt quite unreal now. Clambering awkwardly off the trolley, I set off for the toilets, dragging my drip on its stand behind me like a pro.

After that, events accelerated. Back at the trolley, the nurse had asked Dan to leave the room while she got me changed into a hospital gown. When Dan was allowed back in, he looked horror-struck as the preparations for my op were picking up pace. He said nothing, though, just stayed and watched. I was absolutely detached from it all, but felt extremely lucid and bright. The pain had gone, and that was all that mattered as far as I was concerned. Papers to sign? Permission slips? Yeah, bring them on, I would sign anything right now.

A porter appeared with a new doctor. They discussed briefly where I was to go, and we were off. The porter was wheeling the trolley, the nurse took charge of the drip stand and the doctor led the way. I caught one last glance of Dan standing in the little examination room, holding my clothes and shoes and looking very forlorn indeed, before the door closed behind me.

Chapter Twenty-Six

Down the corridor we went and into the lifts. The porter pressed button B-3, and I giggled again. "Do all the operations happen in the bottom basement?" I asked apropos of nothing, and the doctor smiled, but nobody said anything.

The lift doors opened and out I was wheeled again. There was a whole group of people waiting for me, and suddenly I felt frightened. It was one thing being given a drip, a gown and a chart, and being wheeled through the hospital on a trolley. Seeing all those people in their blue operating scrubs — well, now, that was scary.

"This is Sophie Penhalligan," the doctor introduced me conversationally to the group, as though we were meeting at a party. "She has a spot of bother with her appendix, and I think we had better take it out."

One of the scrubbed-up doctors stepped forward and lifted his mask slightly for me to recognize him. It was the one who had admitted me and made me pee in the third bottle.

"All right?" he asked. "It'll soon be over now."

I smiled shakily as he put his mask back on and stepped back.

The anesthetist introduced himself and explained about needles and going to sleep, dabbing away at the back of my right hand with a moist wipe of some description.

And then—

Another one of the be-scrubbed people stepped close to the trolley, looking at me curiously. Chocolate brown flecked eyes...I had to be hallucinating. I had been thinking about these eyes, and their owner, for weeks. Had had hot, steamy fantasies about them. And their owner. What would they be doing here, I wondered. I had to be mistaken.

Through the drug-induced haze, it hit me. The hospital, *of course*. When Rachel had her swim, she had been taken here as well. I had seen him here before.

My heart was beating faster, and this time not only with fear of the op.

No, hold on, stop. I couldn't be having a romantic moment, right here, in a hospital gown, on a trolley, about to be wheeled into the operating theater. That wasn't right. It wasn't even likely. It was totally improbable.

But nonetheless. Steve lifted his mask to let me have a quick look at him.

"Hello, Sophie," he said dryly. "Fancy meeting you here."

He knew my name. I registered with surprise, temporarily forgetting that I had been introduced to the party. I noticed the doctors exchanging glances, and Steve explained, "We know each other...vaguely, from choir."

"What are you doing here?" I asked quite superfluously. *Obviously* he was going to be part of this operation, but I wanted to hear what he would be doing. He understood me anyway.

"I work as a theater nurse," he said. "I'll be helping out here with your little appendix problem."

"Oh," I breathed. "Okay. That's nice..."

And quite suddenly those lovely eyes swam out of focus as the anesthetic kicked in and I went under.

They were still there when I came back round.

I was in the recovery suite, and there, right by my bedside, was Steve. Still in scrubs, but minus the headgear.

"Was it my appendix?" I asked by way of a conversation starter.

"It was indeed," a voice came from my other side.

Ah, there was doctor man, too.

"We had to perform open surgery in the end, and I'm afraid you have quite a long scar. Your appendix was quite gangrenous."

Yuck.

"Why, thanks," I said, feeling inadequate. "Can I keep it? I mean, in a jar?"

The doctor and Steve exchanged looks, then laughed.

"I'm afraid not," the doctor apologized without further elaboration. "In about half an hour, you can go back up to the ward. Meanwhile, Steve here" — another meaningful exchange of looks — "will keep an eye on you. I'll see you again tomorrow."

And thus he departed. I closed my eyes for a moment, feeling distinctly weird.

"Are you okay?" Steve asked softly. "Silly me, that's a stupid question. What I mean is, are you feeling better than you did this morning?"

"I'm not sure," I mumbled. "I'm really tired."

"That's quite all right. You have a little snooze. I'll—"

I didn't let him continue. Woozy, weird and disorientated I might have been, but I didn't want him to disappear on me a third time. "Please don't go," I squealed. "Or… if you do, at least promise me you'll come back."

Steve leaned on the bed and looked at me closely. He gave a big sigh. "This isn't the right time," he observed. "You're not even fully awake yet. But…" His eyes locked onto mine. "You felt it, too, didn't you?" he whispered.

"I did," I whispered back. "I did, I did."

We stared at each other for what seemed ages. My eyes started to droop again and the effort of keeping them open seemed insurmountable.

"I'm sorry," I said, still whispering. "I can't seem to keep my eyes open…so rude…"

Steve straightened up. "Of course not," he said. "This isn't a good time. I should never have—"

I never knew what he "should never have" as another nurse interrupted us, oblivious to the gossamer-thin bond she was breaking.

"Hello there, Sophie," she said briskly, consulting my chart. "Let's take your temperature, and it's off to the ward."

Steve stood back and let her get on with it, but I could tell he was watching her every move, like he was making sure she was doing it all properly. A warm feeling of delight lodged somewhere near my heart, but it was all too much to take in, so I pushed it right to the back of my mind for later analysis.

Steve accompanied me up to the ward and made sure I had everything I needed, which wasn't much. The one thing I really wanted was a nice big long drink of water, but I wasn't allowed. He brought me some ice chips instead, which was at least a bit of a relief. He also brought me a message from Dan.

"Your friend Dan says he's gone home and to let him know when you're back and awake," Steve read out from a piece of paper. "They probably advised him to go," he added helpfully. "The op took a little while."

"Oh," I uttered uselessly. "Right." Well, this was awkward.

I didn't react to the message itself. Instead, I had an urgent need to explain. "Dan is—"

"I know who Dan Hunter is," Steve offered very gently. "There's no need to say anything."

"But..." I couldn't get my head round this. "How do you know him?"

"I don't know him," Steve clarified. "I know *of* him. Who doesn't? I daresay the nurses downstairs will have been in quite a tizz." He chuckled.

"Me and Dan..." I started. "There's nothing..."

"Shh," Steve interrupted me again, putting his index finger ever so lightly against my lips. "I told you, there's nothing to explain. Let's concentrate on getting you better."

I relaxed into my pillows. "You probably say that to all the girls," I giggled.

Steve was unperturbed. "I do, actually," he grinned. "It's an occupational hazard. Stock phrase, and all that."

Was this man for real?

He caught my look and understood my confusion. Grabbing a chair, he sat down by my bedside. "Look," he said. "I'm a nurse. It's what I do. I'm friendly, and kind, and patient. And when someone has just come out from under an anesthetic, like you have, they may be conscious, but they're certainly not lucid for a while. So, I wouldn't worry too much about talking sense right now. Just relax. I'll fill you in some time on all the funny things you've already told me..."

Funny things? What funny things?

"...and when you're better, we'll talk. Properly. You know...?"

"Okay," I concurred and gave an almighty yawn.

"You grab some sleep. I'll get a message to Dan that you're okay and resting, and that he can see you tomorrow. And I..." he paused, and I swear he winked. Even in my befuddled state, I was sure he did.

"...I will see you tomorrow, too. Good night, Sophie."

"Good night, Steve," I mumbled and let myself drift off to sleep.

Chapter Twenty-Seven

Next time I woke, the ward was getting ready for breakfast. My bedside was empty. I was feeling a little sorry for myself when a nurse strode up to me.

"Good morning, Sophie," she breezed. "You've had a good sleep. How are you feeling?" Seeing me well up, she continued without stopping. "Very soon, you'll be up and about, you'll see. You could have some breakfast, if you wanted? Do you think you'll feel like some light breakfast?"

Once more she didn't give me a chance to respond. "Tell you what, I'll get you some toast and jam, and some nice sweet tea. That'll make you feel better." Thus she was off.

Some of the other patients around me were already tucking into their toast-and-tea, which I eyed with suspicion. I didn't think I would ever want to eat again. But then, Steve arrived with my meal.

Yes, there he was, wearing civvies, carrying my tray, and holding a rose between his teeth. I did a double take. No one, but surely *no one*, could be that cheesy, right?

Steve set the tray down on a rack by the side of my bed, whipped the rose out from between his teeth and presented it to me with a flourish, like a magician. He didn't say anything, but grinned widely, and his eyes were dancing.

I took the rose from his hand and smelled it. Steve was delighted.

"Do you like it?" he asked uncertainly. "It just came over me. I'm not usually that over the top."

I smiled goofily. "I do like it. It's quite romantic. Very Don Juan. Do I get a peck on the cheek, too?"

"Oh, okay," Steve relented. "You're lucky I'm off duty, or else I'd get in trouble." He leaned across and pecked me very chastely indeed on the cheek. He smelled lovely, of aftershave and shampoo, with a tangy hint of man in there somewhere. Hm. Before I could blush too deeply, Steve sat down on my visitor's chair and arranged my breakfast for me.

"Am I really supposed to eat?" I wondered. "I thought after an op one wasn't supposed to. Eat, you know."

"Yeah, well, I wouldn't recommend a Christmas dinner right now, but you've got to try something. It's important to keep your intestines moving, you see?" he informed me, sounding very professional.

"Ugh, too much information," I protested and considered the piece of toast he was offering me. "Must I?"

"Please try," he coaxed. So I took a little bite and chewed it carefully. It went down. It stayed down. A good start.

As he offered me more toast, we started chatting. He wanted to know how long the appendix had been bothering me. I asked him how long he had been working in the hospital—two years—and whether it was really him whom I had seen when I had brought Rachel in—it was. We talked about the choir concert, and having found this common ground, it was like we had been friends forever.

"Isn't it weird," I mused, "this? For weeks I've been wondering when I'd see you again and suddenly..." I petered out.

"I know," Steve acknowledged cautiously. "I feel a 'but' coming here."

"No but. It's just—it's so weird, how we finally meet. And I don't know even really know what I'm talking about. It's like my reality filter has conked out."

"It has," Steve cheerfully informed me. "It'll be a while before it's back. That's the anesthetic sloshing round your system. That's the thing that worries me a little. I don't... I wouldn't..." He paused.

"You wouldn't...what?"

"Well, you're really vulnerable, and I wouldn't want to take advantage of your altered state. Oh gosh, that sounds wrong." He rubbed his eyes, gathering his thoughts.

"I've been thinking about you a lot. And when you turned up yesterday like a false penny, always in the most unlikely of situations, I didn't know whether to laugh with joy, or be beside myself with worry. And now you're here, and we're talking—"

I yawned widely, clapping my hand to my mouth. "I'm so sorry. Sorry! I seem to be yawning at you a lot. I don't mean to..." I yawned again, even wider this time.

Steve laughed. "Don't apologize. You *will* be tired. Look, I'd better let you have some rest. The rounds will be coming later, and the nurses will bully you to get up, and you've got a fairly big day ahead, as things are."

Instinctively, I reached out for his hand, and he gave it readily.

"Will you come again?" I asked in a small little voice. I didn't mean to sound so pathetic, but I was overcome all funny.

"Of course I will. Whenever I can," he reassured me quickly. "As long as that's really all right with you?" He paused, and I nodded, *yes, yes please.* "I'm on duty again later, but I will be back, I promise." He gave my hand a little squeeze and gave me another soft kiss on the cheek.

"Now don't you be going anywhere," he joked, and he picked up the tray and left.

I lay back in a soft rosy cloud.

How odd. How very odd.

But how wonderful, too. Now we simply needed to get to know each other and the rest could be history.

Steve had been right, though. The rest of the day was tough. Soon after he left, the painkillers started to wear off and I was very uncomfortable. The rounds turned up and I was duly examined. Satisfactory noises were being made, notes were being scribbled on charts, and I was told to get up every now and then and move about the ward. Whatever happened to bed rest for the invalid?

In the afternoon, Dan came to visit. Not for the first time, I considered his appearance with mixed emotions. Newly dosed up on strong painkillers, I was finding it hard once more to keep a grip on reality. He took my hand, concern written all over his face. I half snatched it back, then left it. Was that okay, I wondered? Was he still allowed to hold my hand? Did I want to upset him by disallowing little gestures that had become the norm for us? Would I snatch my hand away if he were Rachel?

"Sophie, my love, what's the matter?" Dan couldn't help but ask eventually. "I was so worried for you, and this nurse rang and she said you were doing splendid, and now you're crying…"

He fumbled for a tissue and awkwardly dried my tears.

"I'm sorry," I sniffed. "It's all the painkillers. I was a bit frightened yesterday, and thanks so much for being there… I…" I sniffed back another impeding bout of tears. *Get a grip, woman.* A nurse attending the patient next to me threw me a kind look.

"Now, now," she said across the beds. "It's not so bad, now." And then, speaking to Dan, she offered as though I wasn't present, "She *will* be a little tearful. It's the aftershock, and all the medication." Dan looked somewhat reassured.

"I rang your mum and dad," he said, "and they send their love. They'll probably be here in a couple of hours as well. You gave us all a mighty fright." He grinned his boyish grin.

"Thanks," I mumbled, touched by his thoughtfulness. However, I couldn't hold it in any longer. I was going to explode if I didn't tell him.

"Dan…" I started. "Dan…there's something I've got to tell you." Oh God, those awful words. Dan's eyes were the size of saucers. It had never seized to amaze me how this rock god could look so much like a frightened little boy.

"You remember Steve? You know, I told you about Steve?" I launched in somewhat brusquely.

Dan nodded.

"Well, he was here yesterday. He was my theater nurse. He came up to see me afterwards. And he visited this morning, with breakfast. And—" I couldn't get myself to say the rest. I couldn't read Dan's face. An eternity seemed to pass before a slow smile spread, lighting up his features and making his eyes look that unbelievable shade of blue again.

"Sophie Penhalligan," he teased in a stern voice, "are you trying to tell me that you have been abusing your condition to make eyes at the man of your dreams?"

I didn't respond—I was too busy trying to gauge his reaction. *Was* he teasing, or was he upset?

"How bizarre," he continued, echoing my earlier thoughts. "How really odd that you should meet him, here. Now. Like this. And tell me"—he leaned forward eagerly—"have you talked? You know, like, really talked? Is there something there?"

I nodded my head. "I think so," I said tentatively.

Dan got up and leaned over the bed, trying to give me an awkward little hug around the IV drip.

"I am so pleased for you," he exclaimed, and he sounded genuine. "No really, I am. You've told me all about this moment you guys had, and I didn't believe you, and now you've finally connected. That's so wonderful."

He sat back and rubbed his hands. "Now, tell me everything. Please."

Not for the first time, I asked myself whether Dan was for real and whether I made the right choice giving him up when I did. Not that I was having second thoughts, but he could be so kind, so caring, so selfless that a girl did have to wonder why she wouldn't hold on to this man with all her might. In a rational, hypothetical kind of way, of course.

So I took him at this word and told him everything. I repeated every word and we analyzed the meaning of it all, and Dan honestly appeared happy for me, gleeful even.

And if I had worried, ever so slightly, whether sharing my newfound love for another man with a previous lover would taint the budding emotions somehow…uh-uh, I couldn't have been more wrong. Hearing myself describe my feelings and impressions made them more real, seemed to distil their pure essence until there was nothing left but the certainty that I had found my thunderbolt-and-lightning man. At last.

Chapter Twenty-Eight

My parents arrived later that afternoon, Mum looking pale and worried, Dad pretending to be chipper and cheerful. They were both shaken and anxious, so I tried to make light of the whole thing. After all, the last time we had all met up in a hospital was when Dad had his heart attack, and that had been much more serious. Mum had a long whispered conversation with the nurse and she brightened up immensely. She had brought me toiletries and books and a bagful of chocolate and crisps, which I examined with a slight sense of recoil. However, when Dad offered to get some takeaway pizza for dinner, I didn't say no. I probably wouldn't eat much, but I could fancy a slice of Margherita pizza.

In the end, I was in hospital for five days before they would discharge me. Mum and Dad stayed at my flat for a few days, coming to visit every day. As did Steve and Dan. My bedside was a hive of comings and goings, and I was starting to feel self-conscious about it.

Rachel rang me as soon as she heard and told me off mightily for not looking after myself. We had a little joke about how we both seemed to be drawn to hospitals these days. And one evening, when I found myself miraculously on my own, I closed the curtains around my bed and rang her for a full debrief on the wedding, and everything that had happened since. Including, most important of all, the developments with Steve. Rach was beside herself with shared excitement, and once more I found myself rehashing every last word, every detail, every gesture, every action that had passed between Steve and myself to date.

"Oh, oh, oh, I can't believe I can't be there to witness this," she yowled down the phone. "You lucky dog, you! Finding the man of your dreams in the hospital when you're in for acute appendicitis. I've never heard anything so preposterous."

"I know," I giggled. "We can't believe it either. But Rach…" I cradled the phone between my ear and shoulder while I gave the dressing over the stitches on my tummy a quick rub. It was eternally itchy now and driving me insane with discomfort.

"Rach, it's so amazing. We've not even done anything, obviously, we've talked and he's like my soul mate. He reads me. Like he's known me forever. Tim and I, we got dating and it was lovely and comfortable and all that, and romantic to start with, but there was never that connection. Ever. And Dan, well, that was a whirlwind of excitement and romance and —"

"Sex," Rachel interrupted.

"—and that, too," I whispered, as if all the other patients on the ward might have heard her. "It was all of that, and he did know me really well, and still does, but it was different somehow."

"Are you sure that's not the anesthetics talking?" Rachel probed gently, adding teasingly, "You *do* sound mildly delusional, you know."

"Do I?" I giggled. "Steve keeps telling me the same thing. Not about being delusional, but about the anesthetics and medicines clouding my judgment. But I don't know, I *feel* lucid. I don't feel great, physically, and I'm really tired and woozy and wobbly. Yet lying here, resting, I feel my head is clear and my thoughts are there."

"Hm." Rachel mused doubtfully.

"Anyway," I continued, "Steve is keeping the brakes on until I'm better. He hasn't said, but I can feel it. And even so, it's there, that weird magic, that knowing each other. That rightness."

"*Hm*." Rachel said again.

"Will you stop 'hm-ing' me?" I demanded,

"Okay," Rachel yielded. "It just all sounds so lovely. I'll have to come down and meet this man as soon as possible, I suppose." She sounded like the big brother I didn't have.

"When will you come back?" I pounced.

"Probably next week, or the week after. I've got a few projects to wrap up here, but I'm all better and…what was that you said just now?" Rachel paused as though collecting her thoughts. When she went on, I could practically see her making a Sophie-face as she was talking. "*I feel lucid. My head is clear and my thoughts are there.*"

I snorted. "Don't take the mickey out of an invalid, it's unkind."

"But I'm not," she protested. "I do feel all there. Calm. Ready to go back and face it all. You know, my flat, the places we used to hang out… I've visualized them all in my mind and I can take it. So," she adopted a Schwarzenegger voice this time, "I'll be back. Soon."

We shared a giggle, and I hung up. I was a little exhausted after this conversation, but I felt jubilant.

I felt even more jubilant when, during rounds the next morning, I was told that I would be discharged the next day. Thank heaven! Steve came round soon afterward and he already knew. He said he would take the day off to help me settle into my flat and wouldn't brook any kind of argument. I was touched, and nervous. What would it be like introducing my man to my flat? How would we behave, what would we *say* in a private environment? It was like having first date nerves.

Steve was unperturbed. On the contrary, he was busy making arrangements to ensure that I would be comfortable. We were almost done when Dan turned up, accompanied by a young lady who looked slightly familiar. She was immaculately turned out, wearing beautiful, expensive clothes. She smiled widely and genuinely at me. Yet my heart sank. Steve meeting Dan, *here*, for the first time, and in the presence of this beautiful stranger...

Steve got up and extended a hand to Dan, greeting him openly.

"You must be Dan," he said. "I've heard all about you. It's a pleasure to meet you, finally."

Dan grinned his big boyish smile and took Steve's hand. "The pleasure is all mine," he drawled, then gave Steve a light matey punch on the shoulder. "You must be Steve. Good to meet you, mate," Dan continued sincerely. He was in his best making-friends mode. I had not seen it often, but I did know this was for real. It wasn't his I'm-nice-to-you-but-I-don't-know-you-and-I'll-never-see-you-again brand of friendliness. There was a brief uneasy moment as the two men eyed each other up. The unfamiliar woman broke the spell by clearing her throat and poking Dan in the ribs. Dan sprang to.

"Oh, yeah, right, of course, sorry," he mumbled apologetically. I had rarely seen him so flustered. "Sophie, this is Jodie. Jodie, this is Sophie." He made clumsy back-and-forth hand gestures between me and his sister, and suddenly everything became clear. I had never had an opportunity to meet any of his family before, and he was out of his comfort zone introducing us. Jodie rescued the situation gracefully.

"You social klutz," she pronounced teasingly and playfully poked Dan in the ribs once more. "It's a miracle to me that you're so popular with the ladies." Turning to me, she instructed, "Ignore him. He may be my famous older brother, but he's got the grace of a guinea pig."

She appropriated a chair and sat down while the men were still standing round uncertainly.

I stared in disbelief. "What are you doing here?" I burst out ungraciously, then backtracked. "I'm sorry, that came out wrong. It's lovely to meet you, only Dan said he rarely ever sees you and suddenly you're here, of all places..."

Jodie fiddled with her handbag. "It's crackers, I know. But I simply *had* to meet the owner of the Sophie dress. I'm just passing through London on my way to LA and I couldn't resist."

The dress, oh my God, of course!

"Thank you so much for my perfect little dress," I gushed. "It's divine. It's the most amazing piece of—" *Whoops, hold it, Sophie.* I couldn't call the dress a piece of clothing. I corrected myself quickly. "—the most amazing garment I've ever owned, or ever will. Short of a wedding gown, perhaps." I giggled nervously. "Thank you so much, I...well, I really don't know what to say. When they said in the shop that I could have it for nothing..."

"It was nothing," Jodie stated simply. "I made it for you. I hoped one day you would find it, or it would find you. It did, and that made me happy."

"I know," I sighed. "But still…"

"How are you feeling?" Jodie whispered and cast an appraising eye over me. "You certainly don't look your best."

I laughed, and picked at strands of my greasy hair. "What a relief to hear someone say that," I replied honestly. "For days, everyone has been telling me how great I look, how much better I look, but I know I'm not, and I'm desperate for a hair wash." Jodie made to say something, but I jumped in first. "Don't even go there. I may feel skanky, but there's no way I feel like braving the shower yet. Maybe tomorrow."

Jodie laughed, and I joined in. It was lovely to have some female company, somebody who instinctively knew how weird it was not to wash your hair and blow dry it and look nice day in and day out. She was totally down-to-earth and unaffected, and I had a feeling we would make great friends, given the chance. She was still pondering my beauty conundrum.

"How's about a funky scarf or something?" she offered. "You know, the ethnic look."

"Ah, no thanks," I joked back. "I feel quite ethnic enough as it is."

"What *are* you two girls talking about?" Dan butted in suddenly. He and Steve had been to the vending machines and brought tea and snacks for everyone.

"Lady things," Jodie replied to his question. "Comforts and necessities." She raised her eyebrows at Steve, rubbing her fingers across her scalp in a hair washing kind of motion. Steve caught on immediately. He set his cups and muffins down on my tray quickly and dabbed at my hair.

Right, now I *really* felt like an ethnic freak.

"I'm sorry, my lovely," he said. "It never even occurred to me. That's men for you. And I call myself a nurse."

He looked suitably apologetic. "Shall I get it sorted for you? Because I can, if you want. It's not a big deal at all, I—"

"It's fine," I interrupted. "Maybe tomorrow, at home..." I let the sentence hang, my eyes darting from Steve to Dan and back.

"Good idea," Steve concurred. "Peace and quiet and no rush. We'll sort it tomorrow."

Dan raised his eyebrows but said nothing.

"I'm getting out tomorrow," I blabbed, almost apologetically. "Steve's helping me settle at home. Because I'm struggling to move and bend and I'll probably need some help and..."

Dan held up his hands, palm outwards. "It's okay, you don't need to explain. Steve's filled me in on the plan."

He had? What plan?

Steve grinned. "I did. I mean, I did tell Dan that you'll be getting out tomorrow and that I'll be taking you home. To your home," he amended quickly.

I felt like I was behind some sort of glass wall, not understanding what everyone else was saying to me. "And?" I prompted uncertainly.

"And nothing," Steve said. "Dan's only making it sound grand."

I noted a tone of familiarity, as though the two of them had known each other longer than ten minutes.

Steve continued talking. "It's just that I'm taking you home. That's it." He took my hand as if to make a point. Dan stepped back and watched. Somehow, the moment assumed a special significance, as though a handover had taken place. Steve had stepped up, and Dan had stepped back. I could have sworn the two men exchanged a conspiratorial look.

Jodie noticed it too, because she gave me a big wink. "They're getting on quite well, don't you think?" she uttered in a stage whisper. "Looks like there won't be a fight in the sandbox today."

Dan tickled her under the chin. "Oi, don't you go talking about your big brother like that," he teased. I didn't know whether to laugh or cry.

"I don't get it," I mumbled. "I feel like I've missed a chapter somewhere along the line."

Steve cleared his throat. "You have," he admitted sheepishly. "Sort of. You see—"

"Steve and I went out for a pint that first night you were in here," Dan elaborated. "He'd called me at home with the news that the op went well, and I think I got a bit shirty and rude on the phone, and—"

"—and I said we should meet up," Steve picked up the thread. "I knew about Dan, of course. I mean, come on, the whole *world* knows about Dan."

"Hang on," I burst out. "All the introduction palaver earlier…'You must be Steve,'" I mimicked for emphasis. "Why didn't you simply say you'd met?"

The men were looking sheepish.

"Well…yes…um…it's all mildly embarrassing, really," Steve elaborated hesitantly. "You know?"

"I don't know," I challenged. "Why would it be embarrassing?"

Dan decided to ignore me. "So we went to the pub," he went on. "And we talked. Like grown men."

"Yeah, like grown men," Steve repeated. Now I was getting the embarrassment factor. Jodie and I exchanged a look. I stifled a laugh; Jodie busied herself rummaging in her handbag to hide her twitching mouth.

"And that's that," Dan concluded lamely.

Jodie spoke up. "I think what these two imbeciles are trying to say, very clumsily, is that they met up and put their proverbial cards on the table. It will have been like this." She pulled a face and continued in a deep, wide-boy voice. "Oi, you, you know I've been dating this bird. I'm not dating her anymore, but I won't have her hurt." She pulled a different face and assumed a slightly deeper, macho voice for Steve. "Good to know. She's my bird now. I won't hurt her." And back to the wide-boy voice for Dan. "I'll be keeping an eye on you."

The men stood there, open-mouthed and looking abashed.

"Yup," Jodie confirmed. "It looks like they've sorted out their claims. Lucky you, to have two such adorable men looking after your well-being."

Lucky me, indeed.

Jodie came to the rescue one final time. "Sophie is absolutely exhausted," she observed. "Come on you guys, buzz off. You can come back later." She made a shooing hand gesture, and the men obligingly turned to leave. Steve came back for a quick peck on the cheek, and they ambled down the corridor, shoulder to shoulder.

"I don't believe this," I muttered helplessly.

Jodie regarded me gravely. "Look, Dan cares deeply about you. But he knows you're through. I think he's trying to tell you that it's okay to move on. He's been a bit worried that perhaps…" she faltered, but went on bravely. "That perhaps you wouldn't go after your new man for some weird reason to do with him. Men." She rolled her eyes. "They think they're the center of the universe, don't they? Anyway, all this bravado, that's for show. Really, he thinks Steve is a nice guy."

"That's great. That's cool. But do you know, this matey stuff, that's freaking me out," I confessed.

"I'm not surprised," Jodie smiled. "Just give it some time. Most importantly, give you and Steve some time. I'll sort Dan out, don't you worry. I know where you're coming from. Give this new relationship some time to grow, and you'll find a space for all your old friends, and new ones, too. Trust me."

I smiled back. "Thank you, I needed a little pep talk. I feel a bit overwhelmed." I sighed. "Why is life so complicated sometimes?"

Jodie took my hand. "It feels complicated now, but it won't do, not over time. You know Dan, he's Mr. Chilled-and-Easy-Going. He'll come round, as will you. And Steve. You never know, one day Dan will be godfather to your children."

I snorted disbelievingly. What a notion!

"Don't diss it," she said. "You wait and see. I have a good feeling about this. And now I must fly," she declared abruptly. "Here, have this." She pressed a card in my hands with a whole array of telephone numbers and email addresses. "Any time you need to talk, or if Dan gives you any trouble, give me a call." She gave me bracing poke, then she rose to go. "I must dash, but you go, girlfriend."

She blew me a kiss and she was gone.

I sank into my pillows, feeling as though I had been tumble-dried, all hot and crumpled and discombobulated.

"Give it time," I whispered to myself. "Let it grow."

Chapter Twenty-Nine

Steve arrived after breakfast the following morning. While he gathered together my things into a rucksack, I had a clumsy go at getting dressed on my bed, behind drawn curtains. All done, we waited for the discharge notice to come through, which eventually happened before lunch.

"Would you like to go home, or partake of another hospital lunch?" Steve asked with a big cheeky grin.

"Home, please," I responded simply. I wasn't in the mood to joke about this. All I wanted was to go home, have a bath, and wash my hair.

Steve carried the rucksack while I hobbled to the lifts. As the consultant had instructed, I had been shuffling up and down the ward several times a day, every day, and I could move reasonably well, albeit very slowly, and not for long. But I managed it to the lifts, and through the lobby, and out to a waiting taxi. Steve dumped the rucksack in the back and opened the passenger door for me, holding it wide while the driver looked on. I stood uncertainly, not sure how to get in.

Seeing my hesitation, nurse-Steve surfaced again. "Sit down with your bottom sideways on the seat…ever so gently," he instructed and commented on my progress as I followed his advice. "Right, that's good. Now lift your feet in…carefully, right, good. Now turn on the seat…turn your bottom…well done. And lean back, slowly. Right. There, well done."

He gave me a big smile as he pulled the safety belt down and across.

"Here, strap yourself in, but go easy, now," he instructed, pushing the clasp in my hand. Then he installed himself the back seat, looking at me expectantly. "Ready?"

"Ready," I acknowledged.

Outside the flat, Steve and I stood together uncertainly for a moment. How weird that Steve had never been here before, even though we had talked about our lives as though we had always known each other. How weird that he could confidently take the key off me, unlock the front door, and lead the way into my home, carrying my belongings in his rucksack.

"You go and sit down in the lounge," Steve instructed me sternly, adopting his best staff nurse voice. "I'll make a cup of tea."

"I don't want a cup of tea," I protested. "I really, really want a bath. I feel so dirty and full of hospital grime."

"Oh, all right, if the lady wants a bath, the lady shall have a bath," Steve relented. "But please will you have a sit down while I run it?" So I sat down on the sofa, gingerly, while Steve ran me a bath in my bathroom in my flat.

While I reveled in the bubbles, Steve prepared a little lunch, a few sandwiches and nibbles, which he thoughtfully laid out, buffet style, on the coffee table in the lounge. He also equipped the sofa with my pillows and duvet, and pulled the telly round so I could see it better.

"Your recovery suite is equipped and prepared," he joked as he made me lie down on the sofa.

"It's the middle of July," I protested. "I can't lie around in the lounge with my duvet as though it was the middle of winter."

"You can, and you shall," Steve informed me dryly, then switched the telly on without further debate. He flicked through channels until he found a rerun of Magnum, PI.

"Cool," he exclaimed involuntarily. "I used to adore Magnum."

"Me, too," I agreed. "Leave it on."

Steve settled on the other, shorter prong of my L-shaped sofa and handed me a sandwich. I munched slowly, still not feeling hungry, trying to focus on the TV program and not thinking too hard about the fact that Steve was there, in my flat.

It turned out that conversation was beyond me at that point, as was TV watching. I fell asleep under the snuggly duvet before I had quite finished my sandwich.

When I woke an hour later, Steve had turned the telly off and was busy doing the cryptic crossword in the paper. There was a cup of tea on the coffee table beside him, as well as the discarded sections of his paper. He had opened one of the sash windows and a breeze was gently stirring the curtains. The tableau of domesticity and familiarity was so powerful, so comforting, that I had to catch my breath. Steve noticed me looking and flashed me one of his devastating smiles.

"All right?" he asked simply.

"All right," I replied. Nothing more needed to be said. He calmly carried on doing his crossword as though it was the most natural thing in the world, and I lay on the sofa looking out the window, thinking about nothing in particular.

"Deliver radio for nothing," Steve suddenly shot my way. "Three, four."

"Huh?" I shot back eloquently — not. "What?"

"Deliver radio for nothing," Steve repeated. "It's one of my clues. Three letters, then a four letter word."

My weary brain sprang into action and I found myself turning over words in my head this way and that.

"Something 'free,'" I ventured eventually. "'For nothing' could be 'free.'"

Steve pointed his biro at me like an imaginary gun. "Well done, you," he exclaimed. "And 'radio' is 'set.' 'Set free' as in...'deliver.' We got it." He entered the answer contentedly in the grid, and I felt ludicrously pleased.

"Want to do some more?" Steve offered eagerly.

"I suppose I could have a go," I concurred.

"Okay, scooch over," he suggested and sat down next to me. I leaned slightly against him, my head resting on his shoulder as I was reading the clues from the paper in his hands.

"Oh, I got another one!" I found myself shouting. "Look, 'tax obligation,' four letters." I paused and looked at him to see if he had found the solution. He gestured for me to spit it out.

"'Duty,'" I announced triumphantly, and he nodded his consent.

"Clever girl," he praised, and once more I felt inanely pleased.

Part of me registered that we were sitting there, almost a-cuddle, in contented togetherness like a long-married couple. And another part registered that this was fine. It was more than fine, it was meant to be. It felt right.

And so it went on. As I wasn't really up to anything...physical, we began with all the things that people do when they've been together for a long time. We did crosswords.

Steve went out and bought me some wool, and I took up knitting. We watched silly soaps and scary crime thrillers together until the wee small hours of the morning, me nodding off periodically like an old lady. Steve cooked, and he found a cleaning lady to take over the chores for a few weeks. He arranged his schedule so that he worked early mornings until mid-afternoon. I was amazed that he would go to such lengths for me, but he seemed to think it was perfectly normal.

So with Steve popping by every day, and actually staying over most nights, too—it was that much more convenient that way, and he did sleep on the sofa—it was like I had a three-week enforced vacation with a romantic twist thrown in for free.

Chapter Thirty

"We are totally reverse-dating here," I observed jokingly as Steve and I were getting ready to entertain Dan and Rachel for dinner. It was a Thursday night; I had been out of hospital for two weeks and was beginning to feel better, although I was still on sick leave for another week.

"Reverse-dating?" Steve looked at me blankly.

"We're doing this whole relationship thing backwards," I tried to elaborate.

"We are?" Confusion was written all over Steve's face. It was evident in the way he scrunched his eyebrows and wrinkled his nose; I was getting to know my man fast.

"Definitely. Look, here we are, *almost* like we're living together, preparing a meal for some close friends of ours." I continued chopping onions for the stock of our paella.

"And?"

I giggled. "I'm not explaining this very well, am I? Normally, when people date, they are on their best behavior for weeks and weeks, taking great care to hide all the bad bits. But we've been inseparable for almost two weeks. We know everything about each other. You've helped me bathe. You've seen me naked even if we haven't..." I didn't continue the thought, moving onto safer ground instead. "We've discovered each other's unsavory habits..."

"What *are* you talking about?" Steve interrupted. "I have no unpleasant habits."

"You snore."

"Do not."

"You do *so*."

Steve threw celery and tomatoes into the pot and gave the stock a vigorous stir. "How would you know? I sleep on the sofa in the lounge."

"I can hear you," I commented flatly. And it was true, Steve did snore. Not very badly, but loud enough to stop me from falling asleep. I didn't mind terribly, but I *had* noted the fact.

Steve looked at me and surrendered. "Okay. I *might* snore. Occasionally. But you are anally obsessive with your feet."

I didn't even fight him on that one. I *was* anally obsessive about feet. I hated feet. I found them gross. Therefore, I used a separate foot towel, and I couldn't bear the thought of a duvet being turned head-to-toe and me sleeping with my face where somebody else's feet...ugh. It didn't bear thinking about.

"See!" I pounced. "That's what I mean. We're reverse-dating. We're finding out all the bad bits about each other and the best bits are still to come. Therefore, we're destined for great things." I blushed furiously. For obvious reasons, we still hadn't made out, let alone contemplated sex. Steve made to speak, but I raised my spoon to indicate I wasn't finished.

"And speaking of feet...you, my dear, have a bit of a toenail issue going on."

Steve's mouth hung open. Very slowly, he dropped his gaze to examine his bare feet. I didn't follow. I knew what they looked like and I tried to avoid thinking about them.

"I do?" Steve uttered incredulously for the second time in five minutes. "What do you mean?"

I added my onions to the stock and started chopping chorizo. "They're too long."

"They're too long?" Steve echoed.

"They are. They're like...hornbills." I gave an involuntary shudder.

"*Hornbills?*"

"Birds with very big, curved beaks. Fine on the bird, not so great on your toes. But the point I'm trying to make is" — I turned to face Steve and wrapped my arms around his neck — "I don't mind. I've duly noted the fact and considered it and dismissed it. It doesn't matter. I can't explain why it doesn't matter — it should matter, it grosses me out, but I don't care. They're part of you and..." I ground to a halt. This wasn't the right moment to spout the *L* word. Steve refused to let me off the hook. Merriment was dancing in his eyes as he pulled me closer still.

"...and? And what?"

I swallowed hard. "And nothing. It's just who you are and that's fine."

"Disregarding the fact that my toenails are severely umbraged by your harsh and quite unfair assessment of their visual appearance..." He pulled back and smiled at me, his radiant face belying the purported umbrage on the part of his toenails. "I can see what you're saying and I agree."

"You agree?" My eyes lit up with hope. Maybe he *would* cut them after all.

"I think you're right. We're reverse-dating."

He bent his head forward, and I could feel his warm breath on my face. His arms held me tight and he ran his right hand up my back until it alighted on the nape of my neck. My heart beat wildly and my eyes struggled to focus, so I closed them and surrendered myself to the moment.

Very gently, Steve's lips touched mine, probing, exploring, connecting lightly. They felt warm and smooth and inviting. He tilted his head and pressed against me harder. His tongue appeared, pushing against my lips, my teeth, finding my tongue and dancing with it. I had goosebumps all over my body as I returned the kiss, wishing it would last forever. Steve ran both hands through my hair, mussing it up, cupping my face. I placed my arms around his neck and half-wrapped a leg around his bottom so I could squeeze myself closer to him still. We swayed with the motion of our kiss and toppled against the work surface.

"Whoa." Steve was as breathless as I when we came up for air. His brown eyes looked more than melted chocolate than ever, and a deep glow shone from deeply within. He stroked my face gently with his fingers, then tried to straighten my hair. I lightly touched his nose and smiled my biggest smile.

"I suppose I better run a brush through that," I suggested as I could feel his straightening efforts turning my hair into even more of a bird's nest.

"I like this look," Steve disagreed. "It's messy and very sexy."

The neglected stock came to a boil right at this moment and sprayed all over the hob. Steve and I shrank yet further apart and stepped away from the work surface to save ourselves from getting splattered.

"You go and brush your hair and I'll take care of that," Steve returned his mind to practical matters. "We really must get on with the cooking otherwise our guests will go hungry. And sometime soon…we'll have to get properly dating." He gave me a very meaningful look indeed, and I blushed.

Chapter Thirty-One

Rachel and Dan arrived together, sweeping in like a hurricane of good mood.

"Kiss, kiss, kiss," Rachel shouted and followed through with hearty pecks on my cheek. This was only the second time I had seen her since her return to London, the first time having been very shortly after I got home. She regarded me critically.

"You look much better, sweetie," was her verdict. Dan muscled in energetically.

"My turn," he demanded, and also planted a peck on my cheek. I blushed, not at his kiss, but at the recollection of the first kiss I had shared with Steve just half an hour before. Dan was oblivious to my burning face and busied himself putting the wine in the fridge.

"Sorry I have been out of touch," he chattered away. "We've been in studio. The label has set a date for the next album and we've got to finish producing by January. Beer?"

He turned to Steve brandishing a couple of bottles, and Steve nodded his agreement. "Yes please, a beer would be lovely."

Dan popped the tops and handed a bottle to Steve. He pulled out a kitchen chair and sat down, and Rachel joined him instantly. Steve was at the stove looking after the paella and I laid the table.

"January," I prompted Dan. "That seems an odd time. You'll miss the Christmas sales."

"But we'll be the first launch of the year, which gives us more time to get into the 'best album of the year' charts. Plus we'll be touring from February, and the label has also booked a promo gig for New Year's Eve. Tickets to go on sale soon, not that you'll need any." He grinned meaningfully.

"I should hope so, too!" I teased.

"It's good to see you," Dan changed the subject abruptly. "And you, Steve."

Steve raised his bottle in salute. "Likewise. Sophie's been looking forward to tonight for days. I think she's been bored out of her mind, stuck at home all day."

"Rick's aching for you to come back to work," Rachel supplied on cue. "He's like a bear with a sore head without his star deputy-editor."

"Only a few more days…" I said hopefully. "I really *am* bored. And I miss seeing you and being out and about." I settled myself at the table between Rachel and Dan, who were facing each other. Steve would be opposite me. It was a regular little grown-up dinner party.

Steve added a touch more pepper to the paella, then turned the hob off and declared that dinner was done. He set the pan on the table and started serving. Soon, the kitchen was full of the happy chatter of four people having a fabulous meal and a lovely time. I hugged the feeling to myself. *This* was what life was all about. Cooking with your man, feeding friends, entertaining, being together. A real Kodak moment.

When the evening drew to a close, Dan gave me one his bear hugs before bounding down the stairs. "Gotta fly," he said regretfully. "The guys will be waiting for me in studio, we have a couple more hours' work to do."

I shook my head. "You work weird hours."

He merely grinned. "We work *creative* hours," he retorted with a wink. "I'll see you soon, okay?"

I nodded and waved him off. "Go on, don't be late!"

Rachel, too, made her apologies. "Thank you for a fabulous meal," she whispered in my ear. "I'm glad you look so happy. And your Steve…he's definitely a keeper!" She nudged me gently in the side, and I gave her a hug.

"You take care now."

"You, too!" And she was gone.

Steve and I looked at the debris of a good time and tossed a coin as to whether we would tidy up then, or in the morning. Head said we should do it right away, so we stacked the plates in the dishwasher and put the pan into soapy water for a soak. "Job done," Steve grinned.

He went in the lounge to set himself up with pillows and blankets on the sofa as usual. I looked on with dismay. Steve sleeping on the sofa didn't seem right anymore. We had shared our first kiss, we had entertained as a couple, we had talked about dating…

"Would you like to sleep in my bed tonight?" I blurted out. *Oops.* That didn't quite sound as casual nor innocent as intended.

Steve lowered the blanket he had been shaking out. He considered my question silently, and the moment assumed an unexpected significance.

"In your bed...with you in it as well?" he confirmed before making a decision.

"Yes, please. It's just... It's so stupid, you sleeping here on this uncomfortable sofa."

"It's not uncomfortable," Steve hastened to reassure me. "It's actually quite nice."

I sat down on the sofa in question, obstructing his avenue for further bed-making endeavors.

"That's not what I mean. But it feels wrong making you sleep over here when—"

"When what?"

"When...well, when we're so obviously together. Aren't we?" Now I was looking for reassurance. "I mean, we don't need to *do* anything. That's not what I'm asking. I only want you to be in a proper bed and—"

Oh God, I hated being the one to make the first move, but it was my flat, my bed, my responsibility.

"—and," I continued a little coyly, "it might be quite nice to have a cuddle. You know, a cuddle. Not anything more."

Steve burst out laughing uproariously, but calmed down at seeing my discomfort. "I'm not laughing at you, Soph," he declared quickly.

There, he was using my shortened name, and I liked it. It was good. It said, *I Love You* every time he pronounced it. We hadn't actually got round to declaring our love outright yet, the time simply hadn't presented itself although we had got close.

"I'm not laughing at you," he repeated. "But it was very sweet and funny, the way that came out. And yes, I would love to share your bed tonight, and every night. We'll leave the..."—

significant pause—"something more for when you're all better," he added quickly, "no rush."

I was blushing even more furiously now. This was the second time the matter had come up today; it was obviously playing on his mind as much as it was on mine. However, on the matter of sharing my bed, we were now committed. Steve solemnly abandoned his blankets and we marched to my bedroom. Then we stood in front of the bed, which suddenly looked a lot smaller than I remembered.

"Which side?" Steve asked solicitously.

"That side." I pointed to the far side of the bed.

"Shall I go in first?" he asked politely. I nodded. So he jumped in and, like a modern-day Romeo, stretched out both arms toward me, beckoning me with a cheesy grin.

"Come on in," he invited, now taking over the space as though it was his.

"Okay," I said, and uncertainly climbed in beside him.

There, we had done it. In bed together. I lay in Steve's arms and he pulled the duvet over us.

It was new and unfamiliar, but it was nice. He only wore pajama bottoms and my head rested on his chest.

Okay, okay, I wasn't supposed to make comparisons, but I couldn't help it. Who would? His chest was a nice and smooth one, not at all hairy. Dan, I recalled somewhat inappropriately, had a small spattering of curly hair at the top of his chest, but Steve was smooth and muscular. He put his arms around me and we held each other in a long embrace, breathing deeply. He smelled good, like that first time I had caught his scent in the hospital. I hoped I smelled nice, too, not of illness anymore, but of me.

"Penny for your thoughts," Steve cut into my musings.

I giggled.

"I was thinking that you smell nice, and that your chest is very toned," I confessed.

"Why, thanks, I'm flattered," Steve smiled. "I'd love to return the compliment but..." he tugged at the collar of my pajama top. "I think that'll have to wait. I can't judge, through all that fabric."

We turned the light off, snuggled some more, and I soon felt myself dozing off. It was odd, having an unfamiliar body in my bed, but it was good, too.

I turned over, away from Steve, to assume my sleeping position. Automatically, I wrapped the double duvet around me in one swift movement. A great howl arose from the other side of the bed, and Steve thumped me over the head with one of his pillows.

"Duvet thief," he screeched. "Stop thief! Duvet thief!"

Disorientated, I switched the light back on. There he was, on his side of the bed, completely bare without any duvet at all.

Whoops.

Reluctantly, I gave up half of the duvet and turned the light back off. I assumed my sleeping position, but it was no good without the duvet wrapped around me *just so*. I shuffled and turned and felt miserable.

I must have dropped off, because half an hour later, I was awake again, cold and duvet-less now myself. Steve was snoring softly, having hogged the entire duvet. *Argh!*

Tugging and pulling energetically, I unrolled Steve from within the duvet to get a share back. He half-woke and mumbled sleepily before resuming his snoring. Great. Now I had a bit of duvet, and a big man lying three-quarters across the bed.

I stabbed him sharply in the ribs.

"Oi, you," I whispered. "Wake up, this isn't working."

True love or not, this relationship wasn't going to go anywhere if I couldn't sleep. Steve grunted unhappily but opened his eyes obligingly.

"Do you want me to go back in the lounge?" he said.

"No, of course not." I protested, just before inspiration struck. "But you could go and get the blankets, I suppose."

"Awright," he grumbled and went to retrieve the blankets. He snuggled under his covers, and I wrapped myself up in my duvet. Perfect.

Just as I was dropping off, I heard, from under his pile of blankets, a mumbled declaration.

"I do love you, Sophie Penhalligan."

Hail trumpets and angels! He had said it. He had *said* it.

Steve turned toward me to gauge my reaction, which was probably quite difficult in the dark. I put an end to his uncertainty.

"I love you, too, Steve Jones," I responded. "It's a pity I can't see you."

"Never mind that," he said calmly, giving me another delicious kiss. "We can do this again tomorrow, and the day after that, and the day after that..."

After imparting this life-changing information, he fell straight asleep.

The next day, when he came back from work, Steve carried a bulky bag. "I've brought my own duvet," he announced. "Having two duvets is obviously going to be the secret to our successful relationship."

I giggled, but had to agree. That next night, we went to bed in the same bed straightaway, without further ado. He, under his duvet. And me, under mine.

Chapter Thirty-Two

It was the second week of August by the time I went back to work. Steve and my relationship was almost exactly a month old. Steve saw me off in the morning, walking me to the Tube station and right down to the platform. He kept reiterating that I could easily take another week, that I shouldn't rush back, but I brushed his concerns aside.

As it happened, I got through the day, but only barely just. By four o'clock, I was practically on my knees. Leaving work early, I fell asleep on the Tube and nearly missed my stop. When I got home, the flat was empty and lonely, Steve having to work different shifts now that I wasn't a round-the-clock invalid anymore.

As I sat on the sofa, exhaustion and loneliness swept over me like a big wave. Why hadn't I listened to Steve and stayed at home for a little longer until I was fully recovered? Feeling stupid and sorry for myself, I dragged myself into the bathroom to run a bath. I found a bottle of Orient bath foam on the side, with a label round its neck.

I bet you're knackered, the label said in Steve's scrawly handwriting. *Relax, and I'll be home with dinner by seven. Love, Steve xxx.*

I sat down on the toilet—lid down, obviously—and wept. How thoughtful of my man to leave me this gorgeous bath foam. And, "home." He would be home. My flat, our home. He had come to look at it as home.

And! He would be bringing dinner. *Oh please let it be Chinese takeaway,* I prayed. That would be perfect.

It was Chinese takeaway, and it was perfect. Steve breezed in like a walking ad for good mood and high spirits, and he swept my tiredness away with a kiss. He laid the table and dished up without drawing breath, and he had even brought some wine.

"I think you're allowed again, now," he declared with a twinkle in his eyes.

"Is that so?" I retorted meaningfully, and we both knew we weren't talking about the wine. Steve said nothing more, but it felt like we had come to a tacit agreement about something.

Yet our best unspoken intentions came to nothing that night. The exhaustion of the day combined with a long hot bath, lovely food and a single glass of wine proved too much for me, and I found myself snoring on the sofa before nine o'clock.

"I'm sorry," I muttered apologetically, but Steve laughed.

"We've got all the time in the world," he reassured me and put me to bed.

As the week went on, I realized that I didn't want all the time in the world. I wanted love; I wanted to *make* love and get sexual attention. And urgently, too. All this waiting and getting to know each other and convalescing couldn't go on forever. I would have to persuade Steve, somehow. Properly seduce him, maybe. Take the initiative.

My opportunity came at the weekend. Steve had gone out to get croissants early on Saturday morning and when he came back, he was nervous, somehow, antsy. He kept dropping things and made the most almighty mess with his croissant crumbs, which went everywhere. Eventually, when we had tidied up and I was dressed and ready, he suggested that we go for a spot of shopping and maybe on to his flat.

Aha. My ears pricked up immediately. This was more like it. A visit to Steve's flat. His bachelor pad. Virgin territory. A tiny shiver of excitement worked its way down my spine.

As it was a beautiful, sunny day, we opted to take a bus back toward Putney and raid the delis back there. We ambled down the road together holding hands, and actually this was one of the first times we had taken our relationship for a walk. *The* first time, in fact, if one discounted walking to the Tube in the morning.

We sat on the top deck of the bus together, holding hands. We got off again, holding hands, and we were still holding hands when we perused the shops.

"You look like that cat who got the cream," Steve commented. I smiled back and said nothing but gave his hand a big squeeze.

Steve's flat was on the first floor of a Victorian terrace in a leafy Putney side-street. If I had felt nervous welcoming him to my home a few weeks ago, he seemed just as nervous about showing me his place that day. After all, a flat said a lot about its owner.

We heaved our shopping upstairs and Steve unlocked the door. "You first," he invited, and I stepped in.

It was spacious and bright, very similar to mine. Steve had obviously had a big tidy-round—unless he really *was* that neat—and there were roses in a vase on the dining table. While he busied himself in the kitchen, I had a good nosey round his bedroom. I wasn't looking for anything in particular, just absorbing clues about this man whom I had fallen for so completely. His bed was tidily made, with a cuddly teddy bear nestling on one side. I picked up teddy and smelled him—yes, there it was again, that lovely Steve scent.

One small pine wardrobe was full of his nurse's uniforms, all neatly washed and ironed, ready for a day's wear. The other small pine wardrobe was full of "civvy" clothes, jeans and shirts, socks and underwear. That was all. While the bedroom was quite large, Steve managed to fit all his clothes into two small wardrobes.

Steve found me sitting on his bed. He handed me a small glass of wine and sat down next to me. "Everything to your satisfaction?" he inquired teasingly, and clinked glasses. I spluttered guiltily, having been caught snooping.

"Sure, yes, absolutely. Sorry, I wasn't... I was curious...just having a little look..." I stammered.

"It's okay," Steve laughed easily. "After all, I've been all over your place, looked in every drawer, examined every photo, checked the picture rails for dust..."

"You haven't," I protested, perturbed.

"No, of course not. Well, at least not that last bit. Anyway, are you done? Shall we prepare dinner?"

I nodded, and we moved to the kitchen. Steve had spread out our deli goodies onto various serving plates, and there was an unexpected fat lobster sitting on the draining board.

"Lobster," I shouted gleefully before I could stop myself. "Is that for us, for tonight? Please say yes, I adore lobster."

"It certainly is," Steve confirmed happily, picking up the crustacean and examining it critically. "Only problem is... I've just realized I haven't got any proper implements for getting into it." He grinned ruefully. "I may be an ambitious romantic as well as a man with expensive tastes, but also with a distinctive lack of finesse and requisite tools."

I giggled into my wine. "What are you going to do?"

Steve had half disappeared into one of his cupboards. "I'm going to have to use brute force," came the muffled response. Then he straightened up and turned around to face me, brandishing a hammer and chisel and wearing a Hannibal Lecter grin. I shrieked in mock horror and took a step back.

"That's not right," I protested jokingly. "That's cruel. You're gonna hurt it, not to mention spoil our dinner."

Steve grinned even wider. "Trust me, I'm almost a doctor," he announced and addressed himself to the lobster.

"Never fear, we'll get you right out of your uncomfortable shell in no time." Steve positioned the chisel mid-shell and counted to three.

"One...." Excessive swing of hammer but without follow-through.

"Two..." Same again.

"Three." A gentle tap to the chisel with the hammer. The shell split open obediently, one neat opening right down the middle.

"You've done this before," I observed.

"Does it show?" Steve inquired. "And no, I haven't actually. I've never attempted a lobster at home before." I could have sworn he was blushing but that might have just been the exertion. Or the concentration.

"Right, now for the claws," Steve continued. "What are we going to do about the claws?"

"You haven't got any kind of skewers or something?" I chipped in from the sideline. Steve fixed me with an appreciative look.

"Not just a pretty face," he drawled and went to retrieve a skewer from a kitchen drawer.

Feeling emboldened, I topped up our glasses and it was time to eat. We sat at the dining table overlooking the garden in the back. Steve had laid on his best crockery and cutlery and lit a few candles, and it almost felt like being in a bijou little restaurant. The food was fabulous and even though my appetite was still not what it used to be, I enjoyed every mouthful. We ate in companionable silence and a definite aura of expectation enveloped us. It was heady and exciting, like a date. Which, all things considered, this actually was.

An angry buzzing sound shook me out of my reverie and, being accosted by a big wasp, I jumped up from my chair and retreated to the far end of the room. Deprived of its target, the wasp made for the window and started bashing against it like a demented blue bottle.

"You okay?" Steve asked, surprised.

"Hm-nuh," I responded noncommittally, admitting in small voice that I was terminally afraid of wasps. "They'd be in my Room 101. My own personal hell."

"Best get rid of it," he announced calmly and fetched a clean glass from the kitchen, grabbing a convenient leaflet from his pile of junk mail as he went.

The offending insect was in no mood to cooperate and Steve spent almost ten minutes trying to contain it with the glass, not helped by me shrieking helplessly in the background. A few times, the wasp escaped just before he had it and buzzed around his head angrily. Even Steve was starting to get rattled.

Eventually, though, he managed. Pressing the glass firmly against the window pane, he slid the leaflet underneath to trap the wasp ready for eviction. However, with both hands thus engaged, he couldn't open the window. Trusting him to not release the now extremely angry monster once more, I hastened to his side to slide the sash window up enough for him to throw Mrs. Wasp out.

Coward that I was, fled to the far side of the room again.

"Okay, here we go," he announced. "One… two… three…" He took a swing and flung his hands holding the glass out the window. Whether by accident or intention he wouldn't later say, but he let go of the whole lot at the same time. One second, he was brandishing the glass, and the next minute he turned around to me with empty hands.

"Whoops," he said deadpan, and I burst into helpless laughter.

He stuck his head out the window to ensure he hadn't accidentally knocked somebody out, but came back satisfied.

"The glass isn't even broken," he informed me. "It's landed in a flower bed. Best place for it, I suppose."

"You are officially my hero," I announced, and I swear Steve glowed with pride. There was an awkward moment when we didn't know what to do next.

"Shall we go for a walk?" I pondered out loud, just as Steve said, "Shall we watch a movie?"

"Movie sounds great," I agreed readily, while Steve countered, "what a good idea, let's go for a walk." It was a classic sitcom moment and it carried us over the awkwardness.

"Let's have a movie," I reiterated, fancying a nice little cuddle and some more wine and a little relax.

"Okay," Steve consented, "But you pick. I'll make some sangria."

Sangria, as well. And more nibbles. Was he trying to seduce me, I wondered, or was he trying to put all that weight that I had lost back onto my now skinny frame?

Who cared? I perused his movie collection and made a short list of three. A romantic comedy, first choice; a high brow period drama, for show; and a crime thriller, out of interest. Steve discarded the period drama as too boring and told me the thriller was a bit on the gory side. So the rom-com it was.

"How come you've got these in the house, anyway?" I teased as he loaded the DVD player.

"It's my soft, *metro* side," he told me flippantly. "Can't you tell?" He ran his fingers through his hair in an exaggerated brushing gesture, then rubbed his non-existent sidies into shape. He sat down delicately on the sofa next to me, crossing his legs daintily at the ankles.

"I think you got that wrong," I snorted. "A little too over the top to be metro. You'd better be careful, before I get the wrong idea."

"And what would that be?" he challenged me back.

"Well—"

At this point, two glasses of wine and another of rather potent sangria took over. My rational side said good night and it was all naughty from there on.

"I'd have to check, you see," I sniggered. "Whether all that equipment is there and in functioning order."

Steve was momentarily lost. "What equipment?"

"You know…" I gave a meaningful toss of my head in the general direction of his midsection. "*That* equipment."

Steve looked down at his body doubtfully.

"Oh, *that* equipment," he echoed. "Well, I dunno. It's not been used for a while. It might be defective."

Judging by the way he was prominent through his trousers quite nicely now, it wasn't defective in the slightest.

"How would you test?" he provoked me teasingly.

"Like so," I countered. Before I could stop myself, I had retrieved an ice cube from my sangria and, in one swift movement, hooked my finger round his waistband and dropped the ice cube down inside his trousers and underpants.

The effect was cataclysmic. Steve jumped up from the sofa, howling in exaggerated pain. He did a terrific little dance around the lounge, taking his trousers off to gain access to the over-cooled area. Miraculously, the bulge remained.

Concerned for his modesty, I got up somewhat unsteadily and pulled the curtains. Steve crept up behind me and dropped an ice cube down the back of my shirt. My God, that was cold. I let out an almighty shriek and pummeled his chest with my hands.

"Get it out, get it out," I demanded as he got hold of my wrists and, laughingly, stopped me attacking him.

"Now why would I do that," he asked, "when it's having such a wonderful effect?"

"Because it's co-o-old," I wailed and then his mouth was on mine, his warm lips meeting mine, his tongue exploring gently, probingly. He let go of my wrists and put his arms around me, pulling me close and holding me tight. One of his hands wandered up my bottom and up my spine, sending electric tingles all the way along. I wrapped my arms around his body, pressing against him as hard as I could, going with my needs, feeling, experiencing.

We were so hungry for each other, we never even made it to the sofa, let alone the bedroom. Steve laid me down gently on the thick, squashy rug in the middle of the lounge and lay down beside me, caressing, exploring all the while. We were truly lost in each other, in the sensation of being with each other, and when we finally came together, we created an almighty explosion.

Chapter Thirty-Three

"So…did you have sex with him?" Rachel asked conversationally while she was blowing on her cappuccino to cool it.

We were at our local coffee shop in Tooting to resurrect our old tradition of debriefing each other on our love lives on a Saturday morning. Having overheard her very direct question, the couple at the next table gave me an amused glance. I could feel myself blushing. Instead of a response, I tried a meaningful eye-rolling, mouth-twisting kind of gesture that was meant to say, "well, yes."

Rachel wasn't having it. She wanted to hear it.

"Did you? Come on, you must have done," she teased.

I held my hands up in surrender. "Okay, yes, I did." Muffled snorts from the next table indicated that the couple was still listening to our conversation.

"It was great," I elaborated. Inspiration struck, and I continued wickedly. "Especially when the others arrived." Complete silence next door now. Good.

Rach was confused. "What others?"

I pretended coyness once more. "You know," I said pointedly. "The *others*."

Rachel leaned back in her chair and sipped at her cappuccino. The couple at the next table sat frozen, she with her teaspoon mid-stir, he with his toast halfway up his mouth. Rachel's eyes twinkled. She had cottoned on.

"Oh," she said. "The *others*. I see." She took another sip of her cappuccino while she was working out how to take this charade further.

"I thought you guys had stopped all that kinky stuff."

I grinned wistfully. "We had. But, you know…well, it's quite addictive." She next door had now put her spoon down, her eyes as big as saucers. She was trying hard not to stare, but not quite succeeding. I pretended not to notice.

"Was Big Dick there?" Rachel demanded randomly.

"Absolutely," I deadpanned. "And Bender. And Pussy."

Bender? Rachel mouthed in amusement, but kept going. "Gosh, I'm sorry I missed it. Where did you do it this time?"

"In the cellar," I was quick to respond. I had this worked out in my head now.

"Which one?" Rach asked, as though there was a whole array of S&M places we were both used to frequenting. "The one with the chains and the spikes, or the dark room?"

"The *wet* one. With the water boards," I shot back, totally nonchalant. Rachel drew in a fake breath of horror. "Not the wet room?" she stage-whispered.

A vicious clattering next door suggested that *she* had knocked over her teacup. Out of the corner of my eye, I noticed that *he* put down his toast and got up. Throwing me an extremely dirty look, he pulled his girlfriend to her feet and they left, a picture of moral outrage and disgust.

Rachel and I burst out laughing before the door had closed behind them.

When all was relatively quiet again, Rachel returned her attention to the subject at hand.

"So, did you sleep with him?" she asked once more.

"I did," I admitted, and felt my face splitting into a huge grin. "Of course I did. It was wonderful."

"Tell me everything," Rachel invited, as she would have done of old. I opened my mouth to relate the whole lovely evening but changed my mind. Suddenly, I found that I didn't want to share every last detail, as I once would have done. Stalling for time by taking a big bite out of my breakfast deluxe roll, I pondered this change.

One reason was clearly that I didn't want to make Rachel uncomfortable. But the other reason was quite simply that I didn't feel the need. How to proceed?

"It was wonderful," I reiterated cautiously. "It was warm. And loving. And exciting." I smiled at the recollection.

"You are all loved-up," Rachel observed, also smiling widely. "It's okay, you don't have to share the gory detail. I can see you don't want to."

I swallowed a big gulp of latte.

"I'm sorry," I ventured apologetically. "It's not that I don't want to share, it's not like that. It's just—"

"—not necessary?" Rachel offered. I stared at her. How could she know how I felt?

"It's okay," Rachel said again. "I can tell by the look on your face that you are happy, and safe, and secure. This relationship with Steve, it's doing you good. You're glowing from the inside. I don't really need to know anything more. Besides which, it's none of my business anyway. I'm only after gossip, that's all."

I tried to take all of this in. It wasn't just me who had moved on from the girlie tattler that I once was. Rachel had changed, too, for reasons of her own. A tiny part of me felt a pang of nostalgia for all the giggles we had shared over dissecting each other's love lives. The rest of me realized that we had been bound to grow out of that sooner or later. And we were definitely on the late side as it was.

We ate in silence for a few minutes. Eventually, Rach reached out to touch my hand.

"I'm so happy for you," she said sincerely. "And it gives me faith that you two found each other; it means there's hope for the rest of us."

I smiled and didn't know what to say.

"And do you know what's the biggest tell of all?" Rach mused idly, for her own benefit as well as mine. I shook my head. "The biggest tell is that we haven't speculated about how Steve and you are going to, you know, develop. Whether and when you'll get married, or something. That's a given, and you know it, and he knows it, and I know it, too. And that tells me everything I need to know."

"You make it sound like I'm lost, or going away, or something," I blurted out, suddenly feeling all wrong. "I'm still me, I can still go and have a good time and all that."

"Indubitably," Rach concurred. "But we're moving on, both of us, and that's good. That's life."

This new, philosophical side of Rach was a bit of a surprise. She had always been such a live wire. Only a little while ago, she had given me the third degree about going to Berlin with Dan, sounding quite like her old self. Today she came across so very serene and calm, and quite unlike herself.

"Are you okay?" I found myself asking gently, carefully.

"I'm fine," she smiled. "No, really. I'm good."

And that was when it dawned on me.

"*No!*" I exclaimed, examining her closely. "You have met someone, haven't you?"

Rachel blushed.

"You have, too," I continued triumphantly. "Go on, your turn to tell." But she clammed up instead.

"I've only met him once or twice," she said evasively. "There's nothing to tell."

"You're bullshitting me," I accused her, correctly as it would turn out later, much later. "'Once or twice,' that's a big difference, and you know it. So…what is it, once, or twice?"

Rachel sighed theatrically. I put her discomfort down to the fact that her dramatic break-up with Jordan wasn't even two months old, and that perhaps she felt I was going to judge her to be on the rebound.

"Twice," she acknowledged shyly.

"And? What's he like? What's his name?" So I wasn't quite over the gossipy stage after all.

"He's tall, with brown hair—quite handsome," she elaborated, seeming a touch cagey.

"And? His name?" I prompted again. Surely I was allowed to know his name? I would refrain from asking about their sex life, but—

There was an infinitesimal hesitation before Rachel offered his name. "Charles."

I stared in disbelief. Realizing all the while that I was being terribly judgmental, I nonetheless couldn't help thinking that a "Charles" didn't sound like a Rachel kind of guy at all.

"I call him Charlie," she added as an afterthought.

Ah, now, Charlie; that I could see.

"How did you meet? And when?" I was utterly intrigued.

There was that hesitation again. Followed by an evasive hand-flapping gesture. What was going on? Then I had an idea. "Do I *know* him?"

"*No!*" This, too fast and too forceful. Rachel was looking decidedly shifty, and I knew she wasn't telling me the whole story. Whatever it was, for some reason she was uncomfortable filling me in.

"Okay, okay," I backed down quickly. "Just tell me that I haven't upset you in some way. 'Cause you would tell me, normally. Please say that it's not that you don't trust me anymore?"

"It's not that I don't trust you anymore," Rachel repeated obligingly. "It's complicated."

Oh gosh, not that old chestnut. Now I was having visions of wives, pre-existing children, messy divorces, guys twenty years her senior.

"I will tell you, soon. I need to work out a few things first," Rachel cut into my thoughts. "The real question is, do *you* trust *me*?"

"Of course I do," I assured her without hesitation.

We left it there, even though it was a bit of an effort not to worry away at this revelation. Once upon a time, I would have been merciless, nagging until she cracked. Likewise, she would have done the same to me. Whether it was out of respect for our newfound grown-up-ness, or whether something told me to back off for another reason, I wasn't sure, but I let it be.

We paid up and split up. Not immediately, of course—that would have meant we had had a disagreement of some sorts. No, we ambled down the High Street, engaging in a little window shopping, and chatting away quite amiably. But when we came to the crossroads where it would normally have been a question of "your flat or mine?" we went our separate ways.

I should have persisted. Something had come between us and I should have given this whole interlude more thought. But I didn't, and I didn't allow myself to worry. Whatever it was, I was bound to find out eventually.

PART THREE: BETRAYAL

Chapter Thirty-Four

The weekend before the August bank holiday, Steve suggested that we should go sightseeing.

"Let's be tourists," he had proposed. "Let's do London, in a day."

I chortled. "But we live here. Why would we 'do London?'"

"Because," he challenged, "do you ever bother to see the sights? The London Eye?"

I shook my head.

"The Tower? Tower Bridge?"

More shakes of the head; I was getting the point.

"Come on," he coaxed. "Let's do this. It'll be fun."

I laughed. As far as dates went, this was almost the anti-date. There wasn't a promise here anywhere of a posh restaurant, sophistication and elegance. And yet it sounded like my kind of thing.

So there we were, on a Saturday morning, wandering down Baker Street in double step. We took the ubiquitous hop-on-hop-off bus tour and let ourselves be driven around London for an hour. Steve had stocked up on gummy bears and diet cola, and we felt like naughty teenagers once again, snacking away under the disapproving stare of the commentator. We got off at the South Bank where we ate cheesy pizza bought from a street vendor, sitting on a bench overlooking the Thames and watching the world go by. Afterwards, Steve bought me a huge stick of candy floss from a nearby stall, and I thought, to hell with my waistline.

The queue for the London Eye was long as ever, but Steve had pre-booked tickets. This "on the hop" tourist expedition wasn't as spontaneous as he had made it out to be. I was thrilled, and flattered, and simply deliriously happy. Once aboard our pod with a handful of other people, I stepped up to the railing expectantly. Steve hugged me close, and we stood together as London dipped lower and lower beneath us.

We must have been about halfway up when Steve suddenly turned mildly green, swallowed deeply and announced he had to sit down. My exhilaration turned into dismay as I imagined greasy pizza being returned, right here, without fresh air or any buckets. Still, I sat down with Steve, holding his hand and patting his back.

"Are you all right?" I managed in between deep sympathy breaths. *Keep it cool and steady,* I advised myself. *You can do this.*

"Yes, fine," Steve uttered, looking slightly better.

I must have stared a question mark at him, because he suddenly offered an explanation.

"I get terrible acrophobia," he stated. "I can't stand so close to the window, now that we're so high up."

I was incredulous. "You have fear of heights?" I repeated. He nodded, embarrassed now. I suppressed a giggle. "And you booked a trip on the London Eye because — ?"

Steve shrugged. "I thought you'd enjoy it."

Love him.

"I am enjoying it," I confirmed quickly. "But, you didn't need to do this. If you're that afraid of heights."

"I know," Steve patiently reiterated. "I know I didn't have to do this. But I wanted to. For you. To see your face, when you're all happy, and excited, and relaxed. That's what I came to see."

"I've got to give you a kiss," I announced, and followed through directly. "I love you."

"I love you, too," Steve grinned, relieved and buoyed by the fact that we were nearly down again. An image flashed through my mind of me and Dan visiting the TV tower in Berlin.

"I guess you wouldn't go up a TV tower with me," I ventured, somewhat thoughtlessly.

"Probably not," Steve concurred. "Nor the Eiffel tower. But there are plenty of other things we can do. And it was worthwhile coming, trust me."

He put his arm around me as we stepped out of the pod, and I hugged him as tightly as I could.

"What now?" Steve demanded eagerly. "I'm all in your hands."

To be perfectly honest, doing the tourist trail had completely exhausted me. Just the sheer amount of people we had braved today, pushing, shoving, talking every language under the sun, taking photos—I had had enough. Steve's exuberant and inadvertently suggestive phrase gave me an idea.

"Let's go home," I boomed. Lowering my voice a little, I whispered, "let's make mad, passionate *lurve*."

Steve chuckled. "What, before dinner? How *very* naughty."

And naughty we were.

Okay, so there wasn't a cellar involved, not a dark one or a wet one, and no chains or spikes. But Steve led me to the lounge as soon as we got in. He closed the curtains and stood me in the middle of the room.

"Hm. What have we here?" he muttered, and I went hot and gooey in the loin region. He was undressing me with his eyes, but I wanted him to undress me properly, please!

Steve took his time, stalking around me while I didn't move. "Take your trousers off, now," he said, nicely but firmly.

So I did.

"And your shirt."

All too soon, I stood naked in the lounge, with him still fully dressed. The imbalance of power proved unexpectedly exciting.

Steve stepped up to me and tweaked my nipples. The effect was electrifying, and I gave an almighty groan. I tugged at the button of his shirts, and he slapped me gently on the wrist, grinning widely and mischievously.

"Now, now, young lady, not so hasty," he joked, and I groaned some more.

He stood behind me and ran his hands up and down my back, and soon I was covered in goosebumps of pleasure. He cradled me in his arms as if taking me from behind, and I could feel his arousal pressing into the small of my back.

"I believe we have wood," I giggled, citing a teenage movie from way back when.

"We certainly have," Steve confirmed.

I tried to turn around, eager for a kiss, but Steve held me in a tight arm lock.

"I'm enjoying your behind," he murmured into my ear, nibbling gently at the lobe, then giving it a playful bite.

"And I—"

"Don't speak," Steve admonished me. "It's not your turn to speak. Be quiet." He pressed harder into my back to emphasize his point.

I obeyed, part willing, part unable to do anything else.

"Good. That's good. Now bend over."

"Bend over what?" I wasn't sure what he expected me to do.

"Just bend over and stop talking." Steve spoke in a harsh voice but I could tell that he was brimming with hilarity. Goodness knew what had got into him, but now he seemed to be struggling to stay in his role. He relinquished his hold on my upper body and I bent over and touched my toes. Head firmly tucked upside down between my knees, I could see Steve's still be-jeaned legs planted firmly behind me. The absurdity of the situation made me giggle.

Steve lightly smacked my bare bottom. "This is really no laughing matter!"

Of course I dutifully collapsed in a heap.

"Oi, you, wench," Steve objected, towering above me and clearly also brimming with mirth. "That's not supposed to happen. You're supposed to…

I jumped to my feet and turned on him, raising myself up to my full height and trying to meet his gaze levelly.

"*Yes?*" I inquired in a matronly voice. "What is it that I am supposed to do, young lad?"

Steve snorted through his nose. "I don't think this kinky role play is working for me," he admitted abruptly before he lost his grip and guffawed loudly.

"Me neither," I agreed. "I do like it but it's not doing it for me today. I'm just too impatient, I guess."

I ripped the shirt off his back while I spoke and he took the cue. We fell onto the sofa, conjoined at the hip, while he was still struggling out of his jeans.

Our love making was swift and intense and overwhelming, and so addictive that we had another turn after dinner. This brand of passion was new and intoxicating to me, and I simply couldn't get enough of it.

Steve and I, we had become lovers, soul mates, best friends. We had been together for six weeks. Not a word had been said about our future or about our plans. The *M* word hadn't been mentioned. And yet it was there, between us, as plain as a fourteen-foot billboard. The truth, the obvious. We would get married. We would have children. It was apparent from our every interaction. I couldn't really explain it, but we had mated for life, and we both knew it.

Chapter Thirty-Five

The following Friday night, Steve arrived at my place with a glossy brochure and a rucksack full of clothes. He was excited like a little boy on Christmas Eve.

"Look," he said. "I got us a surprise getaway."

He opened up the glossy leaflet and showed me pictures of a grand old castle with big stately rooms plushly furnished. One featured an enormous four-poster bed with a roaring log fire in the background. There was an indoor swimming pool, a sauna and a spa room, as well as a fancy restaurant.

"There's a beautiful nature reserve round the loch, and we can go for long walks by the water, have pub lunches, come back, rest, sleep, have dinner. It will be wonderful."

His eyes shone, and it was impossible to resist his enthusiasm. I took the brochure out of his hands and looked through it. Steve watched me avidly but said nothing more.

It did look inviting, the perfect place for a getaway.

"It says you can go horse-riding," I latched onto a random detail.

"Yes, it does; you can," Steve concurred eagerly. "Would you like to?"

"I would love to," I said cautiously, "only I haven't actually ridden for years. The last time, I was about thirteen, and I only learned for three weeks or so."

"Never mind," he gushed. "I can't ride either. We can learn together." He took my hand and squeezed it encouragingly.

I let the riding hang for a moment and focused on a more pressing question.

"Where is this place?" I quizzed him. "And how much is this going to cost?"

Steve put his index finger over my mouth in a *shush* gesture. "This luxury getaway castle is up in Scotland, and don't you worry how much it costs. You're getting it on the health service."

"I am?" I exclaimed, utterly perplexed. "Why? How?"

My gorgeous, kind, and thoughtful man blushed. "Well, in a manner of speaking, that is. They are paying my salary, after all."

I took a moment to compute that information, then protested. "No, honey, you can't pay for this, you'll bankrupt yourself. That's not right."

By way of response, Steve cupped my face in his hands and gave me a big kiss. "Trust me, it'll be worth every penny." He paused for a moment. "Let's get you packing," he eventually suggested cheerfully.

"Why?" I hadn't quite understood the ramifications of his grand getaway plan.

"*Why?*" he repeated, half laughing and half exasperated. "Because we are going tomorrow. This trip is all in the bag. We're leaving from King's Cross at midday."

"We are?" I confirmed stupidly.

"We certainly are," Steve repeated gleefully. I sneaked a look at his rucksack which, on reflection, was much too crammed, too full for one night at my flat. *Light bulb moment.*

"You're already packed!" I burst out, and Steve looked duly bashful.

"I am. I'm sorry if I jumped the gun."

"It's okay. It's cool. It's…actually, it's quite exciting," I grinned, infected by his joy.

We set off for the Tube at ten-thirty on Saturday morning to get to King's Cross to catch our midday train. However, two hours, two broken-down Tube trains and one hefty traffic jam later, we arrived at King's Cross minutes after our train had left. Out of breath, hot and flustered after our travel ordeal, Steve looked more dejected than I had ever seen him. Deflated, worn out, and disappointed. I set my bag down and gave him a cuddle.

"Come on, now, it's not so bad. There's got to be other trains," I offered hopefully.

"Yeah, right, and we'll arrive at around midnight," Steve muttered darkly. "How could I be so stupid? Why didn't we leave earlier?"

"Shush," I soothed. "We'll get there. C'mon, let's go." And I dragged him to the ticket office, where we discovered that we could take a train to Edinburgh just after one p.m. We would arrive at six-thirty p.m. and would catch a connecting train to Pitlochry just before eight. Our luck appeared to change, and the nice lady behind the counter even changed our existing tickets to cover the new journey.

Steve was still tense, but he relaxed a little over a quick cup of coffee and a spot of lunch in a coffee shop. Acting on a loved-up impulse, I gave him a big kiss, leaning over the table and nearly knocking over the cups. He smiled weakly.

"What was that for?" he asked, sounding like a husband of twenty years who was taken aback at an unaccustomed display of affection by his wife.

"Nothing. It's just that I love you very much," I declared cheerfully, and finally the hint of a sparkle returned to his eyes.

"I..." He interrupted himself, looking thoughtful for a minute or two while he rummaged around in his rucksack. Then he shrugged as though silently dismissing an idea.

"I love you, too," he said as he sat back in his chair once again, and we smiled at each other.

Things were looking up.

Chapter Thirty-Six

The train journey to Edinburgh was relatively uneventful. However, halfway across the country, the sunshine vanished and grey skies loomed.

Trying to lighten the atmosphere, I declared loudly and brightly, "Never fear, the weather is meant to be really changeable in these parts, I'm sure it'll be fine and sunny tomorrow."

"Och, it's a wee bit o' Scotch mist, lassie," a passing passenger chipped in. "It winna fash ye. The thing to watch oot for is the midges, they're fair ferocious this time o' year."

I didn't have a clue what he had said, but I was too embarrassed to show myself up as a total Sassenach so I smiled apologetically and shrugged.

Seeing my confusion, he took pity. "It's just a bit of rain, it won't hurt you. But watch out for the mosquitoes," he stated cheerily in clear Queen's English. Shaking his head, he continued his journey down the train. I rather wished he hadn't offered this comment. My heart sank to my boots with the thought of eternal drizzle, muddy shoes, damp clothes, frizzy hair, and mosquitoes. I was a real mozzie-magnet and couldn't stand the wee beasties. This time, however, it was Steve who rallied.

"Well, we'll scratch the walks and hole up in our sumptuous accommodation," he whispered in a nudge-nudge-wink-wink kind of way, and I giggled.

When we eventually pulled into Waverley station, we were cold, hungry and dispirited, and we had well over an hour to kill before catching our connecting train.

"Now what?" Steve wanted to know, sounding as though this was all my fault. I bit back a sharp response and continued in *rah-rah* mode.

"Every cloud has its silver lining," I declared staunchly. "We have some time, right? Come on, let's grab a quick dinner somewhere."

The warm and cheerful interior of a nearby pizza place— not to mention the pizza-and-garlic-bread combo we consumed in record quantities—did much to cushion the blow of still being on the road. It proved difficult to be pessimistic on a full tummy and after a glass of wine. Thus it was with relative enthusiasm that we boarded the little trundle train for Pitlochry where we finally arrived at half-past nine, once more weary and bedraggled, but buoyed by the knowledge that we were nearly, nearly there now.

Alas.

The next obstacle proved to be finding a taxi as the hotel was a good half-hour's car ride from the station. It was completely dark and pouring with rain. Obviously, neither of us had packed a raincoat, or even an umbrella. My mood sank again. I wanted to be dry and in bed. I wanted to sleep.

Please, please, find a taxi, Steve.

Steve did the manly thing. He deposited me under a three-way enclosed bus shelter with our luggage and went off in search of transportation. It seemed to take an age, but in reality he was back within ten minutes, drenched to the skin but exultant—a taxi would pick us up shortly.

Sure enough, a hesitant sputtering announced a vehicle approaching along the station road. There were no taxi lights on the green Vauxhall Astra, which was at least fifteen years old and barely roadworthy even by my inexpert standards. Still, at that precise moment, it had to do.

Steve carefully deposited our luggage in the boot and we jointly sat on the back seat, sinking so far into the upholstery that our chins almost touched our knees. The driver appeared to be a relic from a pre-motoring age. He was at least eighty, with crinkly skin and deep set eyes only barely visible behind thick horn-rimmed glasses. His whole skinny frame was shaking incessantly, and the steering wheel wobbled accordingly.

Thirty-seven interminable minutes later, we pulled up outside a gated property surrounded by high hedges. The hotel wasn't visible behind all the greenery. There were no lampposts and no lights, and after Steve had settled the fare, retrieved our luggage and had been dismissed by an unduly cheery "Bye the noo," we were left in utter darkness.

"Are you sure we're in the right place?" I inquired, eying up my black and wet surroundings doubtfully.

"I told the man *three* times where we wanted to go," Steve reminded me. "I can't see how he could have gone wrong."

I shivered, and Steve put his arms around me protectively.

"Well, I don't know," I persisted. "This doesn't look right to me. We're in the middle of bloody nowhere."

Steve suddenly chuckled.

"What could possibly be funny?" I demanded to know, on the verge of hysteria.

"It's quite *Rocky Horror Picture Show*, isn't it?" he offered. I had only ever seen that film once, in the arty cinema off Leicester Square on a Friday night. I had been ill-prepared for it and got absolutely soaked. Nonetheless, I knew exactly what scene he was referring to.

"We're the couple arriving at the castle," I whispered. "Oh God, I hope not."

"*And so it seemed that fortune had smiled on Steve and Sophie…*" Steve intoned in his best narrator voice. He continued, "*…and that they had found the assistance that their plight required…*" He gave a little audio *ta-ta-ta* for the ellipsis before the dramatic rhetorical question, "*…or had they?*"

"Stop it, you're frightening me," I protested. He had a point, though. All we needed was the riff raff to appear and the set would be perfect.

"I'm sorry," Steve apologized dutifully. "I didn't mean to scare you. It's one of my favorite films, and this is kinda great."

I wanted to thump him on the arm to make him stop, but I never got the chance.

"Can I help you?" a brittle and tremulous voice inquired from somewhere in the dark. "Only I have to inform you that you are trespassing."

I shrieked with fright. Steve held my hand very tight, and I could hear him swallow.

"Uh, we have reservations for tonight, and for tomorrow, too," he declared courageously. "In the name of Steve Jones?" He waited for some kind of acknowledgement, but when none came, he elaborated some more. "I booked the four-star Heather suite?"

The disembodied voice erupted into cackles of mirth. "Och aye, the Heather suite?" it repeated incredulously. "You'd better come in. Aye."

The gate swung open with a blood-curdling squeak, and the source of the voice became apparent. The man was extremely tall and his face shone palely like a ghostly moon. A long coat flapped on his gangly frame. Without another word, he led the way toward the dark and abandoned-looking house. I couldn't help thinking that if that was a four-star hotel-spa-resort, I was the Queen of England. There had to be a mistake.

Steve stroked the palm of my hand with his thumb as if to say, *hang in there, it'll all be all right*. But everything was far from all right.

The inside was also like something straight out of the set of Steve's favorite film. It was all blackened oak beams and grimy red wallpaper, with a rucked-up rug running the length of the entrance hall. At least there was an official reception desk, upon which lay an ancient ledger that the…the…the keeper, for want of a better word, now duly opened. I half expected him to load a quill with ink, but disappointingly, he retrieved a cheap black biro from his coat pocket.

"Steve Jones, was it?" he muttered to himself.

Steve nodded, and I elbowed him sharply to speak up.

"Yes, that's right," Steve obliged, earning himself a glare from our host. And what a glare it was. The man certainly was the palest-looking creature I had ever seen. His face was beyond white; the skin was almost translucent. He had deep-set black eyes gleaming like tiny coals under bushy black eyebrows, and an unruly shock of jet-black hair. He looked like a mortician, or something out of a horror movie.

Meanwhile, Steve stood his ground.

"So, the Heather suite, please," he reiterated firmly. Frankenstein's nephew unleashed his scary cackle again. "Och noo, you cannae have that. There's no Heather suite in this hotel," he uttered ominously. "But yer can have our wee best room." He set off immediately, swinging a set of keys in his bony right hand.

"Do you think we should really stay here?" I hissed under my breath, tugging at Steve's sleeve to get his attention.

"I don't know," he admitted in a whisper, "but what else can we do? It's very late and we're not going to walk away from here, and not in this rain, are we?"

"This isn't the right place," I persisted. "Please won't you ring a cab to get us out of here?"

Steve shook his head. "The mobile is dead. There's absolutely no reception whatsoever. We're stuck for the night."

I shivered. "This place totally spooks me," I confessed. That it was also cold, and dirty, and utterly unwelcoming, went without saying.

The "wee best room" revealed itself to be a circular attic room at the top of some kind of turret. Having progressed through a rabbit-warren of passages and stairways, eventually the door swung open on a room that was, in fact, mildly inviting. It held an enormous four-poster bed and a couple of armchairs. There were three big sash windows fully exposed to the howling gale, and rain was oozing in through the frames. Our host quickly pulled the curtains to distract from the water ingress, but dislodged great clouds of dust instead. Evidently, the room hadn't been used for ages. Years. Decades, possibly.

"Breakfast is at eight. You have a good night, noo," the nephew uttered, leaving it open whether he meant "noo" to signify "now" or "no." Then he left and we were on our own.

Chapter Thirty-Seven

I did the only thing a girl could do in such a situation. I sat down on the bed and wept. I was tired and frustrated and disappointed, and I didn't have it in me to hold it all back. However, noticing Steve's crestfallen appearance, and the way he was picking at the curtains trying to mask his disbelief, I suddenly saw the funny side and started laughing instead. Great convulsions of laughter were racking my body, and Steve came over, concerned.

"Oh dear, I think I'm going mental," I erupted. "It's not a laughing matter, I know, but I can't help it." Now I was laughing and crying at the same time. "Come on, you gotta see it. This is a disaster. My goodness, this place is something else. If you saw it in a film, you'd be weeing your pants with mirth. This is *totally surreal.*"

Steve's mouth twitched. We were going places. I lifted the counterpane experimentally, but dropped it back in horror. I couldn't be certain, and I certainly didn't want to know for sure, but it looked like there were mouse droppings on the sheet.

Droppings of some description at any rate. Steve took another look for me and came back grinning.

"Not mouse droppings," he said. "Just mildew marks." He bent over the sheets and inhaled daringly. "Actually, I daresay these are clean. As in, not used since the last time they were washed. They're certainly musty and they don't look great, but I think they're safe to use."

I took a dubious sniff myself. Surprisingly, all I got was a whiff of detergent. Perhaps—just perhaps—this could be braved.

As it was rather late, we decided to call it a day. I explored the hallway to locate the bathroom for my evening ablutions and immediately resolved to go skanky in the morning. There was *no* way I was going to submerge in that bath. Steve ventured forth himself and returned with a similar conclusion. Thus united, we crawled under the blankets, holding each other close, and hoped for morning to come quickly.

That moment turned out to be the best part of the night. Shortly after, the storm picked up another notch and the windows rattled menacingly in their frames. The room proved cold, draughty and damp. And the damp turned into wet when the roof started leaking. Fat drops of water fell from the ceiling, narrowly missing the bed but making an inordinate racket on the wooden floor. The old house creaked and groaned like a being possessed, and sleep proved elusive. Steve and I were both awake—still awake—at the first light of dawn, and I felt gritty and very much out of sorts. Steve didn't fare much better. Silently, we packed our bags in the unspoken agreement that we weren't staying a minute longer. The real hotel had to be found.

Timidly, we ventured downstairs, retracing last night's steps through the unbelievable maze of corridors and stairs. Our wheelie suitcases banged hard on every step, and our approach had to be audible through the entire house. Yet when we recaptured the lobby, it was deserted. All the doors were shut, and there was no evidence of life.

"I suppose we ought to pay," Steve whispered reluctantly. "Awful as it was, it was still accommodation."

I shuddered. "That's injury to insult," I ventured, and Steve grimaced. He pinged the old-fashioned porter's bell on the desk several times, but nothing happened.

Vocal assistance was required. "Hello?" he shouted. "Hello?" His voice echoed dimly around the hall.

"What should we do?" I murmured. "Can't we simply go?"

Steve shrugged, looking uncertain, and pinged the bell a few more times.

Nothing.

I desperately wanted to get away. "Tell you what," I suggested. "Write down your address and a telephone number and they can send us an invoice or something. And then let's go."

Steve was still not convinced. He went across the lobby and knocked at the nearest door, and the one next to it. Still nothing.

"Okay," he finally concurred. "Let's do what you said." He retrieved the biro from inside the ledger and wrote his address and telephone number under his name. Mission accomplished and overcome by the urge to run, we hightailed it out of there like two prison breakers.

"Come on, let's go, go, go," Steve encouraged as I flagged on my way down the drive, and I picked up pace again. Thus we continued for another fifteen minutes, advancing perhaps a half a mile down the deserted country road, before I gave up. We were both soaked to the skin. I could see the muscles playing on

Steve's broad back right through his wet T-shirt as he splashed ahead.

"You promised me a romantic getaway," I panted, "not an all-weather assault course. Slow down, I can't go on this fast."

Under the circumstances, I thought this was a perfectly reasonable observation. However, Steve stopped in his tracks as though I had slapped him. Suddenly, he turned on me.

"Yes, I did promise you a romantic getaway, and I had romance and luxury in mind. This isn't what I'd planned and I'm jolly pissed off. You don't need to rub it in. I'm really fed up," he shouted at the top of his voice. His eyebrows had knitted together in a menacing line and his face was puce.

I had never seen him like this and inadvertently, I took a step back. Bad move! My foot sank into a muddy puddle, my body tilted backwards and I overbalanced. Suddenly I was lying spread-eagled in the mud. Raindrops were falling on my skywards-pointed face and, out of sheer disbelief at my bad luck, I remained where I was, utterly unable to move.

Steve towered over me with a forbidding expression on his face and said nothing to start with. "I suppose this will be my fault as well," he eventually managed.

Duh.

"Of course it bloody is," I snapped, knowing that I was being unreasonable but unable to help myself. "Will you at least help me up?"

"Why is it my bloody fault?" Steve yelled, seriously enraged. "I didn't trip you over. You managed that all by yourself."

"Yeah, because you startled me when you shouted at me," I retorted angrily.

"Bloody woman," Steve muttered under his breath, calmer now. For an instant, I thought he was going to pull me up, but hold on, no! There was no help forthcoming.

He turned away and walked up the lane, dragging his case behind him and leaving me in the mud, my suitcase standing in a puddle.

How dare he!

Ten types of anger were roiling in my chest as I struggled to my feet ungracefully, the mud making disgusting sucking sounds as it reluctantly relinquished my body from its slimy hold. My coat, my trousers, my hair—all ruined.

I lost all rational thought and charged after Steve, ramming into his back at full pelt. He nearly, but not quite, fell. He still wouldn't stop walking, so I grabbed his hand and spun him around to face me.

"Where do you think you're going?" I spat. "What do you think you're doing, leaving me there in the mud?"

"What does it look like?" he responded testily. "I'm going to look for somewhere dry, somewhere where we can eat."

I dimly noted his use of the plural pronoun, but I didn't take the bait.

"You can't abandon me here," I shouted, pummeling his chest with my fists.

"I'm not abandoning you," Steve defended himself patiently. "With that look on your face, you were never going to accept my help. If anything, you were going to pull me down."

I opted for denial and indignation. "Of course not," I protested vehemently. "Why would you even think that?"

For a millisecond, Steve looked dumbfounded but quickly recovered. He laughed softly. "I know you too well, my love."

"Don't 'my love' me, you…you…" I started, searching for a suitable insult, but Steve clamped his hand over my mouth.

"Now, now," he tried to soothe, "don't say anything you're going to regret." He tried to smile and his face almost relaxed, but I didn't reciprocate.

Hell and damnation, I seethed inwardly. If I wanted a blazing row, I deserved a blazing row.

We were locked in this unhappy half-embrace for quite some time before Steve let go. Feeling a red rage at his treatment of me and fueled by frustration and disappointment at the miserable outcome of this "romantic" getaway, I grabbed my case and, head held as high as possible, mud trickling down my back, I splattered down the lane away from Steve without looking back.

Within minutes, I came to a junction where the abysmal mud-path joined a proper tarmacked road. There was even a signpost nailed to a tree directing hapless drivers and joyless walkers back to Pitlochry. It was *only* ten miles. I swallowed down my despair and sneaked a look behind me. There was no sign of Steve.

I went over to the sign post and stood by it, taking shelter under the tree and deliberately facing away from the muddy lane. If Steve did come after me, I wanted him to have a moment's worth of panic, finding me gone. Truth be told, I was awfully mixed up and confused. Somewhere at the back of my mind I was dimly aware that none of this was exactly Steve's fault. Perhaps, I thought, I had better go back.

I straightened up, ready to retrace my muddy steps. Still partially hidden by the tree, I suddenly spotted a Range Rover turning out of the mud road. For a fraction of a second, I got a full frontal view of both driver and passenger. The driver meant nothing to me, but the passenger was Steve. I was stunned with disbelief. What were the odds of a car coming down that lane, of all lanes, today, of all days, picking up Steve along the way, but not me?

With a great lump in my throat, I tried to draw attention to myself. I attempted a wave, but my coat snagged on a branch and the movement was cut short. By the time I had disentangled the sleeve, the car had turned fully and progressed down the tarmacked road toward Pitlochry, its red tail lights bobbing up and down as it traversed the ubiquitous potholes. They seemed to be mocking me as they whisked Steve ever further away from me and closer to civilization.

Now bloody what?

After watching Steve zoom down the road in a dry, comfortable and speedy car, I got angry all over again. How dare he leave me in the wilderness?

Eventually, I started walking along the road toward Pitlochry. The going was slow but I figured that I would get there in about three hours if no lift came my way. My tummy was rumbling most impressively, reminding me that I hadn't had breakfast, and I would have gladly given my life savings for a hot cup of tea.

Fifteen minutes later, a car *did* come along the road heading toward Pitlochry. The driver offered me a lift but insisted on covering her passenger seat with a plastic sheet that she appeared to keep handy in the boot for just these occurrences. Having taken a cursory look at myself in the mirror, I hadn't been able to blame her.

She dropped me at Pitlochry station where I had half expected Steve to wait for me. That, I had concluded during the short drive, would be the redeeming moment. Perhaps he simply hadn't seen me under that tree. Actually, there was no way he could have seen me. *So,* I reasoned with myself, *he had probably kept an eye out for me the entire way to the train station.* And not having found me there, I had somewhat illogically assumed that he would have waited for me. *Surely* he would have sensed that I was behind him, not ahead?

Evidently, he had not. In fact, he had probably consulted the timetable, seen that he had only barely missed a train to Edinburgh, and drawn the only logical conclusion from his perspective—that *I* had left without waiting for *him*. He had to have caught the next train, dieseling ahead of me and leaving me behind in this little place.

Shaking with cold and wet, and beyond feeling anything much else, I took myself off to the restrooms and performed an emergency change of clothing. Somewhat more presentable, I went to the dismal café to have a spot of breakfast and then caught the next train out of there.

A selection of fast and slow trains later, I eventually made it home, taking *only* about ten hours. I was numb with confusion and shock.

Chapter Thirty-Eight

Unsurprisingly, I woke feeling shattered and miserable on the bank holiday Monday morning. The petty argument between Steve and me weighed heavily on soul. There was a leaden taste in my mouth and my tummy churned hot and heavy.

"Stupid, stupid, stupid," I berated myself for letting a misunderstanding escalate beyond belief. Knowing that this was in large part due to me overreacting didn't help matters at all. I added guilt to the mix of unhappy emotions as I stomped restlessly around the flat.

"Why couldn't you have picked me up and given me a hug," I demanded angrily of an absent Steve. "That was all it took. I was tired and disappointed, and I knew you were too, but still, you're the man, c'mon, you were supposed to be in charge, right?"

My reasoning was shaky and I cringed at the self-righteousness of it all. How vulnerable human interaction could be; how easily a situation could spin out of control without either party meaning to.

"Stupid, stupid, stupid," I ranted at myself once more as I stomped restlessly around the flat. What was I supposed to do?

"And why is he not *ringing* me?" Remorse at my own pitiful behavior was beginning to morph into anger at his lack of empathy when the phone stubbornly remained silent.

At lunchtime, I crumbled and tried to ring Steve. He ought to have been at home. He wasn't scheduled to work, I was certain of it. Yet there was no answer on his landline, and his mobile went straight to voicemail.

"Rrrrgh!" I raged, then told myself to calm down. He was entitled to sulk. He probably thought I had actually run away. If only I hadn't sheltered out of sight under the bloody tree!

Becoming ever more agitated, I called Rachel. When I couldn't get hold of her either, frustration drove me out of the flat and toward her house, which was only a short five minute walk away. Once in front her black front door, I rang the bell incessantly for five minutes. Rachel wasn't in.

"Bloody hell!" Tears of misery and self-pity sprang to my eyes. "Where is everybody when you need them?"

I desperately needed to unburden myself to someone. I needed advice. Still standing in front of Rachel's house, I tried ringing her again and this time she answered.

"What's up?" was her familiar greeting, although her voice sounded slightly breathless.

"Can I talk to you? Can we meet? I need to talk to someone." My misery burst out of me in great waves. Nonetheless, there was a small silence on the other end.

"Sure," Rachel eventually responded, somewhat hesitantly. "How about...how about dinner? I'm not home right now but I could be back by..."

Clicking and swooshing noises suggested that she had covered up the handset as though she were talking with someone else. I felt even more alone and bereft. And mystified — what was with the secrecy?

"I could be back by six. How's about a nice takeaway at my place, like the old days?" Rachel sounded cheerful and jolly, but her tone struck me as just a tad over the top. False. Put on. I swallowed. I was probably imagining things.

"Okay. Six is good. See you then," I agreed and rang off. Damn and triple damn. How was I to kill the hours until six o'clock?

I started walking back toward my flat but found myself turning right toward the Tube station rather than left into The Crescent. I desperately, desperately wanted to see a friendly face. Perhaps I would drop in on Dan.

Ha, fat chance, a little voice in my head told me as I sat on the Tube hurtling toward Clapham. *He won't be in. More fool you, you ought to try ringing him at least, give him some warning. In case he has a visiting lady friend, or something.*

I smiled ruefully to myself. *Good point.* I would phone him as soon as I got off the train. And if he was busy, I would simply amuse myself taking a walk on Clapham Common until it was time to meet Rachel.

Alas, my mobile had run out of battery when I retrieved it outside the Tube station. It was one hundred percent completely dead. I weighed my options. It was *probably* a bad idea to visit Dan unannounced. Yet my need for human contact, for conversation, for a friendly face, was so overpowering that I couldn't get myself to abandon the idea. My feet started walking as though with a will of their own and took me down the familiar streets.

There it was, Dan's house. Looking very much the same as it always had. All the windows were closed, and the house had a shut-up kind of feel to it, but that didn't mean anything.

After all, Dan could be in his studio. I stepped up to the front door and rang the bell.

After waiting uncertainly for five minutes, I rang the doorbell another time, even longer. The sound was clearly audible through the front door.

I chewed my bottom lip; I should probably go. If he wasn't in, he wasn't in. Yet a flat, sinking feeling spread through my stomach at the thought of remaining on my own for the afternoon. Perhaps I would stick a note to his door and he might call me later? I latched onto the idea like a drowning woman.

Rummaging through my handbag for a pen and a piece of paper, my fingers closed around a set of keys. Familiar keys, but not mine.

Oh my gosh, I still had Dan's keys.

My gut reaction was to let myself in. After all, Dan had never minded before. Yet technically, I ought to have returned the keys a long time ago. Would he mind if I used them? What if he was out and returned to find me lounging on his sofa? Would that still be okay, like it had always been?

Get a grip, I admonished myself. *This is Dan we're talking about. He'll be fine. The last thing he would want for you to do is lurk around outside his front door.*

That settled it. I inserted the first key into its lock and was rewarded with an encouraging *thunk* when the key couldn't turn the mortise mechanism. Somebody was home. I used the Yale key to disengage the snap lock and stepped in. By force of habit, I put the keys in the bowl on the side table right there in the hall where they always lived, and I took a moment to listen for any signs of life.

The house was quiet. It smelled of furniture polish, fresh laundry, and Dan's aftershave. Feeling like an unlawful intruder, I ambled through the downstairs first but Dan was not there.

Next, I tried the studio, but the door was wide open and there was no sign of recent activity.

Very odd.

Suddenly, I was gripped by an irrational fear. What if he had slipped in the bath and was lying right at this moment unconscious on the bathroom floor? He might have cracked his head. I could almost envisage the blood seeping from a gaping wound.

Anxiety constricted my throat, and I couldn't call out, much as I wanted to. It was like one of those nightmares when you're desperate to shout, scream, warn somebody, get help— and yet you can't.

So instead of calling out, I went upstairs to investigate.

Halfway up the stairs, I realized that the house wasn't empty. I heard a voice, a weird moaning. Dan *had* fallen and was in pain.

I took the remaining steps two at a time. At the top of the stairs, I halted, trying to get my bearings, listening to where his moaning was coming from.

The bedroom, it seemed. He had obviously managed to drag himself in there. Of course, he was trying to get to the phone. My heart was beating furiously with fear at what I would find.

I took a few more steps forward, then stopped again. The bedroom door was only half shut, and Dan's voice was clearly audible now. He was moaning, but he wasn't in pain. He seemed to be talking. There was another voice, as well.

A very familiar voice.

A female voice.

In slow motion, I found myself dragging my feet across the polished wooden floorboards, keen now not to make a sound myself. Without the shadow of a doubt, I knew what I would find but I couldn't help myself. Hesitating at the door, I eventually nudged it open far enough to see.

I had an immediate view of Dan's super-king-size bed.

Dan was in it. Or should I have said, on it.

In a *very* compromising position. He hadn't seen me, but I could see enough to notice that he was wearing his special necklace. Whose companion-piece I was still wearing myself, never mind I had Steve now. It was part of me, and I had never taken it off, really. Weird, how my mind fixed on that tiny detail with utter clarity.

Dan was lying on his back, his legs moving rhythmically, his arms thrust high behind his head. Between the white half-moons of his buttocks, a pale, hairy expanse of scrotum showed, winking at me. *Hello Sophie, fancy seeing you here. Care to join us?*

The absurdity of it all didn't escape me. Human beings mating — they looked kind of primal, in a grotesque kind of way.

And.

On top of Dan —

I could only see her back, but I recognized the voice, and the tangle of tussled, sex-goddess hair.

Rachel.

Oh my God, Rachel.

She was riding him hard. Her pert little buttocks molded perfectly into the curve of Dan's groin.

Time slowed down to a crawl in a way I had never experienced before. I could hear my breathing in my own ears, absurdly echoing the panting coming from the copulating couple. Their bodies were moving as one as they were approaching a climax. Just how I knew that I wasn't sure. I had never even watched a porn movie in my life — it wasn't my thing.

What I was witnessing now; it was sick. It was more than sick. It made me want to vomit.

My best friends—both of them. Dan and Rachel. Together. Really together. As up close and personal as it was possible to be.

It was revolting. My heart beat in my throat and my head was spinning. Hot tears pricked at the back of my eyes but wouldn't come.

Rooted to the spot for what seemed to be an eternity, I suddenly came to and fled. *Down the stairs, through the front door, pull it shut softly, don't let them know you were here, you saw; don't give them the satisfaction.*

Up the road now, quick, quick, don't cry, don't cry, you can cry at home. Get to the Tube, don't be seen, just get home. Just get home.

The tears I had been holding back could be restrained no more. By the time I sat down on a train, my T-shirt was soaked with teardrops, but I didn't care.

How could they? How could they? My best friends. Dan and Rachel. Rachel, in particular. *Was Dan her mystery man?* I wondered. Was he the one she had been so coy about?

I was sobbing now, nearly howling, making quite the spectacle of myself. Thank goodness I was nearly home.

Get a grip, I told myself sternly. *And anyway, so bloody what? You're not seeing Dan, and Rachel's not seeing anyone, and you are definitely in love with Steve, aren't you?*

Damn the rational side of my brain, always playing devil's advocate, always speaking up at inopportune moments.

I don't care, I mentally shot back at myself. *I don't care. I love Steve, and I don't care if Dan shags anything that moves. That's not why I'm upset. But Dan and Rachel? Rachel? Of all people, Rachel? It's sick.*

SICK.

Sick sick sick sick sick.

I took a deep breath. On autopilot, I had alighted from the train and exited the Tube. I was racing up my road and I had inadvertently started talking to myself, talking out loud, hissing that last utterance with all the venom I could muster. A terrified a passerby took one look at me and changed to the other side of the road. I needed to calm down.

And anyway, why should it be sick? Why shouldn't they make out?

Because—

Well, because—

I didn't know why. I couldn't explain it, not rationally. Other than that it was like finding your mum bedding your teacher, or something. Two people you implicitly trusted, but who should never conjoin in lust or any other manner, suddenly doing just that and pulling the rug out from under you with one swift sleight of hand.

Nicely done, really.

Congratulations, you two.

I howled with pain and frustration and outrage. Moreover, I felt deeply embarrassed on their behalf. Angry, humiliated, disgusted.

Betrayed.

My mind finally clung firmly onto that notion. I felt let down and betrayed. Betrayed, by two people whom I would have trusted with my life. By two people who had been the pillars of my adult universe. Dan and Rachel weren't meant to be an item. They weren't meant to have sex. Admittedly, I didn't want Dan anymore, not in that way. But I certainly didn't want Rachel to have him instead. I hadn't minded the parade of women going through Dan's house even while I was living there. They didn't mean anything to him, or to me. *But Rachel,* I mused, as I was stomping furiously down the road toward my house, *Rachel* meant *something. To him, and to me.*

I reached my flat and raced up the stairs, slamming the front door behind me. Anger was now muscling in on my emotions determinedly, doing a good job of eclipsing betrayal for the moment.

How *dare* Dan sleep with Rachel? How *dare* he abuse her vulnerable position, allow himself to be carried away with someone who had only just got back on her feet? And Rachel, the stupid woman! How could she let herself go, knowing, as she did, that she was on the rebound? Knowing that she would end up hurt again. Because no, she wasn't going to reform Dan. He wasn't going to change for her, either. She would be broken-hearted once again in the space of days, weeks. How could she go there? Where were her self-respect, her common sense, her instinct for self-preservation?

Stupid, stupid, stupid, I raged for the third time that day, thumping sofa cushions for emphasis and release.

I had never been so beside myself with boiling emotion before. I was literally seeing red. I had always thought people were exaggerating when they talked about the red mist descending, but I was in that space now.

And I hurt. Oh my gosh, how I hurt.

In my despair, I tried the only recourse I had. I attempted ringing Steve again. I would apologize for my silly behavior, I would grovel, beg forgiveness and ask him to come over. I needed him to hold me and to love me and to tell me everything would be all right. Thus I rang, and I rang, and I rang, but he wouldn't answer or wasn't there.

When the phone eventually shrilled in my hands while I was poised to dial Steve's number yet again, I nearly jumped out of my skin with frayed nerves. Instinctively, my thumb lifted to press the answer button, but caller display showed that it was Rachel calling and I froze. Nah. No chance!

I let the phone click through to answerphone and listened while Rachel prattled on cheerfully.

Hey, sweetie! Her voice was merry and light. How I wished I couldn't hear the undercurrent of sexual gratification oozing out from her every word. *Where are you? It's six o'clock, I thought we were having dinner? Hurry up, I'm starving!*

"*Argh!*"

Faced with such blatant duplicity and deceit, I lost my rag completely. I hurled the handset, innocent though it was, against the wall with all my might. It cracked apart with a satisfying crunching noise indicating terminal damage. However, when I picked it up, the screen was still intact, so I stomped on it for good measure.

I was shaking with fury when I collected up the various bits of broken phone from my lounge. The force of impact had also made a dent in my beautifully replastered lounge wall, and that would no doubt serve as a reminder of this day for years to come. I would have to cover it up with a picture.

Of course, now I was phone-less. *Talk about cutting off your nose.* I howled again, this time with frustration at my own inability to control my anger, and resignedly stuffed the broken pieces into the bin. I would have to replace the phone, of course. And soon, too. I couldn't really be without. It would cost. But.

I seized on this notion gratefully. I would get a new number as well as a new phone. That way, I wouldn't get any more calls from the two cheats. It would be a clean break. End of story. Taking a deep breath, I went to the bathroom to inspect myself. Would I look any different? Emotionally scarred, perhaps? Traumatized?

Not really. I did look, however, as though I had stuck two fingers in a socket and got myself electrified. My hair was standing on end in an untidy mess, and my face was red and blotchy from crying. I recoiled in horror.

The horror was amplified when I realized I was still wearing Dan's necklace. My immediate reaction was to rip it off, tearing the delicate chain with one easy act of vengeance. But I caught myself. I recognized that I had inflicted enough damage on innocent inanimate objects already. Besides, the necklace stood for a long and happy period of my life whose memory I couldn't, wouldn't deny. Even in the darkest depths of my current despair, I knew I was going to regret it bitterly if I broke this precious keepsake. A phone, I could replace. This was priceless.

With trembling hands, I managed to undo the clasp and took the necklace off carefully. I gathered it up in my right hand, looking at it through teary eyes. How had we all ended up in this big nightmare together?

I found some wrapping tissue in my wardrobe. Very gently and feeling quite sad, I wrapped the necklace in the tissue, then put it in its original box and wrapped that, too. Finally, I pulled out my under-bed storage drawers, the ones containing humdrum debris of my life, such as lone shoes, discarded bras, candles and clothes pegs. I placed the wrapped box with its memory cargo right at the very bottom in the far corner at the foot-end, the one that was most prone to dusting up. Let the dust settle on it, that would be cathartic and symbolic. I also buried it under several layers of old clothes, and pushed the drawer back into position.

What a truly shitty weekend. Short of death or natural disaster, I couldn't think of many ways in which a person could have such a spectacularly crap time in two short days.

Granted, the rawness and hurt about my fight with Steve were probably my own fault. Guilt and self-loathing didn't exactly improve my mental state. And why wasn't he answering my calls? How was I supposed to make up if he didn't give me a chance?

But the betrayal by my best friends, that nearly pushed me over the edge. *Epic fail* didn't quite capture how I felt about my life. Bereft, lonely, hurt, abandoned and *very stupid*, that was getting nearer the truth.

In the space of a single weekend, I had somehow lost everyone in London who meant anything to me. Owing to a ludicrous row, my new boyfriend was no longer answering my calls; goodness knew what that meant, but if he wouldn't give me a chance to make up, it didn't look good for us. And Dan and Rachel…well, if I never saw them again, that would be soon enough. My closest relationships, wiped out. There was nothing left for me. What was the bloody point?

Rarely—no, *never* had I been so fed up. I had had enough. I wanted to plug my thumb in my mouth for comfort like a toddler and sulk like a teenager. Actually, what I really wanted was to leave all the shit behind and start over somewhere else, some place happy.

Far too emotionally and physically exhausted to do anything coherent, I poured myself a gigantic neat whiskey, downed it, and crawled under the duvet to seek oblivion.

PART FOUR:
GONE

Chapter Thirty-Nine
~Steve~

Steve banged his glass of wine on the kitchen counter. Hell and damnation, but he was cross. This couldn't go on. He felt like he was stuck in some kind of nightmare. And he had had enough.

Never mind that Sophie hadn't called him or even simply sent a text, or done anything at all. They had a good thing going on. He had waited a long time to find this emotion, *true love*, warts and all. He didn't know exactly what had gone wrong, or what he was meant to do next, but he knew one thing—he wasn't going to let this relationship go under without a fight.

Five days of stewing on the strange argument they had had up there in Scotland. Five days of swinging from anger over self-righteous indignation to despair and worry, and all the way back again. Five long days of mulling and sulking, desperate to call her yet unable to get himself to act, his stubbornness increasing with every passing hour. *Willing* her to make the first call—*what was taking her so long?* After all, *she* had run away from him, abandoning him on that awful muddy lane. How was it possible that the weekend during which he had planned to propose to her had ended in a weeklong separation?

Steve drained the dregs of his wine and set down the glass hard, as if to emphasize a point to himself. He took a second to gather his thoughts, grabbed his keys and left his flat. It was five o'clock. Friday rush hour was still in full swing but nonetheless, if he got lucky for once, he could be at Sophie's flat inside half an hour, and the torment would be over. They would kiss and make up and forget the whole silly interlude. He spotted the right bus coming round the corner and made a run for it.

Steve's heart lifted as he walked up to Sophie's flat. One of the sash windows was open in the living room, and he could hear the radio playing softly. She was in.

He paused for a few seconds, collecting himself. Taking a deep breath, he rang the doorbell. Footsteps clattered down the stairs. Steve tried to smile, forcing himself to relax his facial muscles. A key was being turned in the lock, and Steve took a tiny step backwards.

I should have brought flowers, he suddenly realized, kicking himself for being such an ass. *Well, too late now. Here, the door was opening.*

"Can I help you?" the young man asked politely as Steve stared, his mouth agape. Steve only managed a stupid "um" by way of response, but he delivered it well, and several times over. "Um…. Um…. Um…"

His mind was racing. Who was that man? What was he doing in Sophie's flat? Did she have a brother he didn't know about?

"Are you all right?" the young man asked, looking concerned.

"What is it, George?" another voice piped up and a young woman emerged beside the man, putting her arms mischievously round his back as though they had been in the middle of something else altogether. Which they probably had, Steve realized in a flash, as they were obviously a couple. His face broke into an inadvertent and genuine smile, which he cut short immediately, fearful that this young couple might consider him a bit of a moron. And anyway, the question remained of what they were doing in Sophie's flat.

"Who *are* you?" he burst out, his first coherent uttering. "Where is Sophie? May I see her?"

The couple looked at each other.

"Who's Sophie?" George asked.

"Sophie. You know, *Sophie*," Steve explained, somewhat superfluously, he thought. "She lives here."

"Err..." George continued uncertainly. "No, she doesn't. We live here."

"*You* live here?" Steve laughed. Surely he had misheard.

"We do," the young woman confirmed gently, as though she had understood that someone's happiness was at stake here.

"We moved in today. We haven't even finished unpacking yet." She giggled.

"You moved in today?" Steve repeated dumbly. "As in, you've moved *in here* today?"

The couple nodded, no longer certain what to make of this deranged stranger questioning them on their doorstep.

"But...how? Why?"

"Well, we'd been looking in the area for a while, and the agency rang this morning and..."

Steve pounced on one critical word. "Agency? What agency?"

"The lettings agency, of course," the young woman elaborated. "You know, *YourHome*, they're up the road…"

"You're renting this flat from *YourHome*?" Steve shouted in surprise. George immediately made to close the door, but Steve held up a conciliatory hand.

"No, please… I'm sorry, I'm just so surprised. Perhaps I ought to explain…" He caught his breath, gathering his thoughts. "My name is Steve. The last time I was here, which was last Friday, my girlfriend Sophie lived here. She owns this place." The couple was listening. Encouraged, Steve ploughed on.

"We had a big row at the weekend. Actually, it was stupid and petty. But I've not seen her since, and she hasn't called me or texted me. Please," he pleaded. "Please. I want to make up with her. If you have any idea where she's gone…?"

Mute shakes of heads signified that they didn't know. Undeterred, Steve ploughed on. "Well, if you hear from her, tell her Steve was here, and that I love her. Do you hear? I love her?"

To his great surprise, he had tears in his eyes. All the anger and crossness at the unfairness of the situation, of Sophie's behavior, had dissipated. What was left was worry and despair.

Gone. She had well and truly moved out. She hadn't even bothered to tell him.

Utterly confused, Steve turned away from Sophie's front door and retraced his steps to the bus stop. He had set off with such high hopes and now he was facing the worst nightmare ever. Where had she gone? What was he to do? What did it mean for them?

"The end, you idiot," Steve informed himself dryly and somewhat cynically. Nobody heard him, so there was nobody there to contradict him or soothe him. And yet, even as he said it, he couldn't get himself to believe it. If only he could find her, talk to her, hold her.

Chapter Forty
~Rachel~

With an impatient sigh, Rachel put down the freebie newspaper she hadn't been reading on the seat next to her. She worked on a quality newspaper, after all, what was she doing leafing through another editor's random selection of headlines? Feeling restless and dissatisfied, and needing to do something with her hands as the home-bound train hurtled through the dark tunnels, she rummaged through her handbag until she located her mobile phone. Even though it had no reception underground, she opened her messages folder and checked her inbox. All week, she had been waiting for a message for Sophie, some sign of life explaining why she hadn't turned up for dinner on Monday night, but there was nothing. Complete radio silence.

Sophie hadn't answered her phone that night and when Rachel had dropped round her flat at about eight p.m., it had been in darkness. No response at the door. No one there.

On Tuesday morning, Sophie had turned up at the office bright and early, if somewhat pale-looking, and had closeted herself with Rick for two hours. After the inexplicable and quite unprecedented private meeting, she had left and she hadn't been back in the office since. And she had *completely* ignored Rachel during her lightning visit to their shared workplace. Not a smile, not a nod. Nothing.

Rachel was perturbed, and deeply worried. She had mentally revisited their chats over the previous month or so and had noted with a shock how infrequently they saw each other. In fact, the last time had been when she, Rachel, had dropped heavy hints about her new man. Not that he really was her new man, anyway.

Rachel couldn't really explain to herself what game she and Dan had been playing, and they had both felt quite weird about it in the end, so they had had a few good times and then called it a day. It was over.

Suddenly paranoid, Rachel wondered whether Sophie had guessed. It was a long shot, but...

Nah. She was simply getting herself all worked up over her friend's bizarre behavior, that was all. There was no way Sophie could know. There were no clues, no traces, no overlap. Except for that one time on Monday when Sophie had called her when Rachel had been with Dan. But Dan had frozen in horror and been quiet as a mouse. Sophie simply *couldn't* know. And yet—

"*Argh!*" Rachel growled to herself, voicing her frustration and worry, never mind that she wasn't alone in the carriage. It helped, and it felt good, so she had another go.

"*Mhrrrrwgh.*"

Better still.

The Tube was finally pulling into Tooting Broadway. Rachel alighted, and caught a quick glance of the station clock. It was ten-thirty p.m. She had worked the late Friday shift and she felt exhausted, yet she suddenly knew with absolute clarity that she wanted to, nay, *needed* to see Sophie. Now. There and then. Rachel intended to come clean and clear the air, plead temporary madness and beg forgiveness.

Instead of walking home to her own flat, she directed her steps toward Sophie's street.

Thank goodness, there were lights, Sophie was home. Rachel's heart lifted as she neared Sophie's front door. She was steeling herself for an instant rejection, a door slammed in her face, but she had her first line ready. She would scream it through the letter box, or stand outside the flat and shout to make herself heard, until Sophie let her in. Over a glass of wine or a cup of tea, she would explain.

Full of nerves and ugly, wriggly maggots playing havoc in her tummy, Rachel rang the doorbell. She raised a conciliatory hand in anticipation of Sophie's reaction, and fixed her best smile on her face. There were footsteps coming down the stairs; there, the door was being unlocked.

"I'm sorry I slept with Dan," Rachel blurted out before the door was even fully open. "I swear, I'm so sorry. If you just let me—"

The "in" froze on her lips as she realized that she was staring at a young woman who wasn't Sophie. Rachel took a step back and ran her hands through her hair in a gesture of embarrassment. *Who was this woman?*

"Sorry," she smiled apologetically. "You must think I'm a lunatic. I'm looking for Sophie." She waited for a reaction but the young woman only stood and stared. Blithely, Rachel continued.

"I'm Rachel. Sophie's best friend." She gave an uncertain laugh. "Well, I hope so. If I could just explain... Is she in? May I see her?"

Heavy footfall thundered down Sophie's stairs and a young man materialized next to the young woman, taking her hand protectively.

"Why'd'y'open the door, Maisie?" he whispered impatiently, half turning to face Rachel.

"May I ask what's going on here?" he uttered.

"Um, no," Rachel retorted testily. "But may *I* ask what's going on here? What are you doing in my friend's flat? And where is she, anyway?"

George gave a big sigh. "What is it with this flat?" he asked of Maisie, clearly not expecting an answer, because he addressed Rachel immediately.

"We're renting this flat, as of today. You can check with our agent at *YourHome*. And before you ask, we don't know of any Sophie."

Rachel stood in stunned silence. Sophie was renting her flat out? Through an agency? The implications were complicated and many. *She definitely knew*, was Rachel's immediate guilty thought.

George appeared to be speaking, but Rachel struggled to hear. She shook her head impatiently and the sensation cleared.

"What is it about Sophie?" George was asking. "Are there any more of you likely to come round looking for her? You've got to understand that it's ever so slightly unsettling. Perhaps we need to look for another place?"

"NO!" Rachel shouted quickly, surprising herself and the young tenants. "No," she continued more calmly. "Please stay. I'm sorry to have bothered you. It's just...it appears that Sophie left in rather a hurry, and she doesn't seem to have told anyone and—"

"Yeah, well, we noticed *that*," George cut in sarcastically.

"What do you mean?" Rachel inquired.

"What I mean is that we had a visit not four hours ago from a *very* deranged looking man in search of Sophie, too."

Rachel breathed a sigh of relief. "Dan was here as well?"

George raised his eyebrows. "Dan? Can we expect a visit from him, too?" And, seeing Rachel's confusion, he elaborated, sounding somewhat annoyed. "No, it wasn't Dan who came by earlier. His name was—" He turned to Maisie for confirmation. "Steve, was it?" Maisie nodded.

"His name was Steve. Now *his* story was that he'd had a row with Sophie and had come to apologize…"

Steve? Steve had been there, tonight, to apologize for a row? Rachel was utterly shocked. What had happened to Sophie's ordered life? She shook her head once more to quiet the buzzing that had risen in her ears.

"Steve and Sophie had a row?" she muttered to herself. "Oh God, no, that can't be right. So *that's* why she wanted to meet up on Monday." Rachel could feel the cogs turning in her brain as relief at not having been found out warred with residual guilt and confusion. *Where was she?*

Noticing that George and Maisie were still staring at her, Rachel rallied to close the conversation properly. "I'm sorry," she said. "I'm sorry to have bothered you. I'd better be going now. Please, if you do hear anything from her, tell her I'm sorry, and to get in touch. Please."

Without waiting for a reaction from the couple, Rachel turned and fled. She had to get home and think this over.

Sophie—gone?

What an extreme, and surprising, reaction. Looking deep in her soul, Rachel recognized that Sophie's move was probably not a million miles away from her own desperate bid for change when taking a swim in the Thames. Maybe she had flipped and drawn a line. Without telling anyone.

Well. Without telling her friends.

But she had probably told Rick. No, scratch that. She *had* to have told Rick. She had made arrangements. After all, she still needed to live, and eat, and pay bills. That was probably what her quick visit to the office had been about.

She had flipped and gone, but she had not *flipped out.* Which meant…

Rachel grinned.

Which meant she could be found. She might not want to be found; but found, she would be. Rachel simply had to work out a way so they could make up with each other, and all would be well.

Chapter Forty-One
~Dan~

Dan's alarm clock went off at an uncharacteristically early nine a.m. on a Saturday morning in early September. But, even more uncharacteristically, Dan was already up and dressed. He was in the kitchen clutching a mug of tea when he heard the alarm. He debated for a moment whether to go and turn it off but decided to let it beep itself out. Wearily, he sat at the kitchen table. The deadline that he had given himself after his heart-to-heart with Jodie had arrived. He had until lunchtime to do what he dreaded most—face the music, sort it all out.

Damn.

He didn't consider himself to be a mean man, or a dishonest one. But he knew that was extremely uncomfortable addressing emotions head-on. Explaining the disaster he had wreaked and apologizing for it was his worst nightmare. Finding the right words, speaking coherently, that didn't come naturally to him, not face-to-face. Only in writing songs and lyrics.

Dan sat bolt upright. That was it! He had three hours. Of course. He would knock together a song. Sophie loved his songs, she would listen.

He could write a song in three hours, easy. It wouldn't be polished, perfect, or finished, but it would do. And he would find the right words.

Full of energy now, Dan bounded down the stairs to his studio. He grabbed a notepad and jotted down the thoughts that were jostling for attention in his head, the things that needed to be said. He picked up his acoustic guitar and started strumming idly, mulling over the events of the past few weeks.

When Sophie had started seeing Steve in earnest after she came out of the hospital, Dan had made himself scarce. He had known, from the first time that Sophie had told him about Steve, that she was deeply smitten by him. Dan had patiently sat through many a talk about Steve and had found himself enthusing that Steve sounded a really *nice, kind, wonderful* man. He hadn't wanted to say all these nice things, but he and Sophie, they were history. They couldn't be lovers, it wouldn't work out. That was what she had told him in no uncertain terms in Paris. She was right, of course, but that hadn't stopped him wanting, and regretting. So in secret, and without really being aware of it, he had formulated his cunning grand plan. If he played by her rules, and stuck it out, and stayed her friend, then maybe, one day, just maybe, they could be together again.

Thus he had resolved to be there for her, always, in whatever she was doing, without any sexual complications, innuendos, or anything complicated. It had been hard work, especially when she had moved in with him for a few short weeks, but he had done it, and he had never abused her trust.

When, quite out of the blue, this thunderbolt-and-lightning malarkey had started, Dan had seen no other option but to play along. It hurt him deeply to see Sophie's eyes a-sparkle with love for this different man. In a weird way, Dan had fancied himself in the role of the tragic lover, supporting his loved one and making the ultimate sacrifice. *If you love someone, set them free.*

That had been well and good and *noble*. Yet Dan was of flesh and blood and he had needs. He had felt her loss more acutely than he imagined possible when he had surrendered her to Steve. For weeks and weeks, he had shut himself away, waiting for the pain to recede, the heartache to dull.

Quite randomly, he had bumped into Rachel one day in Harrods. Rachel, who was struggling to put her life back together. Rachel, whom he had known alongside Sophie for years and years. Rachel, who was very much lonely and single, just like himself. They had lunch. They had dinner. They had sex.

It was a tremendous release. It felt good. A little naughty. Possibly just a touch on the spiteful side. *Exciting.* Afterwards, he was overcome with remorse. She was on the rebound after all, was recovering from serious trauma, and he worried that he had abused her vulnerability. She laughed him off. "I know what I'm doing, and I needed this," she assured him.

For a couple of weeks, they coupled every few days. The last time was on the bank holiday Monday, five days ago. That occasion was a watershed, a wild, delicious, bitter-sweet sea-change that had brought their dalliance to a screeching halt. He nearly expired with mortification when, mere minutes after their mutual climax, Rachel spoke to Sophie on the phone.

"This is mad," Rachel declared after she had agreed to meet Sophie later. "I don't know what we were thinking. How am I to look Sophie in the eye? Let's not...let's not do this anymore."

Dan shrugged and concurred. He had loved being with Rachel; she was a fantastic girl. Yet she hadn't captured his heart. Nobody but Sophie could.

"I was afraid I would hurt you," he ventured cautiously.

"You didn't. You haven't," Rachel objected vehemently. "The only person who'll get hurt here is Sophie. We are total idiots. Suppose she found out? How do you think she'd feel?"

Dan's heart sank. That was a terrible prospect indeed. He had never before experienced guilt about any of his conquests even when Sophie knew about them, but he had crossed a line with Rachel.

So they went their separate ways, for all intents and purposes, as though nothing had happened between them. Except he knew it wasn't *quite* as simple as that. Their game was up. He hadn't yet told Rachel, but he knew that Sophie *knew*.

It had taken him a little while to figure it out, but when he checked his phone after Rachel's departure, there were several missed calls from Sophie. He tried to return them, but she didn't pick up.

The following day — Tuesday — when he left the house to meet with the band, he snatched his keys from the bowl in the hallway, only they weren't his set. He knew from the key ring that he held Sophie's set of keys in his hand. His knees buckled and he had to sit on the stairs.

"Jenny," he called out to his housekeeper. "Do you recall Sophie's keys being here?"

Jenny dusted everywhere every day. She noticed things. She would tell him that the keys had been there for weeks. Perhaps she had been here when Sophie dropped them off and —

"Nope." Jenny bustled in, wiping her hands on a dishtowel. "They're new. They weren't here on Friday before I left."

She might as well have punched him in the solar plexus with a rolling pin. The implication nearly killed him. Sophie had visited. She had been in the house. There was no other way the keys would have got there. She had been there. She had probably dropped by the previous day, after she had tried to call him. She had been in the house while—

It didn't bear thinking about. Recalling the moment of realization showered Dan in a thousand types of red-hot guilt, and he shivered.

He had called Jodie that very minute and confessed the sorry mess to his sister. He had wanted a friendly ear and absolution. Alas, her reaction had come as a bit of a shock. Rarely one given to swearing, Jodie had deployed her entire catalogue of insults against him. *Tosser, arsehole, fuckwit, bastard* and *idiot* had been at the harmless end of the spectrum. He had held the handset as far away from his ears as possible and still her voice had resonated, loud and clear all the way from her flat in LA to his house in Clapham.

"Do you really think she knows?" he had asked, hoping against hope that Jodie might say no.

"After everything you've just told me? I'm very much afraid she probably does. It adds up, doesn't it?" Jodie had replied, a little calmer. "How could you *do* this to her? When you love her so?"

Dan had been stunned. "How do you know that?"

"Oh, c'mon, big bro, it's so obvious. For your sake and hers, you go and talk to her. Make sure she's okay."

And he had promised her.

Nonetheless, he had let the entire week pass, cutting it really close to his deadline, before he had found the courage to overcome his inner demons and rouse himself to go to face Sophie.

And that time was now.

He finished his song. He called it, *Undo Your Hurt,* and it contained all the truthful and sincere words from his initial draft, reordered and substituted in places to scan for singing, but the sentiment was there. The tune would need tweaking, and he would have to decide whether to make it voice-and-guitar or voice-and-piano only, but he knew that it would be a simple, no-frills, haunting song.

For his immediate purposes, the guitar version would have to do as he couldn't possibly lug the piano across London.

Chapter Forty-Two
~Dan~

Dan parked his car directly opposite Sophie's flat. Not for him today to turn up by limo. He locked the steering wheel in position and sat back, looking up at her window. It had been weeks since he had been here, and he felt strangely excited despite the apology marathon he was about to run.

He had wondered what to say to make her listen. The core of the truth, he had decided, would be the best option.

"I am a complete bastard," he practiced to himself. "And I am more sorry than you will ever know."

Five seconds. Would that be too long, too much to say? Would she have shut the door by then?

"I'm-a-complete-bastard," he said again, faster, urgency lending conviction to his voice.

Just over one second. Surely, surely he could make her hear that?

Best get it over with. Dan grabbed his guitar from the back seat, got out, locked the car and crossed the road. It was good that he brought music. It gave him confidence, and he knew it was his best chance to get his message across. As long as she let him in, even if only for two minutes. Well, three minutes twenty-six seconds.

Taking a deep breath, Dan rang the doorbell. It was exactly midday.

After a seemingly endless interval, a young woman opened the door. Dan had his mouth open, poised and ready to launch into his first sentence, the crux, the epiphany, the apology—but caught himself before embarrassing himself.

"Hi," he said instead, holding on to his guitar for reassurance. "Err... I'm looking for Sophie?"

The young woman grew pale and threatened to swoon.

"Oh my God..." she whispered. "Oh my God, oh my God."

Dan gave her what he intended to be a reassuring smile, but it seemed to make matters worse.

"Won't you come in?" the girl offered in a voice broken with excitement. "It's much easier to talk inside, isn't it?"

Dan shrugged uncertainly. "Um, yes, of course," he agreed. "Yeah, I'll come in."

He squeezed by her and started up the stairs while she closed the door behind him. Immediately he noticed that something was wrong. The flat smelled wrong; it didn't smell of Sophie, or her perfume, or her things. Also, there were pictures hung on the wall all the way up the stairs. Presumably Sophie could have decided to put those up but they were distinctly un-Sophie-like. They lacked color, focus, and spark.

Meanwhile, the young girl had overtaken him on the stairs and announced excitedly, "George, George, you'll never guess who's here *now*."

George? Dan stopped in his tracks uncertainly, surveying the flat as it appeared from his vantage point at the top of the stairs. The kitchen was unchanged but full of unfamiliar paraphernalia. Surely Sophie wouldn't have acquired *that* much stuff in a matter of weeks? He supposed it might be Steve's stuff. Anyway, the furniture in the lounge was all wrong too. Gone were the new dining table and the dusky-pink sofa, Sophie's pride and joy.

What the hell…?

The young woman emerged from the bedroom, dragging a young man behind her who had obviously only just woken up. He was hastily dressed in jeans and T-shirt and rubbed his unshaven chin.

"Dan Hunter," the girl squealed, jumping up and down with glee. "It's really Dan Hunter. Can I have your autograph?"

Dan stared in bewilderment. For once, he ignored a fan's plea. "Where is Sophie?" he asked determinedly.

"*You* are *Dan*?" George asked by way of response. "We've been told that a Dan might come round, but you are him? That Sophie woman knows *Dan Hunter*?"

Dan gave a big sigh. On the whole, he loved being a rock star celebrity. But occasionally — like *right now* — the whole thing could be extremely wearing. And boring. He decided to disregard the inane question.

"Where is Sophie?" he repeated yet more forcefully.

"Oh, right," George snapped out of his disbelief. "Sophie. Yes. Well, we *assume* that she used to live here —"

"*Used* to live here?" Dan pounced. "What are you talking about?"

"We're renting the flat now," the young woman explained. "From *YourHome*. Since yesterday."

Dan considered that information silently.

"You're the third person looking for her," the woman continued, eager to fill him in and keen to please. "First, we had Steve coming round yesterday about six o'clock."

"Steve?" echoed Dan weakly. How did Steve figure in this nightmare?

"Yes, Steve," George picked up a thread. "He said he'd had a big row with Sophie and wanted to apologize."

Before Dan could compute this information, the woman chimed up again. "And also a girl by the name of Rachel came by late last night, and *she* said she was sorry she slept with...err...you." She blushed furiously as she delivered this blow.

Dan gave an involuntary start as though he had been electrified. Years of media training kicked in and saved him from a disastrous reaction. *Deny or feign ignorance; distract; and remove self from situation with dignified expedience.*

"You must have misunderstood," he declared haughtily. "I don't know any Rachel. And I certainly don't sleep with random women. I came here today to—" What to offer the curious couple by way of a distraction?

Dan's fingers caught on the strings of his guitar, and the gentle strumming sound gave him an idea. "I came here today to take Sophie through our new single. But evidently"—he gestured loosely with his free hand—"something's changed in her circumstances. I do vaguely recall her telling me that she was moving, but I neglected to check my diary this morning before I set off. I do apologize to have bothered you."

Thus he swept down the stairs and let himself out of the flat before the new tenants could say anything else. Knowing that his departure would be keenly observed, he quickly got in his car and drove off.

Befuddled, bemused and utterly confused, he didn't really know where to go next. The only obvious place was to go to Rachel's. Maybe she could explain what was going on.

Chapter Forty-Three
~Dan and Rachel~

Rachel was slightly bleary-eyed when she opened the door.

"Dan," she exclaimed full of surprise. "What—"

"Sophie knows about us," Dan cut in brusquely, despair adding a sharp edge to his voice.

Rachel took a step back to let him in. She grew pale, and a hand flew to her mouth. "But she wasn't there yesterday," she mumbled through her fingers. "How would she know?"

She leveled her gaze at Dan. "Maybe she rang them and they told her?" she mused. She sat down heavily on a kitchen chair, then jumped up again and paced the floor. "Sorry," she offered Dan as an afterthought. "You've no idea what I'm talking about, I..."

Dan interrupted again. "I've just been to her flat. And she's gone. *You* told those people you'd slept with me." His voice was flat, almost impassive, but his frustration bubbled beneath the surface. Rachel paled even more.

"It slipped out before I realized I was talking to the wrong person. I thought Sophie would open the door and…" She gave a big sigh. "I couldn't bear it anymore, Sophie not being at work or returning my calls. She never showed up for dinner on Monday. I was worried sick so I went round…" Something occurred to her, and she turned on Dan.

"Why did *you* go to her flat?"

Dan mussed his hair and exhaled. "I went round to apologize. Because she *knows* about us."

"But how?"

"She was at the house. On Monday. She must have been. I found her keys."

Rachel drew in a deep breath and tried to grasp the implications of Dan's statement. "Are you sure?"

"Of course I'm sure," Dan snapped. "The keys weren't there on Friday. I checked with the housekeeper."

"But that doesn't make any sense." Rachel grasped at straws. "Why would she just leave them? And how do you know she didn't drop them off on Saturday or Sunday?"

Dan's eyes lit up with hope for the tiniest moment, but the glimmer died quickly.

"It's the *only* explanation that makes sense," he insisted. "Plus she'd rung me too several times on Monday. I think she just popped round and…" He couldn't' finish the sentence.

"Oh my God, she knows." Rachel finally accepted the idea. "And you've known that, and you didn't ring me?" She threw him an accusing look, then let the anger go. "Anyway, that explains a few things."

"It does?" Dan arched his eyebrows and Rachel filled him in on what she had learned. His brow furrowed with concern when he heard about Sophie's row with Steve, and more so when he understood that she had not been at work since Tuesday.

"She's well and truly gone," he concluded in dazed confusion when Rachel stopped talking. "That's a bit extreme."

"Hm," Rachel mused, tugging at the hem of her T-shirt nervously. "It might be. Then again, it's not as radical as hurling yourself in the Thames." She smiled wanly and Dan hugged her impulsively.

"I suppose not, but I'm still surprised. It's not like her."

"Maybe she just flipped. Imagine, a row with your brand new boyfriend. Finding your two best friends in bed together." Dan and Rachel jointly winced at her stark summation of their brief affair. "You'd feel pretty crap about that."

Dan inclined his head. "But why not confront any of this? Sophie's a head-on kinda girl. Why run, suddenly?"

Rachel laced the fingers of her hands together and twisted them nervously. "I don't know. Maybe she was done being rational and practical. It's not healthy anyway, all that pragmatic attitude she had going on. Everyone has a breaking point."

The two friends contemplated her viewpoint silently for a few minutes, each lost in their thoughts.

"What do you think happened between Sophie and Steve?" Dan eventually asked.

"I don't know. But I intend to find out." She jumped up and flicked through a pile of purple sticky notes on her coffee table. "Come on, come on, where are you?" she mumbled impatiently under her breath. "Ah, *there!*" She waved a piece of paper triumphantly. "Sophie gave me his mobile number when they started seeing each other in earnest. Let's get him to meet with us."

Chapter Forty-Four
~Dan, Rachel and Steve~

"You did *what?*" Steve half-shouted over the din of the pub, dropping his knife and fork in dismay. "You can't be serious."

"Shush," Rachel hissed on Dan's behalf, noticing the curious stares their group was receiving. "Keep your voice down."

"What did you think you were doing? God, what gives you the right to mess with somebody's life and happiness like that?" Steve sat back angrily, ignoring Rachel's plea for quiet talking and letting his voice rise dramatically.

"You stupid idiots."

"Yes, thank you, that'll do," Dan tried to soothe him. "We feel quite bad enough as it is."

"You feel *bad?* Well, wow!" Steve shouted incredulously, his voice clearly audible over the general chatter of happy Saturday night pub-goers.

Dan shrank a little bit lower in his seat. He had never known his local so busy, and he was a bit nervous. Perhaps they ought to have met at his place, but neutral territory had seemed more appropriate under the circumstances.

Steve was beside himself with livid confusion. All this time, he had thought he had driven Sophie away, and now he found out about this undercurrent of deceit? A betrayal by her so-called best friends, *both* of them, at the same time, in the same bloody bed…? Had these people no common sense? No friggin' shame?

"*You* feel *bad?*" he repeated, utterly aghast. "Who do you think you are?" He had got to his feet and was towering over Dan in a menacing pose.

"I'll tell you who you are," Steve continued, but ruined the effect of his bravado while he was searching for appropriate words. "You are…interfering…scheming…selfish…conceited…arrogant…fuckwits. That's who you are."

"Now, now," Dan retorted sardonically, "don't you go calling us names. Your record isn't entirely unblemished either, is it, my friend? I believe you had the most almighty row with your girlfriend —" He didn't get any further.

"Leave me out of this. Now that I know the facts, I realize I have nothing to do with Sophie's disappearance —"

"Of course you bloody do, mate."

"Guys, guys, calm it down, you're making rather a scene," Rachel cut in, trying to stem the argument.

"SHUT UP!" both men shouted at her in unison. Now Rachel saw red, too. She jumped to her feet and banged the table hard with clenched fists.

"No, *you shut up*, you stupid pricks, both of you!" she shouted back at them. "Bloody men."

Suddenly, the brawl was indeed in full swing. Dan had also risen to his feet, holding both hands in front of him in a defensive gesture. Steve shouted a few more insults and abruptly lunged straight at Dan, fists outstretched in a clumsy pose of attack. Dan dodged the blow easily by stepping to the right, but caught Steve's hand and slammed it hard on the table, sending their plates and glasses flying as Steve was forced to follow through and practically lay down on the table. Rachel shrieked with disgust as a half-pint of beer sloshed all over her top and trousers. Steve reached up from his semi-prone position and grabbed Dan by the hair, pulling at it and forcing Dan's head to come down until their faces were level. Dan let go of Steve's arm, and Steve immediately launched another swing—this time connecting with the side of Dan's face. Dan hit back, delivering a searing blow to Steve's nose, which started bleeding immediately.

All the while, mobile phones were being held up by curious customers trying to capture this event for posterity. No doubt within a few hours, Dan and Steve's disagreement would be all over the Internet. Worse still, flash bulbs were going off from two professional cameras. Several keen photographers caught Dan and Steve mid-swing. Rachel instantly grasped the story the pictures were going to tell. "Guys, guys, *stop*," she tried to pacify them. But it was the sight of blood that finally got the men to stop the fisticuffs. Dan straightened up first.

"Fuck me, mate, but I'm sorry," he muttered sheepishly, searching for something to mop up Steve's nosebleed.

Steve stood up unsteadily, shaking his head in a daze.

"Me, too," he replied, sounding just as meek. "Don't know what came over me." His voice sounded somber and muffled through the napkin he had grabbed to stem the blood.

Rachel pushed the men back into their seats, facing Dan away from the curious onlookers and photographers. "Just a small misunderstanding. Show's over folks, thank you," she announced to no one in particular. Then she swiftly picked up the plates and glasses that the men had scattered during their fight and piled them back on the table.

The landlord came to her rescue. "Show's over, folks," he repeated. "If I see anyone else taking any more pictures, I will personally come and destroy your device, whatever it is, however much it costs. Don't think I won't," he added menacingly. "And if you publish any of your footage, you needn't set foot in my pub again. I know who you are."

Having delivered his threat, he strolled over to the battle-zone nonchalantly as though an angry bust-up between a rock star and another man was an everyday occurrence in his establishment. "Are you guys done now?"

Dan and Steve nodded mutely, and Rachel stepped in again. "Sorry about the mess," she addressed the landlord, still loud enough for everyone to hear. "We seem to have had a bit of an accident. We'll help you clear up, of course. And we're hungry. Is the kitchen still open?"

Dan, Steve and the landlord all looked at her with wide eyes.

"What?" Rachel challenged them. "You've barely eaten anything, either of you. And anyway, now that the testosterone is out of the way, maybe we can finally have that chat?"

"Way to go, girl," muttered the landlord. "If you've beat them, join them. Great strategy. That'll confuse people no end, seeing y'all cozied up here over food now. I'll get your orders sorted straightaway, and don't worry about the mess." He stacked the plates expertly on his arm. "I'll have somebody clear that up post-haste. You sit yourselves down as though nothing had happened."

Gradually, other voices were piping up here and there and within a few minutes, everything had returned to normal. The paparazzi were still hanging round, watching, observing.

"That's good," Rachel commented when Dan asked. "Maybe they'll take a few more pictures of us all having a civilized meal together; that'll confuse them. Either way, they'll watch and learn. Perhaps we can spin it as a publicity stunt? For a new song? Album? Video? Something like that?"

Dan waggled his head, weighing opportunities. "I'll have a think about that, that's not a bad idea. But let's get back to why we got here, after all."

Steve spoke up as well. "I really am sorry, mate." He dabbed his nose ruefully with the crumpled napkin. "I think I was so relieved at finding out that something else had gone on in Sophie's life that I flipped a bit. I had been blaming myself, you see, and…"

So Steve filled Dan and Rachel in on the Scotland trip that didn't go quite as planned. "I had the ring at the ready and everything," he whispered sadly.

The three of them let that sink in, swept up in a shared moment of thwarted romance. Abruptly, however, Steve pulled them back to their sad reality.

"But do you think this was really enough to make her leave everything behind? One stupid argument on one disastrous trip?" he asked, fear in his eyes. "Would you do a runner because of that?"

"Prob-ab-ly not," Rachel surmised. "But I think Sophie felt everyone was against her, and that she had let everything go wrong and destroyed her friendships and relationships all in one go."

"But that doesn't make any sense," Steve protested. "She can't think that everyone is out to hurt her, and then blame herself for it?"

"Who says it has got to make any sense?" Dan pondered. "I think Rachel is right. Sophie lost all perspective on everything, and had no one to talk to."

"So what?" Steve retorted skeptically. "She just leaves?"

"Well, she didn't *just* leave," Rachel threw out. "She seems to have made all sorts of arrangements."

"But I love her. She must know that. Even though I think it's despicable what you did, why should it matter to her when she had me?" Steve shook his head in puzzlement.

"Because," Rachel explained without hesitation. "Because you would have thought that she still had feelings for Dan, which you wouldn't have understood, and you would have argued about that, and it would have been a big mess."

Steve shook his head, but Dan was getting impatient with all the talk. It wasn't getting them anywhere. "Never mind all of that," he steered the conversation back to more practical considerations, "How are we going to put this right?"

Chapter Forty-Five

The ferry bumped gently against the pier and the sailors got busy tying it up. I stood by the railing and stared, trying to take it all in. The wide-open sky, the wheeling seagulls, the dunes, the sheer expanse of nothingness around it all. I had arrived.

My thoughts were free-wheeling as events of the past few weeks flashed before me at lightning speed. I swallowed hard, banishing unhappy thoughts from my mind. *A clean break, a fresh start, remember?*

For better or for worse, and for reasons I hadn't yet quite grasped myself, I had arrived on this tiny, car-free island in the German North Sea. *Langeoog.* Long island, it meant, apparently. I had struggled to pronounce it properly when I bought my ticket at Bensersiel. *Lang – eh – org* had been the best I had come up with so far, but it beat my first attempt, *Lang-eeee-oug*, which had caused much mirth among the locals.

"Moin." A sailor shook me out of my reverie.

"Moin," I responded automatically, having picked up the local greeting quickly. My seeming fluency caused a torrent of words which I couldn't begin to understand with my rusty high-school German.

"I'm sorry," I apologized, "I don't speak German that well... Do you speak English?"

Of course he did, and he told me to disembark and to collect my luggage at the train station. I reluctantly made a move to leave the ferry. I had tremendously enjoyed the ride from the ferry port at Bensersiel across the choppy North Sea to Langeoog. Despite the fresh and gusty wind, I had stood at this same spot by the railing for the entire trip, breathing the salty air, savoring the quiet, and generally letting my mind drift.

Having to disembark now, that made it all real, and I felt a pang of anxiety. What had I done? Where would I live? What would I *do*? I didn't know a soul on the island, which was precisely the reason I had come here. *But now what?*

Anxiety gave way to excitement and a sense of adventure as I followed a small group of passengers down the gangway. I would do this! I would take life by the horns and make a fresh start, beginning with somewhere to live. First of all, I was going to take the island train into the town to find an abode.

Lost in thoughts again, it took me a moment to realize that my name was being called.

"Sophie Penhalligan? Frau Sophie Penhalligan?"

My heart beat faster at hearing my name. I had only been gone for four days; surely I couldn't have been discovered yet? With great relief, I saw a porter heaving my luggage toward me.

"Moin," he puffed. "Sie sind wohl Frau Penhalligan?"

Was I Mrs. Penhalligan, he asked formally—that much German I did understand. I smiled and nodded, yes, I was Frau Penhalligan.

"Ihr Gepäck!" was the next uttering, accompanied by a heavy puffing and proffering of my two suitcases. I smiled again, thanking him for his help and taking my luggage—the ubiquitous pink carry-on case, and a turquoise hard-shell, full-size suitcase. That was it. These were all the worldly belongings that I had packed, in great haste, on Tuesday afternoon to accompany me on my adventure. I had packed clothes and a few books, my trusty e-reader, laptop, and a few CDs that I had acquired after the fire. It was amazing how little one did need, all things considered.

The porter motioned for me to board the little train with carriages painted in all the colors of the rainbow, and I obediently clambered on. Stacking my suitcases in the aisle, I squeezed myself on a banquette and slid across to the window. I felt like a ten-year-old on a seaside holiday adventure. Innocent, excited, fresh. Unencumbered.

The train set off at a sedate pace to make the small journey through the island's *Hinterland* and toward the town. It cut through the dunes, deserted at this time of day; past a mini-golf place and along a hiking path. On the left, I could see a little forest. On the right, there seemed to be some kind of golf course. *Rat-tat-tat-tat* went the carriages as they bumped over joins in the rails.

Gradually, a few houses appeared and we were nearing "downtown" Langeoog. Sure enough, a few short minutes later we arrived at the station. I found myself brimming with excitement when I got off. As I stood outside the station surveying my surroundings, the first thing that struck me was the quiet. I could still hear the seagulls overhead and the tweeting of songbirds. Having lived in London for so long, this was a wholly new sensation for me, and even in my hometown of Newquay, the silence would be steadily interrupted by cars, campervans and motorbikes. This was something else.

I grabbed my two suitcases and wheeled them each down the road as though I had a purpose. Actually, I *did* have a purpose. I needed some sort of coffee shop—I wanted an early lunch and some local information. The best thing to do, I decided, was to amble down *Hafenstrasse* and see what I could find.

Fifteen minutes later, I was still walking. Not because I hadn't come across a coffee shop. On the contrary, I had passed plenty. And restaurants, and bakeries. The problem was that I was simply so enchanted, I couldn't stop exploring, never mind the hunger pangs and the dragging suitcases. Most of all, I wanted to see the sea. I had picked up a map of the island right at the *Bahnhof*, and I could see that the village nestled behind a bank of dunes, so on I lumbered, along *Hauptstrasse*, toward the famous water tower where I stopped for a breather, and up *Westerpad* way, cutting through the dunes and finally cresting before the descent to the beach. The sea, at last. I sat down on my turquoise suitcase and drank it in.

A great peace descended on me, and I could breathe more easily. I felt like I had come home.

I didn't know how long I had sat there, on my suitcase, probably looking slightly odd, before the rumbling of my tummy abruptly reminded me that it was definitely lunchtime now. Satisfied that I would be able to take in this vista again later that day, and the following day, and the day after that, I retraced my steps until I reached the friendly-looking little coffee shop that I had spotted earlier on a street corner. It purported to be *Van Halen's*, and I was thoroughly intrigued.

Chapter Forty-Six

The door closed behind me, jauntily jingling the little bell attached to the top of the door jamb. I was instantly enveloped by the fragrant smell of strong, sweet tea and gulped greedily; I was gasping for a cuppa. *This isn't the time to start feeling homesick,* I scolded myself.

Selecting a spot by the window, I lumbered through the assortment of odd chairs and sturdy tables, feeling like a clumsy hulk. I deposited my luggage in a corner behind my table and gratefully sat down on a blue-and-red striped wooden chair with a blue-and-red frilly cushion strapped to the seat.

Instantly, the waitress bustled over to speak to me, issuing the obligatory "Moin" by way of conversational opening gambit. She was in her mid-fifties, I guessed, although her hair was mostly white. But her eyes were a piercing, sparkling blue, her skin looked rosy and fresh, and she wore a comfy sweater with faded jeans and trainers.

"Moin," I shot back proficiently but added quickly, "I don't speak much German yet. Do you speak English by any chance?"

The waitress wiped the table with a white-and-blue checked cloth that looked clean and starched, even after she was done. Satisfied that all was tidy, she sat down with me thoughtfully, eyes a-sparkle.

"You must be Frau Penhalligan," she offered in flawless English. "I'm Frau Fanhaalen, I own the tea shop. *Willkommen.*" And she extended a hand for me to shake.

My mind absorbed these nuggets of information. First of all, I hadn't been prepared for the island information network and the fact that my arrival would be so *noticed*. Moreover, the teashop had nothing to do with the rock band, *Van Halen*, of course—how could it have? *Van Halen* was the owner's name, pronounced *Fan-Haalen*. And evidently the lady wasn't a waitress, she was the owner.

Frau Van Halen was expecting some kind of response, so I hastily greeted her back.

"Hi. Nice to meet you. Yes, I'm Frau Penhalligan." I laughed uncertainly. "But please call me Sophie." I clapped my hand on my mouth. "Sorry," I uttered from behind my fingers, "That was really rude. You don't even know me. Sorry." I had remembered, too late, that the German code of etiquette was very specific on formalities.

Frau Van Halen simply giggled and shook her head. "What a great idea," she assured me. "So much easier than all our formal stuff. Call me Greetje."

"Greetje," I repeated uncertainly. "That's a nice name." *Doh.* Inane comment alert.

"Thanks," she said simply. "I like it, too." Seeing my discomfiture, she laughed again. "I know what you mean," she elaborated. "It must sound very unusual to you, my name. I lived in London for a few years, you see. I was always coming across people struggling with my name. And of course, I found plenty of interesting names over there. Like..." She scrunched up her forehead, trying to recall. "Like Tamsin, and Wynona."

She had lived in London for a few years. That would explain her firm command of my native language. With a bit of luck, I had found myself an ally who could help me settle in. It also explained the ease with which she offered a familiar form of address.

"How did you know who I am?" I decided to find out, gauging the efficiency of the island communication network. Greetje laughed again.

"You'll have to get used to this," she warned me. "We're a small and very close community. A single English woman, on the ferry, with two big suitcases...and nobody has a reservation for her to stay anywhere... Well, you'll get noticed."

I swallowed, and Greetje patted my hand. "It's not as bad as it sounds. We're nice people here, we look out for each other. And when I saw you coming down the road with your suitcases, I hoped you'd stop by. Else I would have found you somehow. You know, for a gossip and some news about your own island..."

Before I could reply to this invitation, my tummy gave a really loud rumble.

"How terribly rude of me," Greetje exclaimed. "You didn't come in here for a chat, you must be hungry. What can I get you?" She proffered a menu which I dutifully perused but couldn't really do very much with.

"What can you recommend?" I asked instead.

"*Nun denn,*" she muttered. "First day on the island...just having come across the sea... How about something traditional?

My *Fischbrötchen* are very good. Bread rolls with fish, with potato salad and greens on the side."

That sounded delightful, and I could feel my mouth watering. I nodded eagerly, temporarily unable to speak.

"And a nice cup of tea?" Greetje wrote it down, shooting me a quick glance by way of confirmation.

I nodded again. "Heavenly," I concurred, assuming that she was making a concession to my own island heritage.

"Comin' right up," Greetje issued energetically and in a surprisingly authentic accent, jumping to her feet swiftly. I settled back and let things happen.

Within a couple of minutes, Greetje was a back with a tray laden with food. The *Fischbrötchen* was without a doubt the most enormous helping of fish roll that I had ever seen. On a separate plate, there was a lovely fresh green salad and a heap of potato salad.

"Tuck in," Greetje encouraged, seeing my hungry look. "I'll bring your tea through as well. Mind if I join you in having lunch?" She was off again before I could respond. She was definitely my kind of person, and I felt drawn to her forthrightness and her cheer.

Greetje returned once more with her own lunch and with a tray bearing a big teapot, two cups and saucers, a dish of amber-colored lumps that had to be sugar, and a pitcher of milk. She sat down and smiled at me. I couldn't speak as I was greedily eating.

"Hope you don't mind?" Greetje reiterated once more, seeking final confirmation. I swallowed and cleared my mouth.

"No, of course not, it's lovely to chat. But aren't you busy?"

Greetje laughed again. She laughed a lot, this wonderful woman.

"Not at the moment," she explained. "The hungry fishermen have been and gone. They come before they go out to sea. My Klaus is one of them, you see? They'll be back again much later. And passing trade? *Ja*, the locals will come for their *Fischbrötchen* in a little while, but there aren't many tourists at this time of year. So, I have a moment. Just for you."

She looked at me expectantly, and of course I didn't know what to say. But Greetje proved intuitively tactful. She didn't ask me what brought me here. Instead, she focused on the practicalities. Regarding my stacked luggage, she presented another opening gambit.

"I gather you're not just here for the day…" she stated rather than asked. "Do you know where you would like to stay yet? I mean, have you read any of our lovely brochures?"

I shook my head sheepishly, deciding to trust this woman and offer a small part of my story.

"No," I conceded. "I just sort of got here. I didn't really know that I was coming." Greetje received this somewhat unconventional statement with a gleeful rubbing of her hands.

"A modern-day adventuress," she said jubilantly, "how exciting. So. What's your aim? Are you looking for the luxury break?"

I took a deep breath. Here was my opening. "Not really a luxury break, no. I was hoping to find somewhere for a few weeks, a little cottage, or even a flat," I amended hastily, suddenly overcome with fear that a cottage would be way outside my means.

Greetje regarded me with knowing eyes. "A few weeks, huh?"

I nodded, not augmenting this information at this time.

She waggled her head from side to side and passed her hand across her forehead. Evidently she had some kind of proposition up her sleeve and was debating whether to verbalize it or not. Not, for the moment at least. "A cottage?" she asked by way of confirmation. "As in, a cottage-cottage or one with all the mod-cons?"

I gave an involuntary snort at her surprise use of the term "mod-cons."

"Your English is really so much better than my pitiful German," I couldn't resist praising her. "And yes, a cottage-cottage would do. I don't need all the mod-cons. Although," I paused reflectively. "Running water would be good, I guess. And electricity."

This caused an explosion of laughter.

"You're in the wrong century, my girl." Greetje flowed over with mirth. "Running water and electricity." She had to pause as she was overcome again with the giggles. "Of *course* you shall have running water and electricity. I'll even throw in central heating and a fitted kitchen. By mod-cons I meant things like whirlpool-baths with heated towel-rails, built-in wardrobes and Wi-Fi and that kind of stuff."

She calmed down and had a bite to eat. Lifting the lid off the teapot, she had a good long, look, and announced, "Tea's ready."

"Wonderful," I sighed. "May I?" I greedily reached for the pot, but a loud shriek of dismay made my hand freeze mid-move.

"*Halt, halt, halt.*" Greetje shook her head sternly, but still smiling. "This isn't how we do it over here. We have our own little ceremony."

She picked up a little pair of tongs that I hadn't noticed before and dropped three amber lumps into both cups. "*Kluntje,*" she explained as she went. "Rock sugar, I believe you'd call it." I shook my head, indicating I didn't know.

"Kluntje first, then tea," Greetje kept up her commentary. She placed a little sieve on top of my cup and poured the tea through it, collecting tea leaves in the sieve. Finally, she repeated the same for her own cup.

"Now, cream," she concluded and dumped a healthy dollop of cream in our cups.

Cream, mind, not milk. I looked around for a spoon and enterprisingly took one off the table as there were none with our cups.

Greetje chortled under her breath. "We don't stir. No teaspoon needed," she remarked, and took a gulp of her own tea.

"But the sugar is all the way at the bottom," I protested.

"And it is meant to be so," Greetje interjected hastily as my teaspoon remained threateningly poised above my cup. "This is an experience. Your first taste, it has to be plain and bitter. You have the cream at the next taste. And finally, the sweetness of the sugar waits for you at the very end, rounding the drink off with a sensational…sensation."

Well, when in Langeoog, do as the natives do. I took a sip but stopped mid-swallow. Ugh, that was bitter. Greetje erupted in laughter *again*.

"Your face—" she giggled, "—it's priceless. Go on, have another sip. You'll hit the cream next."

I did as instructed and sure enough, things improved dramatically as the cream made an entrance. I gulped greedily, feeling unbelievable thirsty. And wouldn't you know it, right at the end there came a big hit of sugar.

"Welcome to the proper tea ritual," Greetje smiled. "Bitter, creamy, and sweet. That's life, and that's how the tea should be. Another cup?"

I nodded eagerly. Strange it might be, but I could get used to it. Greetje poured us both a second cup, then returned to the business of homing me.

"So, a cottage for Sophie," she mused. "Hm."

I said nothing. I had a distinct feeling she had something in mind.

"There is a cottage..." she started, throwing me an inquiring look.

I gave a slight nod; *go on*.

"It's a little bit outside of the village, but it's beautiful. It's part of a row of cottages right by the dunes. It's got everything you need, even telephone and Internet. It's only —"

I was hanging by the edge of my seat. What was the catch? I was totally hooked, I had visions of thatched roofs and little white roses — wrong season for those obviously, but hey, I knew I wanted this cottage. What was the problem with it?

"What is it?" I finally burst out. "Just tell me."

"*Ach*, it's a bit remote; you know, cut off."

Remote and cut off didn't matter to me, on the contrary. I let that pass and tackled ownership instead. "So...do you own the cottage?"

"Yes, yes, we do. My husband and I. It was my mother's and she left it to us. We rent it out to holiday makers."

"How much is it?" I asked, ever blunt. Might as well get the evil business over and done with; I didn't want to get excited and find I couldn't afford it. Greetje quoted me a figure that was so ludicrous I nearly spat out my tea.

"Six hundred Euro? Is that all?" I did a rapid calculation in my head. That was only just over five hundred pounds. You couldn't get a shed for that money in London, let alone a cottage. "You've got to be kidding," I threw at her once I recovered.

She smiled, and shook her head. "It's off season and nobody else wants it. You'll be paying me normal rent, not holiday rent. So no, I'm not kidding," she confirmed and added, cryptically, "but it *is* cold."

She was letting it dead cheap because it was *cold?* Somewhat hesitantly, I had to find out, "How cold is cold? I mean, will I permanently freeze, or just have to keep the heating on all the time?"

Now it was Greetje's turn to look perplexed. "It's not cold, as such. It's very cozy. But we're letting it cold."

I was still mystified. "You're letting it cold—so I'm not allowed to put the heating on?"

Greetje finally understood. "Silly me," she started to clarify. "I am mistranslating what I mean. In German, when you 'let a house cold,' it means that bills for heating and hot water are extra. If you let a house 'warm,' it means everything is included."

A light bulb went on over both our heads as we grasped our mutual misunderstanding. "Of course you may turn the heating on," Greetje wheezed with laughter, now fully comprehending my dilemma. "That's totally up to you."

Whilst chatting away like long lost friends, we had finished our absolutely delicious meal and put away three cups of tea each. Time had marched on, and lo and behold, the local lunch crowd started arriving bit by bit. Greetje suggested that I should put my suitcases in back for an hour, have another walk around the village, perhaps buy some groceries, and afterwards she would take me to my new home to see if I would indeed like it. So much kindness and accommodation nearly overwhelmed me, and I couldn't help giving her a little impromptu hug by way of thanks. She didn't expect it, but accepted it in the spirit intended and gave me a big smile.

"You'll be fine here, you wait and see," she uttered, as though she could see right into my heart and my head.

An hour later, I returned to the tea shop with a bagful of essential groceries. Milk, bread, butter, jam, cheese, salami, pasta, tinned tomatoes, a couple of pizzas, a few things to tide me over for a day or two. When I walked through the door, Greetje swiftly flipped the "open" sign to say "closed" and stuck a note underneath. "Back in ten minutes," she translated for me, taking me through to the kitchen and out the back door into a yard. There, parked in a little corner and plugged into a power supply, was a dinky little electric van, vaguely resembling a traditional milk float.

"I didn't think there were cars here on the island?" I questioned her curiously.

"There aren't, as such, but some of us have little electric runarounds. You know, to get supplies to and from the ferry, and all that. Here, I've already put your luggage in, look." She pointed to the back of the van and sure enough, there were my pink and turquoise suitcases. "I'll run you to the house, save you walking all that distance with those suitcases. And me." she grinned. "It *is* a little bit out of the way."

Somewhat unexpectedly but entirely welcome, I got a ride in an electric van. Down the road we puttered, left, then right and left again, following the curve of the dunes, passing what looked like a school and a mini hospital or something; then left, right, left and right again; I was thoroughly lost.

"Don't worry," Greetje instructed. "There is a map with directions—in English, too—in the cottage, and you'll easily find your way back. Did I mention there are a couple of bikes, also? So you don't have to walk all the time."

She shot me an inquiring look. "You do know how to ride a bike, right?"

"'Course I do," I assured her, inwardly smiling. This was getting better and better.

Chapter Forty-Seven

Just when I thought the dune road wasn't going anywhere, a little row of cottages came into view. They were nestled in amongst a few low trees and on the inland side of the road relative to the dunes, but they looked adorable. They had a steep hipped roof with red clay tiles and the pretty adornments typical of the island, judging by what I had seen so far. There seemed to be three cottages and, as Greetje slowed down, it appeared one of them was to be mine.

Greetje deftly pulled the van into a narrow driveway in front of the last cottage, the one furthest from the village. It had a white front door, and white mullioned windows including a couple of dormers, and it looked simply adorable. The house of my dreams bar the white roses.

"This is it," Greetje announced, sensing my excitement. "*Na Huus.*"

"*Na Huus,*" I repeated, noticing at the same time that these words were written above the front door. "What does it mean?" I asked.

"Homeward bound," was Greetje's answer, and it gave me goosebumps. I had the uncanny feeling as though the earth moved beneath me, just for a second, and I held on to the van for support.

"Are you all right?" Greetje's voice was full of sudden concern.

"Fine," I smiled. "It's just that the name is so apt."

"Isn't it just?" Greetje acknowledged, choosing to bypass the emotion in my comment. "Let's have a look inside."

Inside, it was perfect. Everything was small but perfect. The front door gave straight into an open plan downstairs, with a fitted kitchen tucked to the right, and a lounge area on the left with a fireplace and two squashy sofas. At the back, a staircase led upstairs, where I found an adorable bedroom as well as a small bathroom. I clocked the shower, but it was the bedroom that had me rapt. It was a dormer room, dominated by a big, comfy-looking bed done out in white linen but adorned by a beautiful colorful patchwork quilt. A big oak wardrobe rested in one corner, and a rocking chair with colorful cushions stood by the window. It was wonderful. Without thinking, I went across and opened the old-fashioned windows, pushing both wings out as far as they would go and securing them with the metal hooks. The salty tang of sea air and dunes rushed into the room and I breathed deeply. And yes! I could hear the rushing of the sea on the other side of the dunes. I would sleep here; I would sleep well.

Greetje stood by the door and observed me silently, a smile playing on her kind face.

"You like it," she stated when I turned back to her.

"I do," I said simply.

"I will leave you now. Maybe I will see you later," Greetje suggested. "Or maybe you will have some rest first, yes?"

I couldn't quite believe my luck, and questions came bubbling out before Greetje could leave. Yes, she confirmed with a laugh, I could really have this place. At the price she had suggested. No, no need to pay her now, I wasn't going anywhere, was I? We could settle the first month's rent next time I saw her. No, she didn't have anybody else lined up, and yes, I could stay as long as I wanted. Now, would I please stop worrying? Greetje gave me an affectionate pat on the shoulder as she pressed the keys for "Na Huus" into my hand.

"The electricity is on, there are directions for hot water and heating in the kitchen, and the bike is in a shed in the garden. I must away, I have some more *Fischbrötchen* to sell."

And thus she departed, leaving me to sit in my new, if temporary, home, marveling at fate. I took another tour of the cottage, delighting in all the little details, and I also inspected the garden. I locked up and followed a random path across the dunes, finding to my intense pleasure that I was mere seconds from a beautiful sea view.

Back at my temporary home, I braved the oven to heat a pizza, ran a bath, and climbed into my new bed, leaving the windows as wide open as I dared. The air grew cold at night, but I was warm and snug under my industrial strength continental Eiderdown duvet, and so I slept.

And slept.

And slept. I slept for the best part of two days. I slept like I had never slept before. It seemed as though I was catching up on a lifetime's worth of lost sleep.

Of course I got up to use the bathroom and to make myself cups of tea or something to eat. But every time, I found myself irresistibly drawn back to bed. I took a book each time, but without fail, I fell asleep.

I was still in bed two days later, and probably would have carried on like this for another couple of days, when Greetje came to see if I was still alive.

The first thing I knew about her arrival was a cheerily shouted "Yoohoo" floating up the stairs and through the door into my bedroom. Initially, I thought I was dreaming but the voice was vaguely familiar.

Next, there were light footfalls on the stairs, and I knew someone was coming. I was still half asleep, cozy, and warm. Somewhere deep down, the rules of social decorum informed me that I ought to get up. But I simply couldn't obey, so I resolutely stayed in bed.

Greetje's face appeared at the doorframe, smiling initially, then crinkling with concern.

"Sophie!" she exclaimed. "Are you all right? It is the middle of the day."

Was it really lunchtime? I cast a glance onto the bedside table where my mobile phone did a stand-in act for an alarm clock. Incidentally, it couldn't find a network out here so it was very much out of action as far as mobile phone services went. It read twelve thirty-four p.m. Lunchtime indeed.

I sat up wearily, rubbing my eyes and yawning widely.

"I am so sorry," I mumbled, hastily covering my mouth with my hand lest I should frighten Greetje away with my doggie breath.

"Are you okay?" she repeated, and I nodded by way of response, although I could feel myself welling up. *Silly me*. I *was* okay, I was feeling better than I had done for weeks. Just very tired.

"I don't know what the matter is with me," I tried to joke lightly, although I could hear the effort in my own voice.

Greetje put down her bag and sat on the edge of my bed. She looked at me, waiting for me to talk.

"I—" I started, but realized I didn't have a clue where to begin.

"You're running away from someone," Greetje started for me. "It's obvious," she stated, as though this was meant to reassure me. "You arrive here alone, call no one, speak to no one, don't send any postcards, keep yourself to yourself, and I find you're still in bed." Her tone was gently admonishing before she changed tack. "We're all guessing why you're running, and who from. You're the big mystery, quite the talk of the island."

I closed my eyes. *Great.* I had come here for anonymity and put myself right in the center of attention. Greetje's next question caught me so unawares, I nearly fell out of bed.

"Did he hit you?"

My eyes snapped wide open and locked with hers, full of concern.

"What? Who? Hit? No!" I let out a wail of frustration at this complete misinterpretation of my circumstances. "No, it wasn't like that. Not at all, on the contrary—oh God, you're going to think me such a wuss."

"A wuss?"

"A person who is sad and pathetic for no concrete reason," I qualified.

"Ah. Well. If you are this wuss, the person who is sad and pathetic for no particular reason, I suggest you get yourself showered and dressed while I fix some lunch. And then you will tell me, so I can put an end to all the speculation and gossip. And you will become better."

Her tone allowed no argument, and I found I quite enjoyed being bossed about by this kind woman. I did as instructed—I had a hot shower and got dressed in jeans and a jumper for the first time since arriving. While the effort exhausted me, I did feel better for being up and about.

When I came downstairs, Greetje had set out the ubiquitous *Fischbrötchen*-and-potato-salad lunch and I fell unto it hungrily. Greetje ate, too, but mostly watched me with barely contained curiosity. Eventually, when I had finished, she pushed the plates to one side, propped her feet on a spare chair, and commanded, "Tell."

My first sentence surprised me as much as her.

"I guess you could say I had a little breakdown," I announced, bursting into tears of self-pity while laughing at myself at the same time. The effect was not pretty, and Greetje hastily passed me a tissue.

"A breakdown," she repeated matter-of-factly when I had overcome my little outburst.

"Yup. I guess that's what you'd call it. I told you I was a wuss."

"A breakdown is neither sad nor pathetic," Greetje informed me calmly. "I don't know why you would even think that. There must have been a lot of stress involved."

"Yeah, well…not to the outside observer, I don't think," I muttered darkly. "Really, this is all a storm in a teacup."

"Good. That's a good perspective to have, now. It means you're getting over it all. But you must have been pretty stressed to start with, and that's all that matters. Do you want to talk about it?"

I had nothing to lose, so I told all. "Do you know," I concluded, "seeing them together *like that* sent me over the edge. I lost all sense of reality. It sounds so stupid now, so unnecessary. But I felt that I couldn't go on with it all. I wanted to run away like I've never wanted to run away before in my entire life. I wanted to be somewhere where none of this would matter, and where I could think about everything."

Greetje nodded thoughtfully, but still I continued. "It seems so…I don't know, so extreme now. But it made perfect sense on that Monday. I went home and crashed, and the next morning I rang my Mum, and cried and cried. She listened to everything; I guess she'd seen it all coming. I said I wanted to run away and she said, totally casually, 'Then why don't you?'"

I sniffed at the recollection, and Greetje gave a little laugh. "Your Mum is a wise person."

"You think?" I retorted. "I thought she'd gone mad. I thought she was playing devil's advocate. But she was serious. She said, why didn't I take some time out to get away from it all for a while? She suggested making some arrangements so I wouldn't lose my job or my flat or anything. She called it 'a safe runner'. She kept saying, 'what's keeping you?' and I didn't have a good answer."

"Does she know you're here?" Greetje interrupted properly for the first time. "Because if she doesn't, she might be worried sick."

I smiled. "I called her every day while I was running scared. From the train station in London and in Brussels, from Hamburg, and from Bensersiel. I told her I was coming here, but I haven't had a chance to ring her since."

"Well, you must ring her as soon as we're done," Greetje told me firmly. "She'll be going out of her mind. But before that, finish your story. You've got me hanging on here."

"Well…" I pondered. "First of all, I went into the office after I spoke with Mum and I talked with my editor. I said I wanted to resign. I insisted, but he refused to let me go. A 'sabbatical' was the best he could do for me, he said." I snorted with disbelief at my own tale when I related the bizarre situation.

"We agreed I would leave until the end of the year. The sabbatical is unpaid but I'm going to write a few features here or there." I shrugged. "It's not much of an income but I'll muddle through, and I have a job to go back to next year. I put the flat on the market with a lettings agent. I managed to find a removals company that could collect my stuff and put it into storage. It's amazing, really, how quickly one can unravel one's life if one has to. I took the last Eurostar that day to Brussels before I could change my mind. I found a hotel by the station and checked in, but I couldn't sleep. So I used their computer to do a bit of Internet searching. I wanted to go to somewhere far away, unusual, remote, isolated. I found a reference to a car-free island in the German North Sea and I had a look and I loved the sight of it all. So, I booked myself on a flight to Hamburg the next day. I stayed there for a couple of days while I figured out arrangements to come to Langeoog. Last Friday, I took the early train to Bremen, the island bus from Bremen to Bensersiel and the ferry, and you know the rest."

Greetje had listened attentively, and she let out a big sigh when I ground to a halt.

"What an amazing story. It's almost like you're gone with the wind...you know, where the wind blows you. Wow. It's quite romantic, really."

"Romantic?" I laughed. Somehow, I felt a lot better. Cleansed. Lighter. As though I had shed a big load. "I'm not sure about romantic. Insane, mad, and cowardly, perhaps, but not romantic."

"You are too hard on yourself," Greetje contradicted me. "I think you did what everybody dreams of doing every now and then. And you took care while you did it. You didn't run. You..." She searched for an appropriate word. "You performed an emergency exit. Planned, responsible."

I thought this over. Put that way, I sounded almost sane. Rational.

"I didn't tell my friends, though," I observed.

"Hm…" Greetje mused. "Rachel and Dan? Do you think you are accountable to them? Did they deserve to know?"

"Maybe?" I reflected back. "They were my very best friends before it all went wrong. Maybe I ought to have reached out to them. And Steve, especially Steve. But now I can't," I pondered. "What if they change their minds? What if they try to get in touch? And I'm not there?"

"Well, they're going to have to put the effort in and find you, won't they? Now that would be telling, wouldn't it?" she grinned at me, and I grinned back, trying to visualize my three friends on this little island.

"Do you think they will?" Greetje asked hopefully, excited by spinning an intrigue and a continuation of my drama.

"I don't know, Greetje, I just don't know," I sighed.

"I guess we'll find out, with time," she suggested.

"I guess we will," I agreed.

"Now, about this 'nervous breakdown' of yours." Greetje rose from the table and started stacking plates in the dishwasher, all no-nonsense and matter-of-fact.

"Yes?"

"Well, maybe it was one, and maybe it wasn't. You don't strike me as the type. You are too practical, too—how do you say? *Pragmatic*. I haven't seen enough wailing and howling to say that you've had a breakdown. I'd say you were fairly exhausted, but now you're up, and anyway, I need your help, so you have no more time for moping about."

She shut the dishwasher with panache, clapped her hands to indicate that her job was done, and turned to me expectantly. "Are you ready?"

I giggled. Her brash, confident, assuming manner was irresistible. And anyway, I had nothing much to do. Apart from phoning my parents, of course. And maybe checking in with Rick. But that could wait another couple of hours. I wanted to get out of the house. I wanted to walk, laugh, and feel alive.

Chapter Forty-Eight

Greetje had me run errands all over the island for the rest of the day. I delivered a late lunch to her husband down at the little fishing port. From there, I picked up a crate of fresh fish that I could just balance on the back of the bike that Greetje had given me for the purpose, and cycled across to the eastern-most restaurant on the island. Next, it was back to the harbor to collect more fish for Greetje's own kitchen. And so it went on. I suspected that Greetje normally did these chores herself, although she did make it sound as if she was going to struggle without me there. Still, I didn't mind. In fact, I was quite enjoying myself, cycling to and fro on the island on this beautiful autumn day.

The sun was shining, and the sea was all around me. At every stop, I was offered a snack and a cup of tea, and there was no hurry, no rush to do anything, anywhere. My first reaction at the harbor had been to dash off as instructed, but the fishermen would have none of it. I got the grand tour of the boats and a little snack of freshly caught, just boiled tiny pink North-Sea shrimp which were sweet and delicious, if extremely fiddly to peel. At the restaurant in the dunes, I had—you guessed it—the grand tour of the premises, the old cow sheds and dairy, and was offered—you guessed again—a cup of tea and a fat slice of cake.

The day passed quickly, the exercise was refreshing, the air invigorating, and the good cheer and calm demeanor of the wonderful island folk was a tonic for the soul. Out here, nothing much mattered apart from taking care of your life and the lives of your family. So what if a trip to the harbor took me two hours instead of the twenty minutes it could have?

At the end of the day, I fell into bed physically exhausted but mentally relaxed, a wonderful, innocent feeling that I had not known since childhood. This island was working its miracle on me with every step and every breath.

Over the first week—the second week of my official holiday from my job at the paper—I explored the island in every nook and cranny. One day, I got a load of sandwiches from Greetje and did the entire island trail, on foot, which took about six hours. I stopped in various places to rest or eat, and I spent at least an hour watching seals play on the beach. Another day, I took a guided tour of the mudflats, marveling at all the squidgy forms of plant and animal life that were found in this brown and slimy environment. My Mum and Dad laughed at me when I tried to explain over the phone that night, chiding me that as a child grown up by the coast, I should really have been prepared for it all. I even tried horse riding, just for the fun of it, and I had a game of mini-golf even though the place was technically closed for the season. Greetje arranged it.

Greetje arranged that, and several other things. On Thursday, over the now customary joint lunch at the tea shop, she asked me slyly if I would consider helping out in the island school. If perhaps I might be able to teach a little bit of basic English to the kids. The school wouldn't be able to pay much, but there might be a small token salary involved, if I was interested.

Feeling extraordinarily nervous, I went for a mini-interview on Friday and was immediately taken in by this friendly little school. The head teacher wasn't overly concerned by my lack of teaching experience. I wasn't to be a teacher but rather a language assistant; "Worth giving a try, not?"

I started working in the school for two hours every morning the following Monday to get myself established before the October week-long holiday. And as Greetje was working hard to integrate me in the very fabric of the island, I found I was also invited to join the choir and the book club. Several times a week, I had dinner with Greetje's family or some other new friends, working my way through the local delicacies and traditional meals, and occasionally reciprocating by cooking English meals like Toad-in-the-Hole. Greetje took me to her favorite fish restaurant on *Hafenstrasse* and an amazing Italian restaurant near *Hauptstrasse*. I discovered the delights of my nearest baker's shop and took to cycling there every morning to collect my fix of fresh *Brötchen* and crusty brown bread for the day. All of a sudden, I had a busy and fulfilled, but wholly uncomplicated, social life. My German improved at a dramatic rate and I was almost competent at conducting a conversation. With all the goings on, I struggled to keep up with Mum or Dad or even the column I had committed to writing for Rick.

A month into my stay at Langeoog, I felt like I had lived there forever, and I found it hard to envisage ever leaving. I was still alone, but I was never lonely. I felt happy and content, but I also felt like I was on borrowed time. Sooner or later, I knew, things would have to change, and I would have to go back. I only hoped it would be later rather than sooner, and tried to push those thoughts firmly from my mind. *Live for the here-and-now, and let the rest come to you.* That was what everyone was telling me.

PART FIVE: COMING TOGETHER

Chapter Forty-Nine

I was working at the primary school on the Monday morning after the October holiday when I got the first inkling that my game would soon be up. All the primary-age children spent the morning sharing their holiday experiences, and little Mattes was very proud to have been to London. He confirmed that the weird language that I had been introducing them to was indeed what was being spoken "over there," and he said he had even tried the odd phrase and it worked. The children were all delighted by this insight and broke out into excited chatter. The teacher smiled at me, and it was an amazing feeling to realize that I was making a difference to the learning of these gorgeous children.

My little cloud of inner peace and glory wasn't meant to last for long, however. Mattes had brought with him a selection of newspapers for the other children to look and read, and we were all leafing through them together eagerly when I spotted the photo.

My throat closed up with anxiety and I felt dizzy, a clammy sweat springing up on my forehead. It couldn't be. And yet—

I took hold of the entire paper and scanned the banner for the date. It was seven weeks old. My heart beat faster as I tried to work out the implications.

"Miss, are you okay, Miss?" one of the children asked me thoughtfully, and I realized that I had sat down on the floor rather abruptly right in the middle of the pile of papers.

"I'm fine," I tried to smile, "thank you so much for your concern." The child beamed at being thus praised and happily went back to her newspaper. I scanned the room for Mattes, only to discover he was right by me.

"Mattes," I started, my voice coming out dry and raspy. "These are a great find. Just where exactly did you get them, did you say?"

Mattes broke into a proud smile. "The hotel where we stayded," he said in German, and I absent-mindedly noted that he was using an incorrect form of the past tense. "The hotel where we stayded, the lady kept all the papers in a big box for putting into recycled, and she let us take as much as we wanted. Totally for nothing."

"That was very kind of her," I confirmed, mystery of the provenance of this old newspaper solved. However, that still left the mystery of what had happened, and I was desperate to read the article.

"There's something here that reminds me of home," I said, addressing Mattes and the teacher at the same time. "Would it be okay if I took a quick photocopy now before it gets inadvertently destroyed?" The teacher nodded her assent, and Mattes nearly burst with pride at having brought in something so valuable to me.

I got to my feet and, on rather unsteady legs, left the assembly hall to use the photocopier. The paper was shaking in my hand as I was trying to make sense of the words.

There was a rather large picture of Dan and Rachel on the front page. Dan was in full profile but Rachel was caught side-on, as though she had turned away, yet there was no mistaking that it was her. Dan looked angry and Rachel looked dismayed. They appeared to be in a pub. I struggled to understand the caption.

Dan Hunter caught in a pub brawl with another man – over this mystery lady?

Man? What other man?

I gave up walking and sat on the nearest chair. I simply had to read the article or I would expire.

Rock Star in Bust Up, the headline screamed sensationally. I grimaced. Of course it would; this was a tabloid after all.

It was a quiet evening in the Thorny Rose pub in Clapham yesterday night until Dan Hunter, lead singer of legendary rock band Tuscq, provoked a fight with an unknown younger man. The two men were seated at a table with an unknown woman who appeared to be the object of their disagreement. When Mr. Hunter launched into the hands-on fight, plates and cutlery went flying and the young woman fled the scene. Mr. Hunter's opponent suffered a broken nose but no police was called and the fight ended abruptly. Eye witnesses to this extraordinary incident report that the two men and the woman were later seen eating a meal together as though nothing had occurred. The fight appeared to center around the woman. Mr. Hunter's agent stated that the event was staged to promote an upcoming video launch. Mr. Hunter himself refused to comment.

My first reaction was one of sheer professional horror at this extremely bad piece of journalism. Badly written, convoluted and uninformative, it was gossip journalism par excellence. No doubt the facts were jumbled, as well, as I could not for the life of me imagine Dan starting a fight, let alone breaking someone's nose. He was much too controlled and much too aware of his public image to risk something like that. And a publicity stunt? I laughed. Certainly not. That was a red herring.

Nonetheless, there was photographic evidence that a fight had occurred. I looked more closely at the grainy picture, and even though it was a great shock to recognize Steve as the other man, it was all starting to make some weird sense.

Or was it?

I stared out of the window at the breezy sky, knowing in my heart of hearts that this would have marked the beginning of the end of my borrowed time. Evidently, there had been a meeting between Dan, Steve, and Rachel. How they got together, God only knew. Whether Dan and Rachel were still together I didn't dare to speculate. Presumably, Steve had been angry with the two of them. I doubted very much, however, that he had been *fighting* Dan *over* Rachel; although if he had, I resolved to remain on this island for evermore.

Whatever happened that night between those three people, I was certain of one thing. They would have talked about me. They would have realized I had gone. And, knowing them all too well, they would have resolved to find me.

I had been gone from my London life for two months. The so-called pub-brawl between Dan and Steve had taken place on what would have been my very first Saturday night on the island. That had given them plenty of time to do some searching.

A rash of goosebumps spread over my whole body as I considered the ramifications of it all. Should I move on and run again? Or should I wait and let things come to me?

I was interrupted in my musings by the teacher, who had come in search of her missing assistant.

"Are you okay?" she asked with genuine concern. "You look like you've seen a ghost."

I tried a feeble laugh. "I have, in a manner of speaking. I'm sorry, I got completely distracted. That was very unprofessional of me. I'll quickly photocopy this and be right back."

The teacher sat down next to me and put a steadying hand on my arm. "Your morning shift has almost finished anyway. Why don't you make the photocopy and go home? We'll see you again tomorrow, won't we?"

I nodded gratefully, seizing on her offer like a drowning man grabs a life ring. "That would be good," I said, "thank you. And yes, I'll definitely be back in the morning."

Having photocopied the incriminating article, I decided to visit Greetje instead of rushing home.

I found the tea shop closed with a note in the door saying *"Bitte laut klopfen."* I knocked loudly, as instructed. Greetje appeared from behind the counter, quickly let me in, casting a suspicious look up and down the road, and locked up again. She bustled back to the kitchen, where she immersed herself elbow deep in some green vegetable that looked vaguely familiar.

"Are you closed?" I wondered, bemused.

"Not really, but the lunch crowd isn't due yet and everyone else can knock. I'm busy. Today it's *Grünkohl mit Pinkel* for dinner," she explained, seeing my incredulous face at the sight of her pile of green stuff. "It's a regional delicacy, you must come and try it."

"Okay," I laughed, "I will. What, exactly, is it?"

"You'll have to wait and see," Greetje teased me. "Anyway, aren't you supposed to be in school? Did they let you out early today?"

I nodded and waved my photocopied piece of newspaper about. "They did; that's why I came. I needed to talk…"

Greetje continued chopping her vegetables with unbroken vigor. "Talk away, as long as you don't mind if I get on. I need to get this prepped because I can't do it this afternoon and it takes a good couple of hours to cook." She motioned for me to sit down at the table, never once taking her eyes of her work.

I sat down and cleared my throat. "Remember I told you about Dan and Steve and Rachel?" Greetje nodded, so I continued. "Well, it appears that they met up a while back in London, all three of them, and had a bit of a bust-up."

"A bust-up?"

"A bust-up…you know, a fight. With fists. *Fäuste*." I tried to clarify, waving my fists about.

"Oh, okay. I see. What about?" Greetje was listening intently.

"I'm not sure, the article doesn't really say. And it doesn't actually matter. What matters is…"

Greetje spun round, pointing at me with her knife and startling me immensely. "They probably talked about you," she cried.

I simply nodded. What else could I say?

"*Ach Du je*," Greetje exclaimed and sat down with me, still clutching her knife in one hand and taking the paper from me with the other. "This is serious, huh?" She scanned the article and took a good look at the picture.

"He's handsome, your Dan," she pronounced.

I smiled sadly. "He's not *my* Dan anymore. And anyway, what about your Grunkohl?"

"Grünkohl," Greetje automatically corrected my poor pronunciation of the umlaut. "It'll have to wait a couple of minutes." She returned her attention to the article. "When was this written?"

"Seven weeks ago."

"So. That means they've had quite a bit of time to get organized, right? And it didn't take them long to notice you'd gone missing. That must make you feel better, not?"

I grinned. "It does, but there's a lot of supposition in there. We don't even know what this is all about."

"Yes, but it stands to reason that it's connected to you. There are three people here who would not normally meet, right?"

"Well, yes, I suppose so," I conceded, pouncing on my own choice of words. "See—I told you it's full of supposition."

"Rubbish, leave me alone with your supposings. Hm." She looked pensive, as though she was withholding something.

"Greetje," I prodded her on the arm. "What is it? What are you not telling?"

Instead of responding, she waggled her head from side to side as if weighing things in her mind.

"Greetje!" I insisted. "What is it?"

She very cautiously got up and placed her sharp chopping knife on a board by the sink. She washed her hands and dried them meticulously at one of her ubiquitous white-and-blue checked cloths. Finally, having run out of displacement activities, she sat down again.

"I was going to tell you a little later but…maybe now is a good time."

"Tell me what?" I prompted.

Greetje rubbed her face with her hands, clearly unsettled by something. She took a deep breath and exhaled slowly.

"It may be nothing, but this morning in the tea shop, a man was asking questions about you. In English."

Talk about dropping a bombshell. My ears started burning and I had that weird hard feeling in my tummy that I got when I heard bad news.

"Are you sure?" was all I could manage in response.

Greetje nodded her head. "Sure. He was quite specific, and he even had your photo."

My *photo*? I gasped, aghast. "Oh my God. Who was he?"

Greetje picked up the article again and examined the photograph carefully. "Well, he wasn't Dan or Steve, if that's what you're asking."

"Then who?" I prompted.

Greetje shrugged. "Maybe they engaged a private detective."

A private detective? This was getting worse and worse.

Greetje saw the shock and confusion on my face and decided to offer a positive outlook. "They must have hit rock bottom when they couldn't find you, and they must have really wanted to find you. Right?"

I stared at her blankly. I supposed that was one way of looking at it.

"I didn't tell him anything, of course, and he won't have gotten anything from anyone else. He didn't speak any German. Talk about a lousy choice of private investigator. And it's a good job the cottage is so far out, huh?" Greetje was rather pleased with herself for managing things so well on my behalf.

"What *did* you say?" I needed to know.

"Well, he was asking questions of my customers, who were very uncomfortable with being thus assaulted, I can tell you." Greetje gave me her best officious voice. "So naturally I asked him to leave. He thrust your picture in my face and asked me if I had seen you. Well, you know I'm totally far-sighted so of course I couldn't see anything on the photo at all, and I said no, I hadn't."

"And then?"

"And then he left before I could throw him out."

"And *then?*"

Greetje smiled a big beaming smile. "Well, Klaus was there while this was happening. So he declared, to no one in particular, that there was no Sophie on the island, and no one fitting your description. And of course the other folks nodded, and left in great haste." She patted my hand reassuringly. "It'll have been all over the island within minutes. You're safe." Her telephone rang in the shop, and she jumped to answer it. I couldn't hear the conversation, but it didn't last long, and she looked very happy indeed when she came back.

"That was Folke from the ferry. Mystery man has given up and is on the way back to Bensersiel."

Even though I had had several weeks of getting used to the island's unbelievable communication network, my mouth hung open in surprise. "How on earth did Folke know that you would want to know when this particular chap was leaving?"

Greetje merely grinned. "Folke was in the shop this morning," she stated simply. "I think you are safe, for now. We haven't given you away."

I shook my head to clear my thoughts. "I'm sure you haven't, thank you. But anyway, I think I need to go home and have a quiet think. It's all a bit much to take in."

"You do that," Greetje agreed, "and don't forget, dinner is at six."

"At six," I repeated.

Chapter Fifty

My mind was reeling as I walked home to the cottage. So they *were* looking for me. Did I want to be found? I supposed the answer was yes; otherwise I would have to run again.

So was this whole time-out-adventure merely a big test, to see if my friends wanted me back and wanted to make up? I sat down on a bench overlooking the dunes to mull this over.

No, I concluded. My time out had been about more than that. My time out had been about me, not them. Ultimately, I had always planned to go back some time before Christmas. Certainly in the New Year.

"But if I allowed for the possibility that they *might* find me..." I talked to myself, "then surely there's no need to run now." And all of a sudden, I knew what I had to do.

I raced back to the cottage, collected my bike, and cycled into town to do some shopping. I bought party food—sausages, crisps, smoked salmon, cream cheese. I stocked up on fresh pizza and fresh fish. I bought wine and champagne. Anna at the checkout looked at me with raised eyebrows.

"Are you expecting company?" she asked, ever curious.

"I am, Anna, I am," I shot back happily, but refused to engage in further conversation. I piled my goodies high in the basket of my bike and pedaled home excitedly.

When I returned to the cottage for the second time, I stopped dead in my tracks, skidding the bike on the gravelly path. The light in the kitchen was on. In fact, it had been on when I had come to take the bike, but I been too distracted to pay much attention to this weird fact.

However, I was absolutely certain that I hadn't left it on this morning.

So.

It was extremely unlikely that I had been burgled. The crime rate on this lovely island was practically nil, and everybody knew that I hadn't brought much worth stealing anyway. There had only been one reported odd stranger lately, and while he had been snooping, I doubted he would have been stealing. But he had certainly paid me a visit.

My heart pounded anxiously in my chest as I contemplated my options. I parked the bike by the fence and did a slow walk around the cottage. All the windows and doors were shut and locked. There was no sign of forced entry.

I cupped my face with my hands and pressed it against the lounge window—nobody there. Same with the kitchen.

Was I brave enough to go inside? I decided to have a try. I unloaded the bike, piling the shopping neatly by the front door, and leaned the bike against the front fence, pointing outwards and ready to go for a quick escape, should I need one.

Thus prepared, I gingerly unlocked the front door and pushed it open. "Hello!" I shouted. "If you're in there, I'm back. I'm going to call the police."

Nothing.

I entered, feeling unbelievably stupid, and did a quick tour of the downstairs. I just about managed to resist the urge to peek around doorjambs with my finger-gun loaded and aiming at any prospective intruders. Nonetheless, a long diet of watching crime dramas on the telly prompted me to shout, "downstairs clear, going up."

I tiptoed upstairs, trying to hear whether there were any suspicious sounds.

Nothing.

Five minutes later, I was back downstairs, confident now that I was alone. I barricaded myself in, locking all windows and the front door *just in case*, even though I was certain that it had been Mr. Private Detective who had performed a totally unlawful breaking and entering on my rented property.

I knew that because he had made one mistake. One tiny mistake. Two, actually, if you counted leaving the light on.

He had double locked the door.

And I *never* double locked the door. Never. Ever. I was simply too lazy.

Mr. Private Detective hadn't paid attention when he had picked my lock, and I hadn't realized the significance of needing two turns of the key when I first unlocked, but now it all fit together.

I sat down with shaky legs, but got up again to make myself a swift cuppa.

"Well, well, well," I said to myself, not knowing what else to say. I had never been the subject of a private investigation before. In a weird way, it was exciting. It made me feel important, and clandestine — like a heroine in a movie or a book.

What was next, I wondered? Now that my three musketeers knew where I was, what would they do with that information?

A certainty popped into my head. They wouldn't ring, or write, or email. They knew I wasn't going to respond, and they would worry that I would disappear again. The only logical answer would be a surprise visit.

How long, I wondered, before Steve would turn up here? Or Dan? Or Rachel? Or would all three of them make the trip?

Who had hired the private detective? It had to have been either Steve or Dan; somehow, it wasn't Rachel's style. But sleeping with Dan wasn't her style either, so what did I know?

I brushed that thought aside determinedly. If they had made the effort to find me, and if they took the trouble of actually coming out here...if they really turned up, I would welcome them, and I would hear them out.

Perhaps Rachel and Dan only had this one encounter. Perhaps they were an item now. Either way, I could see now, with the benefit of time and distance and perfect hindsight, that they deserved to be heard; they were my best friends. Even though I had felt extremely betrayed and hurt, perhaps it wasn't my place to feel thus.

I blushed deeply as I recalled my reaction. It all seemed so futile now, so silly, superfluous. I had totally overreacted. From where I was now, it didn't seem important anymore. Living on this tiny island, in this very different environment with different needs and priorities and a down-to-earth outlook on life *had* done me good. I had regained a sense of perspective that I had lacked, so wrapped up in my make-believe London disasters.

I sighed. I guessed I would have a lot of explaining to do of my own, and quite a bit of apologizing.

Talking of! How would I ever apologize to Steve? How would I find words that would be adequate? Would he ever forgive me?

With that question, I reached a mental wall and found myself staring into space for quite some time. But once again, I reasoned, if he came, he would be ready to listen; and perhaps he would understand and forgive.

Chapter Fifty-One

Naturally, I fell over my shopping as I left the house to go to Greetje's for dinner. In my brave effort at reclaiming my home and my ensuing ruminations on life, friendship and forgiveness, I had completely forgotten that I had left the bags on the front steps. Cursing my forgetfulness, I stored the shopping as quickly as possible in the fridge. I had been running late *before* this unexpected hold-up, having had a long bath and an unscheduled nap, and I knew that dinner would be practically on the table by the time I would arrive at Greetje's house. She was relaxed about many things, but when she set a time for dinner, she expected people to be there.

I pedaled like I had never pedaled before, taking at breakneck speed potholes that I couldn't see properly by the meager light from my bike-lamp but falling off only once. I arrived in the nick of time, albeit sweaty and out of breath. Greetje's fisherman husband Klaus, their two sons *and* their wives and young children were already at table, while Greetje was handling a big, steaming tureen full of an aromatic green vegetable stew. There was no time for idle chit-chat and, having my offers of help firmly declined, I made for the dinner table.

Sitting down expectantly between Klaus and Greetje's empty chair, I eyed the dish suspiciously. Everybody else was full of high spirits and keen to tuck in, but I was feeling a little uncertain.

Grünkohl had turned out to be curly kale, according to my trusty dictionary. I had heard of curly kale, of course, had even seen it in the supermarket once or twice, but couldn't recall ever having eaten it. It smelled fantastic. My mouth watered and my tummy rumbled in anticipation. Greetje put a huge dish of traditional German fried potatoes on the table and we were ready to go.

Being the guest, it was my turn first. I was given an enormous helping of golden fried potatoes, a big ladle of *Grünkohl*, and two fat sausages. It all looked amazing. So far, so good.

That left the somewhat disconcerting issue of the *Pinkel*. I had looked that up as well, of course.

Pinkel was a noun, meaning something like "snob" or "toff." Now, I couldn't really see that the German people would resort to boiling up and serving for dinner the snobs or toffs of the male species. So I had looked a little further down the page and encountered the verb associated with *Pinkel.*

If anything, that was even more disturbing. *Pinkeln* meant "to pee."

Nobody had noticed my hesitation. There was almost complete silence around the table as everybody else tucked in and even the kids were eating with gusto.

Now I had heard about some strange customs in my time but certainly they wouldn't... they couldn't...

Nah.

I speared a fried potato to get myself going before trying the *Grünkohl*. It was amazing. It was by far the best vegetable I had ever tasted in my entire life. Dark green, almost the color of a ripe olive, juicy, succulent, slightly tangy —

Oh God! I choked on my mouthful. Tangy.

Right on cue, Greetje smiled at me. "You haven't tried your *Pinkel* yet," she said encouragingly.

I hadn't? I cleared my throat.

"What exactly is *Pinkel*?" I whispered.

"The sausage," Greetje replied cheerfully, cutting off a fat slice of her own. Clear and fragrant juices were running out of it and quickly soaking into the fried potatoes.

Finally noticing my discomfiture, Greetje lowered her fork and looked at me inquisitively. Her eyes darted between my half-raised fork and my furrowed brow, and she burst out laughing. She laughed so hard that her whole body shook and she had to steady herself against the table. Wiping tears of mirth from her eyes, she eventually managed to speak.

"You looked up 'Pinkel' in your dictionary, didn't you?" she issued, valiantly fighting the urge to belly laugh.

I nodded, sheepishly.

She giggled compulsively again. Her family was mystified, their English not being quite as fluent as Greetje's. Klaus spoke up, asking for an explanation, and Greetje rapid-fired her answer back at her assembled family. Within seconds, they were all exploding into hysterics, and Greetje was patting me on the arm to reassure me that their mirth was good-natured and that they were laughing with me, not at me. Even though I wasn't quite sure yet what was so funny, I found myself drawn in by their hilarity and for a good few minutes, everybody was convulsing helplessly with great gales of laughter.

When eventually we all calmed down, I inquired as to the exact nature of *Pinkel*. Greetje speared another piece of sausage and waved it in my face.

"This," she clarified exultantly, "this is *Pinkel*. It's a type of smoked sausage with belly pork and oats and lots of herbs. No pee, though."

I blushed again at my foolish assumption and made a big show of eating a fat piece of sausage. It was unexpected, quite grainy, but absolutely delicious.

"You cook the sausage with the cabbage, you see," Greetje elaborated. "That gives the dish its fabulous flavor."

I nodded, too busy chewing to waste any time on talking. Now that I had the taste of it, I couldn't get enough of it. Everybody else got back to eating, too, and silence prevailed until we all had our fill. I had seconds, and feeling gross and greedy, I even had thirds.

When we were clearing up after dinner, Greetje raised the subject of the private detective man snooping around and asked me whether I was okay. I filled her in on the events of the rest of the afternoon and told her that I thought I was looking forward to seeing my friends again. Greetje looked at me with those kind and wise eyes of hers.

"Good," she pronounced. "That is good that you feel that way. It makes me glad. It is time for you to make up with your life, and your friends."

Her astute assessment brought a lump of emotion to my throat, and I swallowed hard. "Do you think they will come?" I asked, looking for affirmation.

"I should think so, don't you?" Greetje replied, as I had hoped, while she was placing leftovers into little dishes ready to go in the fridge. "Why else bother?"

"That's what I thought," I conceded. "I guess now I'll have to wait."

Chapter Fifty-Two

The next few days passed in a blur of anticipation. I had allowed a day for the investigator to return to London and make his report, another couple of days for any travelers to make arrangements, and another day for them to actually get here. Therefore, four days after the appearance of Mr. Private Detective, I was braced for the big reunion. But the hours passed and the day drew to a close without incident. I felt a tiny stab of fear—had I miscalculated? Were they not coming?

Greetje didn't bring the subject up again, but I knew she was watching and waiting with me, on standby for assistance if need be. By the following Monday, I was beginning to give up hope and, in unspoken agreement, the subject of my friends' arrival was not discussed between Greetje and me. I felt a little bit hurt, but I also felt like perhaps I was getting my comeuppance. I was the one who had vanished. Why should they come running after me?

Or maybe, my rational voice supplied, *they need a little bit of time to make arrangements.*

As speculation was fruitless, I decided to carry on with my island life as best I could. The weather had changed dramatically, and a cold, steady wind was howling in off the North Sea night and day. The fishermen still went out, but they were watching the sky with frowns and expressions of concern. The weather forecast warned of a big weather front brewing out in the North Sea, bringing the potential for hurricane-style storms. The notion sent shivers of excitement through me. I was partial to a bit of natural drama, and there was nothing I liked more than the thought of a terrific storm. All within reason, of course—I didn't want anyone to get hurt or anyone's house or possessions to get damaged. But I loved the idea of wild, unbridled winds, of waves crashing against the beach and reaching up against the dunes in a foaming, primal, unbreakable rage, of dark skies and howling winds and torrential rains, brazened out in the safety of a warm and dry home, sitting by the fireside, perhaps by flickering candlelight, with hastily prepared thermos flasks of tea and marshmallows to toast on the fire. I had a very romantic notion of what made a good storm.

On the other hand, if the bad weather hit in earnest and disrupted the ferry, then my friends, if they were indeed on their way, wouldn't be able to make it after all. They might be stranded out in Bensersiel for days on end. I prayed fervently that this wouldn't happen.

"Hurry up, you guys," I whispered on a Wednesday night before going to sleep. "Hurry up."

I was woken at five a.m. by rain lashing against the window. Great gusts of wind rattled the frames and at times the entire cottage seemed to shake. I opened the curtains but the island was in darkness and I saw nothing but blackness. I didn't think I had ever seen such blackness before. Leaving the curtains open, I returned to my bed, shivering half with cold and half with delicious anticipation. The storm was here.

I snuggled back under my duvet, savoring its warmth and feeling cocooned and safe. Snoozing on and off, I marveled at the force of nature. At six thirty, I heard the central heating clonk into life and gave a little sigh of relief; the electricity was still working, and I would be warm and dry, never mind the storm outside. Grudgingly, I got up and dressed and ventured downstairs to make myself a cup of tea and some breakfast. By the time I had to leave for school, the rain was falling more heavily than ever. The clouds were so low that it was barely possible to discern where land ended and sky began. Cycling would have been madness, so I walked. I had ferreted around in the storage cupboards downstairs and, lo and behold, found a bright yellow sou'wester with a big, sturdy hood and matching waterproof trousers, beautifully complemented by my own flowery wellies.

Half an hour later, I squelched into school feeling windswept and frozen to the bone. Most of the children and the teachers were already there, having been properly prepared for this kind of eventuality and consequently having left much earlier than usual. The corridors abounded with abandoned kids' wellies. A weird "emergency" atmosphere prevailed, a proud "we won't be beaten by a bit of rain." The normal curriculum was suspended for the day, and the teachers divided their time between recalling emergency procedures for the kids and doing a bit of local history; tales of historic storms and shipwrecks kept the children fascinated through the morning.

I left at lunchtime and made my way to Greetje's tea shop, eager to hear news of the weather and the ferry. Greetje was in high spirits. It appeared that she, like me, was partial to a good storm, and this one was going to be a whopper, a proper *Orkan*.

"This is nothing," Greetje informed me cheerfully. "This is only the *Sturmwehen*... You know, how do you say..." She frowned, searching for a word. "What do you call it when a woman starts having a baby?"

I shook my head, confused. "I don't know...labor? Contractions?"

"*Contractions*," Greetje pounced gleefully. "These are only like contractions. The proper event is yet to come."

"It is?" Now that I found a frightening prospect. How much worse could it get?

"Yes," she confirmed. "We're all... How do you say again? Battening down the doors," she tried.

"The hatches," I corrected automatically.

"The hatches, then," she repeated impatiently. "When the ferry goes again—"

"The ferry goes in this weather?" I interrupted, incredulous.

"No, of course not, silly." Greetje paused in her sandwich making and laughed at me. "But later today, things will calm down for a while, I should think, and tomorrow morning, all being well, the ferry will make a couple of mercy dashes to Bensersiel for people trying to return home, and for provisions, food, that kind of stuff. There's always the quiet before the storm and everybody uses it to get organized. Unless, of course, if there isn't... In which case we'll improvise."

I tried to take all of this in.

"So you're saying this will all go away later and tomorrow the ferry will run and then it'll get *really* bad?"

"Something like that is usually how it happens around here. Hence the idea of *Sturmwehen*, you see? Early warning contractions. Cup of tea?"

I nodded, having become accustomed to the islanders' almost British obsession with cups of tea to remedy any kind of calamity. If Greetje was right, and if my calculations were right and my hopes were granted, there might be one more chance for my friends to get here, tomorrow.

Greetje was still trying to enlighten me on the specific conditions that would brew up a really bad storm on the island. "At the moment, we've got a westerly wind going on and things are pretty rough..." She paused as a gale-force-strength gust caught the windows as though to emphasize her point. "However, the weather forecast says that the wind will shift to the North West through the day tomorrow. On top of that, on Saturday night, there will be a full moon, which will make the high water even higher. So the worst, if there is a 'worst', is to come for Saturday night. It's of course possible that it'll all blow itself out through the rest of today but..." She petered out, unconvinced.

"And why does it all quiet down first?" I asked, ever curious.

"I don't really know," Greetje conceded. "It's what island wisdom says, and it's usually right. Anyway," she moved on briskly, giving me instructions to protect my life and home. Finally dismissed, I made my way back home and busied myself with a long, hot bath. I flicked the heating on low to keep the house warm and investigated the presence of candles and other emergency equipment. My sense of anticipation had become tempered by twinges of fear. It wouldn't be so great to be stuck in this remote cottage all on my own if things got really bad.

But only a few short hours later, Greetje's prediction came true and the wind dropped. Not completely, but significantly. The rain eased off and the day ended on a dull and dreary but thoroughly unspectacular note, like any other November day.

Exhausted by my earlier exposure to wind and rain, and content to stay in with a good book and a stab at writing another column, I holed up for the evening, lighting a few candles, sipping a glass of wine and even laying a small fire in the fireplace.

Chapter Fifty-Three

Friday morning broke quiet and grey. There was a peculiar feeling in my ears as I walked to school—everything was strangely muted and dense, as if the whole island was holding its breath. The children felt it as well. Where they had been excited and animated the previous day, they lounged sullenly and bored on their seats. We tried to jolly them along as best as possible, but I was glad when it was time for me go home.

The call came at two o'clock. It was Greetje, who had just had word from Klaus that Folke the ferry captain had spotted three English people—two men and a woman—buying tickets for the Langeoog ferry at Bensersiel.

I sat down heavily on a chair, giddy with relief.

Greetje's voice was still emanating from the phone. "Sophie?" she was asking. "Are you there? Are you okay?"

"Yes, I'm here," I responded. "Sorry, I had to sit down. I'm okay, though."

"Do you think it's your friends?" Greetje squealed excitedly. "It's got to be them, right?"

"You would think so, wouldn't you?" I mused by way of response. "I mean, how often do three English people randomly turn up on this island at this time of year?"

"Never," Greetje confirmed. "They've not made reservations anywhere, they're simply coming, just like you. Oh, this is so exciting."

I felt my mouth break into a big grin. "It *is* exciting."

"What are you going to do?" Greetje wanted to know.

"I will wait for them here."

"You won't go and meet them at the ferry?" Greetje threw a big spanner in my mental works. I had never considered meeting them at the ferry.

"I hadn't thought about that," I admitted reluctantly. "Do you think it would be a good idea?"

Greetje um'd for a couple of seconds. "I suppose it would let them know that you're welcoming them, not?"

"I suppose it would," I repeated. "But...it would spoil their surprise. I was going to have food ready when they get here, the table laid, candles and all that... like a party."

"Great idea," Greetje enthused. "I like your style. Let them think they're surprising you, and surprise them with a welcome party. Anyway, I must go, there are some customers. But wait, before I hang up... Folke reckons they'll be on the next ferry so they should get here for about four, just so you know."

"Four," I acknowledged. "That's great."

"Be good," Greetje advised. "It'll be fine."

I gulped. "I hope it will," I said in a small voice. After I had hung up, I repeated it to myself, one more time. "I hope it will."

The day carried on like something out of a spy movie, with me being command central and field agents ringing in periodically with vital strategic intelligence. I got a call at three p.m. that the ferry had left Bensersiel with the three English people on it. At half-past five, when I was going quietly mad with worry, Folke called me directly from the harbor, telling me in an excited stage whisper that the three strangers had arrived and were boarding the train.

Thanking him, I hung up and turned to survey my temporary little kingdom. The table was laid, candles ready to be lit, little dishes of nibbles nestling in between the plates. I had blown up and hung balloons all over the kitchen and even found some streamers in the local stationery emporium. I switched on the oven so that the sausages would start cooking and laid out the pizzas on baking trays ready to go in. I arranged the smoked salmon on a plate so that it would have time to come to room temperature, and I put a heap of fresh Langeoog prawns into a serving dish in the fridge, sprinkled with a little drizzle of lemon and a hint of garlic oil.

All the while, I imagined my friends' progress on the island train, their arrival at the station and their route to the cottage. Had Mr. Snoop provided them with a map and instructions, or would they have to brave the locals?

I felt happy and light as a feather. Finally, finally, finally, I would fix everything that had gone wrong before. Whatever it took, I would fix it. I would laugh and forgive and forget and explain and reassure and apologize and grovel and flatter and hug. All of the above, multiple times over, in no particular order. I would fix it, and we would make up.

At quarter to six, Mareike from the *Seeblick Hotel* let me know that my friends had taken three rooms, one each, and had booked in for a couple of nights. "They seem very nice," she commented but I didn't feel like chatting so I begged to ring off.

The telephone rang again at six p.m. It was Greetje. Apparently my visitors had been pointed in the right direction and were at this very moment walking down the lane. ETA would be ten minutes, and *Good Luck*.

Adrenaline sloshed through my body in a rush of great excitement. This was it.

Music. Did I want music?

I flapped about a bit, shuffling through the few CDs I had brought and eventually deciding on my new Eighties compilation CD. No sooner had the first song started than there was a tentative knock. I did a final check; everything was ready.

I went to open the door.

Chapter Fifty-Four

My two best friends and the love of my life stood side by side on the doorstep of my lovely Langeoog hideaway cottage. Steve was holding a bottle of sparkly, Dan proffered flowers, and Rachel waved a pink-wrapped present. All wore big, beaming smiles.

For a moment, nobody moved. I wanted to say so much, yet I couldn't find the right words to begin. All my preparation and rumination had left me wholly unprepared for the sheer emotion at seeing these three people again.

Rachel finally broke the ice. "We found you!" she screamed and launched herself at me for a big bear hug. The force of impact propelled me backwards and we half stumbled, half fell into the living room.

"Easy, easy," Dan chided teasingly. "You might scare her off and she'll run away again." He threw me an inquisitive look and I shot him a smile back.

"Never," I assured the three of them. "Never." And I meant it.

Steve muscled in, gently disengaging Rachel's arms from behind my neck and moving around swiftly for a hug. Despite my every resolution, my eyes filled up with tears and I blinked hard to keep them at bay.

"I missed you so much," Steve whispered in my ear just as I whispered in his, "I'm so, so sorry." He held me at arm's length to look at me, then drew me close for a hug again.

"I can't believe you're here," he said softly. "What a journey."

"I'm sorry," I repeated again. "I'm sorry I ran, I—"

"*Shh*," Steve hushed me. "Everyone has a lot of explaining to do. One thing at a time."

"Yes," Rachel chimed in anxiously. "I want to go first."

"Hold it, hold it," Dan laughed. "Isn't it my turn to say hello and get a hug, too?" He exchanged a look with Steve, who reluctantly relinquished his space next to me.

"Only one, though," he teased and Dan thumped him on the shoulder.

Meanwhile, Rachel, ever nosey, had been investigating the room and began exclaiming about the balloons and decorations.

"She's having a party," she kept repeating before swooping in on me and taking my hand. "I hope... I mean... We're not coming at a bad time?"

There was silence in the room as Dan, Steve and Rachel contemplated the possibility that their appearance might not be convenient. I looked from one to the other and back again, trying to stop my mouth from twitching. I couldn't contain myself any longer.

"Of course not," I shouted. "The party's for you. I've been counting the hours!"

"You knew we were coming?" the three of them uttered in one voice.

"Absolutely," I assured them. "It's impossible to arrive unnoticed on this island. I knew you were at Bensersiel before you'd even boarded the ferry. Besides..." I grinned mischievously. "That private detective of yours was a bit of a klutz. He totally gave the game away."

Dan looked crestfallen. "You knew about him?"

Aha, it had to have been his brainchild.

"*Everybody* knew about him," I stated simply. "You can't come to a tiny, close-knit community like this, not speak a word of German, and expect not to stick out like a sore thumb." I giggled at the recollection of Greetje's description.

"He was meant to blend in," Dan mumbled.

"Yeah, well, I guess it's hard to learn that much German on a one-day trip," I acknowledged, slapping Dan playfully on the hand. "Anyway, naughty you for setting a gumshoe on me."

"We missed you. We needed to find you. We imagined all sorts of things..." Dan offered by way of explanation.

"Gosh, when we discovered you'd disappeared..." Rachel started, but didn't know how to finish.

"We were distraught," Steve offered solemnly.

"Is that why you had the bust-up in the pub?" I couldn't resist asking.

"You know about *that*?" Steve was aghast.

"Of course," I replied nonchalantly. "They do have newspapers out here." I neglected to omit how narrowly I had missed the story. Suddenly, I realized that everyone was still wearing coats.

"Aw, come on you guys, look at you. Take your coats off and let's have some food. You must be hungry, right? And then we can talk."

Within a couple of minutes, we were happily sitting at the table, pouring wine and bubbly and chatting away while the pizzas cooked and the sausages cooled. We picked at smoked salmon, prawns, and all the other nibbles I had bought, and we caught up with each other.

Rachel bit the bullet first. "Dan and I," she began à propos of nothing, picking up a prawn and waving it about.

My heart stopped for a millisecond but I steeled myself. I was going to listen and to forgive.

Rachel opened her mouth but Dan spoke first. "We slept together," he said flatly, looking a little anxious. "I... We..." He paused, clenching his fists, then unclenching them again before squaring his shoulders. "There really are no good words. We slept together five times."

Rachel quailed at the totality of his confession but she held my gaze. A tear escaped her eye and rolled down her cheek, but she ignored it.

"I'm so, so sorry," she whispered. "I became a floozie. After all this time of knowing Dan, I got drawn to the flame. I was lonely and you were with Steve and I didn't see the harm in sleeping with Dan, not to start with, I didn't, I swear... We never meant to hurt you."

I cried, too. "And why would you? You were both free and single and... I shouldn't have known, it was none of my business, and I just walked in, it was my own fault..."

"Not your fault," Dan interrupted firmly. "This is not your fault. We were being selfish and hurtful and thoughtless. The night you saw us...that was the last time. We ended it before...before I even found your keys." He was emphatic on this point.

I was lost. "What about my keys?"

"You left them in..."

Realization broke over me. "I left them in the hallway when I entered. So I did. Oh God, you must have thought I was making such a point. I don't even remember leaving them behind. What a mess."

Steve cleared his throat. "What I need to understand is..." He hesitated. "Look, I'm not jealous or anything but...why is it such a big deal to you what Rachel and Dan did?

I shook my head. "I don't know. I really can't explain it rationally. It just made me sick." Rachel shrank lower into the sofa, and her face crumpled with tears. I took her hand and squeezed it to show her that I was no longer aggrieved. "I don't know why it made me sick. I'm sorry, I feel really stupid." I grimaced and took a deep breath before plunging into a second apology.

"And while we're on the subject of sorry..." I turned to Steve, fixing my eyes onto his. "I'm sorry I ran away from you." Steve raised a hand and opened his mouth to speak, but I ploughed on regardless. I needed to say my piece.

"I waited for you at the end of the road. I wanted to come back and apologize, but then you whizzed by in the car and I knew I'd gone too far. You weren't at the station when I finally got there..."

Steve couldn't hold back any longer. Surprise played all over his face. "You were *behind* me? I thought you'd gone, taken the first train..."

We stared at each other, aghast.

"Is that why you didn't answer your phone when I tried to ring you? Because you thought I'd left you there in Pitlochry?" My voice was small and tremulous, but I had to see this through.

Steve blinked. "Answer my phone? When? *What?*"

"On the Monday. I rang you at lunchtime and then again…later." I tried very hard not to look at Dan or Rachel while I said that, but they got my meaning anyway.

Steve was shocked. "I didn't know you'd called. I wasn't in."

"I noticed," I responded dryly.

"I…I needed time to think. I was out at Richmond park."

"Without your mobile?"

Steve shrugged helplessly. "I wasn't thinking straight. I was annoyed, too, you know. What a rubbish trip."

I giggled. Then I laughed. Then I guffawed. My friends looked at me with astonishment. I wiped tears of mirth from my eyes. "Ah. Life," I pronounced between snorts of laughter. "You've gotta love it. It's a complete bitch sometimes."

"But thankfully nobody's died," Dan supplied, playing on one of his favorite sayings.

When the moment had passed, Rach turned all serious again.

"Will you forgive me?" she pleaded with me.

"Of course I will, silly moo." We hugged hard.

"And you're not cross?" She needed to hear it again.

"I'm not," I confirmed. "But I won't say I wasn't. Oh my God, I was so *angry*."

We hugged hard again and said no more. Steve and Dan simply looked on.

My turn to grovel, from the very bottom of my heart. "Will you forgive me?" I begged of Steve, hoping that he would see the pleading in my eyes. "Please?"

He said nothing at first and I could feel my face freeze in its hopeful expression. But gradually, a lovely, lazy smile spread across Steve's face and he spoke. "Of course I will, my love. And I am sorry, too. For everything." He held out his arms uncertainly, and I launched myself at him, embracing him into a hug that I never wanted to end. Thank goodness the nightmare was over.

I retrieved another bottle of wine and was busy opening it, feeling flushed and happy and overwhelmed with relief, when Dan threw out the killer comment.

"You look...*well*," he suddenly announced. "Happy. Rosy. Serene. I've not seen you looking like this for... I dunno, for as long as I can remember."

Steve and Rachel examined me closely, and Rachel seconded Dan's observation. "He's right, you know."

I set down the bottle of wine deliberately and lowered my bottom onto my chair.

"D'you know," I started carefully. "It's weird that you should say that. I kind of... Well, I feel that way, what you said. Happy. I feel well. Content. I came here..." I poured myself a little glass of wine and had a quick sip.

"I was all in pieces when I came here. Somehow, I've put myself together again. I didn't even have to do anything, it just sort of happened. Things are different here and you get a new perspective on what really matters. And I've slept so well..."

"Why here?" Rachel burst out. "I mean, it looks lovely and all that...but how *on earth* did you end up here?"

I smiled to myself. *Good question.*

"When I took off that Tuesday afternoon, I simply needed to get away, as far as and as fast as possible. I had no plans beyond that. So I took the Eurostar to get onto the continent. And ...I don't know really. Maybe it was fate. I was searching the Internet and I had this idea that an island would be good, and one thing led to another..." I rolled my shoulders helplessly. While I could recall the steps I took to get here, the reasoning, the logic was elusive even to me. It had simply seemed like a good thing to do at the time.

The three of them hung on to my every word. I laughed uncertainly. "Anyway, the only missing piece was my friends. And what I left behind—the mess. So...if you hadn't come, I would have had to come back. But..." I raised my glass in a toast. "I'm so glad you came. I'm thrilled. You have no idea what that means to me. Here's to being there for each other."

"To being there for each other," Steve, Rachel and Dan echoed and we clinked glasses.

There was the small awkward moment that so often follows a toast, and I experienced the overwhelming desire to do something crazy, to make my friends comprehend the grandeur and effect of this island.

"Hey," I shouted, struck by inspiration. "Let's go to the beach. I want you to feel this place, even if you can't see it."

Seaside boy Steve was on his feet instantly. "Oh, do let's," he agreed. "Some fresh air and some surf. Fabulous."

Dan looked a tad dubious but was quickly overruled when Rachel joined in the fray. "Yay! A midnight walk to the beach," she enthused, always one for adventures. "This is so exciting. And weirdly romantic, don't you think?"

Seeing our bemused expressions, she explained. "Four friends, finally reunited, after a lovely dinner...going to brave nature, going to the beach together in the dark, standing as one against the forces of the wild..."

Steve chuckled. "Methinks you've drunk a bit too much," he ventured.

"Have not," Rachel pouted and swatted at him with her free hand, the one that wasn't still clutching her wine glass. The sudden movement made her spill some wine on the table, and she looked at her nearly empty glass with feigned surprise. "Oh well, maybe I have." She hiccupped and added, "All the more reason for some fresh air, huh?"

Laughing and bantering and teasing each other, we geared up for a quick jaunt down the beach. Sensibly, my three visitors had brought rain gear and sturdy shoes, and I found a selection of torches in the tardis-like downstairs storage cupboard. Suitably attired, in high spirits and full of anticipation, we left the cottage lights a-blazing to guide us on the way back, and set off for the beach.

I led the way, taking my friends up the little path across the dunes, over the top and down onto a big expanse of beach. It was slightly surreal, being out at night in the dunes, on the beach. We stumbled-tripped our way over hidden roots and clumps of grass, unexpected holes and ditches. There was much shrieking being done by Rachel and me, and the men dutifully helped and supported us.

Finally, we reached level ground as we hit the tideline. The sea was going out and there was a thin layer of bubbly foam where the water was reluctantly abandoning its hold on the sand. Owing to yesterday's high winds, the North Sea was still agitated and the surf was booming and crashing ominously. Yet at this moment, the sky was clear and there were tiny pinpricks of starlight twinkling above us. We had switched off our torches, and as our eyes adjusted to the darkness, it was just possible to make out the black hulk of the dunes behind and the vast wideness of sea in front of us.

It was one of those majestic, imposing moments that had helped me find my equilibrium throughout my stay here, and I fervently hoped the others would feel the same. I breathed and I gazed out toward the invisible horizon.

Steve gently took my hand. "Awesome," he whispered, barely audible across the hissing of the surf. Rachel stood on my other side and also took my hand. Dan took hers, and we formed a solid line of friendship braced against the harsh and unforgiving elements.

We stood like this for a long time. Everyone succumbed to the magic of the moment; there was no need for words. My heart swelled with joy and love, and I couldn't remember being happier in my entire life.

By silent accord, Dan and Steve eventually moved toward each other, forming a circle, pulling us into a big group hug. A bond was being forged that was stronger than a thousand words. Misdeeds and misunderstandings were put behind us, and the sea pulled them out with her, washing them away, dragging them under, never to be seen again.

Chapter Fifty-Five

We got back to the cottage feeling windswept, with rosy cheeks each and a distinct tang of salt on our lips. As we removed layers of outer clothing, it suddenly struck me that we all looked stripped to our bare selves. Not in a literal sense, of course. Dan was in sweatshirt and jeans. Steve, ditto. Rachel wore no makeup but her skin was glowing, her hair was tousled and messily contained in a butterfly grip, and she looked beautiful.

Rachel caught me eyeing her up and gave me a grin. "D'you know, I don't think I've ever seen all of us so relaxed," she echoed my thoughts. "There's definitely something about this place."

I smiled and was about to reply when Steve was in front of me on bended knee. Rachel exhaled sharply and Dan whistled softly. Steve said nothing to begin with, he just took my left hand and regarded me with his kind, soulful melted-chocolate eyes. Blood roared in my ears and I could hear the sound of my own breathing, turning shallow with excitement.

Steve turned my hand palm up and studied it carefully, as if he was hoping to read my destiny from it. He gently caressed my heart line with his thumb, then turned my hand back over and planted a kiss on the back of it. Raising his eyes to meet mine, he finally asked the question.

"Will you marry me, Sophie?"

Rachel exploded in gleeful squeals and jumped up and down like a child on Christmas Eve until Dan stepped across to calm her down. I looked at the two of them, now loosely hugging while awaiting my answer, and I retuned my gaze to Steve. A succession of snapshots from the past six months flashed before me. Seeing Steve in that church, knowing he was The One. Glimpsing him in the hospital when I was bringing Rachel in. Having him appear by my bedside when I was in hospital myself. Dan and Steve doing their weird double-act in the hospital. Steve towering over me as I was lying in the mud, refusing to help me up. Steve standing at the cottage door earlier, looking hopeful, expectant, anxious.

Yes, I said in my head. *Yes, yes, yes.*

Aloud, my voice uttered something completely different.

"Why now?"

"*What?*" Rachel gasped before Dan had a chance to silence her. Steve didn't blink or bat an eyelid. Instead, he considered the merit of my question. He remained on bended knee as he started speaking seriously.

"Now, because you know and I know that we are meant for each other." He swallowed and I nodded, just ever so slightly, for him to carry on.

"Now, because you got away once. Because I had planned the perfect moment in the perfect place, and it all went catastrophically wrong." He gave a wry chuckle.

I had an uncomfortable idea that his plans might have had something to do with the Scotland trip, and that I had ruined more than just a romantic getaway.

"So, now…because this is perfect. Because I love you. Because I'm not letting you go again. And because I want your two best friends to be there as we take this monumental step."

There were muffled sniffs coming from Rachel's direction, and when I took a quick peek, it appeared she was crying. She was wringing her hands and waiting for my answer almost as anxiously as Steve.

Dan gave me one of his irresistible smiles. He looked completely relaxed, at ease, happy. *Do it*, he mouthed. *What are you waiting for?*

For a few seconds, my gaze rested on Dan as I was trying to figure out what my subconscious had just registered. The necklace—his half of our ring—it was gone. He wasn't wearing it. We had both sworn we would wear our halves, always, to remind ourselves of what we had. We had been so proud of this romantic notion, but it hadn't worked. Without really noticing, I touched my hand to my own bare neck, and Dan nodded.

"I got it still and keep it safe," he said very quietly. Steve and Rachel were somewhat surprised by this seeming random comment, but my heart soared. I still had mine, too, and was keeping it safe. Dan and I had reached the same unspoken conclusion—it was time to let go. I smiled widely. Time for my answer.

"I—" I began finally, but Steve interrupted me quickly.

"Hold on, I forgot something," he commanded, gesturing for Dan or Rachel to hand him his coat and fumbling frantically with his left hand in one of the pockets.

"The ring." He presented the blue box with a flourish. I giggled and broke the tension. "Let nobody accuse me of proposing in bad form," Steve declared, and opened the box. It contained what looked like a shiny purple shell. I accepted the box and cautiously picked at the shell, eventually lifting it off the cushion to discover that it was a ring, after all.

I raised my eyes, smiling at Steve uncertainly, while I gently turned the ring over in my hands. Steve had proposed with a purple plastic ring. It was beautiful, though in a purple kind of way. And surprisingly heavy, for plastic.

Seeing my hesitation, Steve took the ring out of my hands and poised himself to slip it on the ring finger of my left hand. "May I?"

I nodded, *yes*.

The ring looked good on my hand. Purple and shiny; a definite statement. Very *me*. Even if it was slightly unusual.

"Will you marry me, Sophie?" Steve reiterated excitedly. And this time, I said "yes" loud and clear, several times.

"Yes!"

Steve swept me up in a big embrace, lifting me clear off my feet, and Rachel and Dan applauded like mad.

"Whoop, whoop," Rachel shouted, dancing around us like a pixie. "Congratulations, oh, I'm so excited for you both."

I knew I was grinning like the Cheshire cat, I could feel the smile on my face nearly reaching my ears. Unexpected, this had been, but it was totally right.

Rachel dislodged me from Steve's hug to give me a hug herself, making me jump up and down with her in excitement. "This is absolutely the best day ever," she announced, and her delight touched me deeply.

Dan was doing the manly back-slapping-hand-shaking thing with Steve, offering his congratulations. He looked emotional but genuinely pleased. Noticing me watching him, he took the two steps across to envelop me in one of his big bear hugs.

"Congratulations, my lovely Sophie," he said sincerely, and audibly. "You know I'll always love you, and I hope you'll stay my friend. But I am so happy for you both."

He held me close for another second and gently let me go.

"Thanks," was all I could manage in response, both to him and to Rachel. "I…I am so glad you are here, and…"

I didn't have any more words. This morning, I had been worried about being making up, anxious that Steve wouldn't forgive. Now, I was suddenly his fiancée.

My second engagement. Third, if you counted the twenty-four hours I had been notionally engaged to Dan.

Rachel was reading my mind. "Third time lucky, eh?" she stage-whispered and we all burst into laughter.

"Third time lucky," Dan picked up her thought. "Long may it last. Let's drink to that."

Sure enough, another bottle of sparkly was found, and a toast was had, and another one.

We moved from the kitchen to the lounge, and Steve busied himself with kindling and matches. Sitting in front of the fire, we sipped champagne and toasted marshmallows. It might sound odd, but it was perfect.

Until all of a sudden, an ear-splitting shriek from Rachel broke the atmosphere.

"I got you a present, too," she exclaimed. "I nearly forgot. You must open it. Where is it?"

I shook my head, indicating that I couldn't recall what we had done with it.

"There it is," Steve came to the rescue. "It's hiding on the sofa, look."

Sure enough, there was Rachel's pink-wrapped box. I retrieved it and sat back down among my friends excitedly. Sensing Rachel's impatience, I tore open the package and found it contained a beautifully crafted pink box with a white and silver pattern of blossoms. Inside a box was a big notebook of the same design. I took it out and flicked through the thick creamy pages, pristine in their blankness. A little piece of paper fluttered out; it read,

Sophie's Little Book of Notes and Anecdotes
To Help Me Write My Second Book

"It's beautiful," I managed uncertainly. "But what does it mean?"

Rachel giggled gleefully. "Dan showed us your book," she informed me.

"My book?" I repeated.

"Yeah, you know? The one you made for his birthday. It's brilliant." Rachel nudged me with her elbow as if to jolt my memory.

"You *read* it?" I burst out, completely nonplussed. I hadn't really intended it for a wider audience than Dan.

"I didn't read it," Rachel began to clarify, and I breathed a premature sigh of relief. "I devoured it. In one sitting. It's bloody brilliant, and I want another one. Please?" She proffered the notebook at me.

"I'm told that writers need something to set down ideas when they come to them. Organize thoughts. Write down anecdotes. So this is perfect. Or," she mused, "if that's not what you want, you could use it as a wedding planning diary. It *is* pink, so it fits wonderfully."

"It's gorgeous," I hastened to reassure her and gave her a big thank-you hug. "It's just so unexpected. I never thought about writing... I just...well, you know, they were only scribbles."

"Well, they were jolly good," Steve commented from his prone position on the floor and I nearly passed out with shock.

"*You* read it, too?" I squeaked, resolving to murder Dan at the first opportune moment.

But hang on! Steve had read it, and he still proposed?

"I certainly did," Steve confirmed. "And very interesting it was, too. Explained a lot. Well written, I might add. And funny."

You could have knocked me over with a feather.

"As we're on alternative career news and monumental announcements," Dan chimed in from *his* prone position on the other side of the fire. "There's something else you ought to know."

"Oh yes," Rachel squealed, "I forgot about that. Tell her!"

I held my hands up in a gesture of defeat. "I don't think I can take any more," I protested, only half-joking, but my friends elected to ignore me.

"You must know," Steve told me. "Otherwise you'll be in shock when we leave."

"That sounds a bit ominous," I muttered, confused.

"'Love Me Better,'" Dan continued his announcement. "You know, the song?"

"You mean the one that we recorded in private, with me merely standing in for a female artist to be found later? The one that was subsequently released? *That* one? Yes, I remember," I said, a little tartly.

"It's gone platinum," Dan said. "You're famous. Somebody made the connection and it went all over the net."

Platinum? A single? With *my* voice?

"You're having a laugh," I stated flatly.

This was too much. It was totally ludicrous. *All over the Internet? How could I not have known?*

Dan was still trying to get his message through to me. "I'm not having a laugh. You were gone a long time and life carried on."

"But, but, but! The single is ancient. We messed about with it in, like, June. That's five months ago."

"It was a slow burner," Dan acknowledged. "But it got there in the end." He couldn't suppress a smile.

Oh God. He was serious.

"I'm marrying a rock goddess," Steve realized. "Well, I never. Lucky me."

Rachel toppled over with hysterical laughter, but I was still not buying it.

"This is too much," I objected. "And anyway, I thought it was all meant to be anonymous? Huh?"

"It was," Dan acknowledged somberly. "Yet somebody let the cat out of the bag. It wasn't me," he held his hands up defensively. "Uh-uh. It turned up on the Internet one day and that was that. And now the press is looking for you."

I shook my head to clear the fog that had descended.

"In fact," Dan began, but Steve intervened. "Best leave it there for now, shall we?" he suggested gently. "I think it's all been a bit much."

"Of course," Dan conceded immediately.

"No, tell me," I protested, but Dan shook his head.

"Not now," he reiterated. "We have plenty of time." He consulted his watch and gave a startled gasp. "My friends, it is almost two o'clock in the morning. Perhaps it's time for bed?"

"Brilliant idea," Rachel agreed instantly, trying to suppress a wide yawn but giving in eventually. When she finished stretching her jawbones, she got to her feet. "What a day it's been. I know I'm totally overwhelmed, poor old Sophie must be reeling. Come on, Dan, we have a cozy room waiting for us each." She pulled Dan up to his feet while Steve helped me.

"Is it all right if I stay?" he whispered in my ear.

"Totally," I whispered back, feeling unaccountably naughty. "I wouldn't have it any other way."

Chapter Fifty-Six

Steve had come vaguely prepared. Tucked into the voluminous pockets of his outdoorsy coat were a pair of tightly folded pajama bottoms and a toothbrush.

"I'll have to be stubbly in the morning," he joked as we were getting ready for bed together, for the first time since...well.

"But I didn't want to bring a big bag and look presumptuous. And I didn't know whether I'd get a chance to propose this time, and if it all went wrong, I didn't want to have the added problem of an overnight bag speaking volumes on my behalf."

I gave him a big hug.

"I love you, Steve Jones," I said sincerely. "And I can't believe we're getting married."

"You'd better believe it," he admonished me teasingly. "Besides, you've got the ring to prove it."

I waggled my left hand in the air, admiring the glint of purple as the ring caught the light.

"Do you like it?" Steve suddenly asked. "It's a bit unusual…"

"Yeah, you can say that," I interrupted laughingly.

"It's only a stand-in," he clarified. "I've picked three proper ones, you know, but I wanted to see if you wanted to choose the final winner. Just in case."

Ah. A stand-in.

"That's a bit of relief," I admitted. "It's just a bit on the clunky side."

"That, it is," Steve conceded. "Still, they don't make them much smaller. I guess it gets a bit fragile if they make it more slender."

"Fragile?" I retorted. "Why would a plastic ring be fragile?"

Steve looked at me, completely aghast. "You think this is *plastic*?" he asked, his voice an unusually high pitch.

Oh dear. Bad mistake. I obviously had committed quite a serious faux pas. "Is it not?" I whispered in the smallest, most apologetic voice I could muster. We were still standing side by side by the sink, looking at each other in the bathroom mirror, and now Steve nudged me gently shoulder to shoulder. It was a kind, indulgent kind of gesture. One that said, *I know you're a philistine but I'll marry you anyway.*

"No, silly," Steve said very tenderly, caressing my face as he spoke. "No, it is not plastic. It is, in fact, a classic Lalique Cabochon ring."

I swallowed. *That* sounded expensive.

"Lalique, huh?" I repeated.

"Lalique," Steve confirmed. "But that doesn't mean anything to you at all, I can see it on your face."

We both burst out laughing, clinging on to each other for dear life.

"It's a crystal designer ring," Steve managed to clarify in between howls of laughter. "Crystal. And I love that about you, that you haven't got a clue. Oh, Sophie," he chuckled. "I do love you more than anyone in the whole wide world."

I cupped his face in my hands and pulled him close. "I love you, too. More than anyone. You are my thunderbolt-and-lightning man. And I'm sorry it took us such a roundabout way to get back together."

"Nah," Steve laughed again. "Best to get these things out of the way before we tie the knot. But now…" he pulled me toward the bedroom. "Let's make mad, passionate love."

"Consummation before the act, huh?" I teased. "That means I can't marry in white."

"You can't marry in white anyway," Steve teased right back. "And I don't care. You could marry in red as far as I'm concerned."

"Or scarlet," I suggested. "I could be your scarlet woman."

"Now that's going a bit too far," Steve admonished. "Come here, you, and let me teach you some manners…"

Needless to say, we did make mad, wild and passionate love. And tender, considerate love. And hungry love. Several times. It was as if we were making up for lost time. We erased the past weeks from our mental and bodily memories and celebrated our engagement in the most worthy of manners. I would have to John-Wayne-walk the following day, but who cared?

It was bliss, sharing a bed with Steve again. I had forgotten, or had tried to forget, how comfortably my body fit into the curves of his big frame, and how cozy it was to snuggle like spoons, cocooned under two duvets.

I didn't really want to go to sleep, I wanted to hold on to this moment forever and ever. Ecstatically happy, content, spent and newly engaged to the right man. I hugged myself under those duvets, pulling Steve's arms close to me as well.

"You do know they are actually attached to my shoulders and won't, therefore, come off?" Steve muttered sleepily in a halfhearted protest.

"Are you awake?" I whispered back superfluously. "I can't sleep, I'm too excited."

"I'm not really awake," Steve grumbled good-naturedly. "But I'm excited, too." He kissed the top of my shoulder and I snuggled in closer again. I had to have fallen asleep mere seconds later, because when I next opened my eyes, it was light outside and the bedside clock read ten a.m.

"Morning, sleepyhead," Steve greeted me from his side of the bed and I turned around swiftly to make sure he was still there, right there.

"Morning, stubbles," I greeted him back, caressing his sandpapery chin.

"Stubbles," he smiled. "I like that. Nobody has called me that before. It sounds kind of cute."

"It's meant to be," I confirmed and sighed, stretching luxuriantly under the warm duvet. The window did its now-familiar rattling act and I pulled the duvet high against my chin.

Another gust shook the windows all over the cottage and there was a peculiar howling that I assumed was coming from the chimney.

"Storm's coming," I announced like a veteran islander, and Steve didn't contradict me. We lay contentedly for a few minutes chatting about nothing in particular, until a sharp volley of knocks against the front door indicated that one or the other of us would have to get up.

"That wasn't the storm," Steve observed dryly.

"I guess we have company," I declared. We looked at each other.

"You go," we said at the same time.

"You go, and I'll tidy up downstairs and sort out the fireplace," Steve offered. "No doubt there'll be ash all over the place with the wind catching into the chimney as it is."

"Deal," I confirmed and jumped out of bed with surprising alacrity. Pulling on my dressing gown, I bounded downstairs to let in our visitors. Steve followed not far behind, wearing yesterday's jumper to complement his pajama bottoms.

Of course, it was Dan and Rachel.

"Ah, look, the lovebirds were still in bed," Rachel teased me, and stared accusingly at Dan. "Told you we should have come later."

"I'm hungry," Dan protested. "I couldn't wait any longer." He handed me a big wicker basket laden with food stuffs. It had Greetje's handiwork written all over it. I took it curiously and stepped back to set it down on the kitchen table. Rachel and Dan entered gratefully, and the wind whipped the door out of Rachel's grip before she could close it softly.

Ka-bang!

"Sorry," Rachel offered apologetically, but I shrugged.

"This is going to get much worse," I told her cheerfully. "We'll have to batten down. Now what's this?"

"Morning, you two." Steve bustled in full of cheer. "Apologies for my fiancée's *very* rude manners..." He winked at me as he planted a kiss on Rachel's cheek and shook hands with Dan.

"Morning, morning, morning," I added hastily, dispensing kisses all round. "So what *is* this?" I returned my attention to the basket.

"Present from someone called Greetje. She says to come and see her later." Dan was a little surprised at the familiarity with which Greetje had addressed him—"She knew my name. How did she know my name?"–as well as the generosity of the present. The basket contained everything for a proper brunch, and more. Bacon, eggs, croissants, and Greetje's famous homemade pastries, jam, honey, butter—everything. I unpacked packet after packet of delightful goodies, and Dan grew more and more cheerful by the minute. "I love Greetje," he announced. "I'll have to tell her properly later. Shall I get on and make some breakfast?"

Chapter Fifty-Seven

Three hours later, the storm was picking up pace by the minute. Thick grey clouds were scudding across a darkening sky, the wind was phenomenally strong, the rain spectacular. I switched on the telly for a while, and we caught the end of a severe weather warning for the region.

"Not looking too good," Steve observed, and I launched into a rendition of Greetje's insights into storms on the island.

"I'd love to have a go look-see," Rachel suddenly announced. "You know, before it gets so bad that you can't set foot outside anymore."

Needless to say, I was all for it, and we convinced the boys that it would do them good. Once more we togged up, and this time I equipped the visitors with spare wellies from the storage cupboard.

As soon as we got outside, it became obvious that our venture was one of pure madness. It was almost impossible to stand upright.

"Are you sure we want to do this?" Steve hollered.

"Les—ha—loo—" Rachel's voice came from the left, the wind tearing at her words, and she took my hand and dragged me forward. Holding on to each other, a little bit like last night, the four of us struggled and wobbled up the uneven path once more. For a brief moment, the going got easier as the dunes protected us from the worst of the wind, but as soon as we crested the hill, the storm hit us full force. Rachel was nearly swept off her feet with the unexpected impact, and Dan and Steve had to hold on really tight.

When we reached the top, we stood and stared. It would have been sheer folly to go any further.

Gone was the beach. Where we had stood a mere twelve hours before, there was a foaming, seething mass of swirling water. The storm was driving the waves sideways across the beach in a spectacular display of natural histrionics.

"The tide should be going out," Steve shouted into my ear, obviously having done his calculations. I nodded. "This is going to be bad, really bad," he continued his observations, and I nodded once more.

"We ought to go back," he instructed, pulling vigorously at my hand. "This isn't safe."

"Okay," I shouted, tugging in turn at Dan and Rachel's hands. A little reluctantly, but seeing the necessity of it, we all returned to the cottage.

"That was quite something," Rachel enthused, once we were all safe and dry.

"That wasn't even the half of it," Steve muttered darkly.

"You realize we're on the lee side of the island?" I posited cautiously.

"Even worse," Steve retorted. "If this is what it's like on the sheltered side, what will it be like on the weather side? Have you got candles? Storm lanterns? Matches?"

I acquiesced to each of his requests and filled him in on Greetje's emergency instructions. Faced with the inevitable, we turned necessity into virtue and hunkered down for a mammoth game of Monopoly.

It turned out to be one of those priceless, perfect afternoons. In between bursts of playing and bartering, we toasted more marshmallows, although only on candle-flames as it was far too risky to light the fire with the wind howling down the chimney. We made pots of tea and I got an opportunity to educate the newbies in the delights and exigencies of the local tea ritual. We tried to watch a movie but gave up as my gorgeous friends struggled with the German dialogue and reception became more and more disrupted. We laughed. We sang. Yes, we even sang *that* song, all of us together, voices only with no instruments. We played charades. We were happy, and we had almost forgotten all about the storm.

At six o'clock, the phone rang, startling all of us out of a little afternoon snooze.

Greetje. "When are you getting here?" she demanded without preamble.

"Who? Where? What?" was all I could muster in response, not having the foggiest what she was talking about.

"You, all of you, of course. To *your* engagement party."

I turned to face Rachel and Dan. "My *engagement party*?" I repeated in English for their benefit, then switched back to German. "What do you mean, my engagement party?"

Greetje erupted into bursts of agitated speech that were beyond me, and quite uncharacteristic of her.

"Slow down," I tried to get a word in edgewise. But she was talking to someone else in the room with her.

"Right, sorry," she offered, sounding slightly breathless when she returned to me. "I gather your friends forgot to tell you...or maybe they didn't understand. Anyway, I've sent Arne to come and get you."

Arne was the horse-and-carriage man. In all the time on my island, I hadn't had an opportunity to take a trip in the horse and carriage, although of course I had done my little stint of horse riding. I had met Arne then, seeing as that he owned the stables. But why would he come and get us?

"We've got you a little party going in your favorite pizza restaurant," Greetje finally explained. "We're all here and waiting. Which is a good idea anyway because I'll be much happier with you out of that remote little cottage. You never know." Another fabulous non-sequitur, but I was following her logic. She was worried about us landlubbers out here in the cottage on our own.

"Arne will come and get you so you don't blow away, okay?"

I grinned. Greetje could fix anything on this island. "Okay," I said. "We'll be ready. And...thank you."

"It's nothing," she said graciously, "just get here and don't keep your guests waiting."

Three faces looked at me expectantly.

"Why didn't you tell me there was a party going on for us tonight?" I chided Dan and Rachel, but only as a matter of protocol.

Steve gave me a hug. "You must have made quite an impression on these people for them to do so much for you," he surmised.

"Of course," Rachel exclaimed. "Everybody loves Sophie." She was making a dig at a TV series that I quite used to enjoy, but I didn't rise to it.

"We'd better get ready, I don't think it'll be long until our lift gets here," I suggested.

"Our lift being the horse-and-carriage?" Dan confirmed curiously. "How exciting." He was remembering our last horse-and-carriage journey, and so I quickly disabused him of any notion that this impeding ride would be even remotely as luxurious.

Already, there was a knock at the door.

"Arne is here, come on, quick now," I bellowed, rushing to open the door. Arne gave me a quick smile but his manner was serious.

"Please to lock all the windows and shutters if you can, and turn off electric and light. Please to bring blankets and torches with you. And please to hurry. I stay with the horses because they are quite pretty frightened." He doffed his hat and returned to his team of horses, patting their noses gently.

I tried to catch his attention to gesture that I would have to shut the door, but failed miserably. Feeling mean, I shut the door anyway and relayed his instructions. Dan and Steve immediately bounded up the stairs to take care of windows and shutters there. I heard muffled swearwords and much banging about but within minutes, all was quiet and the men returned. Rachel and I sorted out downstairs, flitting about like headless chickens, turning off lights, extinguishing candles and gathering up blankets and lanterns. All in all, it took us about five minutes, but poor old Arne was properly drenched when we got out.

"Occupational hazard," he grinned affably as we piled into the carriage and set off. "I'll be collecting more stragglers from all over the island before the night will be out. We like to stick together, you see, get people from in the most remotest houses into the village. Just in case. You know?"

We nodded, feeling a little better at not being the only source of Arne's discomfort today. Arne drove us to the Italian restaurant, then swiftly turned the carriage around to conduct his next mercy dash. We hurried inside to escape from the weather, clutching our blankets and torches. The restaurant was on two levels, ground floor and basement. Previously, I had always enjoyed sitting by one of the glass doors looking out at life while I enjoyed my food. Tonight, however, the ground floor restaurant was deserted and the action was downstairs.

We were greeted by the amazing smell of pizza, loud voices, and cheerful music. Balloons and banners had been strung criss-crossing the room, and there was a great centerpiece made up of pink and white heart-shaped balloons.

"*Überraschung*," Greetje shouted when she spotted us and hastened across the room to say hello. "Surprise! We thought for a moment you weren't coming." She hugged me briefly and whispered in my ear, "I am so pleased for you, congratulations."

She turned to Dan and Rachel. "Hi, good to see you again. Did you forget about all this?" She gestured loosely at the balloons and the party. Rachel had the grace to blush.

"I don't think we quite understood what you were telling us, I'm afraid," she admitted.

Greetje took this in her stride. "That's why I rang the telephone," she grinned.

"Thank you for the amazing gift basket," I suddenly remembered my good manners. "And this is Steve, of course!" I tugged possessively at Steve's sleeve and Greetje beamed at him.

"Very pleased to meet you, Steve," she said solemnly and shook his hand. "How do you do?"

"Nice to meet you, too, Greetje," Steve responded, managing to pronounce her name correctly. "Thank you for everything. For, you know, looking after our Sophie."

Greetje waved off his praise with an airy disregard. "Oh no, she was looking after herself all by herself," she exclaimed. "Now then, I think the food's about ready. We've ordered pretty much everything on the menu and it's going to be a big buffet, so help yourselves."

Sure enough, at this moment the chef came through with the first load of pizzas. He had abandoned the normal serving-size pizza trays and was presenting huge rectangular trays full of party-size pizzas. A loud "oh" and "ah" went through the room as folks realized that food was arriving. Dan and Rachel joined the fray immediately but Steve and I hung back for a little bit, observing.

"Who are all these people?" Steve wanted to know. There were probably about fifty or so adults and children at the party. "How did you manage to get to know so many people so well in such a short time?"

"I didn't," I conceded, trying to identify the folks around us. "I don't know everybody here, like, personally. Let's see…" I subtly pointed out individuals as I saw them. "There's Greetje, obviously, and her husband Klaus… Their two grown-up children and the grandchildren… Folke, the ferry man… Anna from the supermarket… The teachers from the school… The postman… The bank clerk… The pharmacist… Some of 'my' children from school and their parents… Oh, and the choir of course…"

I grinned at Steve. "On reflection, I probably do know everybody here."

"You joined a choir?" Steve asked in surprise.

"Of course! I missed singing. I wasn't very good at their style of music, but they didn't mind."

Greetje bustled toward us, munching a slice of pizza and waving energetically with her free hand. "What are you doing, standing here at the back? You are to eat, and to be merry." she mock-scolded, dragging me by the arm toward the buffet. Steve followed us, bearing a big smile. He appeared at ease in this environment, he seemed to positively revel in the hustle and bustle. I was glad.

There was a lot of admiration for my purple "plastic" ring which of course I had to show off, and Steve wasted no time dining out on the story of how I mistook his designer gift for a plastic ring. I took the opportunity to have a quick chat with Greetje.

"Thank you for organizing this," I said humbly. "I can't believe you've all come, and all this food and everything…"

"It's nothing," she assured me. "We wanted to celebrate. Besides, I suspect that you'll be going home to England soon?" She looked a question at me, and I nodded my head reflectively. Yes, I supposed I would.

"So this is a kind of farewell, too." She beamed. "Everybody has greatly enjoyed meeting you and hearing about your wonderful escapades."

I cringed, but only slightly. In reality, I had quite enjoyed the good-natured interest that everybody here was taking in everybody else's life. It meant that people were looked after.

"And lastly, before you get too overwhelmed by it all, it's only partly for you." She tried to appease my discomfort at the grand and unexpected celebration of my engagement. "We come quite often together like this in bad storms. It means all people are in a safe place and we can look out for each other and everybody is less scared. There'll be more people coming soon, Arne is—"

"—collecting them all," I laughed. "Yes, he told us. What a wonderful tradition."

"Isn't it just? And it distracts the children from the howling and wailing of the storm. Why sit at home, where it may be cold and there's nothing to do?"

I shook my head in amazement. I would miss this island and its fantastic little community quite a lot when we left. But this wasn't the time to dwell on departures. Steve had been to the buffet and returned with pizza and wine for both of us, and I tucked in gratefully.

As Greetje predicted, more people arrived over the next hour or so until the restaurant was packed out. Steve and I were duly toasted and celebrated, but the islanders also went about their business of resisting the storm and making merry in the face of adversity. When the rush on the food subsided, we cleared a big space to create an impromptu dance floor and the music cranked up. Adults and children alike were bopping and dancing and singing along; it was quite raucous in a harmless kind of way. The evening was a whirl of colors and food and dance while the ferocious storm outside hit and battered the island. High tide was due at eleven p.m., and if there were going to be waves crashing over the sea defenses, they would be at their worst then. We feigned ignorance and carried on.

By and by, the children drooped and faded and the adults created a big sleep area in one corner, bringing out sleeping bags and blankets. Incredibly, despite the music, the kids went off to sleep, having tired themselves out with wild dancing, running around, and lots of food. We turned the music down a bit but kept it going, and the mood changed, became a little more grown up, more serious. Couples appeared on the dance floor, holding hands, even doing proper rock'n'roll or jive-style steps.

Dan, Steve, Rachel and I were in the middle of showing the islanders the proper circular, arm-round-next-person's-neck, foot-swinging way of honoring the classic "Come on Eileen" when the power went off. The room was plunged into darkness and silence.

A male voice immediately started issuing calm and precise instructions. I translated for my three friends.

Everybody stay calm.

Stay where you are.

Folke, find the lanterns and light them.

Within a minute or so, he had lit the first storm lantern, and another man joined him to light the others. Soon, twenty or so oil lights were dotted about the room, casting a cheerful and cozy glow entirely belying the natural havoc occurring outside.

The restaurant also had a number of oil heaters which were set on a low heat. More blankets and duvets made an appearance, and soon we were all sitting on the dance floor in a big circle. Greetje had organized left-over food and drink to be brought in the middle alongside a few lanterns, and the effect was one of a midnight campfire picnic.

Now that the music was no longer masking the sounds of the gale-force wind, we could hear the impact of the storm. There was a dull thudding that we assumed would be waves breaking over the defenses further out on the island, and the wind was howling incessantly. It was eerie and surreal and everybody listened in reverent silence for a few minutes. The atmosphere took a distinct dip into gloom and doom.

Suddenly, Greetje piped up, adopting a jittery, brittle old man's voice and speaking half in German, half in English for our benefit.

"This is nothing," she cackled. "You should have seen the Great Storm of 1962. For days it raged and the island was flooded, the dykes were breached —"

Klaus nudged her affectionately. "You weren't even born then, you fraud."

"I'm being my Granddad," Greetje informed him in a stage whisper. "He'd launch into this story at every opportunity, even the slightest hint of a breeze."

"Go on," Rachel encouraged her unexpectedly. "I'd love to hear the story."

And so Greetje recounted the story of the Great Storm. She was a great storyteller, and we hung on her every word. The howling of the present storm punctuated her tale and for a while, we felt as though we were living the great disaster of the past. When she finished, she looked around us all, one by one, to milk the atmosphere. Gleefully, she clapped her hands and said in a loud, bright, voice, "See, there's really nothing to worry about today. The dykes are much higher, the wind isn't as strong, the weather system isn't as vicious and anyway, we'll get through this."

There was an audible sigh of relief as she lightened the mood. Greetje picked up one of the wine bottles, checked that it was empty, positioned it in the middle of the floor and spun it vigorously. We watched, mesmerized, as it spun itself out, finally coming to a rest pointing at no other than Dan.

"Ha. Your turn to tell a story next," Greetje pounced. "English is fine, isn't it?" She regarded her fellow islanders encouragingly and everybody nodded. Dan scratched his head.

"Does it have to be a storm story?" he asked. "Because I haven't really got one of those."

"Nah," Folke chimed in. "Tell us about you."

"Yes," Greetje reinforced this notion. Never one to miss an opportunity for drama, she informed the islanders that Dan was "famous, he makes rock music." There were astounded mutterings among the people until a young woman piped up, "I thought you looked familiar. Oh, this is so exciting."

NICKY WELLS

Dan flashed her one of his professional smiles, and she nearly swooned, but was swiftly brought in line by an embarrassed husband.

"Yeah, Dan, tell us a rock story," Rachel challenged with a mischievous smile. Dan scratched his head again and conceded defeat.

"Let's see. There was this one time when we were just up and coming... We had an album out and it had done quite well and we were touring the country up and down. We didn't have much money so we used this ancient crappy camper van to take us and our equipment from place to place. One day, we turned up at a venue somewhere and we hadn't had a chance to sleep or wash or anything between gigs. We must have looked pretty rough. And..." he coughed with embarrassment. "We probably didn't smell too good, either."

That admission earned him a laugh.

"Anyway, so we walked in there with our stuff and security threw us straight out. So we were stood outside like idiots. Of course, those were the days before mobile phones so we couldn't send a text to our manager. I had to go off and find a phone box five minutes down the road and scrabble together some change to ring the venue, put on my poshest scratchy voice and demand to be put through to Jack in the changing room."

He stopped, teasing us with a break.

I elbowed him in the ribs. "And?" I prompted.

He chuckled. "The money ran through faster than you would believe, and when Jack *finally* came on, the beeps were starting. So all I could say is, 'come outside, man' and the connection broke."

Everybody laughed at Dan's comical rendering of his own voice and surprised expression.

388

"It worked, though," he defended himself. "When I got back to the place, Jack was outside with the rest of the band waiting for me. The best thing about this was the look on the face of the security man when he had to let us through after all."

There was a round of applause for the story, and it was Dan's turn to spin the bottle.

All through the stormy night, I sat with my friends new and old, sharing anecdotes, spinning yarns, laughing, joking, and eating. I nestled sleepily into Steve's arms, feeling content and secure despite the unusual circumstances

"Aw…. Look at the lovebirds," somebody shouted, and the focus of attention shifted from outrageous tales to my engagement to Steve.

"Have you got a date?" Greetje demanded of us quite abruptly. She had probably been holding that question back for the entire evening.

"Will you keep your nose out of their business?" her husband scolded her lovingly. "For goodness sake, they've barely been engaged for a day."

Greetje looked suitably crestfallen, so I stepped in quickly. "We haven't really talked about it," I admitted. "It's all happened so fast… But…well, I don't know. Maybe in the spring? What do you think?" I turned to my fiancé.

"Spring's fine," he agreed.

"No," Rachel howled. "That's not nearly enough time to get everything organized. It takes six months for your dress alone." She was, of course, speaking from experience.

"Not for mine, it won't," I assured her.

"Are you using your Mum's?" Anna chimed in. "That would be nice, wouldn't it?"

I cringed. Mum's wedding dress was all flouncy and full of lacy frills. Besides, it was probably much too small for me.

"Err.... probably not," I admitted. "But I want something simple and—"

"—and anyway, there's always my little sister, she's a nifty one with a needle and a bit of tulle," Dan tried to come to the rescue.

Rachel and I jointly flinched at "tulle," but I appreciated the sentiment. Of course, the islanders had no idea that Dan's sister was a fashion-guru, but *they* liked the idea of a "homemade" dress.

Conversation reached a bit of a lull after this as tiredness overwhelmed everyone. It was almost three a.m. More sleeping bags were rolled out, blankets spread out and all lanterns bar two were extinguished.

"Good night, sweetheart," Steve mumbled as we lay snuggled together under a heap of blankets.

"Good night, stubbles," I whispered back. "I had a good day."

"Me too," came the nearly-asleep response, and thus ended our truly one-of-a-kind, once-in-a-lifetime engagement party.

Chapter Fifty-Eight

It felt like we were the cast out of a twenty-first century nuclear disaster movie when we gingerly mounted the stairs the following morning to venture outside and inspect the damage. Having been so insulated from the ravages of the storm in our basement refuge, we expected the worst, but things weren't too bad. Although a brisk wind continued blowing, the force of the storm had relented with the outgoing tide. The sky was grey and it was still raining, but not nearly as heavily as the previous day. The locals were chatting in the street, wearing their trademark yellow sou'westers and wellies, and from snatches of conversation I gathered that the sea defenses had not been breached. There were a few fallen trees and obviously the electricity was still out, but the island had come through relatively unscathed. Greetje and her family were nowhere to be seen; they had left at first light of dawn, such as it was, presumably checking on houses, boats and shops. I resolved to visit the tea shop later, if it was open, to see how things had gone and to thank her again.

With weary feet and gritty heads, the four of us trudged into the direction of the cottage. As expected, it was in darkness and fairly cold, but the shutters were intact and in place. We stumbled inside, switching on our torches until the men had an opportunity to open curtains and shutters. I made an emergency bed for Rachel and arranged Dan's make-shift sleeping place on the sofa, then Steve and I went upstairs into my bedroom, and everybody caught up on a few more hours' worth of sleep.

It took another couple of days for island business to return to normal, for the electricity to come back and the ferry to resume running. I used those days to show my friends the island as best as possible and to introduce them to all my favorite people and haunts. We did a fair bit of helping out with broken fences and flooded cellars, and our participation was gratefully received and noted. I also settled my affairs with Greetje, paying outstanding bills, thanking her profusely for everything she had done and begging her to come to my wedding, once we had actually set the date. It was weird and good to have my friends with me as I had to prepare to leave.

Well, obviously I didn't *have* to leave. Nobody was making me. I could have stayed indefinitely as far as my job, my flat, or my parents were concerned. But I had always considered this a temporary exile, and now that my friendships had been restored, now that the crisis point in my life was well and truly beyond me, now that I was *engaged*…I had to go back. It tore me apart, but it was the right thing to do. Had Steve, Rachel and Dan not been there, I didn't think I would have managed, or bothered. But they were there, and their presence altered matters, altered my perspective. Suddenly, I was more of a tourist than I had been before, speaking more English, doing strange touristy things.

Greetje was her usual philosophical self when I confided my discomfort at our parting meeting. "Of course it's awkward," she told me. "Two very different parts of your life are colliding head-on, and that's never easy. But you came here for a reason, your mission is accomplished, your time out is over, and now you must go back. That's how it is." Her smile took the harshness out of her words, and I hugged her. She grinned even wider.

"I shall be missing you and your hugs. You got the whole island hugging. You must come back some time and keep the tradition going."

I snorted through the tears that had suddenly welled up in my eyes. I hated goodbyes, and this one was a heart-wrenching one.

"Now, now," Greetje admonished me. "What's with these silly tears? You came here in tears, you shouldn't be leaving in tears."

"Ah," I sniffed, wiping my nose on a napkin for want of a proper tissue, "but they're different tears. These are happy tears. Well, you know. 'I had a great time' tears."

She laughed. "You're so funny. 'Happy tears' indeed. Well, be off with you now and don't forget to stay in touch."

And that was that. She waved me goodbye from the steps of her tea shop and I went home to the cottage one last time. The other three would have finished packing their things up, and mine, and doing a spot of dusting and cleaning. We were catching the midday ferry and would be gone from my beautiful island refuge within two hours. It was the middle of November, and all things told, my little escapade, my sabbatical, my time out, had lasted just over two months. It seemed a lifetime.

I stood at the railing where I had stood before, insisting on keeping my eyes on the island until it receded beyond the horizon. Finally, I gave in and we went inside to take shelter from the weather, and the others started chatting and laughing to cheer me up.

And I *was* happy, though I was a little sad at leaving. I was a different person to when I arrived. And one hundred percent more engaged. My lovely Steve, always tuned into my moods, took my hand and planted a kiss on it.

"All right?" he whispered.

"All right," I whispered back and leaned against him to show my thanks.

At Bensersiel, a big black limo waited for us, causing much excitement among the locals. Dan lifted his hands in an apologetic gesture but said that he had to get back to London as quickly as possible. Not only were the band mid-recording, they were also rehearsing for some upcoming shows, and the lead singer and front man disappearing for a week would have caused a tremendous setback. It wasn't a problem, he hastened to reassure me, he simply needed to get back now. His boyish grin told me that he had enjoyed his little island jaunt, but his body language also spoke of tension and stress.

The last sound we heard to remind us of Langeoog was the hooting of the ferry as we piled into the car. When the door clunked shut and the engine started, even that was drowned out and it was as if we were entering an alternative universe; one where motorized transport and noise and speed were the norm. It would be as big an adjustment to go home as it had been to settle there in the first place

The limo took us straight to Hamburg airport, and we were all back in our respective homes by the end of the day. Except for me, of course, because I needed to give my tenants notice. So instead of going *home* home, I went to Steve's flat. It was quite fitting and romantic in a way. My prince had come to rescue me from a faraway island and was taking me to his home and his castle.

Mum and Dad were delighted that I was back in the country and genuinely pleased at my engagement. It turned out that Steve had paid them a visit while I was missing in action and had even spent the night with them, making friends and casually asking my Dad for my hand in marriage, should Steve manage to locate and convince me.

Shortly after we had all returned from Langeoog, Dan had convinced me that it would probably be best if we did some sort of press conference together to appease the curious journos and to stop the never-ending requests for photos and comments. "Love Me Better" was still at number one, and it was weird hearing it on the radio and in almost every shop or pub I went into. Without fail, I would get this weird, "my God, that's me again" jolt. To be honest, it was quite amazing to find myself at the number one spot even though I had never planned to get there. But the curiosity of the press was tiring, and quite instructive for me as a member of the press myself. I resolved to stop pestering people forthwith if they didn't ring me back after the third prompting call.

Thus I had let myself be talked into a brief public appearance with Tuscq. To give Dan credit, he had kept the media circus to a minimum, and we had rehearsed the exact story that we wanted to put out there, so it had all been over and done with in ten minutes.

Naturally, I went back to work and Rick slipped me back into the ordinary schedule as if nothing dramatic had occurred. I kept my office, but my door was always open, now. Naturally, there were a few whispers here and there but Rachel and I overcame them together by being totally nonchalant and debonair about it all. Within a couple of days, it was almost as though I had never gone away. Apart, of course, from the big purple ring on my finger. Steve insisted, though, that we had to pick a proper ring before Christmas. Rachel thought it was very sweet. "You are made for each other," she laughed. "You'll always come round to each other's views."

Speaking of, Rachel had returned from her Sophie-retrieval-mission to find the most unexpected news on her Facebook wall.

"He found me, he found me, he found me," she sang as she bounced into my office one morning and sat irreverently on my desk.

"Who?" I could only ask, knowing from her face that this was a significant development.

"Alex! He sent me a friend request."

I was momentarily confused, but quickly I remembered. "What, Alex? *The* Alex? Your thunderbolt-and-lightning Alex? The one that got away?"

"The very selfsame one."

"Wow."

We contemplated this momentous event in silence.

"Did you accept?"

"Of course," she squealed. "We've even been chatting. A bit. He lives in Manchester, would you believe it…"

"So he is alive and back in the country," I confirmed, just to be absolutely sure.

"He is."

"Wow. And have you—" I couldn't even finish my sentence before Rachel started speaking.

"I have," she cut in quickly. "Totally and unreservedly. Apologized, explained, and groveled. He's not great about it, but it was *him* who found me and made contact, so he wants to get over it and…we're…we're working on it."

I got up and gave her a hug. "That's so great," I told her, looking at her intently. She had that sparkle in her eyes, the one that said she would get herself into trouble.

"Just do me the one favor," I begged her. "Take it easy. Take your time. Give him time."

"I am, I will, and I am," she sing-songed as she hugged me back. "But I know…if I'll let him come to me, he will. I know, I know," she raised her hands to deflect my impending response. "Gently does it, I know. I'm not going to mess it up again if I can help it."

We grinned at each other.

"Is he as gorgeous as you remembered?" I teased her.

"More so. Ruggedly handsome…" she gave a mock swoon, and I playfully prodded her arm.

"Get away with you, we're meant to be working."

So things somehow got back into their own swing, and it looked as though finally, finally, everybody's life was back on track.

Chapter Fifty-Nine

Oh yes, there was one more loose end. How could I not have mentioned this before?

It involved the small business of the single. The song, the one that had gone platinum. And Tuscq performing it at the big New Year's Eve gig at The Arena.

Ever since my return to London, I had been looking forward to this gig. Actually, "gig" didn't quite capture it—it was *the* end-of-year event to attend, and The Arena had been sold out for months. In honor of old times, Dan had put me on the guest list, and Steve, too. He had suggested turning up some time around five for the tail-end of the final rehearsal, just before the sound check. After all these years of knowing him, even after having been on tour with the band, the prospect still filled me with excitement. I guessed I was a rock chick at heart, and always would be. Steve jokingly said that I would probably still go out rockin' with Tuscq when I was a granny using a walking frame, and we had both found the prospect hilarious; all the more so because it was most likely true.

At the same time, Steve had no hesitation or qualms about coming along and rockin' out with me, and that was one reason why I loved him so very much. So we made our way to The Arena from his flat by Tube, in no particular hurry, knowing that we would be early anyway, knowing that we had a free pass to enter whenever and wherever we wished. I proudly wore my VIP pass around my neck all the way.

And still I was taken aback by the fact that there were literally thousands of fans camped out in front of The Arena waiting for the doors to open. Of course I knew that Tuscq was a global phenomenon—who better than me to appreciate the stature and glamour of the band first-hand? But there were always fans more keen, more eager than me, and it never failed to surprise me.

Steve took one look at the crowd and frowned. "Now what?"

I giggled. He was obviously new to the scene. I took his hand and whispered, "Follow me." We skirted the crowd until we hit the security fence on the far side of The Arena, where I sweetly and confidently beckoned a security guard to come over. I merely had to wave my VIP pass in the air before he invited us to hop on over the fence and let us in.

The band greeted us with great cheers. However, the tension was palpable and I recalled that it wouldn't be likely to ease until they were due to go on. We had arrived before the sound check but Dan insisted that he wanted to rehearse one more song, one final time. So the band surrendered to their leader and all of us obediently trudged on the stage, Steve and I included, just kind of swept along in their slipstream. If the roadies were surprised, they didn't let it show and quietly relinquished the stage to the maestros. I made a move to lead Steve off stage and into the auditorium, but Dan motioned for us to stay where we were. Which happened to be a pretty awkward spot quite central on the stage, but *still* I didn't latch on to his plan.

As the band launched into the opening chords of the final song Dan had so desperately wanted to rehearse, I hummed and swayed along. That was only natural—I was a huge fan, after all.

When a roadie pressed a microphone into my hot and sweaty palm, I accepted it without thought. And why not indeed. If I was already on the stage, I might as well—

Sing!

What me? Here? Later tonight?

In front of *twenty-three thousand* people?

I nearly passed out with shock as realization had *finally* hit me.

Stupid, of course. I should have seen this coming. It had been totally obvious. Even Steve thought I had realized Dan's grand plan, which is why he hadn't bothered to bring it up. He hadn't wanted to make a big deal of it, lest I should suffer from some kind of stage fright or something. He had thought I was okay with it.

Heck, I wasn't.

Recording a single in the privacy of Dan's studio had been one thing. But standing on this stage, opening my mouth and performing in front of actual people, thousands of them?

I opened my mouth and offered the only reasonable response. I threw up all over the stage.

There was a small moment of silence followed by a lot of blatant ignoring of my shaky condition. Someone appeared from nowhere with a bucket and mop while I stood petrified.

Dan was steely in his determination. I had never seen him like this before. He walked across to me, carefully stepping around the puddle around my feet. A roadie who was evidently familiar with the protocol relating to actual on-stage hurling proffered a bottle of water, and Dan took it, dampening a towel to wipe my mouth and making me take a few small sips. He looked at me, his eyes a clear, icy blue, and he told me, in no uncertain terms, that I would sing.

I wanted to cry. Where were the compassion, the understanding, the sympathy?

One hundred percent absent, that was where they were. *Sorry, Soph, no can do. Not on duty tonight. You're on your own.*

"Sophie, listen to me." Dan's voice was intense and his eyes locked and bored into mine. "You can do this. And you will. *You will.*" He raised my face to his by lifting my chin with his index finger, and the touch of his skin, warm and soft, against the clammy ice-cold of my face, drove home to me how scared I was. Yet that look in his eyes and his voice were hypnotic. It was like a visitation from The Mentalist.

"Sing for me, now," he instructed. "There is nobody there now apart from us."

I finally found my voice. "But there will be, later."

Dan only shrugged. "You won't see them. The spotlights will blind you and the din will be massive and they'll all blend into one. They won't matter. But what *does* matter is that you do this, for me, and for you."

He pressed the mike back into my hand and so I sang, before the show. I opened my mouth and moved my lips. Afterwards, Dan gave me a big thumbs-up and Steve hugged me tight.

Two-and-a-half hours later, after the warm-up acts had done their thing and Tuscq's show was nearing its end, I was waiting in the wings for my cue. The crowd was wild. Tuscq had just gone off after the second set, and the lights were low. This was the usual pretense that the show was over, and the fans rose to the occasion with loud and insistent shouts of *Encore! Encore!*

The band were, in fact, changing instruments and clothes and having drinks of water in the three short minutes that they were off stage. I nearly peed my pants in my position at the side, but I wasn't going to be sick again. I was done with that.

Why am I doing this? I asked myself for the thousandth time.

Because you've always wanted to, I answered myself, also for the thousandth time. And it was true. All my life, I had dreamed about dating a rock star, and I had done that a few years back. All my life, I had dreamed about becoming a rock star, and I was about to have a go at it. So bully for me, and away with the nerves.

Right? *Right.*

The band was back, waving as the crowd erupted into delighted cheers. You could almost feel the excitement, and the adrenaline rush was totally addictive. Dan did his customary little bit of chat, which used to be my favorite part of the concert, but I couldn't concentrate on it today. Joe counted the band in by tapping the drumsticks against the cymbals, and "Love Me Better" began.

My moment was imminent.

Dan came in on his part and sang in his beautiful throaty voice, his powerful vocals carrying clear and strong even at the end of the show. Until he hit my part.

Dan made a big show out of looking around, shielding his eyes, turning this way and that, with the band blithely playing on until he waved for them to stop. One by one, the instruments halted, on a discordant note here or a half a beat there. Totally rehearsed, of course, but it sounded real.

The crowd let out a groan.

"What?" Dan challenged. "What will you have me do? I can't sing this song without Sophie."

A great shout rose from the twenty-three thousand concert goers and within seconds, they were chanting again.

We want Sophie. We want Sophie!

Dan let this continue for the calculated minute or so, until he made the universal "calm down" gesture with his outstretched hands. When the hall was as quiet as it ever would be, he asked, as though requiring confirmation:

"You want Sophie?"

"Yes," came the obliging response.

"I can't hear you... You want Sophie?" Dan really was an extraordinary showman.

"YES!" the crowd roared as one.

The lights went out completely bar one spotlight.

"I give you Sophie," Dan announced and the resulting cheer drowned out his voice completely. *That* was my cue.

The spotlight had come across right to where I was waiting in the wings, enticing me to come out. I took a first tentative step, and another, and the light followed me all the way. I was a little self-conscious, being dressed only in humble jeans and T-shirt, but Dan had thought it would be perfect.

Now another spotlight picked out Dan, and three more spots focused on one of the remaining band members each. The stage looked as though the sun was extending fingers of light through a dark thundercloud. Steve told me later that the effect was breathtaking.

On unsteady feet, my throat as dry as parchment, I walked across the length of the stage until I reached Dan, and he gave me a huge hug, lifting my right hand high in the air as though we had already finished and were celebrating.

The crowd lapped it up.

And of course, Dan had been absolutely right. With the lighting arranged the way it was and with the audience noise coming in a solid block, it was impossible to make out any faces or voices. In front of a crowd of thousands of people, it felt as if we were performing for ourselves.

Softly, softly, Joe counted us in once more and the song started over.

What can I say?

I did it. *Oh my God, I did it.*

It was one of the most amazing moments in my entire life. There was so much adrenaline in my body that I thought I would take off and float away. I felt elated and wired and high, and I was addicted to the feeling. I wanted to do it again.

The single was three minutes and forty-two seconds long, the extended remix another minute and a half on top of that. A live song was a different matter, though.

I was on stage with Dan and Tuscq for about ten minutes by the time we had gone through all the twists and turns and changes and repetitions, and yet it felt like a single second.

Dan kissed me and thanked me, and the crowd roared, and I laughed, and I cried, and then Dan invited Steve on stage as well to collect his fiancée, and the crowd cheered even louder at this hilarious turn of events; it was a great success.

The concert ended there, so I got to go out again for final cheers and we all trooped off to the dressing rooms.

Dan looked at me with eyes full of pride and admiration.

"That was a brave thing you did, Sophie Penhalligan. I don't know if I could've done it, but you did great."

I gave a great gasp of horror when it dawned on me what he had just admitted, and I bashed him over the head with a convenient cushion much to the amusement of the rest of the band. Steve stepped in between us like a mother separating fighting toddlers and bid us to apologize and make up, increasing the merriment factor even further.

The after-party lasted into the wee small hours of the morning and despite my best intentions, I did not get an opportunity to reflect on the year just ended. I was too busy feeling happy. I was too busy feeling like a star.

I was thinking of the future, though. Of my life with Steve, my wonderful thunderbolt-and-lightning man. My true love. This year would bring our wedding day and who knew what else.

This year, which started on an unbelievable high, would only take me to greater heights still. This year, I would have my husband, my best friend Rachel, and Dan the rock star all looking after me.

This year would be my perfect year.

Rock on!

Epilogue

Between them, Steve, Rachel, Mum, Dad, Dan, Jodie and Greetje organized the Jones-Penhalligan wedding without me having to lift a finger or make any decisions. Rachel, my bridesmaid, had also taken on the role of wedding planner, taking all the stress off me. She, who had so loudly declared that four months was an impossible timeframe, pulled together the perfect April wedding.

Before Christmas, very shortly after our joint return to London, she had sat me down and bombarded me with a long list of questions, not unlike a psychometric profile for a random job application. None of her questions had appeared to have any apparent context, and as we had been consuming vast amounts of wine in the process of answering them, I wasn't now entirely sure what to expect of the big event itself.

Big or small? (*Small*)
Near or far? (*Near*)
Green or blue? (*Blue*)

Professional or home job? (*Um, that would depend...what? Oh, okay, home.*)
Over the top or au naturel? (*Either*)
Loud or quiet? (*Dunno*)
Long or short? (*Long*) (*Or possibly short. What on earth are you talking about?*)
Boho or hippie? (*Neither, thanks*)
John Lennon or David Bowie? (*What? Okay, if I must...Bowie*)
Garbo or Monroe? (*Monroe*)
Cups or mugs? (*Mugs*)
Favors or flavors? (*Both*)

And so it had gone on, pages and pages of stuff, until I hadn't known whether I was coming or going. That was the last of it. I heard nothing further. I put my complete faith into my friends and family, not least my groom, and did the unthinkable—not plan my own wedding. I didn't even choose my dress. Jodie made it for me, based on some of the bizarre questions whose answers Rachel had forwarded to her. Four months had passed, and today, all would be revealed. Today was my wedding day.

I was at my flat with Rachel and Mum. Steve was at his flat with his best man and Dad. Yes, we still had the two flats—but we had also bought a proper home for the two of us together, and we had exchanged contracts on a small but lovely Victorian terrace in Barnes only two days ago. In about four weeks, we would move into our first joint home.

Anyway, I was at my flat with Rachel and Mum, and I was already in my wedding dress which Jodie had delivered and fitted first thing this morning. It was stunning. It was a beautiful ivory organza-and-satin creation, with a tightly fitted bodice, thin straps and a long, flowing A-line skirt. It wasn't dissimilar to my "perfect" dress, but much more weddingy. It was amazing. Jodie had done herself proud, and me, too.

Rachel helped me with my hair and makeup, keeping it simple and close to what I normally looked. She fizzed with anticipation but wouldn't disclose any more detail. Then she changed into her own bridesmaid's gown. It was a beautiful dusky pink and it suited her perfectly. Shortly afterwards, the florist delivered our bouquets and the men's buttonholes, and once more, dusky pink featured alongside white and ruby red roses, dressed with simple greens and baby's breath.

The wedding car arrived to whisk me off to an unknown location for the wedding ceremony.

No, I really had not had a rehearsal of any kind. Yes, I knew this was unusual. I was aware how weddings worked. So once more, no, there had been no rehearsal. I had met with no registrar or vicar. I had no clue what was coming, except I had been given a completely anonymous description of the proceedings which I had had to memorize. These suggested a church wedding but I wouldn't know for sure until I got there.

You think this is strange?

You think I'm making this up?

Absolutely not. It was like a mystery wedding, except, of course, I knew the groom. And I loved it. It was romantic. Everybody had made such an effort to create the ultimate surprise party, and all I had to do was to enjoy it. *There was no stress.* I wasn't worried about the flowers in the church, because I didn't know whether there would be any. I wasn't worried about the caterers, because I didn't know what kind of food there would be. I wasn't worried about any of the hundreds of things that could go wrong on a wedding day, precisely because I didn't know what they were.

I was the world's most relaxed bride. Short of getting out of bed in the morning and flying off to Vegas for a totally impromptu event, I couldn't think of a better way for the bride to tie the knot.

The wedding car was a beautiful kit car, although I only knew that because the driver told me. He told me the make and the exact provenance, too, but I couldn't recall them even a minute later. All that mattered was that it was shiny, old-fashioned and spacious, decorated with white ribbons and perfectly perfect. Dad and I sat in the back, Dad radiating pride, and the car gently drove off. Rachel and Mum followed behind in a similarly bedecked, slightly smaller car of the same make. We had our own little procession, and other drivers tooted their horns and waved at us as we drove through the sunny London morning.

The route was familiar and I guessed we were going off to Putney. My mind raced furiously over the possibilities and I suddenly guessed that we were headed for St Mary's Church, Steve's parish church right by the Thames. It was a gorgeous old church, squat, sturdy and solid. Sure enough, that was where the car pulled up after a swift and unencumbered journey, and my heart soared with joy.

Dad helped me climb out of the car without creasing my dress or stumbling over the veil. I straightened up and took a look around, taking in the gnarled old tree, still bare of leaves this early in this spring, but the blossoms of daffodils and crocuses dotted all over the lawn. Spring weddings, symbolic of new life, and life eternal. I was overcome all weird, but Rachel was by my side to give me final instructions. I took Dad's arm and we moved slowly to the gate, him shortening his strides to match mine, me sticking out my knees first like a robotic doll, putting my feet down heel-toe as Jodie had instructed me. Rachel was chatting away next to me until we reached the church door where I was greeted by a kindly looking vicar, who did a lightning introduction, and—

Dan?

Rachel clapped her hands with glee, and Dan smiled broadly as he leaned across to give me a very chaste peck on the cheek.

I couldn't get over it.

"What are you wearing?" I burst out before I could restrain myself. For Dan was clad in a traditional morning suit— except it was dusky pink.

"I'm your mate of honor!" he said seriously and Rachel laughed excitedly.

"Mate of honor? Get it? This was my idea," she gushed. "Don't you love it?"

Suddenly, I understood Dan's odd attire. "Your suit matches the bridesmaid's dress," I declared, stating the obvious, and Rachel rolled her eyes with feigned impatience.

"She got it," she said to Dan and Dad as though I wasn't there, and I pretended to whack her with my bouquet.

"Watch out, you," I mock-threatened her, "I might relegate you to the back of the church and have Dan do the whole bridesmaid's job by himself." I giggled. "He'd need a bouquet, though."

"Oh yes, I left that in the car," Rachel realized and shot off to fetch it.

"*Mate* of honor?" I gently teased Dan. "And you went along with that? Aren't you worried about your reputation?"

"I thought it was a fab idea," Dan protested. "One hundred percent appropriate. Besides, don't I look rather dashing in pink? When do I ever get to wear pink?"

"It does suit you," Dad chimed in, and we all chuckled. Rachel was back, handed Dan a slightly slimmer version of her own bouquet, and we were ready to go. The vicar opened the church doors, the organ burst into life and we processed down the aisle, the vicar leading the way, then Dad and I, followed by Rachel and finally Dan.

I vaguely took in that the church was rammed with people and that there were beautiful flowers. I noted the color patterns on the floor and on the wall made by the sunlight streaming in through the stained glass windows. I took in the church scent of incense and flowers and innocence. But mostly, I was focused on my wonderful groom, my thunderbolt-and-lightning man, Steve, waiting for me at the altar, his best man and childhood friend, James, by his side.

My wedding day passed full of love and colors, friends and family, food and wine. After the ceremony, we went on a riverboat down the Thames. Initially, I thought the reception would be on the boat but it turned out to be just a mode of transport for us, the happy couple, and all our guests. I had a small moment of worry about how Rachel would feel being here, on a boat, reminding her of everything that had gone wrong, but she appeared oblivious to the connection.

The trip took only about twenty minutes, but it was a welcome breathing space and an opportunity to meet all the guests. I was overwhelmed to find that Greetje and Klaus had made the journey; and of course I was ecstatically happy that they helped weave the run-away part of my life and courtship with Steve firmly into the fabric of our wedding day. It was lovely to catch up with Jodie, and to chat with James, the best man, whom I had met only very briefly a few weeks before.

The boat finally moored in Greenwich, right by the Cutty Sark, which was where a photographer appeared to take a few pictures. The reception itself Rachel had organized to take place in the Royal Naval Cottage, although apparently the choice had been mine.

"You said blue rather than green, and I know how much you wanted to get married by the sea. And you also said near rather than far. So this is the perfect answer because here the Thames is still coastal. So you are *technically* getting married by the sea," she explained to me in a brief whispered conversation.

Our reception hall had been decorated by Rachel, Dan, Steve, James, Mum, Dad, Steve's parents, and Greetje and Klaus, during the night before. They had done a grand job with dusky pink and silver table runners on white linen, balloons, streamers and flowers to pick up the color scheme, and little bags of freeze-dried raspberries and strawberries alongside white chocolates truffles adorning every setting.

"You said 'both' to 'favors and flavors,'" Rachel supplied by way of explanation and I told her how beautiful everything was. She blushed deeply and waved my adoration off with an embarrassed flapping of her hands.

The food was inspired. Steve, Rachel and Dan had worked their way through many a tasting—God knew when they had fitted those in—and eventually decided on baked salmon in a creamy sauce with a potato dauphinoise to die for and crunchy green vegetables on the side. There was wine on every table but also plenty of champagne. Dan had told Steve that he wanted our wedding to be fueled by love and bubbles, and had provided several crates' worth of the real deal.

It was after a short performance in our honor by Tuscq— including Dan, of course—that Greetje sought me out, taking me by the arm proprietorially and walking me gently but firmly out of the room.

"What is going on?" I teased her, but she shushed and smiled. She led me out of the college, but I ground to a halt at the gate.

"Where are we going?" I demanded to know, and she finally relented.

"It is a German tradition to abduct the bride from below her groom's nose on the wedding night, so that he has to find her and rescue her. It brings good luck. And now I am doing that for you."

I giggled. "You are abducting me?" I confirmed, slightly incredulous. "Where to?"

"I don't know," Greetje chuckled. "We will have to find a pub or something."

"What, with me in my wedding gown?"

"Absolutely," she assured me.

"But I will be so obvious. And anyway, how is Steve supposed to know?"

Greetje had the answer to that, too.

"Rachel has been informed. She will gently guide your husband to the realization that you are missing after a due amount of time, and Klaus will tell him that you have been abducted and need to be found. You see, all is taken care of."

"Your husband is in on this?"

"Why, of course. He suffered this indignity at our wedding and has not missed an opportunity to pass it on. Of course, it was worse for him, as German men know that this will happen and swear they will not leave their brides out of their eyesight for even a second. And still…"

She smiled in remembered excitement.

"I was taken to a pub, too," she explained. "But do you think my klutz of a husband saw me sitting in a bar? He walked in and asked…" Greetje paused to adjust her voice to mimic her husband's, "'Has anyone seen a bride?' So of course everybody said no, even though I was sitting right there, and he walked straight back out."

"No!" I gasped, and "Yes!" she repeated. Meanwhile, she had started walking me into downtown Greenwich, and we picked the third pub we stumbled across. We caused quite a stir when we walked in, but we played it cool and sat down at a table in the corner. I was quite enjoying this little jaunt; it was weirdly romantic. How long would it take to be found?

In actual fact, this was a welcome break. There was something I needed to do. I waited for Greetje to return to the table with our drinks, and excused myself to go to the ladies' room, where I took a long, hard look at myself in the mirror. "This is it," I told myself quietly. "This is it."

I locked myself in a cubicle and hung my dolly bag on the back of the door. I was so nervous that I struggled to undo the string. But eventually I managed and gingerly received the stick. I had read the instructions at home and I knew exactly what I had to do.

Gathering up my skirts and positioning myself just so, I took a long pee, trying not to think what kind of figure I would cut if somebody were observing me.

Done.

I straightened up and flushed, closed the lid, and took a seat. Now for the wait.

As I had no watch, I counted to sixty twice, very slowly. All the while I contemplated the ornate ceiling light, looking anywhere but at the stick in my hand.

Surely, two minutes had passed.

I let my gaze slide down, down, down until I caught sight of the result window.

The door to the ladies' room opened and a very worried-sounding Greetje called for me. "Sophie? Are you all right?"

I stuffed the pregnancy test back into my dolly bag and hastily unlocked the cubicle.

"'Course!" I smiled, probably looking slightly goofy but I didn't care. "I'm absolutely fine."

By the time we returned to our table, the search party had arrived. Rachel, Dan and Jodie were talking animatedly, and Dan gave me a big, tender smile and a wink. Mum and Dad were at the bar, and Steve's parents had just walked in. Steve was only a few steps behind with his best man and Klaus.

My close and extended family, my nearest and dearest circle of friends, had all congregated here for us, for me. I looked at each and every one of them, experiencing a rush of emotion such as I had never thought possible. I smiled radiantly at my new husband stepping in to reclaim me.

"You ran away again," he admonished me jokingly. "This is the fifth dubious establishment we have searched for you."

"I was abducted," I corrected. "I had no choice. But you rescued me. You are officially my hero."

I gave him a big kiss on the lips to the delighted cheers of everybody around us.

"Any time," he said gallantly. "We're a team for good now, you and me…"

I raised myself on my tippy toes and whispered in his ears, softly, so very softly.

"…and now we are three!"

Love Me Better
(Sophie's Song)
by Dan Hunter

Voice 1 (Me)
You and me / We were meant to be
Now it's history / Why can't you see

Voice 2 (Sophie)
You and me / Were never meant to be
Can't you see / There's no history

Chorus (Together, in harmony)
But the time we spent together / Was magic in every way
No one else could love me better / Make me cherish every
day

Me
I let you go / You couldn't know
That it would break my heart / Tear my life apart

Sophie
I sent you away / Miss you every day
I felt so strong / Now I know I was wrong

Chorus

Me
You and me / We were meant to be
I will get you back / I can't leave it at that

Sophie
You and me / We were meant to be
Now the time is not right / But our future's bright

Coming in September 2013
Rock Star Romance, Part 3

Sophie's Encore

Welcome back, my friend! *Sophie writes*. Thank you for joining me in this, the grand finale of my rock star romance adventure. Hasn't it been an amazing journey so far? In the first story, *Sophie's Turn*, you met my boyfriend Tim, and Dan, my favorite rock star, and you supported me while I was trying to make sense of a bizarre double proposal from the two very different men. When I made my decision, I could practically hear you cheering; thank you!

In *Sophie's Run*, you watched me fall in love with Steve, truly, madly, deeply. And then you witnessed the ultimate betrayal from a really unexpected source. I hope you weren't too surprised by what I did next; wouldn't you have wanted to do the same?

Thank you for coming to my wedding in the end. I had the best time, and I hope you enjoyed yourself, too. Dan told me only yesterday that he'd want a wedding just like it, if he ever...*got there*. I was intrigued, but he simply laughed and changed the subject.

However. The story of me and my rock star doesn't end there, of course it doesn't. If you've just finished reading *Sophie's Run*, you might have picked up a few things about Dan that I don't really comprehend yet. I heard a rumor that he has been secretly in love all these long years. So join me as the last part of the Rock Star Romance Trilogy unfolds right here, in *Sophie's Encore*... coming your way on 7 September 2013.

Rock on!

Acknowledgements

What a difference a year makes! When I launched my debut novel, *Sophie's Turn*, I was in it, more or less, on my own. The past year has been an incredible journey of learning and discovery—in more than one sense, as I had the privilege, in February of 2012, to sign *Sophie's Turn*, with the amazing US publisher, Sapphire Star Publishing. As a result, there are many, many people to whom I owe big thanks. Therefore, in no particular order other than alphabetical, please allow me to honor and embarrass the following wonderful people.

Chris Longmuir, for supplying proper Scottish expressions just when I needed them.

Deborah Smith, for being a real-time beta-reader, for offering unwavering support and for being my official photographer.

Gordon Brown from Bluesdacious, for reviewing relevant sections and offering feedback—thank you for the local color.

Jim Ronnie from Iron Claw, for inspiration and support, and for sharing real-life anecdotes that added real spice to Dan's exploits. I look forward to using the rest some other time.

Jon; I love you; what more can I say?

Kaufhaus des Westens (KaDeWe), Berlin, for granting me permission to send Sophie and Dan on a totally fictitious shopping trip there, to meet with a fictitious personal shopper and buy a fictitious dress from a fictitious designer.

Linn B. Halton, driving force behind *loveahappyending.com*, for being an amazing source of guidance and encouragement.

Everyone at **loveahappyending.com,** for being a fantastically supportive team of authors and readers.

Marleen Heine of **Kurverwaltung der Inselgemeinde Langeoog**, for sending a large amount of material about the island and patiently answering all my questions.

Everyone at **Sapphire Star Publishing**, especially Amy Lichtenhan and Katie Henson, for signing all three parts of the Rock Star Romance Trilogy, having faith in me and my work, answering a million questions, and coaching and guiding me along the way. I am honored and humbled to be part of the Sapphire Star family. A big thank you also to my editor, Ellen Brock, for her detailed read, perceptive comments and energetic prompts.

Sharon Goodwin, wonderful blogger and friend; for showing me the ropes when I was in danger of falling off the cliff. What would I have done without your timely, practical and sensible guidance? You rock.

Shirley Mukisa, for being an ace beta-reader.

Sue Fortin, fantastic writing buddy and friend; for always being there, for reading and commenting, making stellar suggestions and cheering me on.

THE HUSH BAND, for their music, photos, and general rocking support.

About the Author

Nicky Wells writes *Romance That Rocks Your World*!

Born and raised in Germany, Nicky moved to the United Kingdom in 1993. Having received two degrees, Nicky spent six years working as a researcher and project manager for an international Human Resources research firm based in London and Washington, D.C.

Nicky left work in November 2004 to write her debut novel, *Sophie's Turn*, before the birth of her first baby. Nicky currently lives in Lincoln with her husband and their two boys and is now working on the concluding third part in the *Rock Star Romance Trilogy*. When she is not writing, she loves listening to rock music (or simply the radio), reading books and eating lobsters or pizza.

Visit Nicky at http://nickywellsklippert.wordpress.com/ where you can find articles, interviews, radio interviews and, of course, an ongoing update on her work in progress. You can also follow Nicky on Twitter and find her on Facebook. Nicky is a featured author on the innovative reader/author project, loveahappyending.com and has joined the Romantic Novelists' Association. Nicky also has author pages at Sapphire Star Publishing, Amazon and, of course, Goodreads.

Also by Nicky Wells

Sophie's Turn (Rock Star Romance Trilogy, Part 1)
Sophie's Encore (Rock Star Romance Trilogy, Part 3) — Coming 7 September 2013

Lightning Source UK Ltd.
Milton Keynes UK
UKOW05f1304131113

221014UK00001B/139/P